The
Mystery
Man
Murders

Special thanks to Mikita Brottman, whose delightful book titled *The Solitary Vice: Against Reading* introduced me to the idea that a *grimoire* must be read backward if you wish to erase its spell.

The Mystery Man Murders

First book in the series titled
**Grimoire - the Bros Grim
Breakfast Serial** - a story in pieces

By Jon Rieley-Goddard

BaldyBooks
Buffalo, New York

Photo of the author by Cathy Rieley-Goddard

Drawing and cover photo by the author

First Edition 2011

1 2 3 4 5 6 7 8 9 10

ISBN 978-0-9829378-0-8

To Tom
-- first and best reader
(tnx, too, for Jeanne's poems).

To Cathy
-- who said one day on her way to work ...
"... you are a writer now."

(April Fool's Day) is marked by the commission of good-humoured or otherwise funny jokes, hoaxes, and other practical jokes of varying sophistication on friends, family ... work associates, etc.

-- Wikipedia

My Spy Boy and your Spy Boy
 sittin' by the fire,
My Spy Boy told your Spy Boy
 gonna set your house on fire.

-- traditional song

Part One

April Fool's Day.
Now **that's** funny.
Every day is April Fool's Day, for me.
And every day is a day in April, the cruelest month.
How fitting it is that these daily posts begin on such a funny day.
A day when you know that you can trust no one.
Most people find that amusing.
Not me.
I have had a lifetime of such days, one after another.
And I am sick to my soul of duplicity.

Dear Diary: April fools in the rain
|01April08|

It was a dark and rainy night, after a heavy, dark, and rainy day.
The rain had started at dawn, at first light, and continued past lights out.
I was driving home from my home away from home, a used bookshop called **Caspar's Books and That**, in the northern part of my city, Buffalo-nya, at the eastern end of Lake Eerie. Don't ask me why (because I will lie just for the fun of it, or because I have something to hide, or because I live by my wits and I don't know you), but I stopped across Delaware Avenue from President's Park.

Maybe it was the lights and sirens.

Maybe it was the presence of persons I wanted to watch.

I do like to keep my friends close and my enemies closer.

Maybe it was for reasons that I will share as time goes on.

Whatever.

Police and detectives were interviewing four or five agitated people beside a city bus. A body-sized lump lay under a tarp.

The curious stood at a distance.

The rain covered all. The few street lights and the many colored lights on the patrol cars and Crown Vics, and an ambulance or two, reflected the misery of the moment in puddles of water.

I wanted to look under that tarp but knew that I did not have that option. You well may ask why I wanted to look under that tarp, and I could tell you why, exactly, or I could lie and say that I was worried about a friend I had not heard from lately.

Who knows?

I do. You do not.

But I will not leave you alone in the dark.

This tableau toward truth will endure as long as our connection does.

≈ ≈ ≈

A youngish man of maturity roamed in the zone between the gawpers and the ones sworn to serve and defend. He looked familiar -- black wide-sided glasses, punk-short but natty hairdo (dripping wet), and a trench coat.

A trench coat. Yeah, a trench coat.

He watched with the care of a trained observer, which is more than I could say for most of the locals. When he went among the cops and detectives and EMTs and the rest, no one said, **Hey, Bud, get back.** His eyes focused on nothing and everything with the studied ease of a gatekeeper standing in the gap.

We made eye contact, the man in the trench coat and I.

"Whazzup," I said.

"Not much, he said.

"On the job?" I said.

"Is it that obvious?" he said.

We smiled and shook hands like each had found a brother.

"Goose Grim," I said, "late of our country's covert corps and currently in exile in this fair city."

"You can call me **Stranger**," he said. "I've seen you around, Goose Grim. Call me, Stranger."

And so I did.

Call him, Stranger.

Yeah, I think that I just might call you Stranger, too.

Here is a hint for you, Stranger.

Watch it if I say **trust me** or **honestly**, that sort of thing. Ok?

≈ ≈ ≈

These daily posts, over the course of a year, or thereabouts, told my closest friends and associates the story of how the Stranger and I became friends, and colleagues, and where we went from there, and who went with us, and who tried to stop us. Now, you get to read the story.

You had best fasten your seatbelt, Stranger, for it may be a bumpy ride, particularly until we get to know one another a **bleep** of a lot better.

Black/white and read all over
|02April08|

This story ran as the lead story on the front page of this morning's **Daily Afterblatt, Lake Effect edition:**

Police in a pickle
Details elusive in suspicious death in the dark and rain

The morning after a middle-aged male was killed on a rainy night by a metro bus, Buffalonya police say they have few, or no, clues about the identity of the victim or why the man was standing, motionless, in the traffic lane of busy Delaware Avenue near President's Park.

"We would appreciate any help we can get on this one," said lead Det. Joe Blucote of the Buffalonya Police. "We have absolutely nothing, except vague reports from a very few shaken up eyewitnesses that the victim was facing the oncoming bus, as still as a statue."

The night of the tragedy, which occurred in mid-evening, was a dark and wet one. An inch of rain fell in the hour surrounding the unidentified man's death, according to the local National Weather Service office.

The victim was wearing a dark suit and overcoat of good quality and had all the appearances of a successful business executive, according to Blucote.

No wallet was found on the victim, who was declared dead at the scene.

Blucote would not comment on reports in local media that items in the victim's clothing were giving police the only clues that they had.

He also refused to confirm whether the victim was wearing a wedding ring or any other jewelry.

Blucote refused to identify the bus driver, either by name or by gender, or any of the four passengers said to have been on the bus.

"They are victims, too, and we are protecting their privacy. The bus driver is on leave and is not expected to be able to return to work for a long while."

An autopsy is pending and toxicology reports may shed some light on the darkness surrounding the case, according to Eerie County Coroner Bruce Backstaff.

"The cause of death was obvious," Dr. Backstaff said, "but there may have been contributing factors such as drugs or alcohol."

Dr. Backstaff said that it will take weeks for a full toxicology study to be completed at the New York State Forensics Lab in Albany.

Police ask anyone with information on this case to call the non-emergency number at the main police station downtown.

-- compiled from staff reports

I once knew a man in dark places
| 03April08 |

I once knew a man, a covert man, like that man who got grilled by the bus outside President's Park and came up with the wrong answer in the dark and rain. He was a snappy dresser, too, when there was need of that. He could blend in by standing out. He could change the tone of an encounter by changing his tie and cuff links. He could lead, or go along, in the highest levels of ruthless social interaction. He could run with the bulls, for he was one himself.

If the victim without name or identification was my covert friend (and I have no doubt after reading the news story), the local police would never know it, because his was a shadow life and ours was a friendship that never was, in any discernible or provable way.

Operation Beloved, that is what we called our time together.

He was like an iceberg, and no one had seen his submerged side except for a few peers and his handlers.

Some things are best left in the dark in the park, and by the side of the road, as roadkill.

One detail from that ham-fisted news story was enough to confirm any suspicions that I might have had to the contrary about who the victim was. If you knew what to look for, you could see his stamp, big as life, embossed on the weak denials and thin leads Det. Blucote doled out to the media.

Granted, the one detail was far beyond what was subtle, and only apparent to those who knew where to look.

I could see its aura, but the wisp of a clue was not being seen by the local talent, Buffalonya's finest or not.

The detail was mine to notice but never to disclose.

Too much was riding on disclosure of any sort.

The truth can kill, but only if you hear it
| 04April08 |

Suddenly, I am mourning this man who will have no name save a case name, of my choosing, right now.

For the sake of clarity, so to speak, I will refer to him as **Mr. Darke**, first name **Parke**, middle name **Eno**.

Parke Eno Darke.

Clearly, I made up that name, and as clearly I am making jokes at the edge of a volcano that could take us all out, my two brothers Grim and I, and my precious partner Eve and the rest of the old farts at **Caspar's Books and That**, to say nothing of our fair city by the lake.

My Pop taught me well, to make fun of the things and people and situations that bring terror and despair near to us.

It was a lesson from one clown to another -- sharing huge, changeless face-grins and laughing at the ever-fluid face of evil because otherwise we might have started to tremble and weep. I mourn my covert friend Mr. Darke, and I will find out what happened to him, and I will keep to myself the one detail concerning his demise.

I will keep to myself the glories of his life-work among the shadows and the spirits of the night.

I will keep to myself the knowledge that the local police so very much want and that I so very much will never give them.

I will learn the rest of his story, for my own satisfaction and my own obsessions, and my silent and private grieving.

I will be like a ghost shadowing another ghost, visible only to such persons as myself. And I will tell Eve all that I know.

This Grim's *Grimoire*
|05April08|

> Grimoire: French word ... (GRIM - wah) -- book of spells, black-book; secret language; uneasy scrawl (v. *Cassell's French Diction-ary*, c. 1962).

There is an ancient tradition concerning the **Grimoire** that says books are dangerous and that books set traps for the unwary. The only antidote, it was said, was to read the offending book backwards, to free oneself of the spell.

The book in your hands is a Grimoire, too, because it is written by one who has the name of Grim, and because this Grim has wiles that may trap you, and because my narrative will require some unraveling before you understand it, and because it sounds like good, clean fun to tell my story backwards as well as forward. Like this -- **... End. The ...** .

However, as fun as that might be, I'm only joking about beginning at **The End** and backing up like a driver caught in a stop-start-stop traffic jam who comes to an on-ramp and backs his way out. I will proceed in a fairly straight-forward fashion. I promise (**trust me?**) that I won't jump around too much (whatever **that** means).

My life partner, Eve -- Eve Green, if you must know her full name -- owns **Caspar's Books and That**, which is home to a mountain of books in condition ranging from mint to minced, and a cat named **Wild Billy**, and a collection of spookish old farts who worship the ground that Eve walks upon and sits upon, and everything else about her.

Compared to my brothers and me, Eve is younger, a bit shorter, and much better-looking than we are. Eve is generally considered to be the kind of woman that others, men and women, want to be close to, for her attractive qualities, essential goodness, and intelligence. Her upright carriage is well-upholstered, her once-blond hair is a sexy salt-and-pepper fall to her shoulders. Eve smiles a Buddha Girl smile of sweetness and blessing that can light the way in dark places. Eve gives everyone the same honorific. She will call you **Dear**. Repeatedly. Eve and I share, with the old guys in her train, bitter memories of a life lived in the shadows of a not-so-enchanted country that we will call **Spookistan**. The old guys around here treat Eve like the **Lady of the Castle** and tolerate me as her consort.

Rounding out the roster are my brothers, **Jim** and **OtherJim**, both of them, like me, Grims. The old guys answer to the colors of the rainbow -- **Mr. Red, Mister Blue (AKA Mister Ed),** and **Mr. Black** (currently missing and the subject of some concern among us).

The Bros Grim and how they grew
| 06April08 |

Our Pop, now dead, who was a spook during and after the Second World War, was a horny little cuss. I say this because the family history bears out that description, and Pop would have owned the image himself, if anyone had ever indicted him in that way.

He was, truth be told, **not high but mighty.**

About fifty years ago, and a little more, Pop while serving his country in the covert realm, in Spookistan, met a lady, and another lady, and another lady after that. With each one, he had carnal relations to the point of pregnancy. Pop was hopping from bed to bed so frequently that he barely had time for his day job.

It was Pop's own rogue **Operation Pogo Stick.**

The result, in a rush, and days apart, near the middle of the year in the middle of the century, were three little boys whom their mothers (whom Pop refused to his dying day to refer to by name) named **August**, the oldest, and **Jim**, the middle son, and **Jim**, the youngest. In a mirror image of Pop's piggy attitude toward women in general and these three mothers of his sons, in particular, the three dumped their babes in Pop's lap and left, never to return.

It was like three trains running on parallel tracks, aiming for one junction.

The collision generated a gratifying amount of noise and confusion.

≈ ≈ ≈

Pop, with the aid of an amazing young woman named Mrs. McFeather, or Missus Mac, or simply **Ma**, raised us on his own. Actually, Pop was gone more often than not, and it was Missus Mac who raised us. Pop was a lot more like **the presence of an absence.** As time went on, and we gained in awareness of the world around us, we were grateful for his shyness toward his sons.

Pop, you see, sucked at parenting.

One of our early memories was the day that Pop called us together, and said that two Jims were one too many.

"You," Pop said to the middle son, "will be **Jim**, and you," Pop said to the youngest son, "will be **OtherJim**. And you," Pop said to me, "will continue as you were, as **August**. Got it?"

We did get it, though by acclimation I quickly became **Gus**, and shortly after, **Goose**, which stuck like goose poop does to the shoes of the unwary.

Why **Goose**? you well might ask.

The answer is that Pop said I was a honker of a talker. **Goose** came along not far after. Also, he liked to say my name as **Au-GOOST**, like that.

"**August**, lately **Gus**, I now dub you **Goose**," Pop said, "and may your newest, and last, name stick like mud and certain other substances that jump out to snare those simply slogging through life. Be not a slogger, my son, but one who flies over the heads of those who do so."

Pop was like that. He loved to play with his words, like his sons loved to play motorboat with their mealtime glasses of milk. He loved to brandish new nicknames like sparklers on the Fourth of July. He loved to tell stories, particularly when he could pair a good story with some sharp teasing.

We liked Pop just fine, and we liked one another a lot more, and we fiercely loved Missus Mac.

As soon as we could find the courage to leave, we did, and for thirty years and more we wandered in the motherless desert, and we lived lives that could no longer be called even roughly parallel, because we had no knowledge of one another. The Internet in the form of some strategic ISO messages, left in a number of Internet places, brought us together again, in the city of our birth and younger years. We were still getting to know one another again, and my brothers were hanging out with the rest of us at **Caspar's Books and That.**

The amazing and imposing Missus Mac
|07April08|

We loved Missus Mac the way a son is supposed to love his mother, and she loved us the way our mothers could have, and should have, but didn't.

Missus Mac was short and wide, and young in a rude, red way.

Her breasts seemed to our young eyes to be the size of two respectable islands separated by a dark channel. They should have had names. She wore simple cotton dresses and worn-out flat shoes. She cooked and cleaned and disciplined with an efficiency that money could not buy. She came, she said, from the **Old Country**, and we accepted her at her word. At some point, as we grew, we one day just knew that she meant the Baltic states in general and Lithuania in particular. When it was that she had left the Old Country and why, she never told us. Ma had an accent that can only be described as thick, and she was in reasonable command of her English idioms, but not entirely. She was wise, as one who had been educated to some degree, augmented by native curiosity.

Goosey, she called me, and my brothers Jim she called **Jim Ruby the handsomely one** and **Jim Diamond the sharpish one**.

Missus Mac never mentioned our moms. We attached ourselves to her as babies and as children, and as young men eager to disappear and never return to the place of their birth and raising.

We were damaged, my brothers and I, but we did not know that we were, and Missus Mac did an amazing job of raising us as if we were a family.

But we were not a family, in the strict sense of the phrase.

Pop - a rambling man with the words
|08April08|

It was Pop, on one of his verbal rambles, like one who walks on the waters of speech because he knows were all the nouns and verbs are, who explained to us that we, the three little boys sitting before him like three little braves, and Missus Mac, hovering nearby (whom he knew better than to label as **Squaw**), and himself the **not high but mighty** (my words) **Big Chief**, were more like a tribe.

And not just any tribe.

Pop said that we were like a tribe, or band, really, of Apache.

Pop plucked **Apache** from a place of pleasure in the sound of his own voice and delight in his own words.

Pop did not know the first thing about the Apache.

I have looked into their history, however, and I think that Pop was onto something, if he only could have let go of the **Big Chief** thing. And, thank the Dear, he did not have to let go of the **squaw** thing because he never brought it up. We would have scalped him if he had said such a thing (though our fear of his lordly ways would have probably saved him until we reached our mid-teens, at which point we would have cheerfully shorn him for saying any such thing about Ma).

When Pop was gone, as he usually was, Missus Mac was the queen, and we were her knights. The image is still top down, and not Apache-like at all, but among ourselves, as we grew together, we three boys were like a band of little Apache who led by example and who followed by inclination rather than out of fear or any sense of coercion.

I was generally the leader of our pack, because that is my gift, and not because I am smarter or the oldest but because I am smart enough. My brothers, each of them, were, are, and evermore shall be smarter than I am, by a step, but I can keep up with them.

Three little pigs ... or *Duck-Duck-Goose*?
|09April08|

It is with the eyes and ears and mouth of a man of maturity that I say these things. As children, however, we had no such eloquence or insight. Pop was no help. To him, we were **Duck-Duck-Goose**, or the **F-Troop**, where the **F**, Pop said, stood for a four-letter word that will in this narrative go by the circumlocution of **bleep.** Pop would wave his middle finger in our faces and say that finger stood for the number of our collective I.Q. And we would giggle, and Pop would say, "Laugh you little bastards. Laugh!"

And we would giggle again, because we chose to believe Pop was joking.

That is what Ma told us, anyway, and we three wee ones trusted Ma at all points to tell us the truth.

Ma taught us a lot about truth. Honest.

It came to pass that we, a tribe of Apache-like equals, learned to be like the Calvary that could not contain those same Apache. We delighted in having secret meetings of the **F-Troop**, and we had a secret sign that we used for voting. We would touch the tips of our middle fingers together and thrust both thumbs in the air, to signal assent. Since we in Apache-like manner decided things by consensus, we did not have a gesture for dissent.

We loved to call the vote, which was **pro-forma**, so that we could raise our thumbs and flip our touched middle fingers.

Life was Grim in name only
| 10April08 |

Although you may not be able to see it from what I am saying, life for us was Grim in name only. We had a lot of fun, and Pop loved to pun around, and he loved to tell silly stories. His giving of nicknames, I was convinced, was an affectionate act. It was only later that we realized that the naming game that Pop played had both a sunny side and a dark side.

Take **Goose**. As Goose Grim, I could do things that August or Gus, even, could not do. **Goose** was assertive, like a stick, a leader's name. **August** was a fop's name, and **Gus** was dismissive, as far as names go. **Goose** was empowering. **August/Gus** was diminishing.

Jim, chosen to be the one whom Pop said could keep his given name, had an advantage over **OtherJim**, whom Pop differentiated with a nickname rather than a given name.

We lived into our names, and our nicknames, and into the implications of the naming.

There were unintended consequences, and I could speculate on what other names or nicknames would have yielded, but that strikes me as a singular waste of time.

Taken together, when we were young, we made a single, well-rounded person with a number of pleasing and penetrating abilities.

Woe to any kid who said **here come the fairy brothers**, and woe to any kid who called us, even in innocence, **a bunch of bastards.** It was our prerogative, and ours only, to joke about **who's the bastard now!**

When we scattered to three points of the compass, in our late teens, we had to learn how to make our way, like three chocolate bunnies that life had taken a bite from. One bunny said **What did you say**, because his ears were gone, and one bunny said **Ouch** because his butt was gone, and one bunny said **Let us be in odor** because his nose was gone.

Our fairytale childhood of Grim proportions included a dark, grim forest that Missus Mac could not chase away with her love and care. We got lost in that dark place and for many years we were separated, and we wandered, and we did not know the way back.

All in all, though, we were lucky to have the names and nicknames that we had.

You don't want to hear the names that Pop reserved for our absent and angry moms -- and all the other women who came and went in his life.

We decide to become a company (band?)
| 11April08 |

The ghostly, shifting stories that we three brothers embody would take forever, almost, to tell, and by the end you would be almost as confused as I am about the details, such as they are, and the facts, let alone the rumors, lies, and damned lies we told about the years we were apart.

In fact, we are still telling one another, slowly, about those years, and I for one will keep to myself the darker and more important details of my story. My brothers have no idea that I had been a spook, like Pop, as had Eve and the others they met in the bookshop. I am afraid to tell them these things. The spook thing, I decided, is just too dangerous a thing to know if you do not need to know, and I still am coming off all those years in a desert of deception of God, self, and others -- **Spookistan**.

The back-story that I wrote for my brothers was that I had been a private investigator and had met Eve in the course of that work. That has been good enough for the preliminaries of getting back together and catching up on what each of us was willing to release and watch as it ran for the horizon like some wild creature with something of value clutched in its teeth.

"From what I can see so far," Jim said, "our stories go too quickly to bad places that we don't want to talk about, so let us just love one another and the sisters, if any, that we never knew."

"Let us be," I said, "comfortable with a middling sense of one another."

"About a buck-three-eighty's worth," Jim said, "but no more, certainly."

We decided to enjoy the ride together.

"Yeah," OtherJim said, "getting there is at least half, if not all, the fun."

In keeping with Jim's **buck three-eighty**, we also agreed that we would not try overmuch to make sense of ourselves, one another, or situations past or present. We are still catching up with one another, and frankly (**watch it when I say that word**) we are not that concerned that we might not ever get a full sense of what is missing. Being, and simply being together, is of much more import and importance than making sense. We are, frankly, sick of trying to make sense. After living our lives in various shadows, nothing really makes that much sense anyway.

"We were raised to laugh at life no matter what happened, be it good, bad, or ugly," Jim said, "so I say we can take seriously the words to live by that our Pop gave us."

We shouted, in unison, in Pop's angry falsetto, **Laugh, you little bastards! Laugh while you can!**

The F-Troop rides again
| 12April08 |

"I will remind you," I said, "that this meeting will be in odor."

"Yes, Mr. Chair Sir," Jim said, getting into the old spirit.

"Yeah," OtherJim said, "I detect and decry the odor of the day."

"Whazzat?" I said.

"What we are going to do with ourselves now that we are back together again," OtherJim said. "Riff on that whiff."

"I like the private investigator idea," Jim said. "We can call ourselves **The Bros Grim.**"

"I like," I said. "It's Ok to give yourself a name like a brand name, which isn't a nickname, which we all know must come from another person."

"I like **The Bros Grim** as much or more than I like myself," Jim said.

"Are you ready to vote?" I said. "Those in favor signify by the usual sign."

All three of us gave the F-Troop salute and collapsed into giggles.

We sat there grinning at one another like three balding bobbleheads.

"**The Bros Grim** is good, but the **Frosty Flakes** would have been even better," Jim said.

"Yeah," OtherJim said, "and more descriptive."

"I sure like these little F-Troop meetings," I said. "They put the grin back in our Grim and -- in your cases -- ugly faces."

The next order of F-Troop business
| 13April08 |

"The next order of business," I said, "is a slogan to go with **The Bros Grim.** We need, as of yore, to divorce ourselves from the idea that the Bros Grim have anything to do with faeries, just like in grade school. We don't want that old problem to become new again, do we? Well, do we?"

"No!" Jim said.

"Hell, no!" OtherJim said.

"Ok," I said, "let us brainstorm a business name. Something like **The Bros Grim: Exiles on Main Street.**"

"**The Bros Grim: Slim, Trim, Bald,**" Jim said.

"**The Bros Grim: Smiles by the Mile,**" OtherJim said.

"**The Bros Grim,**" I said, "**We Got Your Back.**"

"**The Bros Grim,**" Jim said, "**We'll Git Your Wife Back.**"

"**The Bros Grim,**" OtherJim said, "**We're Back, Jack!**"

I said, "**The Bros Grim: Happy to Help.**"

Jim said, "**The Bros Grim: Beads, Bells, Incense, Bananas.**"

OtherJim said, "**The Bros Grim: Hippie, Dippie Dicks.**"

"Look at it this way," Jim said. "We can't really improve on **The Bros Grim: Private Investigations.**"

"Yeah," OtherJim said, "except let's use a double tilde instead of a dash or colon between the first and second parts."

He wrote "**The Bros Grim ≈ Private Investigations**" on a piece of paper.

"To those in the know," OtherJim said, "our slogan will be, **We are roughly equal to your pressing need.**"

That got three F-Troop salutes and more giggles.

"I move," I said, "that we put a permanent classified ad in the **Daily**

Afterblatt, Lake Effect edition, announcing **The Bros Grim ≈ Private Investigations** and seeking clients."

My motion put us in motion, and we sent our ad in that very day.

The meeting of the old F-Troop stretched on.

We were on a roll, enjoying the ride, lost in the moment.

Found, hours later, upside down in a muddy ditch.

Listen, Stranger, and yet live
| 14April08 |

There is still that category of truth that I cannot and will not ever tell my brothers, whom I love beyond understanding. Jim and OtherJim have my back, as I have their backs, but I have their backs in ways that they cannot ever know or hear. Then why, you might ask, am I telling you, a stranger like a stranger on a plane or train or bus or boat, about things that would mean certain death for my brothers to know. Perhaps it is not too late for you to run in the other direction, Stranger, though the danger to you is slight. **Trust me**. Just don't grow fond of me. That will put you in danger.

The power of the story, and the too-strong hands that hold that story, lies in the threat to my treasures in earthen vessels. Those hands threaten to become a Grim reaper if I break the **Rule of Silence**.

Keep some distance. You should be fine.

Besides, I am an old hand at this deadly game.

Frankly, if I start calling you **Dear Stranger**, you might want to run.

So you might well ask again -- why you?

Perhaps it is because a secret corrodes its container and leaks sooner or later. You will be the judge of that. Perhaps it is because we probably will not meet again, or because no one would believe you if you told them the story that I am telling you. You will be the judge of that, too.

I know that people joke about their little secrets and say **I would tell you, but if I did I would have to kill you**. A woman once gave me that as the reason for keeping secret her favorite recipe for cherry tomatoes and pesto. I am no longer a violent man, and I do not make idle threats willingly. Add to that my gratitude that you seem willing to listen to this story that leaks from me like battery acid -- a story that might be true, about things that I would rather forget, and perhaps partly have forgotten, or distorted, in the details. The story invades my dreams and slams me back among the wakeful, screaming.

The container has become the thing contained. And it is leaking.

≈ ≈ ≈

Yeah, I know who the local police are dealing with, and I can guess with high likelihood of accuracy about the things that the locals are probably holding back -- among them the reflection of that one detail that sealed for me the veracity of my surmise about my dear, dead friend Mr. Darke. I knew that if the locals were to get any warmer the hammer would come down and smash their **window into the darkness of truth**, like a baseball bat smashing safety glass into a million round and harmless pieces of sundered clarity with all sharp edges removed. I have seen the hands too strong for anyone to withstand wield that baseball bat of interruption. I have coached that batter a time or two.

I love my brothers, and our little meetings of the F-Troop, and their narrower range of memories about Pop. My brothers bring balm to my soul, and I trust them as far as I can safety take them toward the place where those overpowering hands reside, on deck and waiting, baseball bat in hand. There are stories -- devoid of puns, wordplay, or laughs -- that I will not share with my brothers.

I sure could use a brotherly pun right now.

It is not that I would have to kill them if I told them but that the knowledge would put their lives in a vice that would crush them slowly, resolutely, without mirth or remorse.

These are the stories that I will tell you something of, Stranger.

Are you willing to hear them?

≈ ≈ ≈

I am sure that my brothers have their secrets, and I know that their secrets are such that one would chuckle and shake one's head, in affectionate wonder, like Pop would do when we learned the kind of life lessons that skunks teach boys who have too much energy and not enough sense.

A mark of my secret life is access to information about and the ability to find out more concerning persons of interest to me, either professionally or personally. That is why I know that I will learn the truth about my old friend Mr. Darke. That also is why I must -- as always -- lead a double life and that is why I know how to do so. My life, and the lives of my brothers and Eve, depends on my ability to live in two parallel universes that must, like one's wives and girlfriends, never come to any knowledge whatsoever of one another.

Duplicity is how we say *I love you*
| 15April08 |

I believe I know why my old friend Mr. Darke is as dead as a toppled stone statue. The worlds inside him collided somehow, and I am determined to know the story, or die in the attempt to collect the facts and fictions that killed him. I cannot go into that dark wood, where hope has lost its way, and hope to come out the other side, without calling upon the skills and wiles of a lifetime. I cannot walk away, either, because that would be both dangerous and life-denying. I am who I am, and I do not want to be anyone else, nor can I turn my back on the dictates of who I am, and survive. I can either act, or die. The truth is a dare that I cannot, and will not, walk away from. Too many lives depend upon my choices.

The little P.I. agency that my brothers and I are building in such a spirit of glee is partly cover, so I can stay near them in a way that does not threaten their safety and in a way that I hope will heal them of the hurts that their lives have dealt them. Also, I know that being in the business, even in such a laughable capacity, is good cover for those other tasks that I cannot share with Jim and OtherJim, or anyone else.

The duplicity? The duplicity is necessary.

It was Pop who recruited me and honed my skills.

Pop took my dubious native ability and made of it a duplicity to behold.

It was Pop who gave me that **sick sixth sense** that ensures survival.

By playing P.I. with my brothers, and giving them hope by giving them work to do, and by shielding them from harm ... I hope for a good harvest from bad seeds planted and tended in the dark.

What my brothers don't know can't hurt them, if I remain in dual focus.

And if my foci falter, the danger to Jim and OtherJim will lift in that moment of blinding light that comes in time to all spooks like a blaring metro bus barreling out of the dark.

Courtesy of the dependable U.S. male
| 16April08 |

About two weeks after Mr. Darke's death, I received a package in the mail. No note, just a black notebook, well-used and battered, in a padded mailer. The return address was **General Delivery**. The package was not ticking, so I opened it. Was this someone's idea of a joke? I looked at the writing, strange but legible. I was mildly interested.

Here's a sample --

I have done a good job of reflecting on EXILE, but I still need to play with the idea of the saving grace of a core self and one's sense of it. My friend Mr. Black believes, without reference to cover, that faith and a core self occupy adjacent cells in the DNA of life ... or, the prison of existence. Both ideas are available as core stories (back-stories?) to describe life. The two have allure at different times and places of the self. The question is, do some persons actually lack this (saving) sense of core self? The saving ability is a separate journey but possible once one makes the discovery of one's ONE. God, yet a third journey, can be found on this same path.

I paused. The journal was written in a style that echoed in my mind. It was familiar, like a familiar. And Mr. Black. **Mr. Black?** I read faster now --

But what of those who can't, won't, or simply don't find their core self? Some people are simple, perhaps, and able to resist introspection. Those blessed and cursed with introspection may resist acknowledgment of a core self as wishful thinking. Or they may have different ways of knowing and different paths to follow.

Mr. Black?

Or my old friend Mr. Darke?

I read on, with slowly dividing attention --

What is a core self or "core sense of self" anyway? A more important question is this: Can a person who is blessed/cursed with introspection be able to exist, endure or even prosper without a specific idea of who one is at the depths? How long can such a one endure without hope? What happens if Sisyphus never learns to be happy in his work? One must imagine Sisyphus happy. Whoever said that is right. Or wrong.

My thoughts?

Re: "... Whoever said that ..." -- **Camus**. Camus said that, you dummy. I used a hard word for the writer, because I felt a kinship. I realized that I wrote those words dimly remembered and many years ago, on another planet, in a galaxy far, far away. I had become a stranger to myself, speaking across time in the weighty words of a man much younger and far older than myself -- and greeting myself with a holy kiss. But watch! In the nanosecond that it took for my thoughts to form and flee, I felt the horror of exposure.

Someone had me in their sights.

Who!

I realized, as quickly as I went on **Code-Oh-Crap**, that an enemy would not have sent me the original of so shortsighted a thing as a written record of my covert life.

An enemy would hoard such a treasure until an inconvenient time.

There were countless good reasons for the **First Rule of Spooks:**

Never, ever put anything in writing, about anything.

Why break the rule? In my case, because the white canister of a shroud that covered who I really was, while I did spook work for **The Man**, had no safety valve, and the pressures could become enormous.

So, a friend sent me my old journal, but who?

≈ ≈ ≈

I knew a man, way back, in **Operation Beloved**, a preacher who had the case name **Mr. Black**. The Rev. Mr. Black. He knew me as **Mr. White**, the Rev. Mr. White. Our case names spoke of our closeness and our contrasts.

I call him **Mr. Darke**, now.

He might have been the one who sent me what was once mine, in tone and in possession. The timing is arresting, if that is the case. Perhaps he knew that something lethal for him was afoot. What is the message, then, from getting this old but still dangerous journal in the mail?

The Rev. Mr. White wasn't **Goose** to anyone back then. I was posing as a pastor, just as Mr. Black was. It was perfect cover for the work we were doing among liberal, left-leaning churches. My time as the Rev. Mr. White was one of the many black bag jobs that I wish now that I had never done.

But it was **The Job** and I did it, for **The Man**, perhaps to chase away the evil and cleanse the quarters where I would have lived, if I had been a member of and not a shadow of that community.

At least that is what I bought and sold, at a discount, at the time. But memories and mendacity aside, who sent me that journal? If not Mr. Black/Darke, then who?

Where had it been lying, so full of truth and other tales?

Who fired that rusty missile from that forgotten silo?

I have some ideas. I have my suspicions.

Always.

Black/white and read all over
| 17April08 |

From the **Daily Afterblatt, Lake Effect edition.**

Unclaimed, unnamed
Police remain in the dark in death-by-bus

Almost three weeks after a middle-aged male was killed on a rainy night by a metro bus, Buffalonya police say they have no new information.

Police say they continue to know nothing about the identity of the victim or why he was standing in the traffic lane of busy Delaware Avenue near President's Park.

"It's like he dropped out of the sky, right in front of a bus," said lead Det. Joe Blucote. "Someone knows this man, but they are not coming forward."

The night of the tragedy, which occurred in the early evening, was a dark and wet one. The victim was wearing a dark suit and overcoat of good quality and had all the appearances of a successful business executive, Blucote has said. No wallet was found on the victim, who was declared dead at the scene.

An autopsy has been conducted, and toxicology reports may shed some light on the darkness surrounding the case, according to Eerie County Coroner Bruce Backstaff. However, Dr. Backstaff said, results are still days or even weeks away.

"These tests take a lot of time to develop results."

Police ask anyone with information on this case to call the non-emergency number at the downtown district station.

-- compiled from staff reports

The Darke File: Into the light
| 18April08 |

Let us start a file on my old friend Mr. Darke.

It will be his dossier, **for our eyes only.**

I know that this file, and the subject of this file, will certainly be Mr. Darke. I also know that the file and its contents will be about me, and about every spook who has ever lived and moved and had some sort of being in that place I'm calling **Spookistan.**

The contents of the file will come from my writings, present and past, and I will dispense with dates and just give you the essentials about this **Everyman of the Darkness** that we are calling Mr. Darke.

BTW, the official inquiry is going nowhere. It seems wrong to stay silent, except concerning the locals. If I didn't know Det. Blucote, I would feel sorry for him, but I do. Know him. One of the unexpected gains so far has been the subtle enjoyment of Blucote's public admissions of cluelessness. Mr. Darke would join me in my well-harnessed and very private glee at the sight of Blucote, clueless.

Sooner or later, I'm sure, we will get a visit from the clueless lead detective himself, and his silent partner, Det. Bill "Joe Bob" Schmidt.

How a spook walks to the store

He couldn't not look.
To the left.
To the right.
Behind.
Above.
He might not have noticed his own looking.
The habit of pragmatic paranoia had stolen into his deep, dark core. He had ordered it to go there and lurk like security software.
The habits of a long life in the shadows.
Lines of sight.
Lines of fire.
Escape routes.
Suspicious persons. Most importantly, the drab ones who blend in and do dirty work. And walk away unnoticed.
Bulges, certainly.
Even the clichés -- man reading newspaper, man reading upside-down newspaper, man looking in store window, man with mirror-finish sunglasses. Repeat sequence and substitute the word **woman**.
Your life may depend on political correctness.
Women who showed him interest from bar stools. Repeat and substitute **man**. Because this is about them, not you.
He couldn't help exercising his lifelong habits, because he didn't want to stop.
Life is spooky when you are a spook. That would never end, until he did.
Once a spook, always a spook. It's the training.
Boo!
Boo hoo.

The Darke File: Operation Beloved
|19April08|

My sins are ever with me, and many of them fall under the category of **Operation Beloved.** This well-aimed and -timed operation of domestic spook work featured the work of two men, whose case names were **the Rev. Mr. Black** and **the Rev. Mr. White.**

Were we ordained? Were we educated? Did we know our Greek and Hebrew, our modern theologians, our pastoral care?

We knew all these things, and we had the doctored documents and files in friendly places to prove it. A seminary education from bad seed.

≈ ≈ ≈

The aim of the op called **Operation Beloved** was to collect information on churches in cities that shall remain nameless. These were churches that **The Man** deemed to be leftist, or left-leaning, and therefore dangerous. The zenith of the op was the Vietnam War years. Many church people, clergy and laity, joined the antiwar effort as time went on, and Operation Beloved aimed to collect information on such activities in the church community.

We collected information from the top, after we gained positions as pastors in local congregations that our handlers were targeting.

The work had its joys, because one cannot do covert work without being as close to the truth as one can be, with the one exception that the real reason for being there, the spook work, had to remain secret.

In other words, we loved our work in the fields of the Lord. We loved, like good shepherds, our flocks. We preached with zeal, and we marched with conviction. We met weekly with our handlers to be debriefed.

After our country pulled out of Vietnam, there were some lean years, but our handlers encouraged us to perfect our pastoral skills and to harden the hold that we had on our churches. The idea was that we were positioned in places where leftist ideals would meet liberal theology, in a number of ways, over time. We continued with our surveillance of those whom we purported to serve as their shepherds, and the hot button issues came and went, with our churches always finding a place at the table.

We were a goldmine of domestic material for many years on countless issues such as feminism, academic freedom, liberal-driven fallout from Watergate and the departure of Nixon, the rise of investigative journalism, the Reagan Years (especially the radical increase in saber-rattling and police actions in such places as Grenada), and the looney-tunes time of the Clintons.

Operation Beloved prospered until the unexpected happened.

≈ ≈ ≈

Our churches, which had always gotten a kick out of our names -- **Black** and **White** -- and our long relationship, personal and congregational, insisted, when they learned of our impending 20th anniversary of ordination, on a celebration.

In good (or bad) time, as we lived out our tangible, duplicitous calls to ministry, the necessary curtain between our lives as ministers and our lives as spooks, was rent for each of us. We no longer could live both lives, and we resolved to embrace the real one. I and my brother in Christ, the Rev. Mr. Black, began to believe -- really believe -- in what we were preaching.

The God whom we had mocked grabbed us and shook us, and gave us, in a rush, the Holy Spirit.

You should have been there. It was intense.

The next weekly briefing, after our conversion from spook to believer, was the last. To no one's surprise, we were drummed out of the covert corps so quickly that we had no time to pack our bags or catch our breath. Though we should have seen it coming, our handlers even stripped us of our bogus ordination.

We lost, at once, our cover **and** our calling. More than we bargained for.

In rapid succession, we were convicted and justified by the living God and were thrown out on the street by forces of darkness.

We did not even get to say goodbye to our churches. Our handlers took care of that, as the last chapter of our back-story. They inserted the story that the Revs. Black and White, gay as the day is long, had run off together to live in sinful bliss away from the prying eyes of God and Church.

≈ ≈ ≈

We survived, in exile. Separately.

Eve was my redeeming savior, my **goel**. Without her love -- which I stumbled upon like a wandering man in a dark wood where the straight way had been lost -- I would not be alive to tell you this story.

My life, at the end of my covert life, would have crushed me.

For many spooks, including the Revs. Black and White, who generally are forcibly retired at some point, the road to exile ended in Buffalonya, through the work of a man who went by the venerable case name of **Caspar**.

It was not only Caspar himself that I loved but also his bookshop jammed with used books and the haven that the used books and shop provided.

The used bookshop is half of the story. The other half is what used to be described as **my better half**. When I found the bookshop, **Caspar's Books and That**, through muttered stories from old colleagues and such, and when I had made contact with Caspar and had gotten the green light to come join his little community of ex-spooks, I met Eve. That was 10 years ago, and we have been what was once described as **keeping house** most of that time.

Caspar's Books and That - the long version
| 20April08 |

Caspar's Books and That started out as a cover story for over-the-hill spooks accumulated by Caspar (a prince among handlers) in his retirement.

Caspar's own personal **Operation Bookcover** was the capper of a career that flew in the face of the wisdom that said spooks and their handlers were like oil and water, town and gown, Spy vs. Spy, ammonia and bleach.

Caspar had the ability to respect and protect his operational charges, and no handler ever lost as few as Caspar did, and when he retired he continued to have the care and feeding of cast-off ex-spooks as his prime concern.

Never again will there be in play such a man as Caspar.

He really was the **Friendly Ghost**.

At first, Caspar promoted us as spook trainers on a spot basis, with his cut being a certain percentage, but none of us had that much zeal about training snot-nosed young spook wannabes, so Caspar, always the resourceful one, trained his attention on what had started as cover -- the used bookshop -- and made a go at being a bookseller for fair.

With Eve's help, both with the books and with her meta-friendly presence, the bookshop became profitable, and we settled into a pattern of hanging out -- one eye out for trouble and one eye out for the work at hand.

I embraced the change from **fields of the Lord** to **folio folds of the tome**.

A few years ago, Caspar decided that his time in the frozen north was running out, and he passed on to Eve the ownership of the bookshop, for a consideration. He moved to **Florida, Baby**. He had slipped one too many times on the Buffalonya ice and snow, and his already-aching patoot wasn't going to withstand any more of such violence.

That was his story and he stuck with it. **Buffalonya's winters usually get you in the end**, Caspar said, and left.

Spooks as a rule hate their handlers, and wish them in hell with a vehemence that surprises first-timers and outsiders. However, when Caspar left for FLA, nevermore to lead us, at first we were lost, and then we were afraid, and finally we took control of ourselves -- and the **Tribe** was born, or resurrected, from the Apache dreams of childhood with my brothers Jim.

≈ ≈ ≈

When you walk into the bookshop, you hear the little bells that dangle from the plate-glass door. We spookish booksellers hear the bells, too, and that sound divides itself in our minds into two feedback loops -- one loop exciting a level of paranoia and vigilance (**that** never changes) and one loop exciting the hope that you will browse and buy.

Over the years, we have seen enough oddness to warrant the first feedback loop and enough sales to warrant the other feedback loop.

When you approach the bookshop, you see a pile of books in the display window and the stacks further inside. As you walk in, you smell that mixture of dust and mold that all used bookshops exude like cheap perfume.

When you look down, you see pre-war floor tiles that curl at the corners and shatter when abused by heavy objects.

Someone will greet you, and it probably will be the gruff and red-faced **Mr. Red**, and if he is not there, probably the avuncular **Mister Ed**. In either case, the bookshop cat, **Wild Billy,** will add a greeting to the human one, and you will make your way into the stacks.

Most visitors go to the aisle on the left and work their way down and back up the center aisle to the front and down the right side aisle. Behind the main stacks are our backroom and the room where the dollar books and a slightly more pronounced bookshop odor reside. We have a back-back room for junk. The back door opens from there.

The door to the backroom, usually open unless top secret business is going down, has a small sign on it that says **The Bros Grim ≈ Private Investigations ... We are roughly equal to your pressing need.**

As you make your slow way down the aisles, you notice a few old men intent on the titles, or straightening the books on the shelves, though their work is never equal to the need. Books occupy the shelves, from the floor to the 12-foot ceiling -- books of every type and at every angle.

Disorder is the order of the day.

≈ ≈ ≈

If you came in with a box of old books that you were sure that we would want, you might be in possession of a few dollars of store credit (you didn't see the small sign that says **We are offering store credit** _only_ **... until further notice** until someone like Mr. Red pointed it out to you).

If you insisted on cash for the books we accepted, we gave you pennies on the dollar, but if you took store credit, we gave you 25 cents on the dollar, based on what the books you brought in would be marked at -- on the first white page after the **ffep,** or **first free end paper,** and in pencil, dammit, with those quirky and meaningless numbers and letters called the **SKU,** or **stock-keeping unit.** Pencil, because ink is **Enemy No. One** of books. If you were vain and put your name in the book, in ink, dammit, we handed the book back to you because that made the book worth a fraction of what it would be worth sans signature.

When you cashed out, you got 10 percent off without asking, and 20 percent off if we, or Wild Billy, or both, had taken a liking to you.

And no tax.

We cover that from the cash flow.

As likely as not, if you did have some books to sell or whatever, you probably met Eve, who is the one person whom the rest of us trust to buy with wisdom.

The rest of us are hopeless in evaluating the value of used books.

Eve sets prices at a range of five to ten dollars for most titles, with a few that are more scarce, or more desirable, running up toward a ceiling of twenty-five dollars. Any books deemed to be worth more than that go in the locked glass-front cases up front.

We specialize in just about anything, as long as it has either proven value or evident whimsy. And we do have an imposing number of spy novels and mystery novels, plus a quirky offering of theology and philosophy. Math and science make a reasonable showing. In the bargain backroom, the titles run to fiction and the prices rarely run past a dollar. Some of our customers, jangling the coins in their pockets, make a line for that room without hardly looking to the left or the right.

≈ ≈ ≈

Once in a while a **book scout** will barge through the front door with a big box of books that he wields like a battering ram. The scouts lay siege to our cash reserves with a verve that has to be seen and heard to be appreciated. Yes, the book scouts do get cash, and we are glad to give them cash because they will take pennies on the dollar in the knowledge that they can keep a high volume flowing into the used bookshops on their routes.

If they take store credit, it means that we missed something they didn't.

I've been to book sales, estate sales, library sales, and the rest, and I don't know where these book scouts come up with their offerings, but a good scout can come in with a huge box holding as many as fifty books and sell every one at an average price of a few bucks.

They are as loud as they are astute, and they love to tell stories about each book and where they found it and a fibber's version of what they paid for it, and you just stand there and enjoy. The whole thing lasts less than ten minutes and they are on their way. The best book scouts tailor their offerings to the used bookshop that they are entering, so they spend a few minutes motoring through the stacks and noticing what is missing and what hasn't sold.

Next time, they will bring what was missing last time.

Having a bricks-and-mortar bookshop means we don't go to any book sales. People come to us, and the book scouts are the best of the crop. Thank the Dear that they do not have any interest in opening their own stores, or even in selling online. If they did, they would drive us out of business.

≈ ≈ ≈

One final fact about **Caspar's Books and That.**

The name itself.

Caspar was fond of telling about a shop that he saw once, when he was walking around in a large eastern city. The sign over the door said **Twelve Steps and More Store.** This was the beginning of a collector's urge to find as many of these retailers as he could who did not trust their core offerings to carry the day, without the promise of **... and more.**

But that only gets us halfway there.

We still need to understand how **... and more** became **... and that.**

Caspar in his hanging around in used bookshops noticed that a lot of the calls that the clerks received ended with **... yeah, we got that.**

Caspar, also something of a connoisseur of accents and regional idioms, had noticed that in parts of our land folks would end their sentences with the phrase **.. and that.** As in, **We went to the store** and that, **and we bought some eggs and milk** and that. **Then we went home, and watched TV** and that.

Caspar's Books and That stands as a monument to Caspar's perfect pitch in matters of retail and idiom.

Eve kept the name when she bought Caspar out, because bookshops are like that and because **Caspar** was Caspar's beloved case name. Unless you start a bookshop from scratch, you stick with the name that will get you all that good will that you just got done paying for. That means you don't have to go downtown and get your pocket picked by every disorganized crime artist in the city's employ, as well as the official fees and such that you would pay if you were so silly as to want to change the name of your new used bookshop.

The Darke file: Emphasis added
| 21April08 |

File this in the Darke dossier --

I once asked Mr. Darke what he felt was the essential difference between **salvation** and **redemption**.

"Bleep off," he said.

"No, seriously," I said.

"A numb-nuts like you, Mr. White, could not feel the difference," he said, "let alone comprehend it."

So I asked Eve.

"Eve," I said, "what's the difference between salvation and redemption?"

"It's like two ways of saving," she said, "one with Green Stamps, the other with Blue Chip Stamps."

My lips twitched. She noticed.

"Green and Blue stamps," I said. "A bit before your time, I would say."

She smiled, perhaps at the always startling reminder that men are never too old to flirt with a twitch of the lip. Her old guy was one such, certainly.

I should know.

"Not really," she said, "just actually, but one hears things from one's elders, such as yourself, and one finds these crumpled little strings of **Blue** and **Green** stamps in shoeboxes in the attic."

I was standing at the front display case in the bookshop, clad in brown coat and cap. Snow was falling. Eve was in her old man's gray cardigan.

She always is, except for the one day of the year when summer comes to Buffalonya, usually on a Wednesday.

My lips twitched again, close to a smile.

"Which one -- salvation or redemption -- gives **Green Stamps**?" I said. "And where is the redemption center for all these saved stamps?"

Her lips twitched back. I love it when she does that.

"Whichever one," she said, "that you like, you Silly Old Fart!"

I once asked Mr. Darke, "Have you never been in love?"

"**Bleep**-you," Mr. Darke said. "I don't deal in abstractions with the likes of proto-people like you."

He always answered that way, making one word of the **bleep**-you phrase and putting the stress on the first syllable.

So much for the company of friends who would rather be strangers.

What can you do when your double really doesn't like you?

We go back to the onion patch
| 22April08 |

Here is another indication of the distance that I go back, with Mr. Darke.
You could file this in my file, if you needed a place to put it.
Or we could start a file on you.
We had files on everybody. File this in my file, your file, and Mr. Darke's dossier, with appropriate cross-references.
This piece comes from my black-clad journal **book of spells for spooks** that that **other** I wrote when he worked in the shadows with Mr. Darke --

Of lemons and onions - the father of the man

Boy-spook, learning to be an onion, and to act like a lemon. Understanding in time all the fruits and vegetables, and their nature and uses.

Variations and expectations, figure and ground. Deception and exile.

The Lemon Boy and the Onion Boy are two, until the boy learns the secrets of both and chooses on the fly to be both. For survival.

The onion, bringer of tears.

The lemon, provider of puckers.

Both seeking, and finding, a response from others -- a strong, sometimes even violent, response.

Most of us settle for one nature or the other, onion or lemon. The spook, the occasional mutant, chooses both, at a young age, feeling forced to understand how to seem like the one, or the other, in effective ways. For survival.

Is this your story, too? Good.

The lemon, impossible to eat, but a delight to the senses.

An important skill.

And the onion, impossible to eat, but a delight to the senses.

Another important skill.

But deception demands the layers of the onion more than the juice of the lemon, or its zest. These are things of the surface only. In Spookistan, one can be a lemon for a season, but one will return to the onion. One learns to **do** lemon and **be** onion. Thus are spooks made, in the stew pot of living day to day, with a purpose and an agenda.

Add heart. Leave the lid ajar.

Exile awaits anyone who acts out of a personal purpose and agenda.

Such ones of onion and lemon are saviors or heroes, in their own minds, and sometimes are even effective. Such ones learn how to survive, always in an alien place of someone else's choosing.

To survive, one learns tricks.

To prosper, one learns to love the irony of the onion and the lemon.

One learns to live apart from one's joy, to survive rather than prosper.

Still your story, too?

Say some more, then.

Ok, then. I will speak for both of us.

You will need purpose and agenda. You will not need to explain these things to self or others, but you will need these things. Good news is, the Quick can do this, and the Dead cannot. Others will ask you what your purpose and agenda are. You will learn tricks, since you probably should not give an accurate answer, ever, and you will learn that self-knowledge becomes a shroud if you give your self-knowledge away or if someone entices your self-knowledge from you.

You will learn how to shed a layer and go into exile, emerging as the self who you, and few others, know to be the self-same. You will be like a serpent, which in some alternative views, such as the Gnostic, is also the Savior or Hero, the bringer of knowledge, and like Prometheus with a purpose beyond rebel joy.

Trickster.

Wanna know what you're playing for?

Asking is Ok, but you must play.

And you already know the answer.

So share your self-knowledge.

This is your life.

This is our story.

Back then, I heard voices and had conversations with them.

And now, years later, we do the same.

Det. Blucote drops by
| 23April08 |

"Detective Blucote!" I said. "To what or to whom do we owe this visit?"

Blucote glared at me. I said it like **Blue-Coat**, because I knew it would irritate him and because my brothers were standing around, on deck, as per usual, like pundits with pun-bats.

"Bluecoat?" Jim said. "Looks more like a Redcoat to me."

"Yeah," OtherJim said. "Turncoat, more likely."

Blucote's face matched Jim's dig.

"Look, you jerks," Blucote said, "it's **Blucote**. silent **T** and **E**, not **Blue-Coat**. And **Detective** goes in front. And who the hell are youse, anyway?"

"Blucote," I said, "I like to joke around, and my brothers do, too. You know that about me. From now on, we'll just call you **Detectif T-and-A** and be done with it. You can call the wise guy Jim and the handsome one OtherJim. My brothers. Boys, this is **Detectif T-and-A**."

"I know more about you than I wanna, Grim," Blucote said, "but I have this feeling that it ain't all there is to know, and I'm not talking about these overgrown little brudders of yours, neither."

"Always the kidder wid da gud grammar," I said. "So whazzup wid youse?"

"I needed to see a man about a bus, and I was in the neighborhood, so I thought of this charming establishment and its equally charming proprietor," Blucote said, nodding to Eve. "I didn't hope to see you here, though you are on my list of low-lifes to talk with sooner or later."

"My brothers and I are hanging out our shingle here together. You will be overjoyed to hear that we have formed a private investigations firm," I said.

"**Skips 'n' dips**, huh?" Blucote said. "I haven't heard worse news since the day the pig ate my baby brudder. I suppose it's hanging like a dingleberry from your license. They don't look like they have licenses, or shots."

Blucote was talking big, like he had brought his partner with him, but that particular public servant (his partner Det. Bill Schmidt, a self-described M.O.T, as in Native American/Seneca, whom most people called **Joe Bob** because that is so far from the mark) wasn't in evidence.

Jim and OtherJim started to wander in Blucote's direction, like junkyard dogs setting up a pincer movement on a midnight intruder.

Quick-eyed Eve intervened.

"Always good to see you, Dear," Eve said. "Read any good books lately?"

Getting Blucote in the back
| 24April08 |

We gave Blucote a chair in the backroom and grabbed seats for ourselves.

"I'm here," Blucote said, "because I'm at the end of the string on a case that you might have heard about."

"No, Dear," Eve said. "What case is that?"

"It's a case about a guy who was struck and killed by a city bus a few weeks ago. We have no idea who this guy was," Blucote said.

"Who is **we**?" I said.

"My partner and I," Blucote said. "We're getting nothing but grief from the bigger fish. No one seems to understand that we have no handles -- no fingerprints, DNA zip, nothing on him like a wallet. We're not even holding anything back, because we gotta nada."

"But how could we be of help?" I said.

"This little shop," Blucote said, "has always had some characters passing in and out. More than books change hands. We have always known that. Caspar was an interesting and complex man, and Miss Eve is, too. This is one of those times when we hope Miss Eve and her regulars will tell us anything that they hear. Same goes for you Grim mutts."

Before we reacted, the little bells on the front door began to sing.

Eve went out see who had come in.

We looked at one another, like big, fat universes at ease.

Blucote stuck a finger in an ear and sat there as glum as we were Grim.

Hey, everybody, it's Joe Bob
| 25April08 |

Eve returned, Joe Bob in tow.

"Better go," Joe Bob said. "We're double-parked in an unmarked."

Blucote got up, took his finger out of his ear.

"Call me if you find out," Blucote said, "-- **anything**. And thanks for the laughs. Always a pleasure, Miss Eve."

The detectives left the backroom.

The little bells confirmed that they had left the building.

We looked at one another. Well, my brothers looked at me.

"Would someone tell me what the bleep is going on?" Jim said.

"Yeah," OtherJim said, "but don't pipe up all at once."

Eve looked at me, and I looked at Eve. I had a flash that we were playing **What's My Line**. Would the real friend of Dets. Blucote and Schmidt please stand up. Everyone would laugh and clap. Those who had guessed wrong would ruefully shake their heads. Bennett Cerf would say something witty.

Wrong channel.

The brothers looked Grim.

They were waiting for answers.

I cleared my throat and got ready to pitch a story that could be true to the extent that they bought it and that could be modified according to their reactions as we went along.

I hoped that Eve would follow my lead.

"It's this way, Dears," Eve said. "Your brother is a liar, and a damned liar, and can't be trusted to tell the truth. No wonder I love him. You do, too. You just don't know why, so I'm going to tell you some things that may startle you."

Truth is, I would have stretched it a bit
| 26April08 |

I was nonplussed, upstaged, and utterly without the ability to make any comprehensible sounds.

I wandered off to flip the OPEN sign so it said BACK IN 10 MINUTES.

It gave me a sense of power to play with Time like that.

Mighty metaphors make me mighty, too.

Well, I felt a little better, anyway.

Eve could be sketching a death warrant with room for four names.

I still thought that to know my secrets put those whom I love in far too much danger. I tried to keep my cool, but my heart was pounding and my mouth was dry like a desert killing field under a heartless sun.

I was trembling, too, as though the sun had died, leaving Absolute Zero.

But ... . The fact of Eve's continued life in this reality was a counter-argument to my fears. She knew the broad outline, the important particulars, and the important generalities of who I was, am, and ever more shall be. And yet she lives. That said, shaking the dice over the lives of my family made me shake.

There was no way around that.

The truth, frankly, scares me more than anything, because I have so little trust in truth. We never did like one another much.

I locked the front door. I could wait a while longer before hearing what Eve had to say about me. I killed time for a while -- another way I have of feeling mighty in the face of that mighty metaphor.

Me and Big Ben, we go way back.

Back in the backroom, I felt like Huck Finn, listening to his own funeral, while listening to Eve finish telling my covert story to my brothers --

- I was in the doghouse, as Huck often was.
- I had a sharp need to scratch, but I dasn't.
- I liked her version of me just fine, but I would have added some stretchers.

"... so your Pop took Goose aside and invited him into the shadows. Goose was a spook for most of his adult life and the last bit of his adolescence. You guys never noticed a thing, did you," Eve said, "about Goose or Pop."

"We didn't," Jim said. "Goose was Goose. And Pop goes the weasel."

"Yeah," OtherJim said, "Goose was never Geese. And Pop was a lot like a weasel whom we loved anyway."

"And as a girl goose," Eve said, "and not a gander or a weasel, I concur."

I could see that they were taking this well.

They were giving me two thumbs up and two fingers sideways.

All three of them.

Eve was cracking wise, too, which is as rare as good cheeseburgers.

"Goose," Eve said, "it is time to get serious about our guy who got hit by the bus. You know who I mean, and I knew him as well as you did, and your brothers grasp the implications of his death and who he was. And who Pop was and who you are and were in relation to the victim and to me, and to so many others, including Caspar, whose friendly ghost inhabits this shop."

"We need," Jim said, "to take this on as our first case."

"Yeah," OtherJim said, "or we just might not have any other cases. We get that, Goose."

"So Eve told you," I said, "... the whole story. The whole truth and nothing but the truth."

"Don't get your truths in a wad, Dear," Eve said. "I told them the story you told me. You tell us if it's the truth. I'm not concerned about that."

"Friends," I said, "Pilate is my co-pilot. Recall his question: **And what is truth?** I can't and won't promise to tell the truth, but I will promise to work my ass off to save yours and mine."

"The wise know that there are **true stories** and **stories that could be true**, Dear," Eve said. "You find yourself in a dark wood where the straight way is lost -- that is given -- but you also find yourself in the dark with the three persons in the cosmos, **A-hole**, who understand, accept, forgive, and love you, Dear."

"Maybe I can't wax poetic about dark woods, but I can quote Pop," Jim said. **"Truth is a cheetah that is well-nigh impossible to run down. And watch out if he turns and runs back at you. Your job just got more difficult, not easier. Because cheetahs rule.** Pop said that, or should have. Our father the spook."

"Yeah," OtherJim said, "and I don't usually get more eloquent than chiming in with a pun or a one-liner, so I just say this: Truth ... schmooth. Let it lie. If we win, we can lie and we don't have to make any sense. If we lose, we'll be lying there senseless. So let's do something!"

Memo to Stranger: Things not seen
| 27April08 |

I guess I should have told you that Det. Blucote and I have had some interactions in the past. It's a long story, but I thought you might like to know, since what I'm about to tell you won't make a lot of sense otherwise. Here's hoping that you and I come as quickly and cleanly to a meeting of the minds as I did, with Eve's help, with my brothers.

Just remember --
• When I use the word **frankly**, check your wallet.
• When I stop calling you **Stranger**, run.
• The truth and I have a nodding acquaintance.

Truth is (watch it when I say that, too), for a long time now Eve and I have been running the shelter that Caspar built for aging spooks through the bookshop. Caspar retired from a long career in the shadows, maintaining certain connections with certain generally friendly countries and their generally friendly secret services. His selling of the bookshop to Eve was more of an act of respect than any kind of necessity on his part. Eve took some semi-public pains with the purchase price as a balancing fiction to maintain cover for many persons.

The one thing that is real is that we all love books.

Such things do make cover easier to maintain.

The old guys who hang around the bookshop figure into this story I'm pitching to you, in ways that might surprise you. Suffice it to say, you should not make any sudden moves in their presence, and you absolutely should not make any gestures or movements, or negative or disrespectful comments, to Eve. You just might get a cupped collection of angry fingers in the Adam's apple.

At a minimum, that hurts like a bitch.

In keeping with my preferred way with facts and figures, I'm going to tell you things as they occur to me, in the sure expectation that over time I will brief you fully, or as fully as I want to, and that you will enjoy the ride and be glad when we reach our destination (whatever **that** is; I have not idea what it is).

I could apologize for keeping you in the dark and feeding you manure, but the **mushroom theory of management** is axiomatic to covert operations and procedures. This is a fact.

I'm like a friendly fecal-forker, aren't I. That won't change.

Still, I do promise that I will both instruct and delight you with the story that is unfolding. Just trust -- if not me -- my zeal for telling a good and satisfying story that is short on sense and long on whimsy.

Think **Onion Man**. Layers upon layers upon layers with a void at the core.

≈ ≈ ≈

That said, on to Blucote and those like him.

The local police agencies have a dim and derived notion that **Caspar's Books and That** deals in more than just books and other explosive devices for the mind. However, you must understand that the local police agencies also know the stolen-goods fences and their feeders, and the husbands who are currently and probably will be continuing to successfully avoid any consequences from having off'd their wives, and the unmentionables who are not only selling drugs to our children but doing so in and outside the schools and bragging about it.

Add to that the inevitable errors of judgment that some law enforcement types are prone to, as ones who understand the criminal mind the best, and usually from the inside.

In other words, there be many a slip between the cup and the lip when it comes to law enforcement.

As a nation, we Americans tell the naive a fiction about the rule of law that rivals our fictions about the wars we wage, not for freedom or self-determination but for high ideals such as the inward flow of foreign oil.

Those in power are there because they control the definitions of the words that we use to describe reality as we think we know it.

When you understand that the run sheet on any given day at any given precinct station only describes the tip of the iceberg of citizen criminality, you also begin to understand why we could run spook agents on a consulting basis on occasion from the dusty, friendly aisles of the bookshop, mainly in supplying spot helpers for friendly foreign services on a fee basis.

The usual cover is **professorial** or **pastoral**.

Old spooks never die.

They just change their white sheets for black robes that remind one of shrouds. With passports to match.

≈ ≈ ≈

One reason for our continued life under the radar is that we were, up until Mr. Darke's death, protected in part by domestic counterparts of the persons and the agencies whom we served in this occasional capacity.

And we still have the protection of a powerful cache of dirty little and not-so-little secrets that Pop bequeathed to us and to which we have added fresh dirty little secrets.

Let us call this **The Vault**. That certainly is what we call it.

Because of our connections, any local law enforcers who get too close to being a nuisance are warned off in no uncertain terms by their masters.

We are like plankton sending threats via sharks using whales as muscle.

Or were ... . Something went terribly wrong that night when Mr. Darke caught the wrong bus on such unequal terms.

His statue-like stance in the dark street had its genesis in some dark place where evil people know how to control the minds and actions of others.

Our challenge is to figure out **who**, **how**, and **why**.

Once we know the answers to those questions, we just might know what questions to ask next. Answers would help with the trembling, too.

Some things never change
|28April08|

You might think that the size of the threat that we sensed would have stopped our gobs as far as puns and playing around are concerned.

Think again.

We were up against a life-devouring foe, but we were not going to let that change who we were. That meant that rather than a war council or strategy session or **come-to-Jesus** meeting, we rounded up the usual suspects for a meeting of the F-Troop.

The first order of business?

Inducting Eve.

"Mr. Chair Sir," Jim said, "I move that we bring our sister Eve into the family, the firm, and the stay-alive enterprise and tribal adjunct known as the **F-Troop**, and I further move that the usual hazing be at bay because said new member lacks the anatomical profile necessary for the traditional hazing of this body."

"Yeah, Mr. Chair Sir," OtherJim said. "Second."

We signified by the usual sign.

Eve's expression teetered between a smile and a frown, and her utterance was something like the unnatural offspring of a laugh and a groan.

It might take her, and us, too, a while to adjust to the new situations --
• Her first **F-Troop** experience (I had never explained the **F-Troop** to her).
• Becoming a sister to my brothers and to the man with whom she slept.
• Meeting death threats with high hilarity.

She sputtered for a while before breaking into coherent speech.

"I knew," Eve said, "that Goose was crazy, but I didn't know that you two Dears were, too. I accept your kind invitation to join the **F-Troop**, and I say **balls** to the idea that I shouldn't be hazed."

"Looks like our sister Eve is in on all fronts, Mr. Chair Sir," Jim said.

"Yeah," OtherJim said, "she's clear as a bell and not hazy one bit."

"So moved, so ordered," I said. "I've never been so moved or so ordered."

"Well, then, our joy must be complete," Eve said. "Can we save ourselves now, or soon, at the very least?"

Why all the numbers are afraid of 7
| 29April08 |

Because **7 8 9**.
I'm still making that point about seriousness.
We are not afraid of **7**, because we are not **9**.
And because we are not going to be **8**, either.
We are much older by the numbers and perhaps much wiser.
Pop was right.
If you don't laugh at the things, persons, and other forces that want to destroy you, you are already invisible to others and about to become invisible to yourself.
If you can't laugh at terror, only God will be able to find you.
And Pop was right that if you don't laugh until you shake your house on its foundations, you will tremble until the house tumbles.
The earthquake is all.
Choose your shaker -- the salt of laughter or the pepper of fear.
Eve's laptop once declaimed, in an error message concerning its infrared port -- **The computer has offended the printer.**
We need to be that offensive, and that hilarious, if we are to survive.
We need to bite like binary -- and let our yes be **1** and our no be **0**.
That is our code of honor.
We need to be as those who live on the fringe and leave the whole cloth as a shroud for those who would be careful.
We need to stop making sense and start making the big money.
We need to ... .

Chopped and channeled
| 30April08 |

"Goose Dear!" Eve said. "Come back to this universe from whatever one you are floating in!"
"Sorry," I said, "I was just giving myself a peptalk -- channeling Pop."
"Pop was short, like someone had chopped and channeled him," Jim said.
"Yeah," OtherJim said, "he looked like a product of God's chop shop."
"You boys will understand if I only tolerate this and not join in," Eve said.
"Only," I said, "if you can tell me why all the numbers are afraid of 7."
"Because, A-hole, **7 8 9**, Dear," Eve said. "Can we focus now?"
"I'd rather **foci**," I said, "but I can focus, too."

Some decisions will have to be made
| 01May08 |

I like dealing with intelligent people. Pop was, my brothers are, and Eve outstrips us all. In all modesty, of course.
If I had seriously said to them that **some decisions will have to be made**,

they would have chased me into the wilderness and thrown **Strunk and White** at me for good measure, like grim grammarians of the scribe tribe.

I liked it that Eve was kicking my ass, because I know and trust her abilities more than most and better than anyone else. I know more about those abilities, which increase day by day my admiration and reliance on her gifts as well as my own. I had to learn how to trust others, beginning with Eve.

I did not come easily to such a stance. I had been like a prizefighter getting up just before the count of 10. I was unsteady on my new legs, post-Spookistan, and Eve's love and challenge made all the difference -- then, and now.

You might think that I had been trained to trust others, to trust the team, but the reality was that I was the team, and I trusted no one, including myself, especially myself. I have always had self-knowledge, but it was Eve who taught me that I could use my understanding of myself to seek good and mutual outcomes rather than solitary, twisted, covert outcomes that meant nothing good to anyone.

≈ ≈ ≈

When Eve embraced the new order, I was glad, because it is frightening to merge one's family of origin with one's family of choice. If the new and the old don't mix, the choices shatter peace and joy.

My brothers are warming to Eve, whom they have known as a colleague and their brother's partner for only a while. I can lead alone, leading myself alone, but in these later years I also have learned how to share leadership. Eve taught me that, gently and over time, by example. Her covert life has been, and is, as mine is, a varied, rich, and surprising rainbow of lies, damned lies, and just plain good and cunning storytelling.

The depth of Eve's story, just like mine, needs to be a secret to most if not almost all. In our line, however, someone has to know, because no covert role has any truth without a genius in the background, writing the back-story and adjusting the details and coaching the covert actor day by day in his lines and in her aims.

And my brothers are in. Events they cannot control have thrown them on the ropes of my punched-out prizefighter's life. In or out? They are in.

I know that to love even three, let alone a thousand, opens me to a thousand sorrows, but I cannot and will not and do not want to turn back. If we go down for the count, it will be together and because we by our own efforts have not carried the day. I like the odds, and so I do not turn back.

So when Eve called us to heel, I fell in with my brothers.

After a few more puns and funnies, we got seriously down to the new business like junkyard dogs with a bone.

Some decision will have to be made? The four of us, English majors or not, know the passive voice when we see it.

We will have nothing of such passivity. When we begin to plan, we will also act -- kicking ass and taking names. The question is, **Who to kick?**

Who is the donkey trying to kick us in the head, by kicking our old friend Mr. Darke into the next reality?

Who is naughty, who is nice?

|02May08|

The four of us agree --

- That someone, singular or plural, is behind Mr. Darke's violent death (making it murder).
- That someone nice, perhaps Mr. Darke, sent me my old black book journal. A foe would have withheld the thing for evil uses later on.
- That our lives in continuation depend on identifying the person or persons who killed Mr. Darke on that dark and wet night. This we see as seminal.
- That the identity of the friend who sent me the notebook might be helpful for us to know. If it was Mr. Darke, it possibly speaks to his state of mind. At the least, it is a provocative detail to pin down, one of the few butterflies that we can see to chase at this point.
- That we are on our own, and we can trust no one, friend or foe. Friends would be put in danger and foes would become more dangerous if we take anyone else into our circle of intention.

We made a list of the things we know so far --

- That Mr. Darke, AKA the Rev. Mr. Black, is dead.
- That we know what Dets. Blucote and Schmidt know and more, probably.
- That there will be weekly updates in the **Daily Afterblatt** for a while yet. This can help us.
- That my brothers will work together, carefully, with ears open and mouths shut. They will be back to back at all times, like a parody of the two-backed beast, when it comes to watching out for one another.
- That Eve and I will work solo. That is our way and our training, and the safer option for us.
- That we all will be carrying -- cell phones, that is. My brothers will be carrying otherwise. Licenses? Oh, please ... . Ask the drug dealer living and working on your street if he has a weapon permit. His answer will be priceless.
- That I will start with my memories of Mr. Darke, beginning with the most recent, and write a memo to brief the others.

"We need a bar," I said, "or a club."

"We have the **F-troop**," OtherJim said.

"We have the **Dew Drop Inn**," Jim said, "and **The Office**."

"I think Goose is talking about leverage," Eve said. "We need a strong bar and a good fulcrum if we are going to get anywhere with the type of bad guys we're dealing with. These are heavies, no doubt, and they don't move just because some old spook sneaks up and yells **boo**. We need a club to fight back with."

"Don't end a sentence with a preposition," Jim said.

"Yeah," OtherJim said. "That is something up with which I and Mr. Churchill here shall not put."

"Eve sees the prize," I said. "We are up against a strong and immoveable foe, and we are in a position of weakness because we cannot trust our normal sources without testing them."

"Right," Eve said. "We will need to do some double-blind tests to begin a short list of persons to trust."

"It's business as usual in Spookistan," I said. "This stuff is second-nature to us, and the stakes are the usual."

"The **Big Casino**," Jim said.

"Yeah," OtherJim said, "the whole farm and all its animals."

"You get the picture," Eve said. "We'll build an Ark and populate it one or two at a time. Then we'll bring on some rain and see who or what bobs up."

"In other words," I said, "we'll be running in the dark."

"And being glad," Eve said, "when something trips us or someone sinks. We have no leads until we make some."

"Do you old spooks," OtherJim said, "always mix your metaphors? You're like bull elephants in a glass candy store."

We sorta knew what he was driving at. Like he had said, **Do you** see **what I mean** and like we had answered, **Yeah, we** hear **you.**

Hold out for sense and you will get pennies or nothing at all.

We need some big-bucks transformations.

Thus absurdity and anarchy are the watchwords.

Black/white, and read all over
|03May08|

From the **Lake Effect edition** of the **Daily Afterblatt.**

Habeas corpus
Police have body but little else, detectives say

A month after a middle-aged male was killed on a rainy night by a metro bus, Buffalonya police are still in the dark about the identity of the victim or any of the circumstances surrounding the case.

"We have no new information on this case," Det. Joe Blucote said, "and we don't expect any information to be coming forth at this point either."

A clearly frustrated Blucote, and his partner, Det. Bill "Joe Bob" Schmidt, who mirrored Blucote's frustration, met with reporters today at the main police station downtown to discuss the investigation.

Eerie County Coroner Bruce Backstaff appeared briefly, saying toxicology reports had returned from the lab but there was nothing substantive to report.

"No drugs, no alcohol were detected in the victim's system," Dr. Backstaff said. "The mystery continues on all fronts."

"If I knew anything about this case, I would call the police," Blucote said. "No one deserves to die without a name. No one is without a family somewhere."

In answer to reporters' questions, Blucote said that searches of national computer databases have not yielded any missing-person reports that shed any light on the case, which insiders have dubbed "The Mystery Man Murder."

When asked why insiders are calling the case a murder, Blucote said, "I can't control how wags' tongues will wag. If they know anything helpful, they should share that information and leave the jokes to trained professionals who actually know how to be funny."

Insiders also say that a Coroner's Inquest will be convened in the case in the next few days.

Blucote had no comment. Backstaff did not return calls.

Police ask anyone with information on this case to call the non-emergency number at the main station downtown.

-- compiled from staff reports

In or out at the inquest?
|04May08|

The Coroner's Inquest sounded like a must-see event for us, but we could not decide how to handle the exposure that a public gathering would pose for us. It wasn't that we weren't known to the authorities but that the locals would take note of our presence and wonder why we were there. Knowing who showed up was an important thing to possess, if we could possess the information without selling the farm or tipping our hand.

We decided to set up outside, in cars and disguises, to see if we could see anything provocative.

The **Daily Afterblatt** would have to provide the rest.

"We're in a funny place," I said.

"Yes, Dear," Eve said, "funny like a sick joke."

"Like **how did Helen Keller burn her fingers?**" Jim said.

"Yeah," OtherJim said, "**can Johnny come out and play home plate?**"

"Yeah," I said, "like **put your tulips on my organ, said the organist** sick."

"I know as much about your sick jokes as I do about this case," Eve said, "and that suits me in the former and vexes me in the latter."

"Well, put your latter up against the former and climb up and see if you see anything we might have missed," I said.

"I'd rather run that story about Mr. Darke in the **Afterblatt** up the flagpole and see who waves what at it," Eve said.

"Not much there," I said. "Blucote isn't lying when he sez he has less than zero. The questions is, who is interested enough to call for a follow-up story every few weeks? Does someone at the **Afterblatt** know more than is seemly?"

"Seems or seams, it matters not," Eve said. "There isn't a crack for them to pry at, smoke out, or peer into, and we need to keep it that way."

The Darke File: Cover stories
|05May08|

I had homework to do, so I took a walk around the block. I walked over to the corner deli and got some coffee and a donut. I walked to the news dealer and got a newspaper. I wandered around in our stacks, looking at titles. Finally, I sat down in the backroom and opened my little black book, written long ago, to refresh myself some more on Mr. Darke as was. God, I miss the SOB.

Put this in his file, cross-referenced to mine and yours.

Looking into this mirror dimly helps me see both him and me.

Cover stories and such

Cover stories were what you made of them, and like the Rev. Mr. Black's pre-destination mixed with a dash of Process Theology, one could extend a cover story or be lured into new spaces by a handler.

Co-creation was the way to a satisfying life on the stage of cover. Subject and observer worked to make the inevitable effective, and if a new direction felt spontaneous to the subject, the machinations of his observer/handler didn't have to lessen the joy of discovery, as long as one could continue to celebrate the size of one's pleasure dome and didn't run full-tilt into the hard skin of the biosphere in which he lived and moved and had his being. Hitting the outer skin of the biosphere gets old fast.

The trouble started when one no longer could accept these limits.

Some of us had friends, but none of us had family. That would have been im-possible. We were a danger to anyone whom we touched and a curse to anyone whom we embraced. Over time, we made peace with our limits and wrote **family** out of our stories, watching from a distance the ones whom we loved, knowing that contact would leave spots that would fester like leprosy.

Some of us were able to find love on the job, like AIDS victims living and lov-ing with AIDS victims, confining the danger to a population that could not be harmed. Who was to say that such a compromise as this fell any shorter than any other human choice did.

The challenge for spooks was the necessary layer of cold calculation in our DNA -- an infection of auto-focus that attacked -- mindlessly -- vulnerability, ambiguity, and threat. Nothing was simple. No one was safe.

To call us control freaks would have been a stab at an accurate description of the armor that clothed us, even in our nakedness.

Our women tended to narcissism at a minimum and borderline personality disorder at the other end. Our men tended to have sociopathic edges. Other types, such as those who wallow in their precious feelings, didn't reach old age in this business. They either fled or were destroyed, either by their own hand or in the vast shadow of their misalignment with the demands of our craft.

Fleeing was always an option and more easily done during the early years.

Some even wrote books about it.

For those with enough bent skills to become effective in the cold and the dark, leaving meant a journey, with no one watching your back, through the **Vale of Paranoia**. At some point, those who continued on found little difference be-tween going, staying, or continuing as usual. We had learned to love our chains rather than bite down on them, and we enjoyed what warmth we could find.

We learned to love the dark wood that Dante talked of, where the straight way was lost, in the middle of the journey of our life, Mr. Darke and I, the Revs. Mr., as was.

It's knot funny when your string runs out
|06May08|

When I came to the end of my life as a spook, I also came to the border of Spookistan. My string had run out. I stepped into another reality. I dropped the cord that had led me and fed me for so long. I had to find a new song, a new string, some new chords. I was not ready for the change, nor did I want to be anything but what I always had been. And at the same time, there was a nausea about me. I could no longer stand the memories and the realities and the demands of the shadow life.

And I was lonely to the bottom of my soul.

Said it, saw it many time
| 07May08 |

I needed someone to love me, though I could not love myself.

I could not find my self, only my shadow.

Either the Rev. Mr. White or the Rev. Mr. Black would have said that this is the terrifying juncture where one is finally ready to meet Jesus Christ in great power to amazing effect.

The Rev. Mr. Black did, and I did, too. We led others before we finally, unwillingly and unawares, led ourselves to the intersection of sharp human need and God's good provision.

Really.

No one was more embarrassed than I was, except maybe the Rev. Mr. Black. Said it, and did it, too. Our cover became skin. The man and the minister merged, forging a bond both vertical and horizontal.

The Onion Man became the Lemon Man.

If you say it like you mean it, in time you really can come to **mean it**.

We were playing at priestly behaviors to the point where we were playing no more. Talk about playing with the whirlwind.

When I walked out of the life of shadows, mirrors, and stories that could be true, what came into my life -- late, and almost too late -- was Eve, my **Morning Star**. Jesus with skin on, and curves, too.

Lord have mercy.

Eve teaches me the morning's lessons
| 08May08 |

I found, as I wandered, weeping as I walked, like the shades in Dante's Hades, that I could change my Zip Code but that I could not change my nature. Just as the Post Office could always catch up with me if I left a forwarding address, so too could my essential nature catch up with me, with even less information than the mail carrier needed.

I was my own carrier. I could not escape who I was, though at this remove, after meeting and loving Eve, I have come to re-embrace myself and who I am at the core. Eve helped me learn that who I had been -- layers over a void like the onion -- did not foreshorten my options as a person in this world.

I caught the good infection, so to speak.

I learned to sort out, and celebrate, what was good, bad, and ugly about me, with Eve's love and leading, and I am now who I was, and more.

Yet another self to greet over the psychic fence.

Thank you, Jesus. Really, as strange as that might seem.
God covers me like skin. I wonder if I'll ever get used to that.
Or whether I want to.
Lord have mercy.

The first time ever I saw her face
|09May08|

The **general** experience of Eve is this: To know her is to love her.

For me, in the state that I was in, when first I saw her face, the experience was **specific** and overwhelming.

When I walked into **Caspar's Books and That**, on a cold and snowy day, I was inhabiting this world and walking in another, at the same time, like an Indian brave on a vision quest at his elders' bidding.

Like having **someone else's blues**.

At least someone very like me was walking here, and there, too.

I seem to recall.

I was lost in all my worlds. Awake to the blues and unable to rest.

None of my passports was valid.

But Eve's face, that I remember. It was her face, dawning like the Eve she is, that jolted me into one space and consolidated all my worlds.

To me, her face is like the sun, and the moon, and all the stars.

Others say less but still enough to validate the observation that Eve pleases those whom she encounters.

No one would say that in reference to me or most of the people that I have known, loved, hated, or been indifferent to. But Eve is different. Perhaps that is why she is named after the **Mother of All Mothers** and of **All of Us**. Her spirit is strong, true, and satisfying. The absolute best.

She has her faults, but to ignore the towering power of her spirit would be a greater distortion than to insist that she is perfect.

Honey, I'm home, I said to myself, as I looked at her, that first day of the rest of my life, in her old man's gray cardigan and all the rest, but especially her green eyes, windows not only into her soul but for me also a mirror of all my hopes and dreams.

My heart, which I had lost touch with, beat strongly, like an organ that had found its organist somewhere out in the deep cold of space and was sending sudden and urgent messages to the mothership.

The fear of loss, for me?

If **God is dead** were more than a crazy metaphysician's metaphor for our indifference to the Ground of Being and Ultimate Concern, I would only be slightly more bereft than I would be to lose Eve. When one person is resurrection for you, it is hard to take risks, even when you know that there is no other way to live, really live, your life.

Sometime I'll tell you how long it took for her to see me as anything approaching how I saw her. It's a good story, but right now I have to see to our survival. That Coroner's Inquest approaches.

We need to see who cares about a dead and nameless man whom we know as Mr. Darke. AKA Mr. Black.

We need to see who is hoping to infer who we are, or what we represent.

We have a sedate way of savings ourselves, it is true, but it is time to act.

CU, C me - outa sight
| 10May08 |

"We will be in order," I said.

"We will order out," Jim said.

"Yeah," OtherJim said, "and we will be inordinate, though I'm not sure what that means."

"**Tending to, or likely to exhibit, immoderation or disorder**. Your wisdom exceeds your understand, OtherJay," Eve said. "Congratulations."

"Mr. Chair Sir," Jim said, "I apprehend that our fair sister has found a pleasing noun of direct address (and a clever nested nickname) for our fine brother. I move its immediate and widespread adoption, with runners dispatched, now, carrying suitable proclamations to the provinces."

"I will recuse myself later, in private," OtherJim said, "and I don't really know what that means, either, though it does sound like a solo sort of hands-on exercise in self-solitude."

"Excuse yourself," I said.

"Excuse me," OtherJim said. "Forgive me, for I know not what I say."

"So ordered," I said. "And now the vote."

Thumbs up x3, with one abstemious recuser with a new nickname.

"Get your cell phones charged," I said. "We will need them when we go downtown for the inquest."

"I get a charge out of you, Dear," Eve said.

The brothers grinned, and we were off.

Only time would tell us how much we were off by, or how much we were in the dark about very important things.

This was the plan for the inquest caper --

- See.
- Be not seen.
- One static post (OtherJim).
- Two chasers (Goose and Eve).
- One rover (Jim).
- Cell phones stuck on.

The hue and cry of color madness
| 11May08 |

The Coroner's Inquest is a matter of life and death for us, but we had a hard time with all the aspects. Even finding out the time, place, and date was hard, because we felt that we could not just ask.

After saying **This is dumb**, Jim called the Courthouse and asked for the time, place, and date of the Inquest. He got what he asked for, and no more, for which we were grateful.

On the day of the hearing, we took our appointed places, remembering the meta-rules --

- See.
- Be not seen.
- Cell phones stuck on.

You've been to the Courthouse, I'm sure. You know the layout. The street outside is an urban box canyon among tall buildings. That's where we stationed the static post, which was OtherJim, cell phone stuck to his ear, loudly trying to get someone to come and tow his disabled car. Hood up for verisimilitude.

OtherJim was not alone. Jim, the rover, drove around the block, like so many people do every day, letting someone off and circling the block until they came back out. Jim had OtherJim's back. Eve and I were in our cars, a block away at the edge of the traffic circle in front of City Hall.

We could tail any persons whom OtherJim flagged for us, up to a maximum of two.

My brothers, who were fairly new in town, had put on some funny hats and old clothes to minimize their being noticed and recognized by the few persons such as Dets. Blucote and Schmidt who had seen Jim and OtherJim up close in my or Eve's presence.

We realized that we would have to take someone into our circle, because to have no one inside the Courthouse would make the rest of our preparations useless. Our inside man was Mr. Red. We knew that we could trust Mr. Red, and we knew that he knew his business.

Eve and I go way back with Red.

\<Begin aside> Mr. Red - what's in a name?
| 12May08 |

Our names are the colors of the rainbow -- in **kid kolors.**
Red red.
Black black.
White white.
Green green.
Blue Blue.
Each color stands for a life that takes a stance at the other end of the spectrum, where shades and hues and tones are ambiguous and easily elide into other shades, hues, and tones in a way that is, well, colorful.

It is one of our many little jokes.

Mr. Red? In a moment.

It's time for you to meet the whole palette of old spooks who haunt **Caspar's Books and That.**

Colors make for strange, lurid bedfellows
| 13May08 |

The color guard will be livid that I'm telling you about them, but their love of Eve will keep them in line. It did with Mr. Red, when Eve approached him. Red quickly saw and already knew that our and his safety, and continued presence on the planet, are parallel concerns. This kept him from exploding in his usual volcano of rage. Our universes are in alignment on this one. Someone has killed one of us. That paints a target on each of our backs.

This is the line-up --

• **Caspar,** the friendly bear handler for a well-known, seldom loved Company. Like the rest of us, he is retired, in a way, and useful in certain narrow situations, still -- at least he was, before he moved to Florida. For us, Caspar had been more than an excuse to gather. He was also a person to enjoy. He was a handler, and we were bears, but there had never been a better handler than Caspar. Sometimes, before he decamped to the Sun Belt, Caspar himself would be behind the display case at the front of the bookshop. White to a fault, from his groomed beard to his full head of hair, to his pink face, he was a white ghost. A spook. And the energy core of a cell of exiles from the ends of the earth. The charge we got from Caspar lasts a lifetime.

• **Eve,** our Lady and the reason for our being. Eve is the one that we all would die for. She sometimes goes by the last name of Green, like her eyes.

• **David**, the bookshop's young man of all works. He wears his cover so well that patrons assumed he is a minimum-wage bookstore wog or wallah. David, as yet, is without color.

• **Mr. Red**, our math genius, from Mother-bleeping Russia (he learned a version of gutter English from drinking buddies who relished their role in his corruption into English as spoken in low-rent whorehouses, serious alky bars, and the mean streets and alleys of our or any city).

• **Mr. Blue AKA Mister Ed**, an expert in the Fifth Estate and a towering presence in our midst.

• **Mr. Blac**k, born-again, pious, foul-mouthed, and as kind as Eve, but only in secret and at random. Currently missing, feared dead. AKA Mr. Darke.

• **Mr. White**. Speaking. Writing. Whatever.

The verdict on the Coroner's Inquest
| 14May08 |

The coroner has stepped in because our friend Mr. Darke, or whoever it was, did not die in a hospital or with a doctor in attendance.

The coroner's job: Set the cause of death and begin, if indicated, the laying of blame, right on up to the level of criminal culpability.

This is what we knew and what we could infer from what we knew --

• Dr. Backstaff had some suspicions that he did not want to keep to himself but must in due diligence share with a special jury of his calling. My guess.

• Their job (the jury): Bring back a verdict more closely defining the cause of death -- as **natural**, or **by the hands of person or persons unknown**, or **by criminal neglect**, would be options. A matter of law.

• One provocative detail: The victim stood in the road, in the rain and dark, like a statue. True, according to press reports of police statements.

Why was the question for the coroner and his crew to answer, to indicate a direction that might lead to an answer, and anyone can tell you that **why** questions are generally unfruitful. For example, a chubby person can know all sorts of reasons about **why** he eats too much and he will still reach for another donut. A coroner could figure out **why** Mr. Darke died the way that he did and still not know if it was murder.

Toxicology reports, which always are a case of **garbage in, garbage out**, and administered usually to detect the presence of restricted or dangerous drugs, had given no clues in Mr. Darke's case. The tests are ordered by persons who do not know what they are looking for. That means that a substance could still be a factor in Mr. Darke's death, and that that substance could be innocuous, such as couch syrup or anti-histamine or two aspirin in a glass of carbonated sugar water. That sort of thing.

The coroner's jury by rule would confine itself to **means** rather than **motive** or **opportunity**. One piece of the puzzle could fall into place.

May the jurors and the detectives chase their tails for a long time. The longer the bad people think that no one is close to figuring out their game, the safer for us and the more time we have to approach them in the dark on their blind side. In the tall grass where the snakes wait.

No one can see much right now.

May this night be long.

<End aside> When you don't have a map
| 15May08 |

We were in our places in the Courthouse and outside. We noted who was coming and going (many, many persons), and we noted a few odd persons, but we came up with nothing.

We had no map, so we had no idea of the territory.

We found nothing because we were lost.

Mr. Red told us what he could of who was present.

Jim and OtherJim were in place, and they had nothing to report.

Eve and I followed countless persons, but only with our eyes, until they were out of sight.

Mr. Red had reported over his cell phone, by going into the men's room, that only the coroner, a clerk, six jurors, and Dets. Blucote and Schmidt were in attendance. And a woman with a notebook whom he identified as a reporter for the **Daily Afterblatt**, based on overhearing her ask Blucote for a comment and writing it down in her notebook.

Mr. Red said they seemed to know one another.

Mr. Red was in a mild disguise -- pressed suit, clean shirt, hairpiece, and variable-tint glasses.

He looked nothing like he does at the bookshop. We were hopeful that he would not be recognized.

Of course, we had no idea who we were guarding against.

Mr. Red spent the time reading a newspaper on a bench next to the door to the room where the inquest was held.

He could hear what was said but did not have to take the more drastic step of going into the room and sticking out like a bald guy in a cheap wig at a coroner's convention.

The hearing took 10 minutes.

Mr. Darke deserved more, but we were the only ones who could unlock his secrets, and we had thrown away the key.

The score was zero, all around.

One thing was certain, however.

The coroner, Dr. Bruce Backstaff, asked for and got a verdict of **death by suspicious circumstances by a person or persons unknown.**

Mr. Red said that Backstaff told the jury that in his opinion there was something not-right about the unknown person's death and that he wanted the file to stay open, pending any developments in any direction.

Backstaff said that toxicology reports merely check for certain substances.

"All I know," Backstaff said (according to Mr. Red), "is that this man died in a fashion that raises questions. His stance in the rain, as described by witnesses, indicates that something was not right with him, but what that was we do not know. I, for one, will not leave him dead by the side of the road without a good-faith effort to pin down the particulars. If I died and no one knew who I was, I would hope for as much from those who found me."

Mr. Red said that Backstaff spoke into a mike.

There could be a recording of the hearing.

Mr. Red promised us a transcript of what he recorded with a tiny recorder hidden in his shirt pocket.

You never know.

According to Mr. Red, Backstaff said that there would not be a burial until there either are developments in the case, someone comes forward to claim the body, or such time as he decides that the public's interest would not be served by any further delays in putting the man and the case file to rest.

Black/white and read all over

| 16May08 |

This article appeared below the fold on the front page of the **Lake Effect edition** of the **Daily Afterblatt.**

It's murder for sure

Coroner's jury concurs in 'Mystery Man' case

By Jeanne Wheenin
Afterblatt Staff Writer

It was a case of not knowing whether to groan or applaud.

But the six men and women who sat as a Coroner's Inquest jury in what is now widely know as the "Mystery Man Murder" case gave it their best Friday morning, with their game faces on.

Dr. Bruce Backstaff, Eerie County coroner, explained to the jurors that he had called the panel into session to help him sort out a baffling case of a man killed by a bus on a downtown Buffalonya street, on a dark and rainy night about six weeks ago.

In the time since, Buffalonya police detectives have been unable to find or release any details about the victim, such as age, ethnicity, name, or address.

The two detectives assigned to the case were in attendance, making up the lion's share of those present for the hearing, which was brief though not necessarily to the point.

Although the case has garnered some attention in local media, some City Hall observers have already questioned tying up what amounts to 25 percent of the detectives assigned to the downtown district.

The coroner sounded like one who would favor the continued use of the two detectives. After all, he impaneled the jury.

"All I know," Backstaff told the jury, "is that this man died in a way that raises questions. His stance in the rain, as described by witnesses, indicates that something was not right with him. What that something was, we do not know. I, for one, will not leave this man dead by the side of the street without at least a good-faith effort to put down the particulars. If I died and no one knew who I was, I would hope for this much from those who found me."

The jury, after the briefest of huddles, returned the verdict that Backstaff asked for -- death by suspicious circumstances by a person or persons unknown.

He told the jury that the case, in view of their finding, would stay open for now, or until someone came forward with pertinent details about the victim, or until the coroner himself closes the file and releases the body for a pauper's burial at public expense.

After the hearing, when asked for comment, the lead detective, Joe Blucote, a veteran of the force with 24 years of service, and his partner, Det. Bill "Joe Bob" Schmidt, had little to say.

"No comment," Blucote said, "and not because I refuse to talk but because I have nothing to share despite constant following up of leads by myself and Det. Schmidt."

Blucote said that he and his partner have been assigned additional cases and have slowed the pace of their attention to the rapidly cooling case of the unknown victim.

The detective said that he and his partner did not dispute or necessarily disagree with the coroner's concerns or the jury's finding.

Although the case has grabbed occasional media attention, no one not connected with the case was at the hearing.

There was no more than a single well-dressed older man on a bench anywhere near the hearing room in an out-of-the-way corner of the Hall of Justice.

Blucote asked that anyone who has any knowledge concerning the "Mystery Man Murder" case to call the central police district offices downtown.

Mr. Red takes a great fall (for Eve)

| 17May08 |

It was a grim crew that gathered for a meeting of the F-Troop in the backroom at the bookshop. My brothers and I are Grim under the best and the worst of circumstances. Eve joined us in grimness.

Mr. Red was living up to his name, as usual.

"I can't **bleeping** believe that I get the mentions in that newspaper story," he said. "That could be for the **bleeper-bleeping** death of me."

Mr. Red was thoroughly addicted to the **bleep-word** and all its permutations, and he had no idea that his addiction put other people, even seasoned salty talkers, on edge.

"You took a chance for all of us, and we are grateful," I said.

"If you wanna make an omelet, you gotta break some eggs," Jim said.

"Yeah," OtherJim said, "and if you wanna make an egg, you gotta break a chicken out of its prison."

"I know that you went because I asked you," Eve said, "and, Red, you have to know that I'm grateful and that I knew what I was asking you to do. We're all under a death watch on this, and we all will be taking chances, for the common good. You know this."

"Lookit," Mr. Red said, "I'm just feeling **bleeping bleeped** to see myself in that newspaper. I get over it."

(As amusing as it would be to quote Mr. Red in all his variety of expressions, I will confine myself to **bleep** and variations to describe the particular English-as-a-second-language skills that he learned from bar stools and brothel beds. You'll just have to use your imagination ... or step outside and listen to the adolescents and teens walking up and down your street.)

"Let us get to the point," I said. "This meeting of the **F-Troop**, with special guest noted, will come to order."

"What the **bleep** you talk about it," Mr. Red said. "I don't know from **bleeping** F-Troop. You waste my **bleeping** time and make me **bleeping** angry. If you don't want to get **bleeping bleeped**, get serious of this."

"Red," Eve said, "the bros Grim are crazy. That is given. But they are all we have except for ourselves. We need all the help we can coerce."

Mr. Red continued to mutter.

"Mr. Chair Sir," Jim said, "in view of our hostile witness, I move the adoption of Minute Order No. 1, to wit: We will go short on clownish behaviors and go long on third down."

"Yeah," OtherJim said, "I **Second** the **Minute**, Mr. Chair Sir. I will undertake to be serious, in a serial sort of way, anyway. And I'll pass on third down, too. Skip right to fourth. Be a punter. Stuff like that."

"So ordered," I said. "Next item of business -- grilling Mr. Red."

Mr. Red began to glow again. He was not willing to have any fun with us.

"Red," Eve said, "this is their way of getting to work. Maybe you could just make a report."

"Alright, Eveie," he said, "I'm of the report."

"Hold on," Jim said, "who is E-V?"

"Yeah," OtherJim said, "who is this **Eee-Vee**?"

"Her," Mr. Red said. "I call her **Eveie** and always would be doing this. You got **bleeping** problem with that, **bleepers**?"

"Brother-boys," I said, "anyone with the proper permissions can modify the nickname file of any of us. It is what makes nicknames fun. And please, **Mr. Beet**, make your report."

Mr. Red again began to glow like a red balloon with a nozzle up its bleep. Eve simply said, "Red."

"Ok," Mr. Red said, "for you, Eveie, I am talking."

Mr. Red sets the seen/scene
| 18May08 |

Eve led Mr. Red back through his time at the Courthouse.

He really didn't give a bleep about the rest of us.

"Red Dear," Eve said, "what sticks out for you in all that you saw?"

"Nothing sticking out, Eveie," Mr. Red said. "There isn't much to tell. I am coming, I am seeing, I am sitting, I am leaving."

"Tell us about the jurors," Eve said.

"Four women and two men," Mr. Red said. "Two old, two very old, and two just right."

Anything stand out about any of them?" Eve said.

"The women's blouses?" Jim said.

"Yeah," OtherJim said, "or the men's bellies?"

Mr. Red continued to live up to his name. Eve pressed on.

"Just that they seemed to be knowing one another. I guess they serve set term, like the six months, so they are knowing one another," Mr. Red said.

"Who was there first, the jurors or the coroner?" Eve said.

"The jurors," Mr. Red said.

"When," Eve said, "did the detectives arrive?"

"About the time hearing starts," Mr. Red said.

"And the reporter," Eve said. "Tell us about this Jeanne Wheenin."

"Now you give me," Mr. Red said, "something nice, Eveie. The reporter was looker, in dark way. Tallish with the heels. And young, very young. And on the plump side of slender. Like you, Eveie. But tight, short skirt, black, with black shoes, expensive, with heels, sharp like spikes. Dark hair to base of neck. Very dark red lipstick. Slutty, frankly, but in pleasing way, if you know the meaning."

"And I think I do," Jim said.

"Yeah," OtherJim said, "we are liking slutty."

"Oh, do shut up, TwoJim," Eve said. "And you, too, OneJim."

Eve was smiling her Buddha Girl smile.

"She was hard-looking, Eveie, and not at all what you would expect for the reporter. She looked smart, I suppose -- sharp intelligence. Was bundle of sexy contradictions, I am of the guessing," Mr. Red said.

"Fine, Dear," Eve said. "We're getting somewhere. Now, who looked at you? Who noticed you? Anyone?"

"Reporter did, Eveie," Mr. Red said. "She is looking right at me, with leer almost with the mouth askew. Can the woman leer?"

Jim and OtherJim were beginning to get interested. How do I know? They let that juicy question go by unchallenged.

"Did she say anything to you, Dear?" Eve said.

"No, Eveie, she sorta smiled, sideways-like and sour like lemons. It was unsettling but in better way," Mr. Red said. "Bitter and the sweet."

"Did she look at you when she left?" Eve said.

"I left just before the people left," Mr. Red said.

"Did she follow you?" Eve said.

"I'm going to say the no," Mr. Red said, "but who is knowing?"

"Indeed," Eve said. "Thank you, Red."

Black/white/red and ogled all over
| 19May08 |

Indeed, indeed.

We had but a few seconds to savor the ambiguity of Eve's benediction on her grilling of Mr. Red.

The little bells on the front door of the bookshop that indicate visitors began to indicate -- nay, herald -- visitors. David, whom we stationed at the front so that we could be left alone in the backroom, tapped on the door frame. He looked pale.

The young woman behind him looked pale, but David looked unwell-pale.

"Someone to see you," David said and departed for the front. Quickly.

Our singular visitor stood in the doorway.

She looked swell-pale.

My brothers looked like junkyard dogs, tongues out, jonesing for a bone.

This was the crop: Black skirt, hair, and high-heel peep-toe pumps, very red lipstick, with a **go-to-hell**, crooked half-smile on her pale face of Punk/Goth elegance.

Jeanne Wheenin, the reporter girl, in the flesh.

Thank the Dear that Mr. Red had immolated the wig and changed into his regular dumpster-derived clothes.

We were about to see how good his disguise had been.

My brothers, staying in their doggie mode, looked like they wanted to lick her, maybe nip at her ankles.

I just wanted to love all 6 feet of her and the two pedicured ones, too.

I wanted a friend, not an enemy, when I look at Jeanne Wheenin.

She was in the right place at what I hoped could be the right time.

Otherwise, we were **bleeping bleeped**, with a **bleep** chaser, to borrow a few frank words from Mr. Red.

We needed a friend in the worst way, but who would look to the **fifth-for-lunch estate** for friends?

Like we had any choice.

"Down boys," Jeanne said to my brothers. "You do do a passable imitation of a couple of bald bobbleheads, though, I will give you that. For free."

She gave them that sideways smile that Mr. Red had described. Bitter and the sweet like lemons. Red had the smile down.

"Hello," she said to the rest of us.

"Nice wig," she said to Mr. Red, who began sputtering and did not stop.

"How did you find us, Dear?" Eve said. "We've been expecting you. We just didn't know when."

Eve gave Jeanne her Buddha Girl smile that said Eve didn't notice, wouldn't notice, ever, how men in general reacted to Jeanne. Eve can be so warm and loving to strangers. Eve looks into the heart.

Looking at Jeanne, heart rate up just a tick, and chest just a bit tight, I wondered if she needed another person who wanted to love her. It all depends on how you define **love**, as **affection** or **affliction**.

"I have a proposal," Jeanne said, "and I expect that you will be surprised, indignant, and pleased, and generally in that order."

"Surprise us," Jim said.

"Yeah," OtherJim said, "and please please us."

We get to, got to know one another
| 20May08 |

"I'll start," Jeanne said. "I'm Jeanne Wheenin, a reporter of dubious distinction at the **Daily Afterblatt, Lake Effect edition**. I don't know you, except by reputation, with the exception of this bald, handsome man, lately bewigged, who is doing a passable imitation of a pregnant dirigible."

"Oh, **bleep**," Mr. Red said.

"Nice disguise, BTW," Jeanne said. "I mean it. Really, I do. No one else saw through it, I'm sure."

"Oh, **bleeping bleep**," Mr. Red said.

"I'm Goose Grim, P.I.," I said, "and this is my brother Jim and my other brother OtherJim, my partners. The beautiful woman of a certain age is Eve, who owns the place, and the man threatening to go **ka-blooey** is Mr. Red. The young man who showed you in is David, who is something of a dogsbody around here, though my brothers, I agree, are doing a good imitation of a brace of bobbleheaded junkyard dogs at the moment."

Jeanne gave us that unsettling sideways smile with the lemons, which didn't do much for the state of mind of the men in the room. My brother-boys were still in the junkyard, I was still monitoring my vitals, and Mr. Red was just that. Eve, bless her, was not affected.

Eve showed Jeanne to a seat and shot me a look, spook to spook, that said something eloquent about the state of affairs. For a couple of old hands in the deception business, this was no more than another in an endless series of a dry runs working up to the **Day of Wrath**. Or so we hoped.

Indignant does not describe the feeling
| 21May08 |

"I figure it this way," Jeanne said. "You either have to hire me or kill me.

There doesn't seem to be any other option that makes sense."

My heart thundered the three brutal opening beats of **Verdi's Requiem.**

It would take more than a moment to sort this out, but the cards were on the table and we had to pick them up. And what goes for cards goes double for those who live inside deception -- keep your friends as close as your cards and your enemies closer. I had no idea of Jeanne's motives, but I knew that for good or ill we would have to keep her close indeed. My brothers would agree. A spook learns early that a functional world has ambiguity at its heart, and as its heart, and your friend today may be your enemy tomorrow but that is no reason to be paranoid, exclusive, or snotty. One merely has to be blessed with a penetrating sense of the moment and the persons and passions at play.

Everyone has a double, and at heart is one, too, so the prospect of Jeanne's playing a double game was not necessarily a problem. The quality of her contribution would be the key, and if she were running a double game, her product would have to be the best. We needed the best right now, however we could get it. The **friend** thing would sort itself out, by itself. It always did.

Eve would have agreed with me, I know, but she was too busy tracking Jeanne to be reading my mind.

My brothers were locked on like junkyard fighter jets.

"It is," Jeanne said, "this way. I hate being a reporter, almost as much as the management at the **Daily Afterblatt** hates my being there, for so many reasons, beginning with the effect I have on others, men especially."

Jeanne gave us that rueful sideways smile again. Bitter and sweet.

"You poor thing," Jim said.

"Yeah," OtherJim said, "I can feel your pain. Just say the word."

"Seriously," Jeanne said, "I'm more than ready to make a change, and my time in the newsroom has taught me a thing or two about investigations. I saw your ad in the classified section -- **The Bros Grim?** -- and have heard all the rumors about this bookshop and who hangs our here, and I thought, **Why the bleep not?**"

"Why not **what?**" I said.

What rumors, I wanted to add but didn't.

"Why not hire me as an investigator or fellow traveler, or whatever," Jeanne said. "I know a lot about the craft, as a newsy fellow traveler, and I know a lot about you folk, which should be a testament both to my skills, my utter discretion, and my utility. And I could help out around here, too. I do love books."

"Jeanne Dear," Eve said, "this is rather sudden, but we are interested -- I can tell that by looking around. We will have some questions, and we will want you to say some more about just what it is that you think you know about us, and we will need to talk among ourselves after that. Fair, Dear?"

"More than fair," Jeanne said. "It's not every day that someone walks in and claims to have blown your cover. That's why I either stay or suffer consequences, and I'm thinking that my being here, with a proposal, rather than taking a short-time payoff and writing it up for the bleeping **After-Blatt,** speaks to my good intentions."

Boom, boom, boom went my heart. **Dies irae** indeed, indeed, indeed.

Testicles are a state of mind, I said to myself. **This girl has a fine set. Brass.**

Balls, cried the queen, had I but two I would be King, I said to myself. **You got 'em if you believe that you do. Jeanne believes that she does.**

"Oh, **double bleep**," Mr. Red said.

"Look," Jeanne said, "I've been poking around, and talking to some people, and putting this and that together. You would be surprised at what a wide-eyed, innocent young woman with big eyes and all can lever out of big bad men who know too much and talk too much."

"I know," Jim said. "Believe me, I know."

"Yeah," OtherJim said. "Do I ever. Let me tell you something."

Mr. Red just said, "Oh, **bleepety bleep bleep**."

"What we really need," I said, "is someone on the inside, if you know what I mean. And I am sure that you do."

"Look," Jeanne said, "I want to go out of the newsroom with my shield on my back, not sprawled out on top of it like a Goth Wars trophy. I'm out of there, whether you take me on or not, but I have contacts there and in the community that will be intact. I can promise you access to a type of information that you may not be able to access yourselves on your own."

If you only knew, I said to myself, **and I think you might.**

I was keeping one eye on Eve, and I was reassured by what I was seeing -- blue skies of serenity, approbation, Buddha Girl bemusement.

I wanted to trust my gut, too, about this womanish girl.

Our choices would spell life or death for us, not her.

Jeanne's offer of inside information was very appealing.

We shot an arrow into the air, it fell to earth we knew not where ... until Jeanne walked into the bookshop. That, really, had been our covert goal -- to throw a **Hail Mary** pass and attend to who caught it and in which direction they ran.

A gambit but not a Fool's Gambit, we had hoped. More of a fling.

"How would you quit?" Eve said. "And how could you come here to work in any believable way?"

"In a rage," Jeanne said. "And I'd hire on, ostensibly, as a clerk in the bookshop **while I sorted out my thoughts and feelings**. That is what I'd tell those who asked me for reasons."

"Don't quit your day job just yet," I said, "but do come back in the afternoon. We'll have a decision for you."

"I notice that I'm **walking** out rather than otherwise," Jeanne said. "I like that a lot. I do."

We all watched as Jeanne clicked her way out the door like a punk princess leaving for an afternoon of shopping at the Good Will.

I had a good idea what the vote would be.

Double or nothing - roll the dice
| 22May08 |

"The F-Troop will be in order," I said. "And we will, as usual, dispense with the reading of the minutes until some one of us learns how to read or write, or both, like good little boys and girls do."

"Second, Mr. Chair Sir," Jim said.

"Yeah," OtherJim said. "Voting **yes** over here, Mr. Chair Sir."

"**Bleep**," Mr. Red said. "**Bleep**."

Eve just smiled her Buddha Girl smile.

"Discussion is in order," I said, "concerning the proposal that Jeanne Wheenin come on board."

"Her arguments," Eve said, "are that she could have stayed away, written a story, and not cared about the fallout for us. I'm inclined to buy those arguments, at full price. And I like the inventiveness of her solution to the appearances, by coming on as a clerk in the bookshop until she sorts out her life. That was smart."

"Handler-smart, perhaps, but I think it was her own idea. I don't see her as a plant or a double," I said. "I go by the adage among the newspaper people I have known. They say that **if your mother says she loves you, check it out**. That's our assignment, and having her underfoot is the best way to follow through to the place of greater certainty. We can't **not** respond to the threat and opportunity that she embodies."

"And so well," Jim said.

OtherJim wagged his head, his tongue, and his tail, in agreement.

Junkyard dogs, the both of them, but I love them anyway. And not in spite of, but because of, who they are and the way they are.

When you say **I love you**, you have to mean all of **The Other** and in particular the hard parts. I hoped this would be possible with Jeanne, too.

"She certainly is not offering herself at a discount," Jim said.

"Yeah," OtherJim said, "and she is worth every penny."

"We are inclined, I take it," I said, "to accept her proposal. I do, certainly, for the reasons that I've given and for the gut feeling that I have about this."

"I, too," Eve said, "see no barrier to taking her on. We don't need to know everything about her in order to do that."

"No," I said, "we certainly can learn on the job better than off, and we can't exactly go ask our friends in various places to run a check on her. She, like Jesus, will be her own witness, and we will be the jury and the Pilate of our own ship. If she is playing us, she will have to give us enough, and a little bit more, to lull us into accepting her because of the quality of her product. If she is selling crap, we'll know it."

"Right," Eve said. "She has to deliver and keep on delivering or we will become suspicious beyond what is normal and usual for people like us. We are in serious need of some good product. We don't have much."

"Ok," Jim said. "OtherJim and I are learning on the job, too, from the two of you, whose experience in these matters is a recent revelation for us. But what about Mr. Red? All I've heard from him is **bleep, bleep, bleep.**"

"Oh, **bleep** you," Mr. Red said. "Is all I am having to say."

"Red Dear," Eve said, "you always were excitable. Relax, this is the familiar ground. We vouch for those whom we can vouch for, and we seek the assurances of others when it comes to new persons and new territory. And when we must, we run our own tests, double-blind tests, and voodoo rituals to arrive at some working version of the truth. You are willing to work with Jim and OtherJim because Goose and I have assured you that they can be trusted. That's how we have always worked. Speaking to that, we will have to brief David about all this. He will need to be in the loop, too. And the others as they wander in."

Mr. Blue would be wandering in but not Mr. Black, I feared.

"I say we trust Jeanne to be," I said, "consistent, and who she is, and that this is the best way to find that out. We are not a secret society but a group of crazies of a particular spookish sort who are hidden in plain sight and up to a few weeks ago hidden securely under God's wings and seemingly with God's sanction if not favor. The fact that she was able to find those wings and take a peek under them is a strong indication of something about her that is very, very promising as well as very, very alarming, at the moment. For whom, we will find out. We are a known quantity, but until Mr. Darke's death we were exempt. We assume that the revoking of his exemption means the revoking of ours, too."

"And if we are ever going to find out," Eve said, "where the threat is coming from, before it's too late, we will need to take the usual chances. The only secure place is between your ears; the rest is a zone of possibility where persons prove or disprove themselves with every choice that they make. I vote with Goose. What about the rest of you?"

"Great legs and smile, et cetera," Jim said. "I vote yes. We must keep those legs nearby and around us at all times."

"Yeah," OtherJim said, "we must, we must. The legs and all the rest, close and closer every day in every way."

"Oh, **bleep** it," Mr. Red said. "Yes. I'm trusting you, Eveie, you alone."

The long and short of it, in briefs
| 23May08 |

"Congratulations," I said, "you have been chosen from among thousands of applicants to share in the joys of the Bros Grim, **Caspar's Books and That**, and related quasi-criminal concerns."

"Thank you," Jeanne said. "I thought that you might see things my way."

"We often look your way, certainly," Jim said. "You bear up well to such scrutiny even on short notice."

"Yeah, OtherJim said, "and we notice and look away but not willingly."

"**Arf**," Jeanne said, smiling sideways.

My brothers, not for the last time, went all pink.

"Welcome, Dear," Eve said. "We will introduce you to the bookshop drill here as things go along, but the covert aspect of our connection demands immediate attention. That much is clear."

"Tell us what you know," I said, "and don't be stingy with the details."

"It would take a long time to tell you what I know," Jeanne said, "but I will confine myself to what I have found out about the bookshop and you who dwell here. I took the liberty of typing up a briefing sheet while I was waiting to come back to hear your decision. I've made copies for all."

"Briefs," Jim said. "I like knickers better."

"Yeah, me, too," OtherJim said. "I long for briefs that encapsulate what is most important to me."

"**Bleep, bleep, bleep,**" said Mr. Red, the little engine that could, barely.

Jeanne shares her brief
| 24May08 |

Memo: From Jeanne
Subject: What I know and from whom, about this and that

Dear new friends, or so I would like to see you ...
The question is, what I know about you and your covert activities.
The answer: Enough that I am ready to quit my job and join you.
Why: Because I am young and impulsive (not really). It is more a matter of fitness – I am not fit for journalism's blind loyalty to the people's right to know no matter what the price to persons.
My motive: That may be murky, but here goes.
I have been working as a reporter on the **Daily Afterblatt, Lake Effect edition**, for a year, after graduating from journalism school. I was born in Buffalonya, raised here, and I went to school here, and now I work on the local newspaper. A lot of the **same old same old**, and I find that I want more.
Eve, and the bookshop, I know from way back, just like any other student who wants to get a book that some prof has assigned and no one has a clue about finding a copy. Perhaps Eve and the others do not recognize me. Back then I changed my hairstyle, clothing, accessories, and look at the drop of a hat, a pair of tall heels to change my height or a neat shade of black lipstick to match my nails. Although you don't recognize me, Eve, I do know you by sight, because you always wear the same old gray cardigan sweater with the buttons on the right, and because I'm a reader. I also remember that guy with the white hair who used to own the shop. Mr. Red, I've seen, and heard, on my visits to the shop, holding forth on mathematics in a loud voice to that poor man in loud plaids whom he teaches.
I love this place and I accept that being a clerk is good cover for what I really can do for you, but I gotta say that I'm very happy being a clerk, just a clerk, in this shop. It's been a dream of mine for years on end. That alone. Sad, I know ....
But more to the point, in my time on the newspaper I began to hear stories, from quirky old-timers, about the city beneath the city and the crazy characters who live there, and the amazing things that they have done. You know the kind of story, full of conspiracy theories and mad dashes of twisted logic. One story, though, included Caspar's Books and That.
"Things are not what they seem there," this one old crusty cop shop hack told

me. "They do stuff for the government, and TLA types are always going in and out -- old guys that don't look the part but talk the talk and walk the walk."

"Really," I said, "tell me more."

And he did. "No one at the cop shop would ever talk to you about it, but there are occasions when word has come down to back off, to play dumb and to ignore that bookshop's dark side," he said, "but that doesn't sit well with local cops. They hate TLAs with a purple passion, because they always come out on top in a power struggle. Three letters, be they **FBI**, **CIA**, **DEA**, **NSA**, or **ATF**, to name just a few, will trump a two-letter agency such as the **BP** every time and Buffalonya cops, particularly the detectives, know it. They have stories on the subject that go back to the dawn of time."

That got me running through my mind images from my visits over the years to the bookshop. Random things that didn't seem just right, like the same cast of characters hanging around and the central-casting demeanor of that white-haired guy, the owner. **Caspar?** I mean he was nice enough, but somehow I didn't really buy that the books were his only passion. It was not something that I could have articulated before that particular talk with the cop shop hack.

"Go get that story, girlie," he said, "and you will have a Pulitzer. No question."

I wasn't cut out for the news biz, but it took a few months on the education beat to make that abundantly clear to me. I started out on the cop beat but was promoted to a more gender-rigid and supposedly more interesting job in the schools beat. I hated that. Call me "girlie" and I don't really care that much, but put me in a softer beat because I'm a woman and the beat is a traditional woman's beat?

You have made a significant and fundamental error.

But it wasn't the pigginess that soured me on newspapers. Men have treated me that way since I was barely showing secondary sexual characteristics, if not before. No. It was the coldness. Ruin the lives of a bunch of retired TLA guys and get a Pulitzer. The newspaper editors wouldn't even see that as collateral damage. Just **T.S.**, if you know what I mean.

For the price of cheap beer on tap at the **Roll In and Crawl Out**, I collected enough anecdotes about the bookshop to realize that I had something there that would make a powerful story, and by the time I had a good bead on the story I realized that I was not about to blow away the bookshop against which I compare all bookshops. Not even for a Pulitzer. No way, at all.

I wasn't going to beat you to death with the pen that's mightier than the sword, so I decided to pitch to you another way to go -- hire me and use me. I do have a reporter's nose for hidden detail, and I know how to dig up the rest, through a combination of hard work and trading on the predicable nature of men. And I write well. That has never been the problem.

I don't know what it is that you have in common with the "Mystery Man Murder," but I realized that if I were to write many more stories about the case I would have to make a career choice. And I am the one they go to for those stories, since none of the hacks see that as a story with any promise. They know if there is a real story there, that no one who wants to stay healthy can tell it or would be likely to be allowed to go to print by management.

By the time they "demoted" me back to the cop beat, as punishment for imagined sins and inattentions to the levels of education and to the innuendos of middle management, it was really too little too late. (That would be **in-your-end-o** to all you punsters out there.)

My last round of buying beers for burnouts with stories to tell garnered the barest of outlines about the "Mystery Man" and a possibility of a connection with the bookshop. It was no more than well-pickled brain cells dimly working out a likely scenario. Although I don't know the specific details, I can see the probability of a connection. And so here I stand.

I remember a very handsome, dark, and well-dressed older man who stuck out like a guy in a TLA windbreaker, and I don't see him anywhere now.

I'm writing this as you huddle over my proposal to come on board, and I'm hoping that the audacity of my approach to you will win the day. I would never forgive you if you found that you had to remove me as a threat (just kidding).

I understand that I will have to prove myself and win your trust.

Jeanne Wheenin

A brief pause between briefings
| 25May08 |

I for one was relieved.

Jeanne understood us, but not as deeply as I had thought and feared.

She was bright, that was plain to see, and she was anything but plain.

My brothers were a monument to her charms. Like an interactive monument, if there is such a thing. They were largely struck dumb but able to make some noises. I hoped they would work this through quickly.

Eve was a study in nurturing femininity. She looked with approval and affection on our newest friendly ghost of **Caspar's Books and That**.

Mr. Red continued in the land of the living, if only to have a place where he could say **bleep** at random times for who knows what reasons.

Rage, and fear, I guess.

I hoped that he would work through his stuff quickly, too.

My brothers suddenly seemed to live only for a sight or scent of our new wannabe clerk/spook. When she would walk, they would follow her like their eyes were on a fiber-optic leash. When she sat, they would stare some more. When she spoke, they would make jokes. That part was reassuring, since it was proof that grim aliens had not entered their bodies.

No one, aliens included, could joke around like my brothers.

We invited David to come back to the backroom for a chat. He was long overdue for a briefing. We wanted to bring him and Jeanne up to the level of their need to know, which was generally the same level. They were like junior partners -- younger, leaner, packed with promise.

Round and firm and fully packed, my brothers Jim Grim would say, if they could but speak.

The mushroom theory of management
| 26May08 |

To treat Jeanne the way we want to, we have to change the way we treat David. Besides, standing side by side they are a matched set.

They are about the same age, and that seems to demand the same treatment. David isn't just some guy off the street, nor is Jeanne -- just ask my brothers. Jeanne in heels is on David's level, eye to eye.

We had chosen David for sensitive and dangerous work. He had not disappointed us, but we had not followed through with a higher level of information. **He is so young**, we told ourselves. **In time, we will brief him.**

The time has arrived.

David was the junior partner. Jeanne would be one, too. We would treat them alike, so that the one could bring the other along. We were in bad need of strength and depth on the bench.

Soon enough, there might be no one but the bench.

Up to now, when we met in the backroom, David had watched the door. We gave him details on a need-to-know basis. He was a junior version of us, but we had forgotten that. He had become what he appeared to be, a bookshop clerk. A doorkeeper. A bookshop wonk and wallah.

We need him to be more now.

We had used the mushroom style of management with David -- feed him manure and keep him in the dark. He hadn't had any complaints, because he didn't know any different. We are that good at the mushroom style.

I was guessing that **Operation Mushroom** would not work with Jeanne.

From the moment David put up the sign that said BACK IN 10 MINUTES, stepped into the backroom, looked at Jeanne, and went into the Bros Grim bobbleheaded junkyard dog trance, he was one of us in a brand-new way.

Make like a bike rider, cycle through
| 27May08 |

Here is an update on injuries.

My list of persons I want to hurry through their changes includes --
• My brothers, smitten and besmirched by Jeanne's presence.
• Mr. Red, acting like he has been hit in the forehead with a two-by-four of fear and loathing with **Jeanne** scrawled on it in deep red lipstick.
• ... and now David, looking and feeling like my brothers.

That leaves Eve and I to provide continuity and safety. With a little help from Jeanne. Or so we hope, fervently.

"I think," I said, "that it's time to bring David into the loop on what has been happening out in the big, bad world. This will serve to give Jeanne a more clear picture of what she has been seeing from the other side."

"Great, Goose, just great," David said to me while staring at Jeanne with the cosmic, brilliant detachment of one sun shining upon another.

Honestly, I counter *truth* with *trust*
| 28May08 |

"This," I said, "is the deal. We are on a high alert because of the death of our own Mr. Black, who the media have dubbed the **Mystery Man**, as in the **Mystery Man Murder.**"

"I knew it!" Jeanne said, "and I bet he was that good-looking old guy with the deep tan who used to hang out here and stick out like a handsome man in a sharp suit in a shabby old bookshop (that I prize above all others). I'm so sorry to learn this. He was an asset. That was obvious."

"Good guess," I said, "and right-on. Mr. Black met with foul play and no doubt about it, in our view. This bookshop and its cast of retired spooks have been under the radar and above the local law for a long, long time. Mr. Black's murder erases our exemption. We need to know who did this, for whom they did it, and why, for starters. Up to now, we've only been able to mark time with puns and such, because we have had no safe access."

"I noticed that," Jeanne said. "And I noticed a few other things, too, like all these sweet little shaggy dogs with their tongues hanging out."

"Junkyard dogs, more like," I said, "but ours none the less."

"Arf," Jim said.

"Arf, arf," OtherJim said.

"Bleep," Mr. Red said. "Oh **bleep**, oh **bleep**, oh **bleep**."

David? Speechless.

Eve just smiled her Buddha Girl smile.

"Jeanne," I said, "we have taken the rather extraordinary step of taking you rapidly into our confidence because we have no contacts that we can use as long as we don't trust anyone."

"Why trust me?" Jeanne said. "You just said that you couldn't trust anyone. I'm not just anyone, but I am a somebody, and you don't trust anyone by any description. So, why me?"

"Look, Jeanne," I said, "we took a big chance by sending Mr. Red into the Courthouse to monitor that Coroner's Inquest with nothing but a cheap suit, a bad rug, and a sour smile. Whether we knew it or not -- at a conscious level -- we were shaking the tree. And you fell out, to the joy of all of us here, for various reasons. My brothers, no comment. David, no comment. As for Mr. Red, the shock of the exposure that our strategy meant, when compared to our exempt status, has all but undone him, for the moment."

"Bleep," Mr. Red said. "**Bleeping bleep**."

My brothers bobbled in a dumbshow of concurrence.

Come-to-Jesus meeting (who knew?)
| 29May08 |

"It's time to get some things," I said, "straight about the truth, the idea of trust, and the way that we do things around here. This will serve as a workshop for some and a refresher for others, and an inoculation for us all. It's time for a **come-to-Jesus moment** right here, right now."

"Talk on, Dear," Eve said. "You're making sense, for once."

Eve gave me her very best Buddha Girl smile.

"First topic, sisters and brothers, and others," I said, "is truth. I will tell you what you need to know when you need to know it, and you, all of you, will do the same back to me and to one another. Truth is a fluid, situational, elusive SOB that never knew its daddy."

"Check, Dear," Eve said.

"Waiter," Jim said, "check, please."

"Yeah," OtherJim said, "check, Mate."

"Second topic, sisters and brothers, and others," I said, "is trust. Another meaningless construct for our Tribe. Here is the real-world version: Trust is an equation based on the operation of truth as we have reframed it -- that is, as a dynamic sharing of pertinent information. The level of truth and trust is set by the common assessment of our interactions. To wit, are we safe, are we focused, are we sealed from the world's eyes, or not."

"Seals know the sign," Jim said.

"Yeah," OtherJim said. "Flippers up or down."

Eve just smiled her smile.

"Third topic, sisters and brothers, and others," I said, "is the way we do things. We trust that each of us will reveal, over time, the truth about each one, to all the others, and that we will act out of the common agreement concerning who each of us is. We will trust that each one will be consistent to who she is and who he is. Variations from the commonly held understanding of the Tribe's members will be cause for pointed conversation and reflection, and the possibility of forced re-education."

"And I think I know the penalty for falling from favor," Jeanne said.

"You got it," I said. "Lights out. It has never come to that, but that is the only remedy for a cessation of the light of truth, trust, and the tribal way."

The uselessness of letters
| 30May08 |

"It strikes me," Jeanne said, "with some force that someone judged Mr. Black to be at variance with a standard alien to our standard and that they applied the one remedy that made any sense."

"Excellent point, Dear," Eve said, "and one that effectively adds us to the list of suspects. Well-done, Jeanne."

"Truth has five letters, as does trust," Jeanne said.

"**I brood over the uselessness of letters**," I said.

"Your phrase is apt," Jeanne said, with her lemony, sideways smile of bitter and sweet."

I smiled at Jeanne. Buddha Girl Eve smiled at me. Jeanne smiled to the side. The rest looked on with flat lips like lifers in a lobotomy ward.

I know the others will be back. And I hope it is soon.

Jeanne is the catalyst we need, but she causes such explosive reactions that it will take some getting used to. I like that she does not make any apologies about the way men react to her. She knows what she embodies with her body and spirit, and she moved on a long time ago.

It's not like my brothers have never been close to an extraordinary woman. They do just fine around Eve. They can learn to be like that around Jeanne, too. David is young. He will recover. I just didn't know how, or how soon. Mr. Red, we will monitor. The shock is not wearing off.

Stranger asks an excellent question
| 31May08 |

You might, Stranger, ask why I was not as smitten by Jeanne as my brothers were, or as David was, or why I was not paralyzed with **the horror, the horror** of it all, like Mr. Red was, stuck in the **Heart of Darkness**. Maybe it was because I was the only one in the room, other than Eve, who knew who and what it was that I lived for.

I would add Red to this short list, but Red had gone missing on us in a very startling way, leaving a colorless space in the spectrum.

Our bond, forged in the dark of despair that lies beyond what the world knows or has seen, gave Eve and I strength, insight, and courage. Our commitment to our Tribe was that we would share from our vision-source, like shamans, giving the people vision, yes, and meaning and purpose. We would not let our Tribe perish because no one had vision. If the people were to perish, it would have to be by violence or old age.

Eve and I had the rest covered, for ourselves and for the others.

Yeah, so my answer is out of whack
| 01June08 |

Ok, so I am a bit out of whack about Jeanne.

To think that it would make a bit of difference whether I am smitten or not, in view of the disparity between a 20-something woman and an on-the-shelf spook riding out early retirement, is a testament to the power that our young partner has with men. We forget the years, the many, many years, that we walked the planet before Jeanne was born. You look at Jeanne, and reason flies out the window, and the sash comes down in a rush, and woe betide any guy who is hanging out, if you know what I mean, and I'm afraid that you might.

My brothers were mooning around like little saturns with rings around their sleepless eyes, but Jeanne got them to come back to the Real.

She walked up to Jim, and kissed him on the forehead, leaving a deep red smudge. She looked him in the eye, and said, "I appreciate your appreciation, **Jiminy**, but come back, my **Little Cricket**."

Then she turned to OtherJim, grabbed him by the shoulders and kissed him on the forehead. "Oh, **OhJim**," she said, "it is time, and past time, that you got serious with us on this, my little **Goose Egg**."

Thus did my brother become **OhJim**, and he is known as such to this day.

My brothers looked anything but grim, but they began to look Grim again. I was encouraged.

Eve smiled like the Buddha Girl she is. She already loved our new junior partner with a maternal intensity. Me, too, in a way. Paternal, that is.

"I am, we are glad to have you back, my brothers," I said. "Go show yourselves to the priests and scribes."

"Back to back," Jim said.

"Yeah," OhJim said, "and belly to belly."

"I'm going downtown to quit in a huff," Jeanne said. "I'll have stories to tell when I get back."

Jeanne left in time to the click of her killer heels.

Jeanne's brief goes on for a long time
| 02June08 |

"Parting is such sweet sorrow," Jeanne said, "but not in this case. I had a fun time twitting the Fifth Estate."

We were gathered in the backroom, like the disciples, with the doors barred, windows shuttered.

Not really. David was doorkeeping at the front, but that was about it.

"Tell your tale from the top," I said, "and do not pass up any chances to embellish the narrative."

"Yes, Dear," Eve said. "You should tell us all that you can, whether it seems important or not. We are in a mode where all facts have the same face, so we have to look into every pair of eyes and hope for a revelation."

"Ok," Jeanne said, "here goes. I drove down to the **Daily Afterblatt** building and parked in the alley next to the cop shop reporters' pool car, an old Yugo with baldness about the rims, low miles, and no smiles. Detail enough so far?"

"Only you," I said, "can say."

"Ok," Jeanne said. "I walked to the front of the building and took the elevator to the floor that the newsroom is on. I went straight to my mail slot, looking at no one, confident that many of those present would be looking at me, especially my bleep of a boss. 'Jeanne,' he said, 'come here when you get settled in.' I took my time with the mail stuff, which had nothing special, and made my way over to Larry's cubicle. He's the deputy city editor and supervises the new hires. Last name is **Harry**. I swear to God it is."

Jeanne's smile was especially long on lemons.

"Describe **Larry Harry**," I said.

"Lawrence 'Larry' Harry. Pudgy porker with a wise-guy attitude, curlicue tail," Jeanne said, "and a bad habit of running his hands through his greasy long hair and any other female follicles within reach. Ambitious to a fault, and vicious to the bitter end. A nasty customer, and one who is not above sexual harassment if he thinks he can have deniability, with his wife and two young children in particular. He likes to dip his paddle, if you follow my drift, and I ain't no canoe to sport in."

"Clearly, Dear," Eve said. "Continue."

Let's get a cup of coffee, Larry said
| 03June08 |

"Larry made things easy for me," Jeanne said, smiling bitter and sweet.

"Larry is consistent over time -- a **revolving SOB**."

"Circular reasoning, sounds like," Jim said.

"Yeah," OhJim said. "Circular but not sound."

"What I mean is," Jeanne said, "Larry is an SOB from any possible angle. Turn him any which way you will and he still comes up looking like and acting like an SOB. And like a cultural/ethnic mutt, with Roman hands and Russian fingers, any chance he gets. In the end, that was the crack that I wedged open and made a scene about, as loud as I could, in the middle of the newsroom. Anyone who knows me knows that the way of the male of the species is not a problem for me. I've been fending for myself, and fending off guys since I was in diapers, it feels like. It's not like I take offense much anymore. Men are consistent over time. Period. Like members of the **Porky Tribe**. Larry, too, thank God. I was beginning to wonder just how I was going to pull off a resignation in a huff. As it happened, all I had to do was generate a high plume of outrage at what I would otherwise ignore. 'Let's get a cup of coffee,' Larry said, 'and we'll talk about your future, in view of the fact that you blew off your last shift without so much as an email or voicemail. **You owe me, Lover**,' he said in an undertone paired with a smirk, and that was all I needed.

"'**Lover**!' I screamed in his face. 'You wish, you rat-tail SOB. I've had it with your oily ways. Get your slimy hands off of me. You'll be hearing from the union lawyer, I promise you. And ... **I Quit**!'

"I did a runway stomp in my heels, out the door and into the elevator, which opened just as I got there. Joey, the burned-out cop shop guy who gave me tips about how to turn youse guys into a Pulitzer, was stumbling out of the elevator. I pushed past him and banged hard on the button with the big **L** for **lobby**. 'Where you going, Jeanne,' he said. 'You look like you just gave someone the air.' 'I did, Joey,' I told him. 'I just quit'."

"Details," I said. "More details."

The overt level - a case of harassment
|04June08|

"I went straight to the Guild rep," Jeanne said, "and spun a tale about sexual harassment that was generally based on the facts, if not the truth. I had the rep on the edge of his seat. He was loving the details that I gave him. Typical male. And who knows, I just might get some cash out of the deal, and my job back, if I want it, which I don't. And told him so. He said that I made a mistake in quitting in front of everyone, since they will take me at my word. He assumed that I would want to keep my job when I came to my senses. You know better."

"Who was there when you had the scene with your supervisor?" Eve said.

"It was early. Just a few of the old-timers, new-timers, and short-timers. The society editor and her puppy, a few secretaries, the city editor, business reporter, and a couple of barely sober copy editors, who have seen it all and couldn't have been bothered to tear themselves from the soaps on the black-and-white television mounted above the Rim," Jeanne said.

"Who was with the Guild rep when you talked with him?" Eve said.

"No one but his secretary," Jeanne said, "who was in the other room. The door was closed. He took some notes and said that he would get back to me as soon as he had talked with the Guild lawyer."

"Who was in the lobby when you came out of the elevator?" Eve said. "Anyone seem out of place?"

"There was one guy," Jeanne said, "who I've seen around town. Don't know who he works for, but he's always showing up at media events with a camera and a creepy smile. He was sitting by the door."

"Did he say anything to you?" Eve said.

"Not a thing. Just the same old slack smile," Jeanne said. "Why?"

"We are looking for diamonds in the gravel," Eve said. "Grab a shovel. There is maybe one diamond somewhere in all this dirt."

"We need to know more about that guy. He may have been freelancing for the bad guys, whoever they are," I said.

"His name, I don't know," Jeanne said. "Media types downtown just calls him the **Twilight Zone**."

Jeanne smiled to the side and held it.

Proof, I need to be seen with your proof!
|05June08|

We were all in the backroom the next morning, staring at one another and at the bottoms of our coffee cups. It was not a pretty sight.

"Proof! I need to be seen with your proof! Without proof, you are of nothing, do you understand? Nothing. No, not nothing. Less than the zero. You, in the other words, are the mathematical impossibility!"

It was Mr. Red, back from the **Zombie Zone**, giving his protégé in funny plaids what-for, like he had been doing for years.

We smiled at one another and at the bottoms of our coffee cups.

We were back at full strength. Pretty much.

"What got into him?" Jim said. "I thought that **Red Red wet the bed** only knew how to bleep like a bus."

"Yeah," OhJim said, "he's like a poster child for belligerent senility."

"You don't know Red yet," Eve said. "Never, ever sell him short. Red has reserves that you only wish you had. He's been through hell so many times that he once threatened to change his case name to **Lucifer**."

"Where's Jeanne?" I said.

"Checking with her sources," Eve said. "Something about a new homicide over on the East Side."

"Another deadly day in the City of Good Neighbors," I said. "Probably a drive-by greeting, one puke to another. **The 9mm wave. The 21-bullet salute. The Saturday Night Special. The Throwdown Hoedown.**"

"Look who thinks he's punny," Jim said.

"Yeah," OhJim said, "and look who don't know from politically correct."

Black/white and read all over
|06June08|

From the **Daily Afterblatt, Lake Effect edition.**

Dumped, bumped
Many drive over body on dark street; man already dead

By Ben Whick
Afterblatt Staff Writer

Buffalonya police were busy yesterday tying up a fabric of crime that kept unraveling on them.

A body was dumped in the middle of a busy intersection on the city's East Side, in the middle of the night, a night of intense thunderstorms.

Before someone finally stopped to see what was lying in the street, several cars and a bus had run over the dumped body.

However, according to Det. Joe Blucote, lead investigator in the new case, evidence collected from the body indicated that a previous round of violence at some other location had killed the person, a male as yet unidentified.

"We're looking for parallels to what you guys are calling the 'Mystery Man Murder'," said Blucote's partner, Det. Bill "Joe Bob" Schmidt. "We still are at Square One on that one."

Schmidt was referring to an open murder case concerning a man hit by a bus in early April on a similar dark and stormy night.

A Coroner's Inquest jury in that case has returned a finding of "death by suspicious circumstances by a person or persons unknown."

That victim has never been identified, according to police.

Police were generally tight-lipped about details in the latest case.

Call out the corps of many colors
|07June08|

"We need to account for our far-flung color guard," I said, "in view of the murder on the East Side and the police saying that they see connections with the **Mystery Man.**"

"I'll call the ones that haven't been in today," Eve said.

"Jeanne," I said, "who is Ben Whick?"

"**Wacko Whick**?" Jeanne said. "He's an intern. My old boss is having some fun with me, and he doesn't even know that I don't care who chases the cop shop stories. Send an intern. Who cares? I don't."

"Can you talk to Ben Whick without raising eyebrows?" Eve said.

"Or hemlines," Jim said.

"Yeah," OhJim said. "Or **himlines,**" signaling the homonym (the punster's bread and butter) with his eyebrows (the punster's italics), which he raised and lowered and raise and lowered until someone chuckled (the punster's just reward).

"I'm already ahead of that game," Jeanne said, "and I don't mean the hem/him thing, either. I called Ben before I came here. He said that the oppressors are still oppressing the members of the working class who write for the **Daily Afterblatt**, especially the **Lake Effect edition** (he's something of a leftist/anarchist, and all of twenty-one). Ben is good. He said he would let me know if he heard anything on the QT."

"But will he raise any eyebrows?" Eve said.

"Definitely not," Jeanne said. "I'm about the only one who takes him seriously. Don't really know why they hired him, except for his brain, which is definitely a right-brain in a leftist body. Creative as hell, in other words, and something of a hacker in his spare time. Journalism student on a full scholarship at Buffalonya State. Total king-hell computer genius. I didn't have to tell him why I'm interested in the case. He sees everything as part of the class struggle. Makes it easy for us."

"**In-terms** and **out-terms**," Jim said. "No one knows the difference anymore. Like left and right."

"Yeah," OhJim said. "Coming to terms with the ins and outs of what is and is not right means enduring outcomes that ensure inwardness, thus do interns keep to themselves. And lean to the left, at least in Ben's case."

"Excellent points," I said, "and nice going. If you wear a hat, or maybe some black electrician's tape in a cross pattern, those points won't show."

Something Mr. Darke would say
|08June08|

"Well," Eve said, "it does make a lot of sense to call the others and make sure that we haven't lost someone. This latest murder has all of my attention. I've heard of drive-bys but a **drive-bye-bye**? Someone went to a lot of extra effort and trouble to kill a guy, schlep him into a car, and dump him in the street."

"Someone may be sending someone a signal," I said, "but my transponder receiver is mute. Moot, even. No signals here."

"Eveie," Mr. Red said, "I tell you this to your own ears, and your ears alone. This has Mr. Black's signing, this **drive-bye-bye** of yours. Mr. Black all over, and him dead. You know what I am meaning, Eveie? I know Black. He teaches me to say the **bleep**, by setting the fine example. I follow."

Eve looked like she had been hit by the turnip truck. Her face was a study in surprise, joy, and alarm.

"Red, you **Beautiful Bald Man**, you have hit the hair on the head, Dear," Eve said. "I didn't think about that, but you are right. See it, Goose Dear?"

"See what?" I said. "All I can see is that the three of us Grim guys have to line up behind Red now in the **Beautiful Bald Guy** sweepstakes, plus **Mr. Black is dead. Mr. Black, he dead. Dead, I said. Heart of darkness, beating no more.**"

"I see said the blind man," Jim said.

"Yeah," OhJim said, "as he picked up his hammer and saw."

"Bleeps to you two," Mr. Red said. "Youse don't have the clue. I talk to Eveie. Eveie understands. Eveie does not play with the words like children with the glass of milk, making the motor boat noises. Eveie uses the words well. The words like Eveie. The words, they don't like you."

"That's sweet, Red," I said. "We all love Eve. If you don't think so, watch your back. And to come back to the point, which is beginning to needle me. What do you mean about Mr. Black's fabled signature?"

"Goose Dear," Eve said, "no one knew better than you. What would he say no matter what you said to him? No matter what you asked him?"

Bleep, bleep, bleep goes the beat
|09June08|

"What would Mr. Black say no matter what the provocation or lack thereof?" Eve said.

"**Bleep**-you," I said. "One word, accent on the first syllable. He would just answer with **Bleep**-you. He was almost as much of a charmer as Red here. His way with words led to one territory -- the **Land of Bleepiness**."

"Sounds like the F-Troop was home for him, too," Jim said.

"Yeah," OhJim said, "or the **Bleep Patrol**, as in **Alpha, Bravo, Cat, Delta, Ernie ... Bleep**."

"Exactly, Dears," Eve said. "That is the signature here: **Bleep**-you **in the middle of the street**."

"Something of a stretch," I said, "but he did have a way of turning the most simple of ideas into a carrier for his favorite phrase."

And he was just like that -- foul-mouthed, especially with those who were closest to him. Those ties did not matter.

Jeanne dreams up some questions
|10June08|

"What," Jeanne said, "are you all talking about? I see a guy in the grime, rained on and run over, over and over again, until dead, though he already was. So **dead beyond dead** was the goal, and perhaps **Bleep**-you was the signal. But Mr. Black? AKA the **Mystery Man**? It fits only if all roads lead from all lanes to the **Land of Bleepiness**."

"For Mr. Black, all roads did, Dear," Eve said. "He was a brilliant man with one message, which he repeated endlessly. No matter the occasion, the meaning was **bleepedy bleep bleep bleep. Bleep**. A one-note samba. Dirty dancing."

"Ok," I said, "and where does that leave us?"

"Did anyone see the first victim?" Jeanne said, "speaking of basic police work. Did any one of you verify that the body was that of Mr. Black?"

"Troublemaker," I said. "Earning your keep again, I see. Answer Number One: No. Question Number Two: How could we? Answer Number Two: Why would we think to do such a thing. He was missing, and there **was** the single detail that could point only to him. Question Number Three: If we were to follow up, how could we do it? And a statement: Don't ask about the detail."

"Easy," Jeanne said. "You walk into the coroner's office and ask."

"Yes, Dear," Eve said, "and whom shall we send?"

"And who will go for us?" I said.

"Here I am. Send me," David said, stepping into the backroom, "but only if you will call me **Isaiah** from now on. I always wanted to have a cool name like Isaiah."

We build an ark for safety
| 11June08 |

"If you are going to take that chance, then we must build an Ark," I said.

"Why an Ark?" David said.

"Yeah," Jeanne said, "you're mixing your prophets, metaphorically speaking. Or, mixing your metaphors, prophetically speaking. You choose."

"Such AC/DC friction might cause an arc," Jim said.

"Yeah," OhJim said, "which can burn your butt blue. Arcs are dangerous."

"Only if they don't float, Dear," Eve said.

"Seriously," I said.

"Yes," David said. "Here I am, having taken one step forward while everyone else took two steps back. I'm volunteering to go see Mr. Black's body. I knew him well, and not just his favorite phrase. What say you all?"

"I appreciate your zeal, David," I said, "and I am taking steps to make it a safe journey for you. Thus the Ark."

"Two by two?" Jeanne said.

"In the dark, especially," Jim said.

"Exactly," I said. "Two by two, and in the dark and in the light, and in all times between. Someone must go with any of you who ventures forth from this huddled mass where we ape the disciples on Day Two, hiding in the dark for fear of the Scribes and Pharisees, to say nothing of the Romans, except we aren't hiding, and we are not particularly scared but merely seriously alarmed. Ours is a **dazzling darkness**."

"Scared? Not so you would notice," Jim said.

"Yeah," OhJim said, "and no **tice** is good **tice**."

"Seriously, I say again, seriously," I said.

(Perhaps you know now how much it hurt me to say that -- and mean it.)

"Two by two," Jeanne said. "I'll go with this young man, as his second."

Jim and OhJim looked sad, for they saw Jeanne as a fine young woman. After all, only a few days had passed since they had returned from the junkyard, at Jeanne's request. They were having a hard time letting go of certain fantasies that old men indulge themselves in.

"You guys will pair up," I said to my brothers, "because it makes sense. Your cover is who you are. David and Jeanne look a lot like a young couple, and that will be their cover. Eve and I have always been like a hand and a glove in this city, so we pair up, or go alone, since we have the tradecraft for solo work. Mr. Red will choose from among the color guard when he goes out. Or he can go alone. His choice."

"I choose nobody," Mr. Red said, "because I stay here, to watch for Eveie. That's it. Period. End of your story. **Bleep** you all, save Eveie."

"Bless you, Red, of course you will stay. Now, David, this is your story, Dear," Eve said. "And this is how Jeanne will have your back."

The youngsters - a pleasure to handle
| 12June08 |

I noticed that Eve took the cue that I didn't give. Eve was ready to say what I was about to say myself, to David and to Jeanne, to prepare them for their trip to the coroner's freezer.

We have been handled by so many master spookmasters that we fall into the handler's role the way water falls from the sky.

This is the kind of gravity that I prefer over saying things like **seriously** to my friends and family.

Eve and I can mix and match the parts of the bear handler, from long acquaintance with them and with one another.

There was a moment of gravity in realizing that this was David's first real gig since we took him on as a bookshop clerk on steroids a year ago.

We had judged David to be quick, in general -- swift of foot, fist, and mind. He was of average build, but that was our preference.

The element of surprise wins the day where slow brute force will not.

David has desire.

That was what we were looking for. And quiet courage.

We all take turns being on duty at the bookshop, to ensure Eve's safety. By adding a younger man to our number who is charged with constant attention and permanent on-call status, to augment our efforts at security, we know that Eve is as safe as ever, and more so.

In the months since taking David on, we have verified to our satisfaction what we had sensed in him.

Now we will hone the edge we set aside.

Spookistan is/goes with the territory
| 13June08 |

You might shudder at our constant watchfulness.

We go by the adage that says you are only paranoid if **They** are **not** after you, and we knew that **They** were always out there with the potential for harm, and we took measures to protect what was most precious to us, Eve.

We knew there was a potential for harm based on our own short list of persons from Spookistan who would come to grief if they crossed our path.

Once someone says to you, **Welcome to the jungle**, do you think you ever really leave?

Answer: Absolutely not. Why?

You are the jungle, and the jungle goes with you, go where you will.

We mobilized to protect Eve not because she is weak, but because she is strong, and good, and everything that we are -- and so much more. She can take care of herself as well as any of the rest of us can.

She is as quick as we are, and a lot better looking.

No, it was not that she was in need of special attention.

It was that Eve is the prime reminder of our need for constant watchfulness. Doing this for Eve makes it probable that we will do it for self and all the others. By externalizing the question of safety, and linking safety with Eve, we make sure that we never forget to be watchful.

If it is just me, sometimes I will forget.

If it is for the keystone to my life, I never will forget.

That is our answer to the question -- **What are you least able to lose?**

Your life? No.

Your life's meaning? Yes.

Simple.

For the others, this zeal for Eve extends to a zeal for me. I am Eve's man, and that is more than enough for the others. Because Eve is precious to them, I am, too. Otherwise, I would be just another bozo on the bus.

As it is, I am a **Bozo Prince among the bozos on the bus.**

More important to me than princely status are Eve, the tribe, and the relationships that we have.

I love the jungle.

Lessons that bring increase
|14June08|

Eve's safety comes first, and no one would put their ego ahead of that.

Any of us would die for Eve, no question, and all of us have lost a step, as they say in the sports world.

Most of us have lost an entire foot.

Although the spirit is willing, the flesh is weaker with each passing year.

When we made our way from Spookistan, like Adam and Eve, east of Eden, we met again at **Caspar's Books and That.** Like middle-sized fish in a big pond or fish tank, we were not food for all but only some, and those larger than us suffered us to gather and prosper in our new roles, with Caspar as our handler and Eve as his able assistant.

We grew fat and happy, though we did not have those words for the sensations that we felt, until Eve taught us that that sensation and those words went together. Eve, giver of happiness, bringer of joy.

What at first looked like the horizon of Purgatory as we wept while we walked, out of that dark wood, that shadowland were no one lives, except for a time, began to look more like Paradise when we settled in, got to know Caspar and Eve, and realized that rejection isn't judgment of us but is a comment on the ones who had rejected us.

We beheld a land of milk and honey that would never have been ours if we had been stronger in the shadows.

Our weakness had become our strength.

Rejection was more like reunion.

The container seemed limitless and friendly.

We accepted containment with joy.

Mr. Black's disappearance telescoped our container and brought us up short, like goldfish looking at the glass rather than through the glass.

Our limits were sudden, and we were alarmed.

Not scared but alarmed.

We were not raised or trained to know fear.

We were trained to be paranoid in a functional, life-sustaining way.

But not afraid. And so we were not.

Spookistan has few old persons. You either die there, when your luck, attention, and exemption intersect with someone else's zeal, speed, and cunning, or you flee from there, or you are told to get the hell out.

Spookistan is the one experience where failure and rejection bring life and joy. Being judged deficient or no longer useful was a life sentence that one could accept with laughter and celebration.

This, in time, was our experience, anyway.

To be cast aside in the shadow world is to be blessed with life rather than cursed with destruction on the spot. The rest you can easily live with.

We were exiles from damnation
| 15June08 |

We of declining reflexes, we were the **Quick**.

The ones who bought their ticket to the next reality were just **dead** there, in Spookistan, where no one lives but only endures, for self, country, family, friends, love, glory, or whatever it is that motivates those who accept the shadow life.

Maybe that is why any one of us would cheerfully kill you in your boots if you convinced one of us that you meant Eve harm.

Being exiles from that land of shadows meant that we were joyful exiles who were aware on a permanent basis concerning just how lucky we were --
  • To be gone from there.
  • To be knights in service of such a fine Lady as Eve.

It is from such experiences that Christians and other sorts of passionate true believers are made, from gratitude, relief, and appreciation toward all of the things that endure.

Eve simply noticed and accepted our fealty, without comment, and this as much as anything cemented our love for her into a bulwark that could not be moved, though we knew it could be eroded by the drip of inattention.

I could see that my brothers and David were feeling fealty to Jeanne, the way we had to Eve, and I was glad, because I knew that it was a good use of their passions and abilities.

Life is sweet when you focus on what you prize and desire most.

Life is especially sweet when you can focus your passion on a person or persons worthy of your life.

This would preach.

And I should know.

I played the preacher for many years.

The Eve of Destruction ... Operation Black Ice
| 16June08 |

Eve brought me back to the reality of the room.

"David," Eve said, "we need to craft a story for you that will cover the likely scenarios you will have to pick among when you go to see the body in the coroner's freezer that we have assumed to this point is Mr. Black's."

"First question," I said, "is Jeanne's role."

"Rock n roll," Jim said.

"Yeah, or Motown," OhJim said. "Something tight with sequins, I think."

"Actually," Jeanne said," I've thought about my role. And what I will wear. I should go as myself."

"And?" I said. "Say some more. Write me a story."

"Well," Jeanne said, "I'm a known quantity at the Coroner's Office, at least because of my being the reporter who wrote up the Inquest for the **Mystery Man**. What is not generally known is that I've quit at the **Daily Afterblatt**. The newspaper is not in the habit of printing its firings and quittings. They only print dirt about other media."

"I know," Eve said, "but is it wise for you to be there, trading at some level on your erstwhile role as reporter? What other options are there?"

"I could walk around in the halls at City Hall, even in the basement," Jeanne said, "without attracting negative attention. No one would think that was unusual, even if it came out that I had not been on the payroll when I was there. And if anyone asks me, who knows me, I'll say that I'm saying goodbye to old sources because I've quit at the paper. That news is not out yet, by the way, as far as I can tell. Only a matter of time, though. The rumor mill never stops grinding out corn."

"It wouldn't hurt," I said, "if the word got out that way that you weren't a reporter anymore. If anyone asks, you can say that you're taking a temporary job at a bookshop to sort things out personally, and you can say which one if asked. The word is going to get out anyway, and those whom we fear, and don't know the identity of yet, will find out in whatever way they use. If they come here, we're ready, and we find out what we need to know, too."

"That raises a couple of points," Eve said, "and I don't mean the type that my dear brothers Jim like to chortle about. I mean that Jeanne is there to watch David's back. That means providing safety and it means noticing who is noticing David. For example, that freelance guy who was outside the newsroom. We'll want as many details as we can pull from you."

"That covers Jeanne," David said. "Now, **what's** my **line?**"

"You," Eve said, "are who you are. You are worried about an old friend who lives across the hall on your floor. You haven't seen him for weeks, and no one in your building has either. The super has checked his apartment and nothing is out of line, but you thought that you would ask to see the body they have in hopes that it might settle the question of your friend's disappearance. You haven't filed a missing person report because you are not related to your friend. You figure that that is the job of others who are related to him, and you do not know who they might be, specifically. You don't even know if there are any at all."

"How do I play it?" David said. "-- dimwit, smartass, or regular joe?"

David smiled through his round glasses, all bug-eyes and teeth.

"It's always best to pick a persona," I said, "that is close to your own and to change details as little as possible. So, you choose. If anyone checks on your building, we will need to improvise some more. We probably can expect a visit from Blucote and Schmidt. We will tell the truth as far as we can and make up the rest. They won't be much of a challenge. With the coroner personnel, use your own name, address, and driver's license if asked. Be who you are, in the essentials, and lie about the situation. Be convincing about both."

"And no matter what," Eve said, "tell them that you can't make an i.d. because it is not your friend. And, of course, if it is or is not Mr. Black, we still will want a carload of details."

"Right," I said. "You will get a debriefing when you return, both of you. Let us worry about that part of **Operation Black Ice**. You just pull off the deceptions necessary to get a look at that body. The rest will be in the dark recesses of the mind. Eve and I know how to get at that."

"And," Eve said, "the rainy-day signal. We can't go off without setting that. In case of dire need of our help, call me here and say, 'Do you have a copy of a book called **The Eve of Destruction**'?"

Still in the dark re: Mr. Black
| 17June08 |

We were sitting around in the backroom of the bookshop, Eve and I, with my brothers Jim and OhJim, and we were waiting for the youngsters to return from their field trip to the coroner's freezer. We do spend a lot of time leaning back on our chairs and shooting the bleep, but that is our way and that seems to be the best way to maintain security and safety for one another.

We know that in the game of rock, paper, and scissors, that paper is as cunning and strong as the other two. We always choose paper, bound and cataloged, as our first line of defense. The pen is mightier than the sword, and our unassuming bookshop is a fortress for us with all the weapons and firepower than we need. We do not brood on the useless of letters; rather, we build of letters, words, and sentences a bulwark of protection, hidden in plain sight -- piles and piles of old books.

Books stop bullets and loosen tongues.

Books make the timid man glad and wise women wiser.

Books confound the simple and make the hip look elsewhere for action.

A tough guy but a nonreader is as uneasy as a cat on a vet's metal examination table the moment that he steps into the bookshop. The alien surface creates a docile pet where there otherwise might be a junkyard dog.

No one is tough or daunting in a bookshop, except the readers among us, and there are few enough of those.

This is our wheelhouse, our place of greatest ease and confidence.

At least one doddery old fart is roaming in the stacks at any given time that the bookshop is open, ready to totter over and lay someone out if necessary, or to provide early warning for those of us in the backroom.

We seem to have a bad case of agoraphobia, but such **seem**s are not always seemly. We are where we want to be, and we are with those whom we want to be with.

And we love being surrounded by the sight and smell of old books.

The threat from outside is not new, just different, and our defenses are the same as they have always been. Our focus is steady, like a bookworm with a pair of glasses and a good novel.

Nothing can move us when we stay in the midst of our books.

Book jackets, not **flak jackets**, that is our motto.

Books not **bullets**.

≈ ≈ ≈

We were having our daily picnic on the edge of the volcano of life as we knew it and loved it.

Mr. Red was out in his favorite place -- a desk for him to spread out his precious paper and pencils, to do battle with facts in figures. Math was his thing, and the higher sort was his favorite.

Every once in a while, he would explode into speech.

Red's protégé in the loud plaids was having a lesson. In what, I'm not sure.

To learn math from Mr. Red is more like buggery by the numbers.

If Red could have punished his charge with raps on the open palm with a steel ruler, he would have done so, but Eve had used her good offices to help Red see how disruptive that was.

Eve knew better than to sally forth against the verbal abuses that Mr. Red was so fond of, and we suspected that the regular customers who wandered among the stacks were amused more than not by his outbursts, which were like the audio part of a good and thoroughly silly Saturday morning cartoon.

≈ ≈ ≈

"Where are they?" Jim said.

"Yeah," OhJim said. "I don't like to go long without seeing Jeanne."

"I'm glad to see that you have your priorities straight," I said. "The poor girl certainly has to pack around a peck of seedy admirers whom she may not have picked but certainly did provoke, by simply being herself."

"Goose," Eve said, "you seem to forget that your tongue hangs out almost as far as your brothers' do."

"My tongue, my dear," I said, "sings your praises and those only. Other women, even our fine Jeanne, get only lip service. **I has spoken**."

The telephone, at least, twittered, even if my audience didn't.

Eve picked up on the first ring and listened.

She frowned and picked up a pencil.

Take this down and check it
| 18June08 |

"Ok, Dear," Eve said, "come back as soon as ever you can. We will check on this at our end."

"So?" I said.

"Surprises," she said. "David has no idea whether it's Mr. Black. They would only show him mug shots of the corpse, which was not a pretty sight. Mr. Black or whoever was slammed into eternity by that bus. The impact did a number on his face and the rest of him, too, I suspect. David said he just couldn't say one way or the other."

"And the rest?" I said.

"They have a name for us to check on," Eve said. "**Bill Zeohn**. Apparently that is the name of the victim found last week in the middle of the street over on the East Side. Jeanne said that she bumped into a friend who told her that much. The friend said the i.d. was from stuff in a wallet, which certainly is no more than suggestive of who the body actually belonged to. And get this. Remember Jeanne's friend the **Twilight Zone**? She says she thinks that this guy is the vic. **Zeohn ... Zone**."

"Still," I said, "there are some similarities with Mr. Black or whoever it was that got grilled by that bus. I'll call Luke Parmgartner and see what he can come up with. I guess we'll just have to take him into our confidence. At least he's TLA. I'd sooner eat bleep and die than help the locals. And besides, we no longer can say with total certainty that we know anything about that body at the coroner's. It's going to take some serious scheming to get any further on that."

"DNA," Jim said.

"Yeah," OhJim said. "The criminal's friendly foe."

"DNA, no way," I said. "No one has any stinking DNA on any of us. Use the brains our Pop gave you. DNA sits in databases; our kind don't like databases. Our kind don't show up on databases. Ever."

"Yes, Dears," Eve said, "if we are to figure out for certain who that corpse was, we'll have to do it the old-fashioned way. And Goose is saying that DNA has been ruled out already; otherwise the coroner would not be getting a zero on all forensic fronts."

"Mea culpa," Jim said.

"Yeah," OhJim said. "Mea maxima culpa."

"**Mea shmea**," I said. "Shut the door. You're latin the cold in."

For the first time in many weeks, I got the F-Troop salute.

I returned it smartly.

Eve smiled her Buddha Girl smile.

"You know, Dear," Eve said, "it might make more sense to call Baldi and Luce. That way we don't have to deal directly with TLAs just yet. Baldi and Luce have excellent sources, including Luke, and I think that if we must start taking chances with someone, they would be first on my list."

Our friends - prosperity and preaching
|19June08|

Luke Parmgartner has something to do with security along the Niagara River. The river separates us from the wily Canadians, not because we need to be separated, like domestic combatants on a hot night with blue lights flashing and a crowd gathered and your cousin on COPS, but because geography is permanent and causes differences, not all of which are necessarily benign, or so Luke says.

Baldi and Luce Cleanue were old friends **under the cloth**.

Baldi anyway.

He and I, along with Mr. Black, had been colleagues in ministry as it is done from the shadows. At least as far as Mr. Black and I were concerned.

Baldi, or **Garibaldi** for long, was a cheerful, rotund, and intelligently wise minister of the actual sort, at least until he and Luce, his big and pretty wife, hit it big in the Lottery.

Baldi, you might guess, is as bald as a Grim ... and, BTW, twice as nice. And about half as nice as the lovely Luce, whom he called **My Light**, sometimes, and **Loose**, sometimes.

Loose is a great nickname for a woman who is anything but.

Since their Lottery win, Baldi and Luce have been trying to hide in plain sight, in the same house on the West Side of Buffalonya that they had lived in before the millions and millions in sinful Lottery money put them on a course of temptation that most of us would kill to experience.

Baldi and Luce always moonlighted in P.I. work, such as skip-traces and such, since ministry in Buffalonya does not really pay the bills.

After the fall of the balls in Lottery heaven, they formed a not-for-profit foundation, the **Ibbity-Ibbity-Bye Foundation**, which funds projects for the public good. The catch is, the projects that they fund must have a significant undercurrent of good old fun, or they do not pay out.

Baldi and Luce are our fun friends.

Imagine *big* and *pretty* as *roughly equal*
|20June08|

When I say that Luce is **big and pretty**, just imagine **big** and **pretty** as twin peaks of equal satisfaction.

And Luce is tall, the tallest person in the room.

Luce has pretty, plump feet that she loves to dip into peep-toe heels and other such earthly delights.

God was generally extravagant in making Luce, and she is a delight to the eye and a source of great gladness for those who encounter her.

Luce is a lot like Eve in that way, just a bit more uptown in her trappings. No gray old-man's cardigan for her. Still, let it be said that no one can make such a uniform work the way Eve does.

If I had the right kind of talk to describe Baldi in the ways that I have found so easy to use in describing Luce, I would be saying equally effusive things about his exterior and interior.

Baldi is a round, red delight of a man, and one of high sweetness.

And just a toe-tad shorter than Luce in her heels.

I knew that my brothers would highly appreciate Luce. They would like Baldi, too. It would be very, very hard to dislike Baldi. And Luce is so much more than a pretty pair of peds and a large set of lungs. She is a savvy investigator and shines at undercover work.

Somewhere in her family tree was a significant link to Buffalo's finest spook, Gen. Wild Bill Donovan, of OSS fame (and a hero of our Pop's and thus the Bros Grim as well).

Improbable connections?

It's a Buffalonya thing. Folks could tell you stories ... .

Just another punk with a big gun
| 21June08 |

Baldi and Luce, after their hit in Lottoland, hired two live-in aides, a geeky guy who ran the computers and security systems and a Punk girl who did the secretary stuff and happened to pack a Glock.

Baldi and Luce, to their sorrow, learned early on that good fences make good neighbors, and their two aides provided what our friends were just too darn nice to do on their own -- virtual and actual protection.

Geoff "BIOS" Botts was a good-looking computer geek who earned his nickname -- short for **Basic In/Out System** -- for his steady pace in certain indoor sports, which is why he no longer works for our friends. That position was open. The other aide, the one with the Glock, is **Jo-Joe**. She stayed on after Geoff was encouraged to plow fields and furrows elsewhere.

After all that money came rolling in, Baldi and Luce pursued a deeper and more interesting sort of P.I. work. It is an understatement to say that they had developed great contacts. But they did have great contacts, clear up to an astonishing number of TLA types, local and beyond. At some point, they met Caspar, who introduced them to the denizens of the **deep thoughts depot** AKA **Caspar's Books and That.**

They were surprised to see me in both places, church and bookshop, and they quickly forgave my mendacity in serving both God and my other master. I like to think that they already knew the depths of my double-dealing under the cloth.

We never talked about that, for which I am grateful. It is not the part of my story that I am proud of.

Baldi and Luce are among the few persons who know the depth of my conversion and utter sincerity in the role that I played for my flock and for my own shepherds AKA handlers.

If Baldi and Luce had learned that some names went down on some lists, because of my being a double-minded man, at the time, I know that they would have been angry with me and would have told me in words of one syllable just how angry they were, but they also would have forgiven me and offered, in the course of the same interview, the right hand of fellowship, with no set term on the lease.

Life is a lot about the need to know.

Everyone needs to know people like Baldi and Luce.

What Would Jesus Drive?
|22June08|

In our Tribe, we joke about **WWJD,** and translate that as **What Would Jesus Drive?** or **Who Wants Jack Daniels?** but Baldi and Luce actually are thoughtful and kind, and wonderful, and they see Jesus, and what he would both do and drive, as their ultimate concern.

What would Jesus drive? A Honda, of course -- **on Pentecost, the disciples were in one Accord.**

I would call our friends with a heads-up as well as an invitation, but I knew they would shun the idea that they could not be with friends in need.

I loved Baldi and Luce before I ever really knew, at Eve's loving knee, what love was. And besides, they gave us our Wild Billy who lords it over all at **Caspar's Books and That.**

Wild Billy is a check on the tendency to think that all is well in the world post-Spookistan where all we do is stay up all night and worship at the altar of love and happiness. Wild Billy will have nothing of such happy fictions, but lovers that we are, we love him, too, even if he is not the sort to talk about or show his feelings. Typical male.

And, of course, Wild Bill -- Pop's idol -- is Luce's family connection with Buffalonya's finest in the halls, dimly lit, of covert excellence. Wild Bill Donovan left a legacy of American intelligence where there had not been anything resembling a covert national corps since the nation's beginning.

It is time for potluck.

Baldi and Luce are folks who despite their towering, sudden wealth still go by the bitty church/wee kirk motto that says, **No meetin' without eatin'.**

Black/white and read all over
|23June08|

From the **Daily Afterblatt, Lake Effect edition.**

Busy streets
Two murder cases stretch into future; police stumped

By Ben Whick
Afterblatt Staff Writer

Bodies in the middle of the street.

That is close to everything Buffalonya Police detectives, at least officially, know about two puzzling murders that are unsolved, one since early spring.

In the first case, back in April, a man -- still without a name or story -- was killed on a dark, rainy street near President's Park when he was hit by a bus.

Witnesses said that the man stood still, arms flung wide, in the traffic lane.

The bus driver has said to the police that he could not stop in time because of the poor visibility.

No charges have been brought in that case.

In the second case, some say it is known who the victim was, but no one is telling detectives why the body, allegedly that of freelance photographer Bill Zeohn, was dumped by someone in the middle of a busy intersection on the city's East Side during the night or early morning hours of June 5 or 6.

Sources close to the case say that the body has been identified from items in a wallet as that of Zeohn, 37, a person known to media types in the city.

Zeohn often covered the same stories as print and broadcast representatives.

Insiders describe Zeohn as something of a hanger-on.

"He was always near the action, always around the ball, and always taking picture after picture with that annoying flash," one media person said.

Zeohn seems to have no local relatives.

No one answers Zeohn's phone, or comes to the door in answer to loud, repeated knocking by reporters.

Neighbors say they haven't seen Zeohn for many days.

As well as refusing to comment on the identity of the body, detectives also were tight-lipped about any possible motive for the killing.

Lead Det. Joe Blucote and his partner, Det. Bill "Joe Bob" Schmidt, had no news to offer when contacted.

"When we get something that we can share, we will call a press conference," Blucote said. "Until then, speculation about who the dead man was is irresponsible and those who are bandying about names should be ashamed."

Blucote was apparently referring to a story broadcast first on BFNA FM, saying that the body was that of Zeohn.

The story broke an informal agreement with authorities to withhold any mentions of names in the case, according to those close to the case and the coverage.

Police have previously linked their interest in this case with the earlier case of the man hit by the bus – the so-called "Mystery Man."

In that case, the coroner asked for and received an Inquest Jury's finding that the man died by misadventure through the intervention of a person or persons unknown.

Neither the coroner nor the jury knows just how the man was induced to be in the way of the bus, but the evidence such as it is points to that conclusion, the coroner had indicated to the Inquest Jury when it met at his request last month.

No one has come forward to claim or identify the body.

"Someone was in here the other day with a lame story about a guy missing from his building, but we sent him on his way after he looked at some mug shots of the corpse. He told us that he could not be at all certain. That wasn't surprising. The body had been badly battered in the collision with that bus,'" said the Eerie County coroner, Dr. Bruce Backstaff, in a telephone conversation with this reporter.

Backstaff said that county policies do not allow viewing of bodies in the morgue unless certain stringent proofs are produced.

He had no identity of the man who asked to see the "Mystery Man" body.

"The guy turned green and ran out the door as soon as he saw the mug shots," the coroner said. "He called from his cell phone a while later to say that he didn't think the body was his friend."

In the event, personnel at the Coroner's Office failed to get the man's name or any details about his friend before sharing the mug shots.

The coroner has refused to release any photos to the media, citing the gruesome quality of the images.

"We are not in the entertainment business like you are," the coroner is quoted as telling one broadcast representative who asked for release of the photos.

"People come in here all the time, wanting to see the bodies." the coroner said to this reporter. "We get a lot of kooks, and this one went away as sick as he came in, maybe more so."

When asked if there had been a serious breech of morgue protocol, the coroner referred this reporter to the police, who had no comment.

"If Backstaff has something to tell us, he should pick up the phone," Det. Blucote said to reporters.

He would not say whether he and/or his partner would follow up on this latest "mystery man" who turned green and ran after viewing photos of the corpse of the original "Mystery Man."

"If we chased every one of these things, we would be very tired in a very short time," Blucote said before hanging up abruptly on this reporter.

Police ask that anyone with knowledge of either case call the switchboard at the main police station downtown.

It is to be assumed that they will not hang up on you.

Green Guy returns to fresh abuse
| 24June08 |

Are you still with me, Stranger?

If you remember Pop's motto, what is about to go down will make a lot more sense. Trust me.

We know two things that stand in relation to one another --

• The Color-Coded Corps and its Young Adult Auxiliary are in danger ...

• ... therefore, in memory of Pop, we laugh to keep from trembling.

When David and Jeanne walked into the backroom, Jim was the first to check in with a quip.

"Hey, if it isn't the **Green Guy!**" Jim said.

"Yeah," OhJim said, "green shading into rookiedom."

"And the newest entry in the local **Mystery Man** contest," I said. "**Name that dead guy!**"

"Long, long may you live, Green Guy Dear," Eve said. "Buck current trends and please us all."

"Bleep you all," Mr. Red said, "except you, Eveie, always except you."

"Hi," Jeanne said. "What's with all the chortling? Is this a meeting of the F-Troop or the **Green Party?**"

"**Going green** is the latest thing, Dear," Eve said.

"I'll take the new name under advisement," I said. "However, for now: While you and David were taking the afternoon off after dazzling the coroner and his minions, your replacement, this reporter Ben Whick, was writing our obituaries. Little creep got my nickname wrong, too. (Just kidding.) Have you seen this morning's edition of the **Daily Afterblatt?**"

"Don't forget the **Lake Effect edition**," Jim said.

"Yeah, "OhJim said. "We would be lost without it, and we may be dead because of it."

"What's not to laugh about," I said. "It sounds like David and you did a good job in a difficult situation. If we survive your replacement's zeal for self-sealed news stories, we will certainly be a stronger crew. By the way, he seemed to have three sources."

"You mean **me, myself,** and I?" Jeanne said. "Ben can make a lot of a little, let it be said by one who loves him."

A word from our sponsors
| 25June08 |

Another selection from my old journal.

White stuff

A story, then, and -- perhaps -- an ironic one (where there is a pleasing, or jarring, mismatch of information and understanding).

A story already populated with characters, with more to come.

Sticking with the color-coded approach, meet **Mr. Very-White**, a permanent resident of Buffalonya and Western New York.

In fact, meet the entire Very-White family – no two alike, like snow flakes in their diversity. The Very-Whites fall into the category of **permanent as permafrost**. They are as cold as your accountant.

Ok.

Snow.

In any story about Buffalonya, one of the characters, who is like a man for all seasons -- one of the main characters -- will be the snow.

More than 100 inches per year, and usually more than 150 inches per year.

Like some people in the spook business, the Buffalonya snow is a now-you-see-it, now-you-don't thing.

The constants are snow and the melting thereof, with some of each on most winter days. Even blizzards leave a darker mark on the memory than on the streets and yards. Seven feet fell one Christmas Eve. A month later, the ground was bare.

You learn to drive by ear. Sucking tire sounds are good. Silence is a loud honk of warning about the black heart of the snow, called **black ice** or **glare ice**. A banana peel ready to send you bleep-hole over tea kettle.

Like fire, ice is good, bad, and ugly. Ice can soothe the summer sweat, or crack the winter coccyx. Snow can make a beautiful landscape, even if the underlying ground is a brownfield.

With the addition of salt, snow behaves itself, to a point, somewhere in the single digits Fahrenheit, where refreezing occurs. Salt saves slip-ups and puts the rust in the phrase **Rust Belt**.

Finally, the snow in Buffalonya, as in other Great Lakes AKA Rust Belt cities and farms and woods and villages, falls in augmented amounts. This phenomenon, called **Lake Effect**, is the bastard black sheep relation, like a **Son of Snow**. Any ice-free water, such as Lake Eerie, in winter, yields enormous amounts of moisture to any sub-zero wind of winter, which adds inches to any general snowfall borne on the jetstream from west to east. When Lake Eerie freezes over, the machine falters.

If Boise bleeping Idaho gets an inch of snow, the same storm can bloat to several inches at any spot on the Great Lakes, particularly long, stringy Lake Eerie (which looks something like giraffe scat, if you look on the map).

Lake Eerie, oriented east-west, in conjunction with the jetstream and prevailing surface winds, generates enough extra snow to bury the open country south of Buffalonya and still turn Buffalonya, which is actually in something of a snow shadow, into a mockery of itself.

That's the best joke of all, because Buffalonya grew into a first-tier city because of its friendly microclimate and relative lack of snow.

Still, the snow that falls makes Buffalonya one of the first major U.S. cities in terms of snow load. No city of 200,000 could cope with the yards upon yards of snow that fall on the farmland and forests south of the city. What goes by the name of the Southern Tier, from Buffalonya's southern edges to the Pennsylvania line, 70 miles south, sees snow for up to six months of the year, with flurries possible into May on one side and October on the other.

And we love it.

The snow, the cold, the adversity.

We actually love it.

Anyone who does not appreciate the adversity moves somewhere else, usually south, and swears to never set foot in Buffalonya again, at least in winter and never for more than a visit. Now mind you, this curse is also likely to pass the lips of those who love it here. Winters are a bitch in Buffalonya, and the snow gets old at some point in the season, for just about everyone.

Mr. Very-White gets bad press and is the butt of mean-spirited ethnic-style jokes everywhere but at home.

At home, Mr. Very-White gets treated like family.

We abuse him endlessly, and we defend him with the stumbling menace of a bunch of mean drunks when outsiders presume to join in the abuse.

To see the snow, mile after mile on the level ground, yields a peace that passes understanding. It is a peace that passes more quickly according to distance from, and experience of, our city of snows.

≈ ≈ ≈

Mr. Black, in his pastorly jokes about **whiter than snow, whiter than snow**, managed to get a chuckle every time and also managed to preach a bit on his favorite topic, redemption.

My text, brothers, and sisters, he would say, **is from Isaiah:**
> **Though your sins be as scarlet,**
> **says the Lord, I will make**
> **them whiter than snow.**

And he could preach it, too, and we needed to hear a **good word**, we who had lied, cheated, killed, and adapted without reference to morality, sin, or salvation for so many years and in so many places.

We had our snow, and Eve, our **Lady of the Stacks**, and we had the dulled edge of guilt and shame that only age can engender and ease. You might ask why we did and had done such deeds in the dark and cold, and our answers would touch on **God and Country**, **Justice**, and even **Mercy**, and would slide on such aspects as outlaw attitudes and anti-social behaviors. That is, if you could gain the knowledge to get a hearing for such questions as **why did you become a spook?** and **how long have you done this work?**

Since the answers were not available, and the answers were a weaving of truth, dare, and bull, I'll answer for all, since this is a story that I am telling you. It is, as you know, a story that could be true.

Perhaps my redemption will be in the telling, because it certainly will not be in the candor or truth with which I address my chosen subject. Those things are in short supply and are generally confined to classified documents in files that you will never see.

Hell, I've never seen them myself.

There is redemption in telling one's story, though, even if the story is a story that could be true. My reality does not stretch any further than that, and truth is a luxury that I have done with and without for so long that I no longer seek it, tell it, or see it, in waking life.

I simply tell stories, and I usually tell these stories to myself.

Just like now.

Question: Do you ever go outside?
| 26June08 |

Sometimes the friendliest sight that I know is the inside of my eyeballs.

You might think that I would want to go outside once in a while, or my brothers or the others, for that matter. We seem to be content to hear stories about the outside world from outriders such as Jeanne and David.

I do go out of this room. Only this morning, I was awakened by the sound of a car stereo rattling the windows and setting off my neighbor's car alarm. Only this morning, I got in the car with Eve, and we motored over to **Caspar's Books and That**, bitching about the heat and humidity.

When I stepped from the house and toward the car, I checked to see who was on the street, the lines of sight of those in view, and my options in case I found myself suddenly in the middle of a rainy day.

Sometimes I wish that I could feel more, that I could have sensations like other people do, and feel fear the way other people do, and walk in a cloud to the car and not give a flying bleep about who is or is not in my line of sight or just off my left flank in the blind spot.

I also wish that I had won the lottery, like Baldi and Luce did.

I wish so many things, but some will never happen. Odd as it might seem, I long to feel the sensation of fear. Perhaps because it has been so long, and perhaps because I wake in the middle of the night, sometimes, screaming, or I awake to eyes full of tears. In my dreams, I run and cannot hide. I laugh and cry, and I feel things in my body.

Waking, I am the Onion Man, who cries but does not feel.

Pop would not be pleased. Pop would want me to bear down and try harder, for my own good. Even in my dreams. And for the time that Pop prepared me for, Pop was right. But now? I don't want **someone else's blues**. I want my own.

I wish so many things, but I will still check the lines of sight out my own front door, because although Pop is gone and his idol, Wild Bill Donovan, is gone, old enemies remain who have counted our cost and found that we are about a **buck-three-eighty** short of paying our debt, both inherited and personally incurred.

So, you see, I'm not afraid of anything that I know of, including the marketplace, and I am not paranoid, because I have the scars and screams to prove it.

I am one of the happier persons that you will meet, because I know the country that I live in and because the monsters that inhabit my dreams and wait just outside my lines of sight and hearing are old friends.

≈ ≈ ≈

The story is told of a boy who wanted to be a samurai. He indentured himself to a samurai master in hopes of receiving training in the arts of the warrior. However, the master handed him, not a sword but a broom, and the master taught him, not to cut with the edge of the sword, but to sweep with the bottom edge of the broom. And the master would sneak up on the boy, busy with his broom, and swat him on the rump with the side of his fearsome sword. And laugh in a way that would have been mean-spirited had it not been a samurai who was laughing.

Until one day, the boy wheeled and struck the master with his broom, full in his surprised, pleased face.

The next day, the boy's samurai training continued.

≈ ≈ ≈

Do I wish for a life of ease and safety? I already have these things.

Do I wish for safety for my Eve and my brothers Jim, and the other members of my Tribe?

Just try to hurt one of them. Then run and hide. And don't breath, and don't bother to let your heart beat, because I will tear your heart out and feed it to Wild Billy, a piece at a time. I'll make up funny stories about you to tell Wild Billy, and Wild Billy will lick his lips and meow for more.

I am who I am, and I am glad for these times of ease and safety, and I do not notice the cost nor the steps that I take to maintain my bubble of peace in a world where most of us are blowing smoke up one another's patoots.

Does the violence of my assurances bother me?

I assume that **you** are bothered by them.

Am I alarmed that I have replicated Pop's uneven parenting and have taken two young ones under my wings, which are nothing like the wings of the Lord, that dazzling darkness that blesses and protects?

No.

I need their eyes and their zeal, to add to the old-aged treachery of my cohort of trembling assassins, of the many colors. I may have enticed the two, with sweet words and kind attentions, but I did not coerce them. And I have grown fond of them and will not let them come to harm, if I can help it, and I think that I can, with the help of my friends and family.

David and Jeanne came on board of their own accord.

Depart from me, Lord, for I am an evil man, I could say. And not be too far off, for I have been convicted by the same **Powerful Presence** as Peter was when he said those words. And I am no more evil or violent than Peter was. That accounts for me. For those who still have ears to hear.

But what think you of my Eve, and the others?

They have abilities where I have blindness. They have scruples where I have only a list of requirements and a perimeter to establish and maintain.

Eve does not wake up screaming.

Something else is bothering me
| 27June08 |

Something else is bothering me, like a persistent rash of self-talk.

You notice that I am willing to spin out fantasies about the wrath I would visit upon anyone who tried to harm a member of my Tribe.

This is the itch -- **but what about Mr. Black?**

Was he or was he not a member of my Tribe?

Why am I sitting in the backroom, telling jokes and sending out youngsters with limited portfolios to do specific, careful things, and report back?

Why does the heart still beat that stopped the heart of my friend, my more than friend Mr. Black?

I do await with interest the report from Jeanne and David. A little bug in my ear keeps buzzing about just who is it that is in the coroner's freezer. If it were not for that one detail that I'm so sure of, and will not disclose, I would say that it could be just about anyone.

As it is, I'm unsure. Some of the time. Truth is, I have no assurances that vengeance is mine to seek just yet. I am becoming something of a Doubting Thomas in this matter, and I will need to see the wounds themselves before I am certain.

There are two bodies, probably linked by the malevolence of one force, or tribe, or syndicate, or whatever, but that is all that I know at this point.

The background levels of the Tribe's daily attitude of being **ready and not ready**, like the sweeping samurai's boy, are enough to provide safety in anything short of atomic holocaust or an industry-leading dream team of a hit team.

So I hold my peace and holster my piece (just a figure of speech ... watch the hands, not what is in them ... watch the donut, not the hole).

Jim meets his maker in motion
| 28June08 |

"I have a motion to make, Mr. Chair Sir," Jim said, "and I'll speak against it for a slight consideration. Or even the drop of a hat, or the slightest glimpse of stocking."

This last he said in Jeanne's directions.

Jeanne affected not to hear.

She did, though, deliver a sideways smile, eyes down, as only she can.

"Yeah," OhJim said. "How about **for a song?**"

"He may be able to carry a vote, but he can't carry a tune to save his soul," I said. "Make your motion, Sir."

"For reasons," Jim said, "that probably will become less and less clear as we go along, I move that we become the **Green Party brigade** of the F-Troop, in honor of our young brother's notoriety in the newspapers, and I quote, 'He turned green and ran out the door'."

"I can explain, Mr. Chair Sir," David said. "I was faking it, and it wasn't easy, either. I had to do something quick. They were about to ask me for a bunch of personal data, and I didn't want to give any out."

"It was brilliant," Jeanne said. "David drew upon his native abilities in a tight place. Not everybody can turn green like that."

"Turn green?" Eve said.

"Some people can shoot peas out their nostrils," David said, "and others can squirt water or milk from their tear ducts. It wasn't anything that you haven't seen on late-night television. My trick is turning green."

"I'd like to offer a friendly amendment, Dear," Eve said, "since our David has more than one new nickname. First **Isaiah**, then **Green Guy**. If the maker of the motion will allow, we will vote also on a single nickname for David-as-was. Say, **Green Guy**."

"I thought that I had a lock on **Isaiah**," David said.

"My young friend," I said, "one cannot confer a nickname upon oneself. One can only accept what others deign to denote. Our Pop taught us that, among a steaming heap of other spectacularly useless information."

"By the way," Jeanne said, "where is Mr. Red?"

"He said, 'I am always hating you, except for Eveie, so get the bleep back there while I watch the door,'" David said. "Oh, and he said that he **called the question**, whatever that means."

"That means we vote without debate or delay," I said, "but I don't recognize Mr. Red. Those in favor of the motion as amended by Eve signify by turning green. Opposed, same sign."

I got the F-Troop salute from the newly named **Green Party brigade**, and we moved on to matters of lesser clarity.

Matters of disinforming and the disinformers who do so.

Disinformation and disinformers
|29June08|

"Moving on," I said, "to the committee reports. We have reports from the Party Committee and the Disinformation Committee. First, the disinformation report. I call on our two disinformers, Jeanne and David."

"What?" David said.

"What disinformation?" Jeanne said.

"Just report," I said.

"Why didn't you just say so," David said. "I've been washing my briefs all night in preparation for this meeting."

"Not bad for a young man of grassland hue," Jim said. "He doesn't short-change his shorts."

"Yeah," OhJim said, "but he is much, much, much too free with his abla-tives and absolutes."

"Who taught you to talk like that, Dear?" Eve said, smiling and shaking her head at the same time.

"Nobody did, **Ms. Cyclops**," OhJim said. "Nadia, maybe -- this little Rus-sian girl who came to nothing in the end. I'm very sleepy now. I haven't said this many words at once in a very long time."

"If the face is pale, elevate the tail," Jeanne said. "I learned that, and a whole lot more, in Brownies."

"Mister Chair Sir," David said. "Permission to rattle on for a long time."

"Permission granted," I said.

"This," David said, "is my story. I walked into the coroner's lab in the basement of the city building and asked to see the body of the man who had been killed by the bus."

"I was outside the door, sitting on a bench, minding my front and his back," Jeanne said.

My brothers leered.

"The person behind the counter looked at me in a funny way," David said, "and asked to see some i.d. I pretended to not hear her and went into my story about the old guy in my apartment building who seemed to have gone missing. She was not nearly as dense as she seemed. She said, 'Sir, I need to see some i.d.' So I showed her my driver's license. The sight of it was enough for her, apparently, because she asked me why I should be allowed to view the **deceased** (her word). 'Your reasons to this point are not sufficient,' she said, 'but in keeping with the public's right to know, I can show you pictures of the head.'"

"Who was this person," Eve said.

"She didn't have a name tag in view," David said, "but she carried herself like a clerk or receptionist."

"Her name," Jeanne said, "is **Johnnie**. A real pain in the bleep. A retread loser from the dark side of the moon. I've had some run-ins with her. She's on a cheap power trip, like most entry-level gatekeepers."

"She seemed inclined to play along with me as far as the photos went," David said. "She only glanced at my driver's license and handed it back."

Reason puts its *but* in the air
| 30June08 |

Ever heard of that bestseller **Under the Grandstand by Semour Butts**?

Reason was about to raise its ugly **but** in the air, and say something like, **But did you make a positive i.d. on Mr. Black or not?**

Eve asked that very question.

David's answer?

"I can't be sure," David said. "And that, frankly, is why it was easy to turn green and run. I just don't know, based on the awful sight of that black and blue face, whether it was or wasn't Mr. Black."

"Ok," I said, "let's be reasonable about this. First question: Did the corpse have any hair?"

"Yes," David said, "but not combed and teased and hair-sprayed the way Mr. Black did. He was a stickler about his hair."

"Ok," I said. "What color of hair did you see?"

"A kind of mousy brown with grey mixed in," David said, "and certainly not Mr. Black's black mane."

"That black mane was the result of chemicals and alchemy," Eve said. "A women knows this sort of thing."

"So we are no further along," I said. "The corpse doesn't have the hair of our friend, but our friend didn't, either, according to Miss Eve, who claims expertise in matters to dye for."

There are dyes, rinses, tints, and frosts
|01July08|

"Mr. Chair Sir," Jeanne said, "I rise in support of my sister Eve, who has a lovely head of hair that has aged with natural grace and beauty. It may not be what her mama gave her, but it is not, I am certain, what some hair-dresser did, either. It's a matter of tints and frosts versus days and years."

"I'd rather be in a warm bed on a frosty morning," Jim said.

"Yeah," OhJim said, "tints don't cover much, even with the flaps closed."

My brothers Jim bobbled for a space of time.

It was plain to see they were pleased with themselves.

"My brothers in arms," Jeanne said, "have hit the peg on her head. Mr. Black, in my opinion, based partly on teen-aged personal observation and partly on recent hearsay, put a rinse on his hair to achieve a plausible black tinged with an unruly undertone, where the black of his dreams and the brown of his roots fought for their place in the sun."

"And," Eve said, "a rinse is just that. Given enough time and water, it departs. Mr. Black, or whoever that is in there, could have started with a silver mane that ended up looking like a brown-gray mop that had sat in a bucket of soapy rinse water for far too long. One must attend to dyeing rituals, or face the consequences."

You gotta suffer to be beautiful
|02July08|

I looked at my brothers, and my brothers looked at me.

This is what I saw.

Two bald bobbleheads with their glassy eyes rolled up in their sockets.

This is what they saw.

A bald bald-guy who grew some hairs in the most amazing and out of the way places. Such as the ears. Such as the nose.

We didn't know from hair, and this discussion was in a code that we could sense but not follow with any confidence.

"Look," Eve said, "it's like my mama said. You gotta suffer if you wanna be beautiful, and Mr. Black wanted that and did the covert work necessary to achieve some tolerable results. He used a hair product, known as a rinse, that leeches slowly from the follicles. You have to repeat the process on a schedule if you don't want to let out your secret. If he had used a tint or dye, or a frosting product, which gives streaks of color, the results would have been more permanent and he still would have had to attend to his roots as they emerged on the top of his head."

"So," I said, "it may or may not be Mr. Black in the freezer, because his hair is all over the place."

"That's right, Dear," Eve said. "You have the details correct."

"David," I said, "and Jeanne, you did fine work down there the other day, and the press account that came out at about the same time was a hoot. Who knew, except for the thousands of readers of the **Daily Afterblatt** (**Lake Effect edition!** everyone shouted at me) that the coroner and the lead detective in the case can't stand each other. We thought that you might get a bit further along, but it was as important to maintain your tribal exemption as it was to get information. Good job."

"We need a plan, Panama," Jim said.

"Yeah," OhJim said. "**A man, a plan, a canal.** I never did get that one."

I flip over Eve ... all over again
| 03July08 |

"And we are back," I said, "to the same question."

"Who will go for us?" Eve said.

"Exactly," I said. "And it was only a few days ago that our own David was saying, **Here I am, send me, especially if you will agree to call me Isaiah from now on.** We are further along, but on a different track than the main question -- is Mr. Black dead or not."

"Like **undead**?" Jim said.

"Yeah," OhJim said. "**Zombies?**"

"Only the two of you," Jeanne said. "I expect better from my fan club." The boys looked glum.

Jeanne looked like a Punk Princess in blacks and reds.

"I tried," David said. "I cannot try again. They know me now."

"I never was in the running on this one," Jeanne said. "My face is too well-known at the Coroner's Office."

"Is this the face that launched a thousand slips?" Jim said.

"Yeah," OhJim said, "and burnt the topless towers of Ilium?"

The boys shared a leer.

"Someone else will have to go," Eve said, "Either Goose or I, methinks."

"What?" Jeanne said. "Our recluses threatening to leave the building?"

"We have the skills, and we all have the need for the information," I said.

"Flip you for it, Dear" Eve said, rising and grabbing me by the arm. The next thing that I knew, I was looking up at her ... well, let's just say that I was looking up at her. Never mind what she was or was not wearing.

You gotta focus on the higher things once in a while.

"You win," I said. "I let you, you know. You gotta see things once in a while from my perspective."

"Doesn't look that way from here, Brother Goose," Jim said.

"Yeah," OhJim said. "Looks a lot like you on the floor, looking up."

"Get up, you self-selected loser," Eve said. "We've a story to write."

"And maybe some **tick-tock**, too," Jeanne said.

You know what Eve was doing, don't you?

Grinning. Like a Buddha Girl.

Me, too. Well ... you know what I was like. I was, like, grinning. Too.

Tick-tock. Love it. Don't really know what Jeanne meant, but I love it.

Eve's many covert faces
|04July08|

"**Tick-tock**?" I said.

"Timeline," Jeanne said. "New slang. Cute, eh? Heard it on NPR."

"I like," I said. "Tick tock."

"I'm partial to **Hickory Dickory Dock**," Jim said.

"Yeah," OhJim said. "I'm partial to myself, because I'm a work-in-progress. I am not partial to partial plates, however. I have a healthy appetite, as you know."

"I need a story and a face," Eve said.

"Like **The Three Faces of**?" Jeanne said.

"Actually, Dear, I have many more faces than just three," Eve said. "It's part of the training."

"Let's begin with the story," I said, "and the face will follow."

"You are a gypsy," Jeanne said, "and you are looking for your man, a tall, dark, handsome hobo man who has gone missing."

"Good start," I said. "However, it may be wise to tailor Eve's look to the profile that you painted of the woman who runs the counter at the coroner's freezer. She is, and I quote: 'A real pain in the bleep. A retread loser from the dark side of the moon. I've had some run-ins with her. She's on a power trip. Just like most gatekeepers.'"

"Nice," Jeanne said. "I like being quoted accurately, being a former journalist and all."

"I once was a former drip under pressure," Jim said.

"Yeah," OhJim said, "and I was a novice, not an expert."

"What is a **former drip under pressure?**" I said

"An **ex-spurt**," Eve said. "Any fool knows that, Dear."

"I guess I'm not just any fool but a specific one. But getting back to some semblance of reality," I said, "what about this Johnnie. Is she gay?"

"Foul, brother," Jim said. "You're profiling."

"Yeah," OhJim said, "most foul, you Turkey. Politically incorrect, politically incorrect. Alert, Alert."

"Boys," Jeanne said, "we are politically incorrect to the core. We would be dead if we didn't profile people by looks as well as behaviors."

"I like your profile," Jim said, "you pretty Punk Princess, you."

"Yeah," OhJim said. "Me, too. Pro-rank, pro-file."

Jeanne favored my brothers with one of her sideways things that starts as a smile and goes east.

Bitter and sweet.

They went all pink.

"So," I said, "is she gay? Is she a queen bee? Is she fundamentally damaged? Is she a mean person who likes to say no?"

"I saw no ring," David said. "Not on her finger, not around her collar. I don't know about her bathtub, and I do not want to know. **TMI** squared."

"Nor are you likely to see any of her rings, handsome as you are," Jeanne said. "She, as a matter of fact, is kind of asexual. I've never heard or seen anything alternative about her. She is your basic bureaucratic small-fry model. And she loves to say no, as a matter of fact."

"So far," I said, "the salient factors are her love of saying no and her lack of passion, in the passionate sense. We need to give her something that she can say no to, and we need to convince her that her **no** was a terrible blow, so when we ask for what we want, she will feel in Eve's debt. And we need to pay some attention to the **tick tock**."

Hey, Stranger, let's make a list
|05July08|

Are you still there, Stranger?

I am making a list of loose ends to attend to, things that I promised and/or indicated that I would visit --

- Call Baldi and Luce for potluck.
- Figure out the size, velocity, and direction of the threat to my Tribe.
- More about my ass-kicking-and-screaming conversion experience.
- Rotate my tires.
- Back-story for Eve.

I can't promise when I'll get to some of these things, especially the tires, but I will do my best. In the meantime, it's business as usual at **Caspar's Books and That** (I did explain the name, didn't I? **Yeah, we got that**) -- open, and ready, for whatever.

Remember.

When in the bookshop, don't let the glasses fool ya, and watch out for old men doddering in your direction, but only if you're making a nuisance of yourself or acting in any way that these doddering old men would construe as being a threat toward Eve. Otherwise, the prices are in pencil on the first white page in the front of each book.

Eve had that look about her that she gets when she is preparing to go out and **covert** someone.

She begins to play with her facial features and with the way she walks, talks, and stands.

For me, it's like having my **Kate and Edith, too**, if you know what I mean.

Jeanne, David, and the boys were watching her with that slack look that denotes surprise, wonder, and joy.

That is the usual reaction to Eve, who really is a lovely person down to her toes. I can't say the same for some of her covert roles, but Eve-as-Eve could teach sugar how to be sweet (which sounds pretty sappy but is nonetheless true. Honestly. [I did warn you about when I say **honestly**, didn't I? This time I mean it. Really. I never lie about Eve, except when it is necessary for her safety]).

My brothers were far more startled by her covert abilities in the quadrant of covert disguises than she ever is when they rattle off a literary reference to something obscure and wonderful.

Mr. Red, at the front of the shop, was ranting at the **bleeping** cat, our beloved Wild Billy, who by the way was sitting on my chest when I came to my senses after Eve took me by the arm and put me in the dirt, so to speak.

On the carpet, actually.

Wild Billy is an affectionate cat, and he shares with all bookshop cats the ability and the desire to absolutely ignore everyone who wants his attention at their bidding, be they customers or those who feed him.

You either love that about cats, or you get a gerbil.

Baby got back to the back-story
| 06July08 |

"Ok, friends and family, members of the Tribe," I said, "let us get back to the back-story that Eve will need downtown."

Billy the wild cat jumped onto Eve's lap.

He rubbed on her old man's-style sweater and settled in for a while.

Eve scratched his ears.

"Try this on for size," Jim said. "You are Eve, owner of **Caspar's Books and That**. You are looking for an old, somewhat elderly and dear customer whom you haven't seen in a couple of months. When they ask for particulars, you give them his name, or a name, and you describe him as well-tanned, tall, and handsome."

"And," OhJim said, "you have checked with his friends, the hospitals, and now the morgue. You have a name on file (fill in the blank) and an address (real or not). You ask to see the unclaimed John Doe bodies. Johnnie the Gatekeeper sez **No bleeping way** or something equally charming."

"Yeah," David said, "so then you ask her, 'Who do I talk to?' And she says, 'Detective Blucote.'"

"Ahhhhh," Jeanne said, **thank you for playing.**"

To which, many puzzled looks.

To which, Jeanne gave her lemony sideways smile.

"I thought,' Jeanne said, "we are not dealing with or helping the locals."

No one wants to make the charts
|07July08|

"Here's the deal," I said. "We can do just about anything that makes sense out front, so let's break it down and make a list of all the options we can think of or wish for and a list of the pros and cons."

"First item," Jim said. "Blucote is a dope."

"Yeah," OhJim said, "and a bleeper. And his partner, too. **Joe Blob.**"

"Noted," I said, "but not quite. Can someone start a flip chart?"

"Someone with pretty handwriting," Jeanne said. "Like you, David."

Jeanne gave David her sideways smile. He stuck out his tongue.

"I gave at the office," David said. "Mr. Red has a nice hand."

"And cute hips," Jim said.

"Yeah," OhJim said, "but only if you swing the same way that they do, and I don't think that you do. Nor does he, for that matter."

"Oh! Sorry, Brother Oh. I got caught up in the moment," Jim said.

"Seriously," David said, "Mr. Red writes well and has a good head on his ruddy red shoulders."

"Where is that bleeping cat," Mr. Red said, thunder-style, from the front of the bookshop. "I have his bleeping supper."

The little bells on the front door tinkled a false alarm, like double-hung windows responding to a bass and booming car stereo.

Mr. Red was in the house.

Wild Billy jumped from Eve's lap with catlike grace and high-tailed his way toward the **Red Presence of Big Voice.**

They were covert pals.

Both thought that it was a well-kept secret.

It was not.

"Ok," Jeanne said, "in the interest of gender-specific craziness, I'll do the chart thing."

"We understand that you are being a team player not some bimbo named **Naomi**," I said. "And thanks."

"It's the least that I can do for the war effort," Jeanne said. "Later, I'll plant a Victory Garden and roll some bandages. For now, hand me a marker pen, Dude."

Jeanne walked her way while we watched her walk.

Jeanne hits the charts at No. 1
| 08July08 |

"This is what we have so far," Jeanne said, turning to her fans and allowing us to see what she had written on the flip chart --

- Det. Blucote and his partner (Joe Bob) are dopes and bleeping bleepers.
- That stipulated, what do we gain and/or lose by talking with the dets?
- Would it make them debtors?
- We can do just about anything, as long as it makes sense out front.
- Although Mr. Red has a nice hand and cute hips, he is not a poofter.

"What else," Jeanne said. "You're on a roll."

"A Parkerhouse roll," Jim said.

"Yeah," OhJim said, "a jellyroll."

"A **role** is more like it," I said. "We need to be clear about our roles, the detectives' roles, and donuts, too (I'm hungry)."

Jeanne turned and wrote --

- Roles (watch the donut, not the hole).

"Add this," Eve said. "We can go public with the true story -- discuss. And this: We can go public with a fabrication -- discuss."

Jeanne turned and wrote --

- Tell the truth -- discuss.
- Tell a lie and say it's the truth -- discuss.

"And this," David said. "Discuss why we want to know who is in the cooler."

Jeanne turned on her kitten heel and wrote --

- Why we want to know who is in the coroner's cooler -- discuss.

"I've got one," Jeanne said, and turned to write --

- What updates re: junior partners' need to know.

I looked at Eve, frowning.

Eve looked at Jeanne, smiling.

"Well-played, Dear," Eve said. "Very well-played. You just put Goose behind the 8-ball."

"The **Mystery Man** downtown," Jim said, "isn't the only tall and cool one around here."

"Yeah," OhJim said. "Brother Jim Grim means that in the nicest and most respectful way possible."

Jeanne turned to the chart and wrote --

- Get clarity on what I'm doing right (Naomi).

"Keep going," I said. "We need to chart the whole, not just part."

"Ok," Jim said, "Who are we?"

"Yeah," OhJim said, "and how did we get here?"

Jeanne gave her two best (they would say firmest) supporters a bitter and sweet smile, turned to the side with catlike grace, and wrote (they -- we -- could watch her do this all day) --

- Who are we, how did we get here, where are we going.

I dangle another existential question
| 09July08 |

"I have a question that," I said, "the lovely Naomi can wrote down."

Jeanne smiled at Eve. Eve smiled back, ever the Buddha Girl.

"You are lovely, you know, Dear," Eve said. "Goose has good taste. After all, he chose me."

Although Jeanne did not go all pink, she did betray a blush. Even the lovely relish being told so.

I never expected to hear Eve signify about me.

"What difference would it make if the body in the coroner's cooler is not Mr. Black's?" I said.

Jeanne smiled at me, sideways, and turned to write --

● What if the body is someone else's -- discuss, take notes.

"Keep going," I said. "This rose has many thorns."

"Go, Lovely Rose," Jim said.

"Yeah," OhJim said, "and tell her who wastes her time and me ... ."

Eve just smiled.

"Had we but world enough, and time," I said.

"This coyness, Lady, would be no crime," Jeanne said.

"You are a marvel, Dear," Eve said.

"I don't have a poetic bone in my body," David said, "but I do like the comics by the name you bandy about in slightly fractured form."

Jeanne turned and wrote --

● Add some rhymes to David's reason.

"One more item, my Muse," I said. "A list of friends to call. I'm thinking of Baldi and Luce, and Parmgartner."

Jeanne turned, slowly, and wrote --

● Call in friends -- Baldy, Lucy, and Parmgarter.

This be the list
| 10July08 |

"This is the list as it stands," Jeanne said. "The canon is closed."

"Shoot a man from that cannon," Jim said.

"Yeah," OhJim said, "or spell out the word so my brother doesn't look any sillier. There are **canons** and **cannons**, Jim-bro. Books have been written about the word, and wars have revolved on the sound of it."

Eve smiled.

OhJim blushed.

He really did.

"I repeat myself," Jeanne said. "The canon is closed. **C_A_N_O_N.**"

"Why didn't you say so?" Jim said. "I know the difference between a book and a bazooka."

"We need," I said, "to make another list of how we will attack this list."

"**O Captain, my Captain**, I am already listing to port," Jeanne said, "but if you call, I will obey."

She turned, turned, turned once again on her cute kitten heel.

She ripped the list from the pad of paper and walked it over to the wall.

Eve handed Jeanne masking tape and a Buddha Girl smile.

"But before we get to the meta-list," Eve said, "I think that Goose should tell you-all about the Vault."

Eve smiled at me. I frowned back.

Something I want to jump over
|11July08|

"The Vault," I said. "That reminds me of a story."

"Tell it, Dear," Eve said. "I'm sure you will be glad that you did."

One story for another.

Not that subtle.

However, I did not want to tell about the Vault. Just yet.

"Once upon," I said, "a time, when I was undercover as a minister, I was at the hospital when a guy ran from the E.R. to the roof and was making people down on the street nervous. So I was asked, and I agreed, to go talk with him. I got up on the roof and eased my way out toward the man, who was sitting on the edge of the roof with his legs dangling down."

"The dangling man," Jim said.

"Yeah," OhJim said, "the existential dilemma. Two horns on a toot."

"What the **bleep**," Jeanne said, "do you mean **undercover as a minister**? Who knew that you did such sacred and unprofane things? There are stories that your story has yet to pen."

"I could see," I said, "that the man was in his right mind and was probably just trying to get next to some sudden bad news about his health or something like that. So to put him at ease, I said, 'Hi. What's up? Feeling a little bit **jumpy**?' The guy burst out laughing and almost tumbled from his perch. Needless to say, he didn't fly but walked back down to the E.R."

"The point," Jeanne said. "What is the point? I am eager, jumpy even, to hear about this vaulted Vault."

"Well," I said, "I feel like that guy, a mixture of intense trepidation mixed with a wild glee."

"Why such a range of feelings?" David said. "The Vault. What is the Vault? **Vault you tell us? Vault's to lose?**"

Our jaws dropped, in unison.

David, a pun, (nay, a brace!).

Amazing.

"The Vault," I said, "is why we are still alive and are still free of fetters. The Vault is why Mr. Black may or may not be dead. The Vault is why we can sit here at our ease and tell stories and pull puns from the peaked hat that covers up a very good point. The Vault, to jump to the quick, is our ultimate insurance."

The youngsters and my brothers looked at me with **vacancy** signs blinking in their eyes. That was fine with me. I wanted to go slow here.

The Vault demands specific responses.

We agree - no *Vault-mort* puns
| 12July08 |

"Promise me," Jim said. "-- no **Vault-mort** puns."

"Yeah," OhJim said. "I'll make that promise."

"But **you** can't, Jim," I said. "You already made one."

"You got me, Goose," Jim said. "One what? Promise?"

"Pun," I said, "Putz."

"I promise I won't make putzy puns," Jim said. "Thought never entered my mind. I was thinking **Vault** plus **mort** equals **pun** to a Harry Potter fan."

"Yeah," OhJim said, "but only roughly equal, as your puns so often are. I think we need a promise from David in particular. He seems to have a sudden appetite for **ham and wry**."

"I promise," David said. "No puns, Putzes. May I be mortified if I do."

I was glad for the diversion, which I had anticipated. After all, this is what we did and how we spent our time. The Vault was not going away, unless we did several dumb things, and I was there, and Eve was there, to make sure that the Tribe knew what it needed to know to avoid stupidity and death.

Meanwhile, we joked on.

A serious moment locked up in honesty
| 13July08> |

"Listen," I said, "Eve and I need to tell you a few things about the **Vault**. We're actually going to be serious and honest, for a change, so you might want to copy off your neighbor's paper, because questions based on what I tell you and what Eve tells you will be on the final exam."

"Right, Dears," Eve said. "This is important enough to suspend the minute rule on hilarity and irreverence, if only for a moment. I don't think any of you could take much high seriousness and utter honesty, especially from your man Goose."

"Be still, my beating heart," Jeanne said, smiling to Eve's side. "I thought that Goose was your man."

"He is mine, Dear, and he is yours," Eve said, "just in different ways."

I love it when beautiful women talk about me, not to me. Doubt it? Try it sometime. It really helps the old self-esteem engine go **toot-toot-toot, chugga, chugga, chugga, woooh woooh woooh**.

"Listen to learn," I said. "The Vault. We speak of things that point to what we, and you, should most fear."

"We are here to hear," Jim said.

"Yeah," OhJim said. "Hear here and here hear."

"The Vault," I said, "was an innovation from Pop, who understood that the spook's life is ephemeral in the extreme, at best, and lived at the whim of persons who run their agendas on our power, with our lives up front on the line for their ends."

"Pop was a wise man," Eve said. "He wanted the best for us all, and as an older and sometimes wiser ghostly presence, he imparted two things."

"The first thing," I said, "was the Vault as **Container**. The white sheet to throw over the fantasy that **all is well in this best of all possible worlds**."

"The second thing," Eve said, "was the need for some things to **contain**. A Vault is useless if it only gives an echo. Pop added the first secrets and made the first courtesy calls on the **Strong**."

"Also," I said, "a Vault must contain secrets, the bigger the better. And Pop saw that secrets have limits as to time. People die. Secrets lose their saltiness. At the same time, **a good secret**, Pop said, **can exert control to the sixth or seventh generation** when it comes to the sins of the fathers and mothers of a powerful family."

"The Vault, Dears," Eve said, "must remain hidden from both the Wise and the Foolish."

"And the Vault," I said, "must be made known, in general terms designed to remind **the Strong** of things that they had thought had been forgotten. They must know that we know and that we can produce proofs for what we know. They must know that we can make them **Weak**. This means making some of us known to them -- permanent exposure in exchange for permanent protection."

"Finally," Eve said, "the Vault's location and contents must be a secret to almost all."

"We will not tell you," I said, "what is in the Vault, where the Vault is, or how many persons know the answers to these things. For example (and here I told a small lie) between Eve and I, one of us knows the answers to some of the questions and the other knows the rest. I don't know what she knows, and she doesn't know what I know. Our safety demands this. There are others (here I told another small lie) who know parts of the answers. I don't know and Eve doesn't know who they are or how many of them there are."

"Pop knew all the answers and imparted them in ways that must remain secret, including who is the heir of the master secrets," Eve said.

"The system is not perfect," I said, "but trying to crack this system would be unwise. Terminally so. The story that we told you has cracks, too. Ignore them unless you have a compelling reason not to."

"Questions, Dears?" Eve said. "We can answer a few ... perhaps."

A good question - more *punch* than *pat*
|14July08|

"Remember," I said, "a good question is better than a pat answer."

"Ok," Jeanne said, "here goes nuffink. Why not just go to the **Daily Af-**

terblatt or **The New York Times** and blow the lid off?"

"Good question," I said. "Eve?"

"It's like this, Dear," Eve said. "The press can cause a bubble of protection that will pop when the focus goes to the **Next Big Thing**. Then we would become exposed and unprotected, which would be bad for our continuation in this particular reality."

"I hear you," Jeanne said, "and that is part of why I work in a bookshop now, I guess. The power of the press does not please me."

"I'm in," David said, "and here are my questions. How will we know that this system is working for us, because you are clear about the layers of secrecy that attend the Vault. And how do we know if we are still in your good graces?"

"Good questions," Eve said. "You know you are in good graces according to the quality of the relationships that you have with the Tribe. And as for the rest, you will trust your Elders."

"I can relate to that, too," Jeanne said, "because family was not a sweet thing for me, otherwise I would have had a different hair color than pink when I was a teen-ager and only the regulation seven holes in my body like most other people not Punk. I'm in, too, because I can't seem to fit in anywhere else. Someday I'll tell you the story of my life."

"We want to hear it, Dear," Eve said.

Eve smiled at Jeanne with a **sisterhood-is-powerful** smile.

Jeanne gave her reply, bitter and sweet.

"I certainly am beginning to understand," Jim said, "why you tolerate OhJim and me in our disregard for solemnity, decorum, and the American way of life."

"Yeah," OhJim said. "I won't wonder anymore why we don't do anything. This right here, in this room, is what we do. It's all about relationships. There is nothing else that matters but the Tribe."

"Here is another question," David said. "What about Mr. Red and the other color-coders? Will they be upset that you told us about the Vault?"

"No," I said, "because they understand that this is how the system that gives us life works. Their zeal toward Eve and I, in terms of our safety and survival, begins to make more sense, perhaps."

I looked at Eve, who smiled at me.

"Still," I said, "there are more questions to add to our list. Jeanne, if you would assume your position."

Jeanne gave me her sideways smile and stood. She was something to behold, in black dress and burgundy peep-toe kitten heels, nails, and lips, with her thick black hair and go-to-hell attitude.

"For starters," I said, "is the Vault in need of new secrets?"

Jeanne wrote --
  • What is the status of the Vault's contents?
  • Are new secrets needed, and if so, how many?

"And," I said, "another question: Is there a link between the body in the coroner's freezer and our Vault?"

Jeanne wrote --
- What is the link -- if any -- between the Mystery Man and the Vault?

"Here's one from me," Jeanne said. "What-if Mr. Black is not dead but is going around killing people for reasons unknown?"

Jeanne wrote --
- Is Mr. Black out there killing people, and if he is, why is he?

"Clearly," OhJim said, "there is a world here that is covert, complicated, and right out there for certain persons to see and know. Who are the minders, the ones who stand in the gap between us and them?"

Jeanne wrote --
- Draw a map of the territory, denoting those who stand in the gap.

Eve gave OhJim her **you-amaze-me** Buddha Girl smile. He blushed.

"And," Eve said, "the meta-question: Is the Vault working as designed?"

Jeanne wrote --
- Is the Vault working or not - discuss, what-if, and spin out scenarios.

"Now that I think about it," Jim said, "I want to hear Jeanne's story. I don't want that to fall into some crack, if you know what I mean, and I am afraid that you do."

Jeanne drew a line under **Add some rhymes to David's reason** and wrote out in the left margin --
- The lovely Naomi tells her ugly story.

Wild Billy's namesake (Pop's favorite)
|15July08|

Talk about the Vault and sooner or later you will be mentioning Wild Billy and the one for whom the cat is named. We named our bookshop cat **Wild Billy** because he was much more the opposite.

Lazy. Aloof.

Always hungry. Never in a rush. Often found on his back, with his back legs seeking separate exits, like a regular down at the local.

That Wild Billy. Usually he can't/won't move. Little modesty, lots of style.

The general public loves Wild Billy. I think that some folks come to the bookshop to see the cat. I have fond memories of times in bookshops that include the endearing antics of cats such as our Wild Billy. I've had them follow me, rub on my shins, jump onto the stacks, jump on my back (had my winter coat on, luckily). You may not be able to judge a book by its cover, but I can judge a bookshop of the used and musty/dusty variety by the quality of its cat.

Or cats.

Seen that, too.

Wild Billy's antecedent, Gen. William "Wild Bill" Donovan, a legend first in Buffalonya and later in the rest of the cosmos, was an Irish American boy from Buffalonya's Old First Ward who rose to the higher levels of overt and later, covert, government -- **O**h, **S**o **S**ecret. A joke, by the way, that Pop would not hear of or repeat.

It's OSS, dammit, Pop would say, glaring like a very senior junkyard dog.

Pop and the General went way back, how far Pop never indicated but to a few, but it was clear that they had been in some things together and that Pop had not and never would forget those times. Pop wasn't a law clerk, but sometimes he played one for Wild Bill. Pop could play many parts; it is part of the deal when you live the shadow life and go undercover to please your masters and further their aims.

Pop had assured Eve and me, and others of the color code, that the General was an amazing man, and not just with the ladies.

Those stories have been told by others. I won't share them in any detail.

And now back to our regularly scheduled plot line.

Once more into the freezer
| 16July08 |

"This meeting of the F-Troop, Green Party brigade, will come back to order," I said. "Does anyone have anything to add to the agenda?"

"Does anyone have an agenda?" Jim said.

""Yeah," OhJim said. "We all do, Grim-bro Jim. That is probably a hallmark of highly functioning persons. I wouldn't know."

"I do, Mr. Chair Sir," Jeanne said, "but I don't know if it is old business or new business. You decide. I got a call this morning from my replacement down at the **Daily Afterblatt.**"

"**Lake Effect edition!**" the tribal troops said in unison.

That seems to amuse them.

"It makes little difference -- old or new," I said. "Let's just talk about it right here, right now. **Robert's Rules of Order** makes provision, obliquely, for the intrusion of reality into a meeting."

"You-all remember Ben Whick," Jeanne said, "my replacement at the **AfterBee**? He's doing a follow story on the **Mystery Man Murder**, or **Murders**, I'm not sure which he is using. The City Editor's **Tickle File** is set for a monthly interval in follow stories. The story is due in three days."

"Why," Eve said, "did Ben Whick call you, Dear?"

"Didn't call her **Dear**," Jim said.

"Yeah," OhJim said, "probably just called her **Jeanne**."

Eve stuck her Buddha Girl tongue out at my brothers.

"He wanted," Jeanne said, "to know if I had heard any rumors since I left the newspaper. I told him that I hadn't heard a thing and didn't want to. It was a short conversation, but I left the door ajar in case we want to use it."

"This is an opportunity to shake the tree," I said. "Who has ideas?"

"I'm working on one, Dear," Eve said. "I still want to know who belonged to that body in the freezer down at the coroner's. Maybe we can get this kid reporter Ben to take a look at what the coroner has beyond what David saw, including the body. We need an angle, though, and I'm not finding one."

"I know," David said. "We could send Jeanne with him on some pretext."

"I could tell him that getting a look at what the coroner has may give him a feature angle to play up for Page One," Jeanne said. "I still have contacts at the coroner's, including the battleaxe gatekeeper we talked about before. No reporter can ignore the possibility of a **P. Oner**."

"Sold," I said. "Call him back and set it up. We'll work on a backup scheme with my brothers. They need the practice."

A cub's obsession with Coyote
| 17July08 |

"And what's more," Jeanne said, "I don't think that Ben will listen to reason, threats, enticements, or anything else. He is onto something, in his own mind, and won't let go of it. He's got Pulitzers in his eyes. The **After-blatt**, for all its faults, has nurtured some gifted hacks who have grabbed that particular brass ring. He is determined to write a story about this secret society that has a dead coyote as its emblem, whatever that means."

"Not logo?" I said.

I noticed in passing that Jeanne had given us a way to buy a lot of time with young Ben. We get him in here, feed him manure, and largely keep him in the dark but give him enough to write something, too. The **Mushroom Theory of Management** strikes again.

"No," Jeanne said. "Emblem. He kept calling it an **emblem**, because, he said, the society is older than logo-talk and Coyote is older than dirt. He's focused like a cub bear trying to do fine work with two big mitts. You should see him fling those things at the keys. It is a lot like boxing but not much like typing."

"Did he say where he heard this?" I said.

That was the **Sixty-Four-Thousand-Dollar Question**.

I shot Eve a look.

"No, he wouldn't tell me anything except that he had talked to some

burn-out in a bar," Jeanne said. "He gave me this drawing, though. The result is eerie, to say the least."

Eve shot back my look.

"It's Ok, Dear," Eve said, smiling at Jeanne with her protégé smile. "**One can always make lemonade from lemons**."

Jeanne gave Eve her lemony smile but with her red-red lips turned down.

"Don't frown, Dear," Eve said. "There are more where that came from. For example, **This is not a crisis but an opportunity**. Or this: **Adversity builds character**."

"Sayings from Pop," I said. "Sicky sweet slop to live by. Mostly stuff that he swiped from one writer or another. Sayings that make you cringe, then think. Pop was a participant/observer/reporter who needed a rewrite desk in the worst way."

"Ok," Jeanne said, "but what about the secret society?"

"Guilty, guilty, guilty," I said.

"Close the door, David. If you will," Eve said, "but first go out and en-courage Mr. Red to close the shop and put out the **Back in 10 minutes** sign up. Or have one of the others take over. Just make sure that whoever stays, their job is to keep the shop secure until we're done back here."

"We're about to have yet another **need to know/come to Jesus** meeting," I said. "This should be fun."

What you need to know (me, too)
| 18 July08 |

"Why now?" David said. "Why not when you hired me, or say, the last time we came to Jesus around the Vault?"

"Some cat or kitten has let the feline out of the bag, to a reporter. We need to know, Dears, who that cat or kitten was, but first," Eve said, "there are some new things that you need to know."

"New from you, anyway," Jim said, "and new to me."

"Yeah," OhJim said. "Me, too. Like the AOL mantra -- **me, too.**"

"OhJim," Jeanne said, punching at the little super cell in her lap, "you are a wiki, wiki boy."

She walked over to Eve.

"Look. **Me, too,**" Jeanne said. "It's immortalized on **Wikipedia.**"

OhJim turned a very pleased shade of scarlet to match the lips that had praised him. We all had a look except for Mr. Red.

"I'm not back here to pick **berries,**" Mr. Red said, "of any color, or any of your **wicked pediatricians.** Bleep all that, and you, too. I'm here because you seem to be about selling the bleeping farm. Eveie, how can this be?"

"It's Ok, Red," Eve said. "It's need-to-know, old friend."

"They know some stuff," I said, "through no fault of ours, and they need to know why they need to keep silent but vigilant about said stuff. And since it comes from a committee of this whole, there is no need for a second, and because Eve and I called the meeting, as the ones charged with the prosecution of such matters, there will be no debate or discussion, or vote, for that matter. **Pop's Rules** trump **Robert's.** You know that, Red, or you don't know bleep-all about anything."

"Bleeps to you, Bird Man," Red said.

A meeting of the Coyote Society
| 19 July08 |

"This meeting of the Coyote Society," I said, "will come to order."

"I know this might be confusing," Eve said, "but there is no way around the up-to-now unknown name and game, which is already afoot."

Jeanne and David were looking like the kind of clouds that cause thunder and lightning when they get close together, and since they were sitting side by side in metal folding chairs (which are surprisingly comfortable but vicious conductors of electricity) they erupted at the same time.

"**Society!**" David said.

"**Order!**" Jeanne said.

"Secret societies are a funny thing," I said. "You can belong to one and not even know it. Such a secret place is where you find yourselves."

"And when you find out, as we all have, in good time, on a need-to-know basis," Eve said, smiling at the slowly bleeping Mr. Red, "the reaction has generally been a Fourth of July thing followed closely by a come-to-Jesus moment of inspiring intensity."

"And so, my brother and sister," I said, "this is the next layer."

David and Jeanne, while still rumbling at a distance, were no longer setting off simultaneous flashes and bangs over the building.

You could count to three between each flash and bang, which was a good forty-five miles of distance, anyway, by the algorithm that I used as a good Boy Scout (every second is 15 miles ... start counting when you see the lightning and stop when you hear the thunder, and when the two occur at the same time, bend over and kiss your patoot goodbye).

My brothers, though they were in the same storm-tossed boat as the youngsters, looked like they had come to Jesus. Short on hair, long on faith.

The story ends with a flash and a bang
| 20July08 |

The weather outside matched the weather in the backroom.

Flash! (... one-elephant, two-elephant, three-elephant ...) **bang!** and the lights went out.

"You Ok out there, Mr. Blue? I said, standing at the darkened door to our lair of secret doings.

"Ok, Goose. You?" Mr. Blue said in a voice tuned to thunder's pitch. "There's no one up here but me and Wild Billy."

I turned to the troops of the night and of all the places in shadow.

"Someone got a candle?" I said. "No? Well, since we are going to tell you a ghost story, this is perfect."

I smiled a Goose smile that no one could see.

"Pop and the General," Eve said, "plus Red, Goose, and I, and you, too, Dears, are part of a loosely connected society of, let's say, **Friends of the Night**, workers in Spookistan, or however you want to describe us. There is no name, per se, so you can pick one or make one up, like Goose did."

"For us," I said, "Pop was the glue that bound us to the secrets, and Pop told us only the secrets that we needed to know. The ideal form of the thing was never that important. Pop was never Platonic, or platonic, either. Just ask any of his three wives."

"The ideal form of the society," Eve said, "was a nameless, invisible, powerful society whose members knew one another through the interpretation of those who held greater or higher knowledge. Here, that means Goose and me."

"We're your bear handlers," I said, "when it comes to the society. You tell us who you encounter and we tell you whether they are in or out. It is a highly important distinction, you will note."

"Then the Vault is part of this," Jeanne said from the dark at the other end of the room.

"That's right, Dear," Eve said, from her spot of darkness.

You could hear the Buddha Girl smile in her voice.

Eve is like that.

"Yes," I said, "the Vault is an important container that is contained by this larger entity that really has no set name, no set emblem (though Ben Whick hit near the mark with Coyote, and we will need to figure out who has been playing **Zen and the Art of Archery** with him), and no roster."

"It sounds like the early Christian Church," David said, "with their secret toes in the dust tracing the fish symbol to gain food and fellowship."

"You have hit the mark and sin no longer, young Mr. Green," Eve said.

"Another important idea or image for the society is the idea and image of Coyote," I said, "which is troublesome in terms of what cub reporter Ben found out while sitting on his bar stool. The connection with Coyote, a trickster figure in many different cultures, is that many citizens of Spookistan relate to Coyote above all other role models. Like Coyote, we work for the safety of persons who do not know or understand us, and sometimes we do strange and terrible things that have unpleasant side-effects for those whom we are sworn to protect."

"Now for the come-to-Jesus moment," Eve said. "You must swear -- to those present as well as to those who will reveal themselves to you in mysterious ways that the elders of your Tribe will interpret for you -- that you will obey the leaders of the society as you know them (that is, Goose and I), and that you will keep secure the secrets that you know and that you will do the same for secrets that you will learn as time marches on."

It was a solemn moment.

"I swear," Jeanne said, "and I accept the contract as revised."

"I agree to this covenant as one who had been wandering in the desert and finds a well with water in it," David said. "I swear."

"I swear all the time," Jim said, "so I have no problem swearing here, too, at this moment. I swear."

"I swear, yeah, when my brother does," OhJim said, "and, yeah, I swear all on my own, too, such as when I hit my thumb with a hammer. May I suffer worse if I fail any of you. I swear."

Later, when I thought of the perfect thing to say, I realized that in speaking of this secret society of the Coyote, we could have as easily talked of the **Onion Man Society**, for a Coyote Society by that name would smell as sweet. Even onion smells sweeter than Coyote. The opaque layers of the onion, and its void at the center, add something real to the trickster image of Coyote.

For the names and images can vary, for the reality that the image you choose will still point beyond itself to the same ultimate concern.

That is, the larger secret community deeper in the shadows.

The cops that bother you ...
... when you drive ...
... usually retire ...
... at 65 ...
  -- Burma Shave

Part Two

Welcome to *VPNistan*
| 21July08 |

Email from Goose to the Stranger --

Dear Tommy (for so it now pleases me to call you):

It's time to huddle over some things, my brother. You might have noticed, and I'm betting that you did, that we just brought to a conclusion something that I call **Part One**, since this story is mine to tell. And the related thing of treating my writing as daily **posts**. **Blog posts**, actually.

That's where we are, and this is how we got there. For the general amusement of the Tribe, I've been writing something every day about tribal living, and David and Jeanne have started posting what I write to what they call a **Virtual Private Network**, or VPN, to which we have granted you permissions to view over the Internet. The kids swear on my life that the VPN is absolutely secure, even over the Internet. They call my virtual soapbox a **blog**.

Blog is a coined word representing the head-on collision of **web** and **log**.

The movement from **web log** to **we blog** to **blog** follows like lights and sirens at a crash scene. As you are my first, and last, outside reader, I feel a debt that will endure. You have earned the right to understand some things. It's like a need-to-know thing based on merit not need.

Some of my posts have harkened far into the past, and some are as fresh and as accurate as that day's edition of the **Daily Afterblatt, Lake Effect edition**. Some posts are invention, and some posts never get a hearing but die without hint or comment for the reader. All this is done silently. I post stories, not truths. And, always, my stories are stories that could be true. So, my friend, welcome to **VPNistan**. And no longer will you be **Stranger**, but **Tommy**. I will be silent on the fitness of the new name, such as whether it is your name or case name, or a name that I just made up. Actually, I like this last. I made up a name for you based on the story of Wild Bill Donovan and thinking about those Tommys in the trenches of World War One. Well may you ask -- in view of my vague way with things such as names and other fictions -- whether the cat, the bookshop, the Tribe, and the city are real, or have I changed things to protect the not-so-innocent? You tell me. I'd love to get your take on all this.

We met, in the dark and the rain on a cold night back in late winter, at the beginning of my story that could be true. You asked me some pointed questions while the red lights flashed in the rain, and I said, **Who are you, anyway?** So you know that I am real (as real as you yourself). And you know my stance toward the truth and lies, too. I hope I am making sense here, my brother.

Honestly.

Fasten your seatbelt and keep your hands inside the gondola at all times. And when we get to the end, here's hoping that you say, **Holy Bleep, what a ride!**

Motherless Brother Goose

Darkness, darkness, draw me closer
| 22July08 |

Until the lights come back on, in the backroom, let us leave the Tribe to its dark devices.
The darkness is friendly to ones such as we.
And the youngsters need the practice.
They need to learn of --
• The difference between dim shadow and bright shadow.
• The **dazzling darkness**.
• And the darkness that **draws us closer**.

Round of swearing makes us shy
| 23July08 |

When the lights came on again, we looked an one another with reticence.
Perhaps it had been better to swear in the dark rather than light a candle, after all. What we settled in darkness had been hard stuff.
Eye contact was as sparse as hair on a Grim's head.
Mr. Red, however, was not fazed.
"**Bleep-it**," Red said. "I go back to Wild Billy and the door. Just don't sell this farm. Leave swearing for me."
"I don't usually give up so much of my freedom," Jeanne said, "but for some reason, and probably the same reason that brought me here, I suspect that I gained a lot more than I gave up."
"Yes, Dear," Eve said, "you stormed our walls to get yourself in, so this is nothing compared to your initial leap."
"We're all glad that you were so determined to be one of us," I said. "It

gets pretty ugly around here with only Eve to leaven the loafers who go by the name of Grim and have faces to match. **Coyote ugly**, you might say."

"No one of us has a corner on the **Grim and bald thing**," Jim said.

"Yeah," OhJim said, "and none of us has a corner on the **street thing** either. And, yeah, maybe someone could interpret to me why I said that."

"Maybe it was a bloody **Type Oh**, or a mental typo," David said, and slowly, softly began to count, "One ... two ... three ... four ... ."

At a quarter to **five**, everyone erupted into laughter.

Another pun from David.

Who knew that he had so many in him?

[Note to future generations: Thus did my brother OhJim attract a new nickname -- **Typ0 Jim** -- for occasional use.]

"Look," I said, "I propose a field trip. We deserve a break today."

"**Field trip**," David said. "I didn't even know that they could walk."

This time he didn't have to count beyond **two** before we laughed.

"Yes," I said, "some wine, some fresh air, some Shakespeare, some park in the dark. **Shakespeare in the Dark** is putting on the **Merry Wives of Windsor** at Play Knoll in President's Park, and we're going to go. All of us, with the probable exception of Mr. Red."

"You have purposes," Eve said, "-- don't you, Goose Dear."

"Yes," I said. "Good clean fun in iambic pentameter. Harmless footsy. We haven't seen the scene of the crime where Mr. Black, or whoever, was run over hard by the park. In the dark."

"What about the security thing? "Jeanne said.

"That's part of the fun," I said. "We will all go in disguise. It will be a training trip as well."

Eve smiled her Buddha Girl smile and said:

> We go in train to see where Darke met bus
> and thereby put the Tribe in fear of fuss.

A one-act play, *In the Dark*
| 24July08 |

Scene: A spot in Buffalonya near **President's Park**, on the street that forms the park's west boundary. All the action takes place here and at nearby **Play Knoll**, the home of **Shakespeare in the Dark**, an outdoor troupe.

The time of day is dusk and just after, in summer.

Characters:

The Rev. Mr. Gander, a wealthy Dissenting clergyman
The Rev. Mrs. Gander, his wife
Mr. Bob Punish, his brother
Mr. Rob Punish, his other brother
Ms. Mitsi Gander, the Ganders' daughter
Master Kit Khat, her suitor

Scene One opens on the street hard by the park.

The Rev. Mr. Gander: It's around here somewhere, My Love.

The Rev. Mrs. Gander: What is, Dear? Out with it.

Mr. Gander: The spot, the damned spot, where our friend Darke had his lights put out by a speeding Metro bus.

Enter Mr. Bob Punish and Mr. Rob Punish

Mr. Bob Punish (to Gander): There's a kiss that is more than just a kiss, Brother Rev. More like a contract with severe penalties for abrogation. More buss than bus. Death, even. Beyond a grilling.

Mr. Rob Punish: Aye, Brother, and I warrant that you would not seek such or return from same. When a bus asks the questions, 'tis a grilling, indeed. But hark, here come the lovebirds. **Twitter, twitter**. What are they doing now? Kissing and kissing, I'll be bound.

Mr. Bob: Aye, Brother, you meant to say **softly, softly**.

Mr. Rob: Aye, Brother, and **catchee monkey**, too.

Mrs. Gander, though she speaks seldom, smiles often -- as she has been doing since the scene opened.

Mr. Gander: How now, Mrs. Gander, how dost thou? We seem to be on a Fool's Errand here as darkness approaches.

Mrs. Gander: Well, Spouse, very well, indeed. Jest with your brothers, Dear, to give the young ones a space apart.

Mr. Bob: A space, you say? A part? The way they play at love, I'd rather give them a nip and a tuck. They know their several parts only too well. Would that they knew their lines at all.

Mr. Rob: Well-said, Brother, but low like the ankle biter that you are.

Mrs. Gander continues to smile, though a stingy frown now plays at the corners of her generous, smiling mouth.

The two youngsters come near, arm in arm, whispering and giggling.

Ms. Mitsi Gander: For sooth, Khat, watch your tongue.

Master Kit Khat: For sooth, yourself, and see how you like it. You are not wont to complain of my lips or my slips. Or my raspy Khat's tongue, either.

They giggle some more. Mrs. Gander watches and beams. Mr. Gander seems frozen, mouth open and head tilted slightly to one side. The frown that tried to jump into Mrs. Gander's cup of smiles has become lodged in Mr. Gander's grim mug.

Darke lie my lover's thoughts
|25July08|

Continuing the fun and play --

The Rev. Mr. Gander, who is looking at something off stage, with his mouth open and head tilted, has become a tableau of surprise.

Mr. Gander: Mark me, Brothers, like a dog with another dog's bone, or a fido contemplating a fire hydrant. Rather, I say, mark me not, in that fashion. But rather, attend to my words, you lusty buckoes with naught but change in your pockets and lint in your bellies. Aye, and the buttons therein.

Mr. Bob Punish: Speak shortly and plainly, Brother, for this is but a one-act play. I hear the **Noises Off** that indicates the Bard's opening greeting on Play Knoll.

Mr. Rob Punish: And mean we not to attend the spectacle, yonder, from its inception? Go we now.

The Rev. Mrs. Gander continues to smile, having mastered and banished the frown that had lately been knocking at the barrier of her teeth. She speaks.

Mrs. Gander: Why gape you so, Husband? Let us be about our business.

Mr. Gander (coming quickly back to a startled sense of self): What! I was looking for that dark spot, that place where friend Darke became electricity, a thing of the air, insubstantial. Dead.

Mrs. Gander (smiling): Talk, Husband Dear, and you will feel better.

Mr. Rob (sotto voce, to Mr. Bob): Brother Rev. feels with his fingers, but not, it seems, to his wife's liking. Practice the thing and often at that, say I.

The two snicker and turn aside -- out of earshot, both theirs and the others.

The two youngsters continue to giggle.
The three groups form the points of a triangle, as they are wont to do.
They sit to watch the play on stage and fall upon their meat and mead.

Mr. Gander (taking up his wife's hand): Darke was a darkling man, and his passing grieves me, for now he will spend eternity biting at his chains and raging at the God who will love him no matter who, My Love.

Mrs. Gander (taking her husband's other hand in her other hand): Yes, Dear, he was a dark and a stormy man, and he was darkness to us, too, in so many ways.

Mr. Gander (startled, dropping both his wife's hands, and gesturing with vigor, off stage): But look, that shadow of a man, that darting likeness. Is it not dead friend Darke, come to haunt the place that did for him?

Here endeth Scene One.

Scene Two, *In the Dark*, on the Play Knoll
|26July08|

Continuing the fun and play --

On Play Knoll -- a scene of gentle disorder, in which wine-bibbing adults on blankets eat pizza from boxes or dainties from home. In the play within our play, actors in the garb of the Bard speak lines that resemble English to listeners who resemble, well, who they are in the light. Spotlights in the dark strive to define and encompass the bounteous ship of fat and fool called **Falstaff**.

The **noises** that were **off**, now much closer, continue in the background as our six characters in search of meaning speak excitedly about what the Rev. Mr.

Gander fancies that he has seen out on the street.

Needless to say, the Play Knoll patrons to left and right, and behind and before, turn frequently to glare at the prattling parson and his rapt listeners.

Mr. Gander (agitated): I swear to you, brothers, spouse, friend, and family. It was Mr. Darke. I would know that profile anywhere.

The Rev. Mrs. Gander (not smiling now but very much wanting to): Speak more plainly, Husband, and use your indoor voice, I beg, not the voice of the pulpit, Dear. Our neighbors grow restless and would have our business become theirs, which would be to fall on us with what weapons that lie at hand and run us off, away from this knoll of fun and play.

Mr. Bob Punish: Rest you, Mistress, that was a very long speech, and you tire easily, like a car that runs on gas, not a talker who puts air in her tank, the better to burst forth in sounds that please, not repel, her listeners.

Mr. Rob Punish: Aye, Mistress, allow those better-versed in the poetics of speaking to do same, by fits and starts, not art or .... .

Ms. Mitsi Gander (to her beau, sotto voce): My but they will be farting in the bag and passing it 'round.

Mr. Kit Khat giggles at his lover's audacity and goggles at her wit, or a spot just lower, perhaps.

Mr. Gander (to the others): I tell you, it was Darke!

Mrs. Gander (now able again to smile): Aye, Spouse, very dark now.

Mr. Gander: No, My Love. -- Darke, as in **D, caps, a-r-k-e**.

Mrs. Gander: Now we are playing at cards, Dear, where **D** trumps all the rest. What suit is **D**, for sooth, My Sweet?

The Rev. Mr. Gander gapes again, partly in the knowledge that he has no response to this sudden outburst of wifely wit and partly because of what he sees, again, off.

Our revels now are up-ended
| 27July08 |

Continuing, and finishing, the fun and play --

Mr. Gander: There he goes again that spritely shade of death (pointing off, toward a reeking row of portable toilets hard by the street).

The Rev. Mrs. Gander (on her feet and not smiling): You will be the death of us, as well, if you don't shut up and sit down!

The scene on Play Knoll, of wine-bibbing playgoers, enjoying their cold pizza and dainties from home, erupts like a crowd of people who came to hear a play. Some yell at Mr. Gander, others yell themselves red in the face at the yellers. Dogs bark, and the actors ignore the pandemonium. Cell phones come out and sirens soon wail at a distance.

Our characters chase after the Rev. Mr. Gander who is chasing after a shadow and a dream.

Here now endeth our revels.

Jon Rieley-Goddard | 116

We dispense with minutes and hours

| 28July08 |

"This emergency meeting of the F-Troop will be in order," I said. "Secretary will read the minutes from the last meeting."

"We don't have anything like a secretary, Dear," Eve said.

"The closest thing that we have is not a thing but a person, me," Jeanne said, "and I only work on the bigger canvases with marker pens. In fact, some of my best work has adorned these very walls."

"Mr. Chair Sir," Jim said, "I move that we dispense with those things that we do not have, such as minutes."

"Yeah, "OhJim said, "and hours, too. If one lacks minutes, I say, one also lacks hours."

"Any fool can see that, Typ0 Jim." David said. "I rest my type case. My body type is weary."

OhJim grinned at the mention of his new nickname.

We all marveled at David's punishment and word-flay.

"**Bleeping bleep, bleep and bleep**," Mr. Red said. "I will see of your blood on the sidewalk."

Red glared at everyone but Eve.

For Eve, he offered the absence of what he gave the rest of us.

"You weren't there, Red," Eve said, "when we went to see the spot where Mr. Black met his end, seemingly. We also took in some of the **Shakespeare in the Dark** play. The **Merry Wives of Windsor**. What we saw was good."

"And **a good time was had by all**, as we used to say in the newspaper biz," Jeanne said. "We used to say that long before I was born, in fact."

"I am talking at you, Eveie, and you alone," Mr. Red said. "Tell me what is this big emergency."

"We are no longer as sure as we once were, Red," Eve said, "that our beloved colleague Mr. Black is dead. Goose is certain that he saw him or someone very like him in the dark in the park, on the street and again near Play Knoll."

"Yes, Red," I said, "it looked a lot like Mr. Black. At least his silhouette, so to speak. Darke against the darkness. Still, I'm almost sure that it was him. I'd know that gait anywhere."

"Yes,' Jeanne said, "you shoulda been there, Red. We gave chase and caused an uproar on the Knoll, to no purpose."

"Speak not to me," Mr. Red said, "for I will not listen to **gits** and **gaits**."

"Your ears are like beets, and you look like a cheese ball," Jim said.

"Yeah," OhJim said. "How would you like to take a cheesy bean dip?"

"Bring on, bald guys, bleepers," Mr. Red said. "You don't know the peril for your Type O. Red will show you red."

"Ok, Red," I said, "that is more than enough. And you brothers Grim, don't antagonize the senior citizens. Around here, it makes them totter toward homicidal behavior. It would not be a pretty sight. He would launch out for your eyes first, and he would see his way to success in that orbit. So don't. See things my way."

"Gotcha,'" Jim said." Blinking over here, Boss."

"Yeah," OhJim said. "These pupils are teachable."

"Focus," I said. "There is a motion on the table. Can you see it?"

Black/white and read all over

|29July08|

From the **Daily Afterblatt, Lake Effect edition.**

Ruckus on Play Knoll – 'noises off'
Costumed group upstages the Bard, exits stage left

By Ben Whick
Afterblatt Staff Writer

Buffalonya police, called by irate playgoers, say they still don't know who the five or six or seven costumed persons were who disrupted last night's open-air performance of *The Merry Wives of Windsor.*

No one this reporter spoke with was merry about the dust-up during a Shakespeare in the Dark performance on Play Knoll in President's Park.

According to police reports, cell-phone-wielding citizens began calling 911 during Act One of the play by the Bard himself. Police said they logged 23 calls from the crowd in the park.

"It was not a fun night," one police source said. "How would you like to field call after call from the park, with people shouting about 'noises off'? No one here had any idea what they were talking about, but we send a few units anyway. It is obvious, from the 911 calls, that there is a hubbub going on."

Police officers, including one canine-assisted officer, reported that their presence seemed to increase rather than decrease the disturbance. The canine officer's charge, in particular, had much to say, so to speak, to other canines in the vicinity, police officers said.

"Our police pooch was only one yip and bark in the dark, but there were a lot of dogs in attendance at the play, and the combined effect was very loud," the canine officer said.

When all the barking and bemoaning were finally muted, the following composite story emerged from witnesses and complainants, officers said:

A group of adults, men and women, dressed in vaguely English period clothing (including one clergyman in a black coat and "appropriate" hat) arrived late, during the first act of the play. Patrons said the group was loud from the start.

As quickly as the group had seated themselves, talking all the while, the man dressed in clergy garb jumped up, waved his arms around, and ran off. The others ran after him, in the direction of the portable toilets that are the blessing and bane of outdoor theatrics on Play Knoll (both their utility and their aroma are legend among seasoned patrons).

Police said one playgoer complained of being hit on his head, which police described as "hairless," by a flying fried chicken drumstick but refused medical attention, saying that he would consult his family doctor if symptoms persisted.

By the time officers arrived, no one had any idea who the loud group had been, where they had gone, or anything else about them.

One of the women was described as a cross between a Punk and a "serving wench," but police said they could not verify this with any other patrons.

The odd thing about the disturbance, other than the insistence on the part of callers yelling "noises off," was the attitude of the actors, police said.

The show went on without any hesitation or faltering.

F-Troupe gets an F-Troupe-A salute

| 30July08 |

"Mr. Chair Sir," Jim said, "I defer to the **Great State of Jeanne, Punk Princess and Serving Wench Supreme.**"

Jeanne gave him her signature sideways smile, which turned him a well-nigh unmanly shade of pink.

"Second, Mr. Chair Sir," OhJim said, "for the Wench is first in my heart."

Jeanne gave him that smile. He matched his brother in hue and cry.

"Chair recognizes Jeanne," I said. "How ya doin'?"

"Thank you, Mr. Chair Sir," Jeanne said. "I have a motion to make and if I get a second, I'll rule it out of order, since I want to put one motion on the floor, not two."

"Take your turn," I said, "but be you Roberts-ruled by me, Mistress."

"I move," Jeanne said, "that we change the name of our tribe to the **F-Troupe**. I point to your Elizabethan bone, that's **b-o-n-e**, mot (to wit, **be you Roberts-ruled by me**) as a case in point. The Bard has been very much with us, of late, and the new name would be an extension of that fine madness, good my Lord."

"**Troop** is not any different than **Troop**," I said. "You seem to be out of order. Nothing will come of nothing, Fool."

"Nay," Jeanne said. "F-Troupe, as in **T-R-O-U-P-E**, Mr. Chair Sir."

"Second," Eve said, "with pleasure. **Troupe** looks if not sounds enough like **toupee** to please me in a mighty fashion. There is a general readiness for such a hairy word among the **Bald Brothers Three.**"

"Discussion," I said, "and this had better be good. Pop used to call the three of us the F-Troop, in honor of the upright single-digit's worth of wits that he said stood for our collective I.Q. I don't want to pull the rug out from under his memory or pull it off of his bald but hidden head."

"It's like this," Jeanne said, "Mr. Chair Sir. After our stellar performance at Play Knoll last night, we owe it to ourselves to memorialize that effort, and exchanging **Troupe** for **Troop** does no violence to the sound of the name but does set up a righteous pun. And other possibilities that have leapt to the attention of our dear second, the first-born Eve."

Eve chose, in love, to ignore Jeanne's fling at **the Garden.**

No Garden of Eden jokes. Eve was adamant about that.

"We like puns," Eve said. "No doubt about that. We be like puns, too. I rise in favor of this motion, Mr. Chair Dear."

Buddha Girl Eve smiled at me.

I didn't turn pink, but I did feel warm and fuzzy. Really.

"Are you ready to vote, F-Troop, perhaps for the last time?" I said.

Yes! they said.

Everyone, the Chair included -- giving **Robert's Rules** the F-Troop salute in passing -- gave the F-Troop salute to the **F-Troupe**. Two thumbs up and two centrally located fingers pointing in, and touching, per voter.

"Mr. Chair Sir," Jeanne said, "I would like to point out that we changed the name but not the salute, which retains its sign-language signal array and its name, both by sound and by spelling."

"The **F-Troupe**," I said, "will still give the **F-Troop** salute?"

"In lieu of having you spell that all out, I will simply," Jeanne said, "say yes, Mr. Chair Sir."

"We also could stipulate that the pronunciation of Troupe be **Troo-PEH**," Eve said. "Frenchified, like. We also could alternatively call ourselves the **F-Troupe-A**, and arrive in one piece and in one Accord."

Only auto in the Bible! everyone shouted.

"We have adopted that idea by acclimation," I said. "**F-Troupe-A**, it is."

"If I could have another go at motion," Jeanne said, "I would march in the idea that Goose could change his name to another animal, that being the deer, Dear. **Buck**, maybe. Or even **Bambi**."

Everyone but me was shouting the same word, the one that follows **first**.

"If I had recognized you," I said, "you might have made such a motion. And I might have had to answer to **Bambi**. However, you did no such thing that I recognize as such, Wench. No blood, still fowl. Still Goose."

We hatch our chicks a plan

| 31 July08 |

"And now," I said, "for something completely different, let us hatch our chicks a plan, one that will serve Gentle Ben Whick, cub reporter, a Papa Bear's portion of disinformation."

"How much is the bear's portion?" Jeanne said.

"As much as the bear wants," I said. "And here's hoping that our Cub Reporter wants a second helping."

"Say on, Dear," Eve said. "This sounds interesting. And I noticed that you dissed the distaff side with mention of **chicks**."

"Only a few punning peeps in passing," I said. "To bring this frivolity to a pass, I will descend from my lofty summit and speak plain."

"I had rather hear the mountains in your yodel," Jim said.

"Yeah," OhJim said, "with a few peaks at your plan."

"Could someone give me a map," David said, "or a chick that I might hide under its wings? I'm lost and don't want to stop to ask for directions."

"Here is the outline of my plan, young Mr. Green, and a map of the territory," I said. "We need to neutralize the aims of Ben Whick, who has been waylaid by Jeanne's promise, lately given, of background material on the **Mystery Man Murders.** You will recall that Gentle Ben, when he went out drinking with Jeanne a few days ago, was babbling about coyotes and secret societies, and vowing to write a Pulitzer winner of a Page One story herald-ing a series to follow. You will further recall the round of information sharing and subsequent swearing that you-all did in the dark right here in this room while **The Dear** threw beer barrels down the stairs of heaven, issuing in flashes and bangs that briefly put out our lights."

"Thank you," David said. "I am clear now. We are all mad -- beyond aid and beyond belief. I don't need no stinking map anymore. Nor do I any longer have any curiosity as to why we are not discussing the ghost of Mr. Black that we saw in the park in the dark."

"You stand near the truth," Jim said.

"Yeah," OhJim said. "Step to one side so that others here might see and be healed as well -- of their need for clarity."

"In your honking-on, Goose Dear," Eve said, "there was the kernel of a corny idea that just might work. And I know just the man to help us."

I nodded.

"BlueBoy! Mister Ed!" Eve said in a tinkling outdoor voice. "Leave the door in the charge of Mr. Red and Wild Billy. We need you, and you alone, in the backroom. Bring your No. 2 pencil, pica pole, and non-repo blue pen. **The Dear** hath need of them."

That sounded very close to a **Dear Buck** or **Bambi** reference, but I let it pass, hoping that no one else would notice.

I braced myself for noise.

BlueBoy AKA **Mister Ed** could make Mr. Red sound like a mumbling old man looking for his misplaced dentures. At the top of his lungs.

Meet Mister Ed, man and beast
|01August08|

I could hear Mister Ed above the din of bleeps coming from Mr. Red -- a case of **loud** and **louder**.

"I'm going back, Red. Cover the door," Mister Ed said, in a voice that made Eve's outdoor voice sound like the peeps of a newly hatched chick. "And watch out for Wild Billy. He's acting like he wants to bolt as soon as the door opens."

Mister Ed could make Mr. Red sound like a phone left off the hook -- irritating and dogged without pause but not really all that loud.

The two, holding forth at the front of the bookshop, acted like an old couple who carried on all conversation, no matter how banal, in thundering tones. They quibbled over Wild Billy like they had joint custody.

Every time I saw Mister Ed, whom we also called **BlueBoy** or **Mr. Blue**, I was struck anew by how well he fit the role of bookseller. Many of our first-time patrons assume that they are talking with the proprietor when they come through the door, to the gentle tinkling of bells, and say a generally timid hello back to the booming explosion of welcome from the large, professorial-looking man in dark turtleneck sweater under a tweed coat of a certain age.

When Mister Ed asks you if he can help you, you want to say **yes**, in answer to the commanding quality of his voice but also in response to the juvenile friendliness this bear of a man projects in all directions, like a transponder guiding rescuers to the goal. You find yourself checking his chin to see if he has the little keg of brandy under there that St. Bernards in cartoons always bear.

In short, and in sum, most who meet Mister Ed are glad that they have.

We named **Mister Ed** after the talking horse of the same name and in honor of his service in Spookistan in various roles of news hack or editor.

Ed has big, hairy ears, the better with which to hear you, and random spikes of hair on his baldish head, mainly tip-top and dead center. He has deep furrows between his eyes, deep and interesting valleys of wrinkles under his eyes, and black circles around his eyes. Mister Ed is like a dependable sedan with high miles and lots of stories.

When Mister Ed takes you for a ride, you enjoy the story that he tells you and you enjoy the comfort of the seats. The odometer mileage isn't that bad, either, when you factor in the size of the machine and the many years and miles of wear on the mechanical systems.

Mister Ed was going to be central to the game we intended to run on Ben Whick. We knew that Mister Ed would be up for it. He loved to play newsy types and had done so again and again and again.

Give Mister Ed a story to tell, or a story to dig up, and he is like a dog with a bone that can deliver some **bon mots**, too.

Mister Ed makes you feel calm, and rattled
|02August08|

"Eve!" Mister Ed said in his voice of gravity and size. "I am here."

Small items rattled in place or tumbled from higher to lower levels.

"I hear you," Jim said. "I see the evidence of it, too."

"Yeah," OhJim said, "loud and clear, very clear."

Jeanne took in the scene with her sideways smile.

I was looking forward to seeing Mister Ed and Jeanne interact.

David was watchful like a sleek animal with sharp hearing and teeth.

Mister Ed, polite to a fault, nodded at my brothers and to the youngsters. He smiled his avuncular smile, giving Eve a much warmer version.

"Eve," he said, and waited, in all his contradictions and contrasts, like a shaggy dog who looks like he can lecture for an hour without notes or microphone. Named after a talking horse, Mister Ed looks like a smart and handy pooch whose bark is much louder than its bite. What he is, in actuality, no one really knows. That is standard for the color-coded corps. However, we do know him to be capable and wise in the ways of the media, particularly print.

Editor Ed has forgotten more than Ben Whick will learn for years to come.

Of such mismatches are good stories made. We intended to write a story to fit our ends, using Ben as the quill and Mister Ed as the guiding hand.

Reality is what you write, right?

|03August08|

The worst was over.

The thunder of Mister Ed's arrival had rolled into the distance.

We were intact.

"Well," Eve said, "I see that you have not lost any of your volume, Ed."

"Not a bit, Eve," Mister Ed said. "I'm a multi-volume set, as you can see."

"I hear you," I said.

Eve briefed Mister Ed on ...

- Our need for a newsy scam.
- What we knew about Ben Whick.
- And what our thinking was to this point.

"Look," Mister Ed said, "this boy reporter with big ideas will bite hard on the right bait. We need to put that bait under his nose. I agree that the best way would be right here in this room. The question is, who should be here."

"I don't think that I should be back here," Jeanne said, "but I should be out in the stacks or at the front, when he comes in. He will expect to see me here, and if he does he will report back to the newsroom, and that is a good thing. It bolsters my story that I am sorting out my life while working at a bookshop."

"Agreed," Mister Ed said. "And I will welcome your presence in my normal, usual part of the bookshop."

Jeanne gave Mister Ed her sideways smile. It was difficult to tell if it had any effect on him. Mister Ed was like that horse that you could lead to water. He had a mind of his own when it came to women. He seemed to be indifferent, but we who knew his story knew otherwise. It's just that Mister Ed was a mystery to most people. He was more of a mule, maybe, than a horse when it came to women, except for the sterile part. His voice was emblematic of his drive -- overdrive would be more to the point. Or maybe more like a donkey, than a horse or a mule, where women were concerned. And that matched the size of his ears, too.

Ed continued to look at Jeanne, and the rest of us, with that calm Uncle Ed air he has when he shuts his thundering trap of a mouth.

"We know more now about who won't be in here for the interview with Gentle Ben," I said, "but we know no more than we did about who will be present. I say that the natural choices are Mister Ed, our resident expert in media disinformation, and Eve, the owner of the bookshop. That leaves open the question of who Ed will be, for the interview -- name and role."

"Leave that to me," Mister Ed said. "I have a stable of such things."

"We also," Eve said, "need to clarify our goals in this. That will set a lot of the parameters, too. I think that we get in touch with young Ben through Jeanne, who was the one who promised him access concerning his story if he would hold off on writing it."

"I can tell him," Jeanne said, "that the interview will be deep background and that he can use the interview to guide his investigation but not describe where the interview was, who the interview was with, or any description of the persons with whom he talked. In fact, I will tell him to take it or leave it, that he cannot write anything about any aspect of the interview in any story that he writes and that he is not to discuss the interview with his editors except on a need-to-know basis down the line. Nothing out front."

"Won't that be a problem, the last part in particular?" I said.

"Ben wants to bust a big one and win the big prize. That gives us the leverage to induce him to bypass what he knows he should not," Jeanne said, "but we do need to be ready for him to disclose the whole thing to his editors later, if he actually comes up with something that he can offer for publication. We can insist he talk to me, or us, again before doing that."

Ben Whick, cub reporter - beer at 7
|04August08|

Jeanne's super cell rang.

"Ben," she said, "how the heck are ya?"

Jeanne even smiles sideways while on the phone.

Who knew?

"Yes," she said, "we can meet for beer this evening. Seven sounds fine. I'll have details for you then. Bye."

Jeanne put her cell in her pocket and that smile, sideways, on her face.

"Well," I said, "that certainly speeds things up."

"We were on a short turn-around anyway," Jeanne said. "One must not irritate the news bears, particularly the cubs. They run to their mothers and whine. I think I have the outline of what I'll tell him, if you agree to what I lined out."

"With one addition," Mister Ed said. "Tell him that the interview you can set up will make a mockery of whatever he learned from that burnout on the barstool who told him about some **so-called** coyote secret society."

"I agree," Eve said. "We need to plant early a big seed of doubt about that and we need, at the same time, to give him something else that seems to be as big or bigger. Bait and switch."

"Yes," I said. "That is what we need to nail down next. We need to put some **dis-** with the **information** that we feed our young reporter. We must make sure that he likes what we cook up."

"I like to start," Mister Ed said, "with what I'm **not** going to share. In this case, we are **not** going to share the fact that **Caspar's Books and That** is a quasi-criminal enterprise left alone by local authorities because of the flux and flow, or not, of information that we have and that **Certain Powerful Persons** know that we have. That is **Fact One** to hold back and protect."

"And that we belong to a quasi-secret society with no name, no officers, no rules, and no clubhouse," Eve said. "That is **Fact Two** to hold back."

Eve gave us her Buddha Girl smile.

"And that we know what the police want to know about our friend we call Mr. Black. That," I said, "is **Fact Three** to hold back."

I smiled into my whiskers.

"This probably covers the waterfront," Mister Ed said. "Now let us list some ways to lure the boy away from these precious things, like mother birds pretending to have broken wings."

Mister Ed's smile was as concise and colorful as his blue pencil.

We search for the broken wing
|05August08|

"You see," I said, "why it is good to start with what you won't be saying."

"Because," David said, "it is not a creative thing but a reviewing and a listing thing. What we have left here is the hard part."

"Fear not," Mister Ed said, "we will have the disinformation covered."

"Well," Jeanne said, "I think the way to go is to convince Gentle Ben that the man who told him about the secret society and the coyote and all, and linked it to the bookshop, was barking mad. If you can get him to discuss the person in any detail, it will give us valuable information about just who the bleep that person was."

Eve smiled a smile of mystery. I was the only one who noticed, and I thought that I knew where she was smiling from.

"Good point," Mister Ed said. "We don't know who he talked to but we do know that that person had some accurate information. On the face of it, it seems like there could be a few, and a few only, who could be expected to have such information."

"However," Eve said, "we know, better than anyone else, that it is not the size of the pool of fish who know but the size of the threat that the Vault represents to the fish, big and little, who know far too much about the true nature of **Caspar's Books and That**."

"So far," Mister Ed said, "the only option that we have discussed is discrediting the source. We need some other options. Let's try for two more."

"He's young," Jim said. "We could just scare him."

"Yeah," OhJim said, "give him the lecture about what happens to persons who threaten our Tribe."

"Here's another option," David said. "We could invite him to join our Tribe, like we did with Jeanne and myself before her. The threats make a lot more sense and carry a lot more weight if you are inside the magic circle."

"A lot," I said, "depends on who Ben is. Pick up the action at that point."

Ben's and Jeanne's understanding
|06August08|

"Jeanne, Dear," Eve said, "tell us about you and Gentle Ben."

"Well," Jeanne said, "Ben and I go back a ways. He is in the same program as I was in college, but a year behind. We both worked on the campus newspaper and got to know one another some. When he came to the

Afterblatt to do an internship, we used to have beers at the **Roll In** after work sometimes and discuss this and that. I mentored him some."

"Is he, Dear," Eve said, "a friend? Or more?"

Eve smiled her Buddha Girl smile, girl to girl.

"A friend," Jeanne said, sideways, "but understand that I do not have a category for men that is any higher or deeper. Men and I go a long way back, and I have known for a very long time that it is better to be at arm's length when it comes to men."

The brothers, and David, looked sad to hear their muse speak this way.

"Cheer up, boys," Jeanne said, giving them a warm sideways smile. "If I would ever break my rule, I would have to go **eeny, meeny, miny, moe** with the three of you. It's just that I have a lot of history to rewrite before I would ever get to that point."

The three began to look like something other than three blind mice.

David managed a wintry little smile.

My brothers shared a high-five.

"There is another thing about Ben," Jeanne said. "He's implicated, at least in his own mind, with a certain Glock-packing Punk-girl bodyguard. I was waiting for the right time to tell you about that. Ben is totally besmirched by Jo-Joe the girl guard who works for your friends Baldi and Luce. She likes Ben but maybe not to the same degree. The guy who worked for your friends was a contender in the prize fight for her heart, Ben tells me."

"Need to know," Eve said. "Good work, Dear. Timely. You learn quickly."

"Well," Jeanne said, "I actually like David's option. We can invite Ben into the Tribe as the way of controlling his flow of information."

"What about his Pulitzer lust?" I said.

"That is the crux, isn't it," Jeanne said, "but don't cross him off for having lust in his heart for something. We all do, and some more than others. (She smiled sideways at OhJim, who went pink.) I think that the two in the room with Ben should be augmented by the rest of us listening to the audio. You can bug yourselves, certainly, if you can bug others."

"No problem," I said. "Mr. Red does bugs like an entomologist."

"This is where," Mister Ed said, "we stand. Eve and I will hold a deep background conversation with young Ben, based on the rules of engagement that Jeanne will get him to agree to. Based on our collective sense of where he is coming from, we will either punch out his lights on the spot, let him go in the certainty that he will do no harm, or make him an agent in place at the **Daily Afterblatt**. Did I leave anything out?"

"Sadly," I said, "no."

Yo Tommy, you got your ears on?
|07August08|

Email from Goose to Tommy --

Tommy, my friend, I'm thinking of you:

You might be wondering why we are contemplating inviting yet another stranger into our Tribe. Perhaps you are wondering why we seem to solve all our problems in this fashion.

Since I'm pulling thoughts from my head that I imagine might be in your head, I'll go ahead and add some more words. The operant phrase here is **keep your friends close and your enemies closer**. Notice that this phrase is not the same as my other favorite:

The enemy of my enemy is my friend.

Still, this phrase is kin to the first. Taken together, they begin to explain the paradox of our frequent additions to the Tribe. You see, it's all about relationships ... and kinship. In a world where **the truth** is more often a way of describing the fantasy set of a given segment of the population, one needs some things that are dependable. If everything is relative, with what do we discern? If truth is next to useless, what actually does have use? If there are **permanent friends,** and **permanent enemies**, in contradiction to other models -- v. Saul Alinsky and his community organizing followers -- how do you decide which is which?

Anyone who has lived, and lived to tell about the living, in the shadows of **Spookistan**, knows that there is one way to decide who to trust.

Trust no one.

As Mister Ed and his ink-stained press ilk are fond of saying -- **if your mother says she loves you, check it out**. Or as Pop always said, **There's liars and there's damned liars**. (I think that he borrowed that from Mark Twain and never gave it back.)

We need information that is accurate, or we need a paradigm that does not depend on truth or facts. We choose the latter, and on that we stand, and paint our picture of reality.

Fool me one time, shame on you.
Fool me twice, shame on me.
Fool me thrice?
Bend down and kiss your patoot goodbye.

That, then, is our theme song. We wrote the lyrics ourselves, in blood. It's more brutal than beautiful, I admit, but then so is our world. If you think about it, this dual way of discerning not truth but direction works well. It acknowledges that among the twelve in the circle, one at least will be a Judas. It also acknowledges that there is no way to discern a Judas until the behaviors appear that we associate with that name (too late, if discerning the truth is your paradigm, except if your name is Jesus, who trusted his disciples to be consistent over time and if they weren't, as in the case of Judas, to adjust and move on, pragmatically giving thanks for what was cosmically useful in the man -- no betrayal from Judas, no Cross; no Cross, no Promise; no Promise, no Hope).

The second principle, **the enemy of my enemy is my friend**, is a way to lighten the dark load of cynical closeness. If one does not add something powerful, but only goes with the first idea, of keeping one's friends close and one's enemies closer, one is stuck with being intimate only with persons who are, **ipso facto**, enemies.

The second idea makes it possible to court the possibility that intimacy is possible, desirable, and attainable. And measurable.

In Spookistan, the Quick go by the first idea only. Those who survive Spookistan by being expelled from it, in my experience, add the second principle. But retain the first. Because you are only paranoid if no one is after you, and if you are a spook in recovery someone is, indeed, after you.

At any rate, you have a short list of kill-on-sight persons you are at some level, and always and forever, after.

I'm not at all certain about what we will decide about Gentle Ben Whick, cub reporter, but I am sadly and ruthlessly certain of the principles on which we will base our decisions.

Goose

Ben accepts our terms
|08August08|

We were all in our places, with bright shining faces.

No one could see our faces, though, because we were hiding in the storeroom, next to the backroom where Mister Ed and Eve were talking with Gentle Ben Whick of the **Daily Afterblatt, Lake Effect edition**.

"I can appreciate your position," Mister Ed was saying. "I, too, was once a member of the Fifth Estate, and I don't mean the fifth-a-day club, either. **New York Post, Los Angeles Times**, like that."

We could hear everything, right down to Mister Ed's annoying habit of smacking his lips before bursting into speech.

Jeanne had made sure that she greeted Ben when he came in, and she came back to our lair after showing him into the backroom and making introductions. Jeanne had told the two that Ben had accepted the terms of the interview, and we were all glad to overhear that.

We had an earpiece receiver apiece.

"Jeanne tells us, Dear, that you heard some interesting stories from a man on a barstool," Eve said.

"Yes," Ben said, "he talked at length about this secret society that he said he knew of, and he was very taken with the symbol of the coyote. He even made me a rough drawing on a bar napkin. I gave a copy to Jeanne."

"I take it," Mister Ed said, "that you are here because of something that this mysterious man said."

"Right," Ben said. "The guy said that old bookshop on the north side of town, **Caspar's**, was a hotbed of this secret society. I guess you're going to tell me about that."

"Never fear," Mister Ed said, "we are going to tell you a lot of things."

In the dim light of the storeroom, with its one small, high window, we looked at one another.

Fear was evident on our faces.

Ben describes his source
|09August08|

"Dear," Eve said, "tell us about the man who told you these things."

"Yes, Son," Mister Ed said, "without in any way compromising your source. We understand that you must protect your source."

"Well," Ben said, "he was medium build, darkish, intelligent, and just a little bit drunk. As was I."

"That is an interesting combination," Mister Ed said. "What made you think that he could be trusted?"

"And why did he tell you his story?" Eve said.

"I'm not sure," Ben said, "that I should be answering your questions, but if you will give me the same terms that I'm giving you, I guess it will be Ok."

"We will," Eve said.

"Yes," Mister Ed said. "Mutual trust is good here, I think."

"So," Ben said, "this guy came and sat down on the empty barstool next to me, in this mostly empty bar that I hang out in sometimes -- the **Roll In and Crawl Out**, over on one of the side streets near the **Afterblatt** building. Both of us had had a few before meeting up, and we had a few more while we talked."

"Did he seem to have an agenda?" Mister Ed said. "It seems interesting that he sat down next to you in a pretty much empty bar."

"It is a small place," Ben said, "but he didn't have to sit right next to me. There were stools nearby, too. But let's get back to that after a while. I want to ask you some questions now."

Once again, we exchanged uneasy glances in the storeroom.

It was wearing us down to listen but not have an active part to play.

I was pleased with young Ben.

He was well over six feet tall and had a gentleness about him that justified the nickname that we had given him.

He was candid and trusting.

Probably a jinx for a reporter.

Where all this was going, I could not guess.

Ben gets to the point and twists
|10August08|

"What," Ben said, "is the truth about this bookshop? I've been asking around, and no one will talk to me, except to say that I should shop elsewhere if I'm looking for tips instead of titles. Stuff like that. Jeanne won't say much, and that really isn't like her at all. Jeanne has a lot to say about almost everything. But not the bookshop."

Jeanne took a bow in the storeroom's half-light.

We mimed applause.

"You can't believe everything that you don't hear," Eve said.

"Right," Mister Ed said. "You may not be asking the right questions."

"Tell me the right questions," Ben said.

"No can do," Mister Ed said. "It don't work that way, Son, and I think that you know it."

"And look at it this way, Dear," Eve said, smiling her Buddha Girl smile, "we probably have no more secrets than you do."

Ben laughed, short and hard.

Loud, too.

"Ok," Ben said, "it was worth a try. And I figured that I had been forthcoming with you, and all. Here's another way of asking: What goes on here that no one wants to talk about it. It gives cred to the barstool guy's story. Though I admit that a barstool is not the same as a witness box, though the truth is probably more often told at the **Roll In** than in the Courts."

"I'm glad that you see it that way," Mister Ed said, "because frankly I don't think that you could sell your editor on a story based on a single pickled source of a pickled young reporter."

"Yeah," Ben said, "he would not like that at all, which is why I'm sitting on the stuff except for some asking around. He's been after me to do another follow story on the **Mystery Man** stuff, and I was hoping against hope that I could work this angle some, but Jeanne warned me off last night and I slept on it. I guess that that Pulitzer will have to wait."

The faces in the storeroom lost some of their pinched tone.

"Sometimes I get this sick feeling," Ben said, "that I'm not in the right line of work. I really don't enjoy turning people's lives upside down. The old salts scoff at me and say I better toughen up, but I tell them that I'm young, and dumb, and full of ... well, I won't say what I tell them, but it seems to amuse them."

"You're right, Dear," Eve said. "You don't have to be a newspaper hack if you don't want to be. Remember what Hemingway said about newspapers."

"You need to know when to leave," Ben said, "or something like that."

"Close enough, Son, close enough," Mister Ed said, nodding stiffly from his waist like a skyscraping construction crane in the air, dipping to grab a fistful of girders. "Close enough for hacks like us, eh?"

Ben goes away sad but not mad
|11August08|

"Well," Ben said, "let's talk some more about this guy who sought me out and told me a tale about some secret society your bookshop is involved in."

"Ok, Son," Mister Ed said. "Say some more."

"So," Ben said, "this guy was probably trying to make trouble for you.

That much is clear. Question is, did he make up that stuff or was he telling some version of the truth?"

"Good question, Dear," Eve said. "What's your answer?"

"My answer," Ben said, "is that it doesn't matter much one way or the other, as long as I get either confirmation or can't find anyone who will say anything about youse guys that is anywhere near what the barstool guy said. Like I said, so far no one will say anything at all. They seem to be afraid of you. Is there something wrong with me that I'm not?"

"Well, Son," Mister Ed said, "I think we are a collection of over-the-hill booklovers who especially like to hang around with Miss Eve here. I can't think of any reason to be afraid of that."

"I'm pretty much hanging out at the cop shop," Ben said, "doing the work that the veterans don't want to be bothered with. I'm sometimes an ear for stories from guys who never tell the truth in anything except ink on a page, if that. And the veterans on the police force are like funhouse mirror images of the news veterans. They all like to lie, and drink, and spread rumors. But about you? They say, **Go away, Kid, you bother me**. Or worse."

"Let's take this case on its merits," Mister Ed said --

• "You get a visitor on the next barstool over (and the next stool after the one that he took was empty, too).

• "He tells you a story about a secret society with local ties. He does not, I'm guessing, tell you why he's telling you what he is telling you about the bookshop."

Ben nodded. Mister Ed made his assenting crane motion.

• "When you go to the veterans -- both news and police -- and ask them in a general way about the bookshop, they know the place and they don't want to talk about it.

  • "Your editor would not agree to run anything based on one source, with no name and no address to follow up on (I'm guessing on that, too).

  • "No one to this point will confirm anything that the barstool guy told you."

"That sums it up, except," Ben said, "for one thing. Why did you not only agree to talk with me but go after me, in the person of Jeanne?"

"What did Jeanne tell you, Dear?" Eve said.

"She just said," Ben said, "that I should come over to the bookshop where she works if I wanted to ask any questions about the rumors that I heard about the bookshop. She said you were wonderful people and that I would see how absurd it was to suspect anything about you other than the fact that you had some cool books for sale for way too little."

"Jeanne is wise for her tender years," Mister Ed said. "You are fortunate to have her for a friend."

In the storeroom, Jeanne took another deep bow, to our applause like the sound of one hand clapping.

"And we," Eve said, "are fortunate to have her for an employee. Her love of books and her depth of understanding are remarkable in one so young."

"If you ever decide that the news biz is not for you," Mister Ed said, "I hope you will come and talk with us."

"Yes," Eve said. "Come and see us. We may have jobs."

"Well," Ben said, "my internship is up at the end of this month and I go back to school for my senior year. I may just do that."

In the storeroom, Jeanne took yet another bow. We were all smiling.

F-Troop (by any other name) meets
|12August08|

After Jeanne, heels in hand, scurried in her stocking feet out of the back-room and re-shod herself just ahead of the departing Ben Whick, and saw him out the door, we gathered for a meeting of the F-Troop.

Excuse me, the **F-Troupe-A**.

"We will be in disorder," I said, "if we do not come to order."

"Why not in **dis** order?" Jim said.

"Yeah," OhJim said, "why not in **dat** order?"

"Other comments," I said, "ones that are to the point, not the issue of too many pints. For example, do you agree with our talking heads' decision to let Gentle Ben go free?"

F-Troop salutes all around on that one.

"What else?" I said.

"Mr. Black," David said, "as in medium build, darkish, intelligent, drunk."

"Noted," I said, especially if the lovely Naomi would consent to take some big notes on the flip chart.

"Why not," Jeanne said, "I do all the scut work around here."

She gave us her sideways smile and rose to the task on her killer heels.

"Naomi?" Jim said.

"Yes?" Jeanne said. "I do remember my own duly constituted nicknames."

"Yeah," OhJim said. "How soon we forgot."

We once again gave her the sound of one hand clapping.

Jeanne wrote on the flip chart --

• Mr. Black? medium build, darkish, intelligent, drunk?!?

"What else?" I said.

"Bring some stuff forward from the last list," Eve said, "like potluck with Baldi and Luce."

Jeanne wrote --

• Potluck with Baldy and Lucy.

"It's **B-A-L-D-I** and its **L-U-C-E**," I said.

"Sorry," Jeanne said. "I forgot."

Jeanne fixed the offending spellings with her red marker pen --

• Potluck with Baldi and Luce.

"There were some other things on that list that were provocative," I said. "Do you have it somewhere to hand, Eve?"

Eve reached into her desk file drawer. David put the sheet up on the wall.

"Interesting," I said, "but let us not forget to add new items from today's frolic with Ben."

The List of Things to Do
| 13August08 |

"Very interesting," Jeanne said, in a lame German accent, using her red marker pen like a huge cigarette, held between her thumb and index finger.

"But stupid," David said. "The reference is from that F-Troop-like series **Hogan's Heroes**, which compare to **Laugh In** spoof of Colonel Klink by the diminutive actor Arte Johnson."

We looked at David in slack-jawed shock and awe.

For a while, no one spoke.

"Sock it to me," Jim said.

"Yeah," OhJim said. "Sake to me."

We turned to the old list.

- Dets. Blucote and Joe Bob are dopes and bleeping bleepers.
- That stipulated, what do we gain and/or lose by talking with the dets? Would it make them debtors?
- We can do just about anything, as long as it makes sense out front.
- Although our own Mr. Red has a nice hand and cute hips, no one in this room is a poofter.
- Roles (watch the donut, not the hole).
- Tell the truth -- discuss.
- Tell a lie and say it's the truth -- discuss.
- Why we want to know who is in the coroner's cooler -- discuss.
- Get clarity on what I'm doing right (Naomi).
- Who are we, how did we get here, and where are we going?
- What if the body is someone else's -- discuss at length/take notes.
- Add some rhymes to David's reason.
- The lovely Naomi tells her ugly story.
- Call in friends -- Baldy, Lucy, and Parmgarter.

"I guess that you had to be there to get the significance of a lot of those entries," Jim said.

"Yeah," OhJim said, "it looks like **Geek** to me."

"I resemble that comment," David said, "but let it pass. It looks more Punk or Goth than Geek to me. After all, Naomi wrote it."

Jeanne just smiled, sideways.

"What comes forward?" I said.

"Well," Eve said, "we do need to touch base with our old friend Parmgartner (that's **P-A-R-M-G-A-R-T-N-E-R**)."

Jeanne wrote large and red --
- Touch base with P-A-R-M-G-A-R-T-N-E-R.

"This is all very good," I said, "... but."

This is all very good ... but titular?
| 14August08 |

"Scrub your **but**, Goose Dear," Eve said. "It is **all** very good. Period. And we can add some things about Ben. Such as, Question: Do we want to invite Ben to join the Tribe, quit the **Afterblatt**, and change his major?"

"Or do we want to manage his stresses for our ends and turn him, in place, as our man inside the **Afterblatt**," Jeanne said.

"I like your mind, Miss. Right on target. The Miss that hit," Mister Ed said.

"And I like the rest of you," Jim said.

"Yeah," OhJim said, "and I, all of thee above, and below, inside and out, within or without."

"I dream of Jeanne," David said.

Jeanne just smiled, to the side.

No one was surprised that Mister Ed could pun better than a talking horse, but then we all knew that he was a wordsmithy and could bang out shoddy **words-work** without much effort. Clip, clop, pun. Under the tree, spreading his chestnuts, the village wordsmithy stands. Cantor at a canter pace.

But how about that David?

I'll stop.

Jeanne wrote, in big red letters --

• Do we invite Ben to quit the Afterblatt, change his major, and join the Tribe, or do we turn him, in place, as our man inside the Afterblatt?

• Question from Naomi: Why do we need an inside man at the Afterblatt?

"Good question," Eve said, "and well-noted, Dear."

"What else?" I said.

"Why," Jeanne said, "would someone want to make trouble for us by spreading rumors that could be true? And why would Mr. Black, if it be Mr. Black, back from the titular dead, be doing such things?"

Jim and OhJim received with gladness any such words as **titular** from the lips of their Muse.

Jeanne wrote a quote of her questions --

• Why would someone want to make trouble for us by spreading rumors that could be true? And why would Mr. Black, if it be Mr. Black, back from the titular dead, be doing such things?

• Mr. Black, dead or alive -- discuss.

"Here's one about Ben," David said. "Who will we be dealing with from the **Afterblatt** when Ben goes back to school?"

"Better the devil you know than the devil you don't," Mister Ed said.

Jeanne wrote --

• Who the devil will replace Ben at the Afterblatt next month?

"What else?" I said.

"We have totally dropped the ball on the second body, the one dumped on the East Side," Jeanne said. "We never did follow up on the similarities."

Jeanne wrote --

• Pick up the ball on the body dumped on the East Side -- who, what, where, when, why, and how.

"I move, Mr. Chair Sir, that we memorialize the previous iteration of **The List** and commend it to the care and feeding of our own Eve," Jim said. "It would be good if this could be done by nightfall, Eve."

"Yeah," OhJim said, "second, by virtue of the fact that my brother spoke before me and by virtue of the fact that nightfall and Eve have a certain ironic affinity, or **ironifity**."

Eve stuck out her tongue at Jim, but not far, since his fling at her name didn't include any reference -- veiled, piebald, or overt -- to the Garden of Eden or any of its heirs or assigns (at least by name).

The List, Boss, The List!
| 15August08 |

This was **The List**, as amended, delineated, and scribbled upon --
• Mr. Black? medium build, darkish, intelligent, drunk?!?
• Potluck with Baldy and Lucy ... Baldi and Luce.
• Touch base with P-A-R-M-G-A-R-T-N-E-R.
• Do we invite Ben to quit the Afterblatt, change his major, and join the Tribe, or do we turn him, in place, as our man inside the Afterblatt?
• Question by Naomi: Why do we need an inside man at the Afterblatt?
• Why would someone want to make trouble for us by spreading rumors that could be true? And why would Mr. Black, if it be Mr. Black, back from the titular dead, be doing such things?
• Mr. Black, dead or alive -- discuss.
• Who the devil will replace Ben at the Afterblatt next month?
• Pick up the ball on the body dumped on the East Side -- who, what, where, when, why, and how.
"Very, very good," I said. "You're right, **Eve M**y, it's all good."
"**Eve My?**" Jeanne said.
"Short for **Eve My Dear**," I said.
"Yes, Dear," Eve said, "and we need to parcel out these posts so that we get some results."
"Ok," I said, "who is going to call Baldi and Luce."
"You are, Dear," Eve said.
"Ok," I said, "and who is going to call Parmgartner?"
"I am, Dear," Eve said.
"And," I said, "who is going to re-brief us on the body on the East Side?"
"I will," Jeanne said.
"Ok," I said, "that leaves some big questions for immediate attention --
• "Mr. Black, he dead (or not) and related questions re: motivation, if any.
• "Several questions about Gentle Ben."

Motions make us seasick
| 16August08 |

"We are becalmed," I said. "Someone needs to make a motion -- and any old song and dance will do."
"**I second that emotion**, Mr. Chair Sir," David said, and began to sing.
"Almost as good as the original," Jim said.
"Yeah," OhJim said, "but different, very different. I move that we accept David's emotion, as amended."
I was suddenly wishing that I had a parliamentarian nearby.
 Turns out, I did.

"I would like to offer my services," Mister Ed said, "as resident expert -- parliamentarian, if you will -- on **Robert's Rules of Order**."

"So ordered," I said. "So speak."

"First," Mister Ed said, "there is a motion on the floor. To wit, that we accept David's emotion. This was the first of several utterances to actually rise to the level of a motion. The first utterance, from you, Mister Chair Sir, was an appropriate invitation for someone, other than yourself, to make a motion. You spoke correctly, since you cannot, as Chair, make a motion, any more than a footstool could; you can, however, entertain one (if you can square that with your lovely Eve). The second utterance, from David, was indeed in the form of a musical utterance, but it did not rise -- though it was in falsetto -- to the level of a motion. David seconded a motion that he posited but that he did not, nor did anyone else here present, actually make. In any case, David could not have seconded his own motion. Jim's comment was just that, a comment, and as such would be in order if you so rule. OhJim's comment on his brother's comment is a motion concerning David's proto-motion. If it were not for the fact that it was a motion, in form if not in substance, and could or should be recognized by you, Mister Chair Sir, we probably should note it in passing as we move on. In summary, there is a motion on the floor. To wit, that we second David's emotion."

The assembly erupted into applause.

"Is there a second?" I said.

"Second," Eve said, "just to see where this goes, Mr. Chair Dear. And I would like to hear Mister Ed say some more about footstools, though I say so in fear and trembling."

"Are you ready to vote?" I said. "Of course you are. I see that we are unanimous in our opinion that someone should make a bleeping motion!"

"I move," Jeanne said, that we take up the question of Gentle Ben Whick first and Mr. Black second, to go from the simple to the complex, in steps."

"Second," Jim said, "and that is a second, Mister Chair Sir, not a com- ment on Mr. Black's apparent position in all this, or Ben, for that matter. I second Naomi's motion, in fine."

"Yeah," OhJim said, "me, too. What he said. Jim, I mean, not the long- winded and shiny Mister Ed. I couldn't talk for that long. I'd be in a coma before the midsection. But brilliant, mind you. Brilliant."

"Let's do it then talk about it," Jim said.

"My brother may be confused," OhJim said, "but I agree. **Do it then talk about it** is a good way to conduct public intercourse in general."

Jeanne gave OhJim a bittersweet smile just for him. He went all pink.

"I regret the mention of footstools, Eve," Mister Ed said, holding his hands about twelve inches apart. "To define the term would bring a flush to my face and would bring the high tone of this body's discourse to the level of a jakes. In a feisty group such as this, mention of the water closet or any of its contents was in poor judgment and in worst taste. I apologize to the body, in mind and spirit. Fie on me. Scat!"

"So noted," I said. "I continue to be Chair, not Stool."

A word for my sole brother

| 17August08 |

Email from Goose to Tommy --

Sole Brother, Sole Reader, Big Fish, hail:

I've been jotting down back-stories lately to share with you.

Eve Green: My partner in life and sole reason for living. Eve has the beauty of a woman of a certain age, which is the beauty that ages gracefully and well. She has a smile and an encouraging word for everyone that she meets. Everyone, to Eve, is **Dear.** This quaint, fanciful appellation for all others fits her age and self-chosen station. Eve wants to be a blessing to each person that she meets, and most people respond powerfully to her intentions. As I have said many times, the old farts who drift around the bookshop like a noxious cloud work without pay or praise because of their devotion to Eve. And, as I have said on a number of occasions, these oldsters are capable of the most shocking violence in defense of their Lady. And their Lady's consort, too (me). Eve is of medium height, tending toward the angular but stopping on the pleasing side, showing a hint of plumpness. **Zaftig** gets at Eve's form. She has center-parted salt and pepper hair that she wears long and in her eyes. Her full mouth is made for smiling, and her large eyes have a direct quality that hints at a stern ability held in reserve. Eve's nose is substantial and glorious. She almost always wears an old grey old-man's cardigan sweater when at the bookshop. The general feeling about Eve is that she could dress in a sack and still be a deeply desirable woman, and a beautiful person. Eve has lived two lives, the first in Spookistan. as a woman of various types, and the second in **Caspar's Books and That**, as the sole owner and resident blessing. The sourness of the former has led, I believe, to the sweetness of the latter. Not atonement, exactly, but close. Her sweetness was purchased at a price, and she does not tell all the stories that she has lived. Her beauty, directness, sweetness, and mystery make her an exciting woman to love. I should know.

Jeanne Wheenin: Where Eve **has** secrets, Jeanne simply **is** secret. Jeanne, our Punk Princess. This was my first impression of her, when she breeched our walls and forced us to take her in and on as a full member of the tribe: **Black skirt, hair, and heels, very red lipstick, go-to-hell half-smile on her powdered-pale face of Punk/Goth elegance.** Jeanne, like Eve, has a signature smile (Eve's being the Buddha Girl smile of blessing). Jeanne's is a sideways thing of ironic glory, bitter and sweet like lemons. It was easy to embrace Jeanne, at least in theory, though we seldom touch her in reality. It isn't something that she invites or rejects, but a friendly distance is her preference on both sides of a relationship. Jeanne is, in words of one syllable, hot, sexy, smart, aloof, and desirable. Her manner can be as blunt as her nose. Men's eyes act like iron when Jeanne walks into a room. She is a magnet, and she knows that she is, and at the tender age of twenty-something she has long since made many decisions about men and about herself. They could look, because they had no choice, and she would be who God made her and not hide her body under a bushel basket or burlap flour sack. There are parts of her story that she has only hinted at, but we know that she had to have had brushes with abusive men all her life. We don't talk a lot about it, but my brothers in particular, with David right in there, will not tolerate any mistreatment of our Punk Princess. Jeanne is a fine bookshop worker, because she loves and understands books, and she has a reporter's way with not only words but concepts, too. She and David are the next generation of the Tribe, and Eve and I see them as our replacements in the fullness of time. Jeanne has full lips and a flat and notice-able nose, and dark eyes. Her black hair, which is the color that her hair is on its own, with no assistance, is thick and straight save for a general and loose wavi-ness. There is something of the gypsy about her. She is not a small or a thin woman. Nor is she big-beautiful. She is substantial and vital. Someday she will be **zoftig**. Just like Eve.

Those are our women. Next the men.

Goose

On the way to the men's room
| 18August08 |

Email from Goose to Tommy --

Hi, friend and reader:

Yesterday I sent you back-stories of the women of our tribe. Today, on the way to the male room, I pause to post a profile of our **Wild Billy**, the bookshop cat. Wild Billy, whose acting parents are the bickering Mr. Red and Mister Ed, came to us by choice via Baldi and Luce. And since Wild Billy chose to stay with us, we were behind the curve from before the beginning. We named him for the General, Buffalonya's own Gen. William Donovan, who earned the nickname **Wild Bill** on the battlefields of World War One.

Our cat earned the same moniker by his extreme contrast with the hard-charging Donovan. I guess it was inevitable that we would call him **Wild Billy**. Patrons love Wild Billy, and they love him despite his tendency to jump from a sitting position on the floor to the back of anyone naive or new enough to bend down to check the books on the bottom row. Wild Billy knows an invitation when he sees one. Despite his surprises, there are patrons who come as much for the cat as they do for the books.

Tomorrow, I promise, the men of our tribe.

Goose

The men of our Tribe
| 19August08 |

Email from Goose to Tommy --

Hi, my friend:

I'm going with one-liners about the men of the Tribe --

Jon Rieley-Goddard | 138

- **Jim** has a Groucho Marx hair top.
- **OhJim** has a tuft about the ears.
- **I** have a lot of hair growing out of my ears.
- **Mister Ed** has a chest as big as all outdoors.
- **Mr. Red** ... in a word, **bleep.** And in a phrase, **Bleep-etty, bleep, bleep.**

And a few things about **David** --

- David and Jeanne are both in their early 20s, and they make a cute pair. When we took David into the bookshop with the idea of developing him for our covert activities, we pretty much assumed that he was a rainbow sort of guy, if you know what I mean, but since Jeanne has come on board David has blossomed in covert understanding and as a hetero sort of guy. I think we were a victim of our assumptions, and I suppose I am being Politically Incorrect to talk about this. So shoot me. David is a handsome cuss of a slight but deceptive build. He is healthy and agile, and so far we have not found him to be fearful in any way.

Goose

Brothers and sisters like you and me
| 20August08 |

Email from Goose to Tommy --

It's funny how the process of sharing like this can take people from being strangers to being in some sense brothers. Sisters, too.

I know that I sound naive, often, but I have decided, like those who decide to follow Jesus, that I will live my life as if others are worthy of trust. It has to do with the second life (isn't there a web site called **Second Life**?) -- the one after Spookistan, or east of Eden, or whatever image you like best.

Life is short by any measure, and **second life** is by definition more precious and probably less in length than **first life**. I never had any friends in my first life. I messed with lives.

I did the bidding of my masters, and I thought that I was doing the work that I myself believed in.

Perhaps it was the experience of being shunned into exile that changed me.

Perhaps it was the stench of the accumulated garbage that my life, my **first life**, had become. Whatever the reasons, or reason, I will live henceforth, I decided, for myself in relationship. I will live for self and others. Eve taught me that.

Goose

Day shift at the olfactory

| 21August08 |

"Let us be in odor," I said.

"You stink, Mr. Chair Sir," Jim said.

"Yeah," OhJim said, "and I don't mean anything by it. Jim does."

"Thank you, brothers," I said. "No offense taken. Not a whiff."

"You mean there won't be any overtime put in at the olfactory?" Jim said.

"Nor the new factory either," David said. "But who nose, really?"

"Spell that, Young Man," I said.

"Why?" David said. "Is he tired?"

The Tribe gave David an ovation.

"I think," I said, "that we agreed to take up the question of Gentle Ben as the more simple one."

"None of us wants to talk about Mr. Black," Eve said, "including me."

"So," I said. **"Black, Black, no trades back."**

"I would like to make a motion," Jeanne said.

My bobblehead brothers looked at Jeanne in hopes that the motion would be something about the hips.

They began a rhythmic clapping -- **Jean-ne, Jean-ne, Jean-ne ...** .

"Not that kind of motion, you Horndogs," Jeanne said, smiling in the sideways way she has that looks something like a cross between a happy person and a person who just sucked on a lemon.

"Your motion, Miss?" Mister Ed said. "We've been over this before. Seems like I recall missing the point."

"That we embrace our young bro Ben," Jeanne said, "and bring him into the fold of our Tribe, or quasi-criminal enterprise, whichever you prefer."

"I was thinking the same thing, Dear," Eve said. "Ben has potential and stands in need of some mentoring."

"And he may be having some woman troubles, too," OhJim said.

"And we stand in need of an infusion of young blood," I said. "We must look to the future."

"My question," Eve said, "is whether he will be amenable. And if he is, my next question is about timing."

"He's not mean," OhJim said, "he's Gentle. We like that about him."

"I mean --, Eve said, but stopped and smiled at my brother instead.

"No," OhJim said, "you no mean at all. You very sweet and good."

"We should wait until he is done at the **Afterblatt**," Jeanne said, "and then we should invite him back. He only has a few more days."

"Is there a second?" I said.

"Where are the big hand and the little hand?" David said.

"OhJim and I will divide the second in half, making fourths," Jim said.

"Yeah," OhJim said. "He means yes. Me, too. And I think that David was making mime fun with the time."

"So odored," I said, giving my signature smile for eyes only.

My smile is a hidden-in-plain-sight smile, like a bird hiding in a bush.

No one has seen my smile. But it is there. The eyes have it.

Have you seen this man?
|22August08|

I was thinking about a slinger with a photo of Mr. Black for placement under windshield wipers up and down all the streets on the West Side of Buffalonya --

Have you seen this man?

**If you have, call Goose Grim at Bros Grim P.I.,
and ask for (you guessed it) Goose.**
It was time to talk about the man, and the subject thereof, that we had been avoiding for a long time. That was at the top of my list for the day.

There was time, however, for some levity in passing.

Jeanne and David made a slinger with the lurid look of a **Wanted** poster.

I added a drawing of the Rev. Mr. Black from the days when we were under the cloth. I was pleased with the drawing of my old, dear friend and the slinger, even if it would not grace any windshields in the neighborhood.

Old and dear?

Well, old, anyway, and important. And maddening. And obscene.

He could make Mr. Red sound like he was preaching to the choir.

And don't say that **foul mouth ne'er won fair maid**, for that would not be true of Mr. Black. In spite of his foul words, his mouth got quite a workout in the gender olympics.

We were revolving slowly around the fixed point that Mr. Black had become in our lives, dead or alive.

It was time to run the questions about Mr. Black through the Tribal think tank and see what came out the old noggin nozzle.

Some righteous puns, at a minimum, I figured.

The book on Mr. Black
|23August08|

"Look," Jeanne said, "it may have been for fun that we mocked up that slinger, but I certainly can show the drawing of the Rev. Mr. Black to Gentle Ben and ask if this looks like the guy on the barstool who talked about the secret society and Coyote."

"True," I said, "but we need to bring Ben on board first."

"Well," Jeanne said, "today was his last day at the **Afterblatt**. He goes back to school in a few."

"Right," I said, "and if you would slip into **Naomi mode**, we can begin a list of thoughts, feelings, and options."

"Roger, Mr. Goose," Jeanne said.

"Just don't call him **Buck** or **Bambi**, Dear," Eve said. "He seems to bristle like a big bore when those names come up. **Roger**, though, seems safe."

"Which," Jeanne said, grabbing a marker pen and rising on towering peep-toe heels, "amuses me, especially when he, once again, reminds us not to call him **Buck** or **Bambi**. Add **Big Boar** to the list of proscribed names for Mr. Chair Sir."

"Be that as it may," I said, "we are in order, like a deck of cards with two cutesy little jokers. That typification suits you both -- hearts and clubs."

"Since we are in session, Mr. Chair Sir," Jim said, "I would like to make a motion that we dispense with the usual and go with the unusual."

"I second my brother's motion, Mr. Chair Sir," OhJim said, "and, yeah, I apologize for not having a smart-ass comment to go with it."

"It takes," Jeanne said, "an entire village to raise a smart-ass. We have let ourselves down by razing ours to the ground ... unless the brothers Jim Grim can find it in themselves to be who they were and puns again can be."

"I rise in support of my own motion, Mr. Chair Sir," Jim said, "and I thank Princess Naomi for her **kine words** to bull-laden old bulls such as ourselves."

"Yeah," OhJim said. "Moo, or whatever a bull would utter."

"Bulls don't have udders, Brother," Jim said. "Heifers have udders, and the little cow dears love to talk."

"You two have found your home on the range," Eve said. "Bull fits you to an utterance. **Moo-hoo** if you don't like it."

"Udder delights they are, my rough-cut Jims," Jeanne said, "even when they become udderwise occupied."

Aside to Tommy: Didn't I say we might pop a few puns along the way?

Jeanne dusts off Ben's doodle
| 24August08 |

The next morning Jeanne showed up with a hangover and a sheaf of doodles, both thanks to her friend and soon to be our friend Gentle Ben Whick.

"You look like a million bucks," Jim said, "all green and rumpled."

"Yeah," OhJim said, "but you're looking good, my brother meant to say."

"Thank you, boys, for your candor and drivel," Jeanne said, smiling to

their side, with effort. "I feel like I look, but it was for the common good."

Jeanne gave us copies.

"This is what -- art class?" I said. "Well, I guess it does look familiar."

"Ben's drawings of the guy he met up with," Jeanne said, "in the **Roll In and Crawl Out**, plus some characters who were hanging around, and the secret society symbol that the man drew on a bar napkin. We didn't give this art its due yet. We got caught up in the Coyote question instead. Remember? Ben will be coming by for a friendly visit later this morning, BTW."

The most important drawing was the barstool guy. I held my opinion, save for a raised eyebrow to Eve, who for just this once was not smiling.

The drawing that I had done in jest for the slinger was of a Mr. Black from many years ago. Ben's drawing was of a man whom he had shared a toot with a few days past. There were similarities, even if you factored in all those years.

Remember, Mr. Black could change a room by changing his tie. He was a master of deception with the trappings that hung from his frame.

The contrast between Ben's and my drawings was helpful for us all.

The baseball cap, the hoodie, the hair sticking out, and the mustache in Ben's drawing were beside the point. We could explain away the difference in jaw line and facial shape. And we noted the eyes and nose.

And the gate-mouth quality apparent in both drawings.

"I think that we have our man, back from the dead," Jeanne said.

"I agree," David said. "The very same. In the flesh."

Mister Ed nodded his horsey head.

My brothers bobbled theirs.

"Probably," I said.

"Very much so," Eve said.

"What now?" Jeanne said. "I'll get my red marker pen."

The book on Mr. Black, back
| 25August08 |

Jeanne, rising on cute kitten heels to channel the lovely Naomi -- tribal, scribal note-taker -- was as ever a sight to gladden hearts.

We needed some gladdening, for the prospect of Mr. Black out there, somewhere, doing who knows what for who knows what reasons, was a sight in the mind that created, not so much a gladness at his living, but fears about things we did not understand.

"Well," Eve said, "it looks like we need to do some serious work."

"Yeah," Jim said, "we are about as eager to work as the legendary Nero Wolf himself. I feel a ton of resistance."

"And yeah," OhJim said, "this is one time it is appropriate to cry Wolf."

"I'm standing by," Jeanne said, slowly revolving on heel point, "ready to jot down work-related calls for action."

Jeanne demonstrated by spinning around once, a single revolution, arms out for balance.

The boys erupted in applause. Eve and I, too.

Jeanne bowed while smiling that smile.

"You haven't heard anything work-related yet, Dear, have you?" Eve said. "Here's one to start with: We will work on the assumption that Mr. Black is alive, not dead."

"Yes," I said, "and here is a second, just like the first but only different, since I and Eve are two, not one. We will work to figure out just who it was who died on the grille of that bus if it was not our friend Mr. Black. I can repeat that if you need, but from the look on your face I'll just stop here."

Jeanne smiled to the side and rolled her eyes. No mean feat.

"Here," Eve said, "is a third, fourth, and fifth -- Why is Mr. Black out there and not in here? Is he working covertly apart from one and all for our protection? Has he simply gone off the Rez and off his rocker?"

"Next item," I said, "is this: What connection, if any, is there to Mr. Black's disappearance and the first body in the **Mystery Man** case?"

Jeanne wrote --

• Assumption No. 1: We will work out of a conviction that the missing Mr. Black is alive and not dead.

• Assumption No. 2: We will work to figure out just who it was who died on the grille of that bus, if it was not our friend.

• Questions: Why is Mr. Black out there and not in here? Is he working covertly apart from one and all for our protection? Has he simply gone off the Rez and off his rocker?

• What connection, if any, is there to Mr. Black's disappearance and the first body in the Mystery Man series?

While Jeanne was performing feats of spinning, listening, and recording, to the rapt attention of my brothers, I was making a personal list in the darkness of my mind, thus confining the anxiety in myself for now --

• If Mr. Black is working for us, why isn't he telling us anything?

• If Mr. Black has gone off in all directions at once, has he become by this a danger in all directions?

• If Mr. Black has gone over to the dark side, what must we do to protect ourselves and others?

• What, if any, are the moral implications in all this?

Black/white and read all over
| 26August08 |

This story ran in the **Daily Afterblatt, Lake Effect edition.**

Trash crew finds body in dumpster downtown

Buffalonya Police detectives today were canvassing the neighborhood downtown that surrounds a dim, dingy alley where an early-morning trash crew making weekly pickups found a body stuffed into a dumpster.

"We got nothing so far," Det. Joe Blucote said. "This is another case that doesn't fit the mold of drug wars and drive-bys."

Blucote, who is investigating the death, with his partner, Det. Bill "Joe Bob" Schmidt, promised that a drawing of the dead person would be made available tomorrow morning.

Blucote would not give any details on the cause of death or any other forensic details. He referred questions to the County Coroner, Dr. Bruce Backstaff.

Backstaff was not available for comment.

"He's busy, as you might expect," said a clerical staffer at the Coroner's Office.

Unconfirmed reports say that the victim was a young adult male of slight build, with curly hair and full beard.

The city's police detectives have been running into brick walls all this year, with two unsolved murders already on the board.

There are few businesses in the vicinity of the crime scene that police established in the alley between Fillmore and Bush streets in the downtown district.

A bar of the seedy, hard-life sort empties out the back into the alley.

Black/white and read all over
| 27August08 |

This story ran in the **Daily Afterblatt, Lake Effect edition.**

Another 'Mystery Man'
Buffalonya detectives release drawings in dumpster death

By Jane Carlotto
Senior Crime Reporter

One day after trash crews found the body of a young adult male in a dumpster downtown, Buffalonya detectives are saying that the case is linked to the "Mystery Man Murder."

That case, last March, was a bus-versus-man accident near Presidents Park.

A Coroner's Jury later ruled that the man had died by misadventure, making the case a homicide investigation. The i.d. of that victim has never been made.

Detectives released two drawings. One drawing shows the face of the dead man, and the other drawing shows a symbol that was scrawled on the dumpster where the body was dumped.

At a news conference, lead Det. Joe Blucote explained that newly discovered evidence in the initial case led to the linking up of the two murders.

Blucote said the body in the dumpster had no identification, so police hope the drawing of the dead man will bring in some essential details about him.

"He was clothed," Blucote said, "but there was nothing of substance in his pockets. We're hoping that someone is missing him and will call us."

An autopsy was to be conducted later today.

Blucote refused to say why drawings were being distributed instead of photographs. Det. Bill "Joe Bob" Schmidt, Blucote's partner, said reporters should check with their editors as to whether they would print photographs of dead persons, but he refused to answer any follow-up questions.

The second drawing that Blucote and his partner handed out at the press conference was of a symbol that had been drawn with marker pen on the dumpster at the crime scene.

The symbol looks like an oval electrical outlet, or a shroud with two long and narrow, lidless eyes.

"We would like to hear from anyone who has seen this symbol," Blucote said.

Little is known about the circumstances surrounding the murder, and Blucote refused to say why detectives were calling the death a homicide.

When asked if the victim was homeless, Blucote said he was not sure about anything except the fact of the man's demise.

"Beyond the obvious, we got zip," Blucote said.

Generally reliable sources say that the victim was a young adult male of slight build with curly hair and full beard.

Blucote referred all questions to the county coroner, Dr. Bruce Backstaff.

Backstaff did not return calls, and his staff would not say where he was or what he was doing.

The city's police detectives have been running into brick walls all this year with two unsolved high profile murders on the board.

There are few businesses in the vicinity of the crime scene that police established in the alley between Fillmore and Bush streets in the downtown district.

A bar of the seedy, hard-life sort empties out the back into the alley.

Ben knows enough to be scared
| 28August08 |

Gentle Ben Whick knew enough to be scared when he saw the drawing of the symbol found on the side of the dumpster. He called Jeanne, who invited him to come by the bookshop as soon as he could.

To say Ben was eager to accept the invitation would understate the case. He was itching to see us.

It is said that **if you lie down with dogs, you end up with fleas.**

Here's hoping that Ben's itch was more metaphorical.

The two articles about the latest body were enough to get the attention of the entire Tribe.

We were due for a meeting of the F-Troupe-A to discuss all the angles, but Ben arrived before we had a chance to call ourselves to order.

When Jeanne showed Ben to the backroom and closed the door, I knew that we would be making a bold move by taking Ben into our confidence. It is one thing to trust David and Jeanne, who earned our love and respect by their steady and dependable ways. Jeanne, in particular, displays not only a fine sense of alternative fashion but also a maturity and fund of knowledge that are both gratifying and startling in one so young in years. Ben is another kind of young person, with more of an edge of need and confusion. Could he be trusted with the secrets of the Tribe?

The penalty for failure is repugnant, but we are the ones who inherited and extended Pop's system -- trust everyone unless they prove you wrong.

In Spookistan, it was easier, because one's safety was the first concern and because so many others wanted to compromise one's safety. Now, however, I want to be more trusting, loving, and forgiving while maintaining a permanent, medium-high level of watchfulness.

As exiles from that land of shadows and shapes, we want to be more like the persons on this new planet that we quickly learned to love and appreciate. We have already decided, leading with our hearts, or perhaps it was intuition, that we would welcome Ben to the Tribe and help him grow into a role here.

I knew that we soon would know the answer to the questions about Ben.

We all were rooting for Ben to be successful. if we were to continue to be successful those around us needed to be successful, too -- and alive.

Black/white and read all over
| 29August08 |

This article appeared in the **Lake Effect edition** of the **Daily Afterblatt.**

Middle 'Man' makes three
Police link a third body to the 'Mystery Man Murders'

By Jane Carlotto
Senior Crime Reporter

The bloody bookends frame a sketchy story that now has a middle.

Way back in March, the coroner suspected that a man hit by a bus in the dark near President's Park might have been the victim of murder.

A Coroner's Jury soon after returned a verdict that was sought by the Eerie County coroner, Dr. Bruce Backstaff, of death by misadventure at the hand of person or persons unknown.

Just two days ago, detectives linked the body of a man that had been dumped in a dumpster in an alley downtown as the work of the same killer or killers.

Now, based on the finding of a strange oval symbol with a circle and two marks inside, scrawled on the dumpster, detectives are saying a body found in June, in the middle of a street on the east side of the city, also belongs in the "Mystery Man Murder" file. The same symbol has been found on a piece of scratch paper in that dead man's shirt pocket, after some rechecking, according to sources.

So, three murders in the so-called "Mystery Man Murders" case, all unsolved.

Det. Joe Blucote, the lead investigator, and his partner, Bill "Joe Bob" Schmidt, now say that a piece of paper with the same symbol also was found in a coat pocket of the first victim, who is still a John Doe.

The detectives refused to speculate on how the slips of paper actually ended up in the victims' clothing.

In the first death, back in late March, a man -- still without a name or story -- was killed on a dark, rainy street near downtown when he was hit by a bus.

Witnesses said the man stood still, arms flung wide, in the traffic lane that the bus was occupying.

The driver has said he could not stop in time because of the poor visibility.

No charges have been brought in that case.

In the second case, a body, that of freelance photographer Bill Zeohn, was dumped by a person or persons in the middle of a busy intersection on the city's East Side sometime during the night or early morning hours of June 5.

Zeohn as a free-lance photographer often covered the same stories as print and broadcast representatives.

Insiders describe Zeohn as something of a hanger-on.

Blucote said it was the discovery of the symbol on the dumpster that sent the two detectives back to the evidence locker to take a closer look at the effects of the first two victims.

The effects of persons found dead and taken by coroner's workers to the city morgue for autopsy can fall through the cracks if the case is not initially deemed to be a homicide, Blucote said.

The rules of evidence are clear in the case of homicide.

In the case of the man killed by the bus, and apparently the second victim, Zeohn, there was initial confusion, police say.

"We overlooked the pieces of paper the first time around," Blucote said. "The delay in deciding that we were dealing with a homicide, not an accident, caused some role confusion. No one actually checked the pockets of the victims."

On another front, Blucote said the county coroner, Dr. Bruce Backstaff, had identified the second body in the investigation as Zeohn within a few days of the discovery of the body but media attention in the case had disappeared and the news was never widely printed or broadcast confirming Zeohn's i.d.

"Zeohn was a man that nobody cared about," Blucote said. "He didn't even rate a filler on the obit page. My partner and I care about him and we would like to hear from anyone else who cared about him."

And so the living remember the dead.

Ben takes a chair in the circle
| 30August08 |

Minutes of a meeting of the **F-Troupe-A** --

The meeting was called to order by our Chair, Goose Grim.

Present: Goose Grim, Eve Green, Mister Ed, Jim Grim, OhJim Grim, David, Jeanne Wheenin, Mr. Red (at the front desk), Wild Billy our cat.

A guest: Ben Whick.

Yours truly read the minutes of the previous meeting.

The order of business was to discuss with Ben recent events surrounding the discovery of a body in a dumpster downtown near, it turns out, the **Roll In and Crawl Out**, the bar where Ben, while a reporter intern at the **Daily Afterblatt, Lake Effect edition**, had a meeting with a mysterious stranger whom we now suspect was Mr. Black, once presumed by our Tribe to be a murder victim from back in March. Ben was understandably anxious about the fact that he had met with a man who may be killing persons and dumping their bodies in public.

We encouraged Ben to --

• Understand that Mr. Black's motives, whereabouts, and even his status as alive or dead are matters that we are actively investigating.

• Bracket his feeling that he should go to the authorities with his information (he doesn't really have any facts).

• Consider joining the Tribe and sharing our secrets.

Each point here noted was the subject of spirited, and sometimes heated, conversation. Ben had many questions and reservations but in the end was persuaded to accept our offer of protection, training, and life focus.

A subcommittee of Jeanne, Eve, and Goose was appointed to shepherd Ben in the process of entering the life of the Tribe and becoming acquainted with the secrets, aims, and overall intensity of said Tribe.

Many motions were made, mostly in jest, with the one motion to extend the right hand of fellowship to Ben duly recognized by the Chair and seconded by Mr. Red (yeah, can you believe it!).Wild Billy spent the meeting on Ben's lap, which was a significant factor in Mr. Red's acquiescence in the motion.

We adjourned in place, and a good time was had by all.

Naomi AKA Jeanne, recording secretary

Let me put it to you this way
|31August08|

For reasons that I have yet to understand fully, Gentle Ben Whick, formerly a cub reporter intern with the **Lake Effect edition** of the **Daily Afterblatt,** has come to monopolize this narrative of mine.

You have seen Jeanne's minutes of the meeting just past, where we inducted Ben, in mutual fear and trembling, into our Tribe.

As an aside, you might be wondering why we are now taking notes of our little meetings of what we fondly and madly call the **F-Troupe-A.** A very good question, and one that is answered by the **No. One Plan** around here: Winning through intimidation.

In our arrogance, we assume that no one can hurt us, so we do pretty much as we please, and we do some things that in the eyes of the world look like foolishness, such as acting something like President Nixon and taping our deliberations at will, and taking notes, writing about our quasi-criminal deliberations in red marker pen on 2-foot by 3-foot flip chart paper, and posting to a secure VPN stories that could be true about what we do and do not do.

In our defense, all this stuff goes into the Vault, where its value has to do with its true content. And as long as the Vault is safe, we are, too, and so are the foolish things that might be true that we set in stone, put on paper, or cut out with scissors and put on the fridge.

Ben is the latest person to put our arrogance to the test.

My fear and trembling is that the Tribe demands a lifetime commitment without any wavering, and I am deeply unsure of these youngsters' ability to commit to what they do not really understand. Wisdom is not a function of youth any more than cyber security is a function of computer chips.

We know this.

Ben's fear and trembling has to do with the mechanics of avoiding whoever it is who is killing young men and dumping their bodies for others to find and figure out.

A related sort of fear and trembling for the older members of the Tribe is this: Time's winged chariot is hurrying near, and we know that we must recruit wisely, well, and quickly or the Tribe will become like a church sliding into the grave as one old member after another moves on to the Promised Place and no one is there to replace the ones lost.

In my work under the cloth, I saw this happen time and again, with all the grief and anger attendant on the passing of yet another Body that would no longer be **Christ with skin on** for a hurting world.

I want a better outcome for my assembly, and I use the same techniques that I did when I acted a lot like a minister in my covert days in **Operation Beloved** -- personal invitations one person to another.

It is said that it takes ten years for a person to fully enter the life of a congregation. The same is probably true for a quasi-criminal enterprise such as ours.

The moral? Work and play, and hope, and watch. This is the way of things and will not change. Someone will always be exiting and someone will always be entering. Pick good teachers. Get going.

Don't look back unless it is for your learning.

This means that in our version of succession we lay hands on persons whom we think and feel will **probably** work out.

We take chances based on experience and intuition.

I know, too, that Eve and I are spending significant time devising new ways to part with ones who may not work out short of the expedient methods that Mr. Black, it seems, is using in the community for reasons we cannot yet understand.

Someone is laying on hands too strong to withstand, and it is not Jesus.

Eve and I are courting the idea that tightly focused intimidation done for our safety can somehow allow persons to depart from us, life intact. We need assurances, but those, we hope, can come from the Quick rather than the Dead.

There has been enough of killing and maiming, and narrowing of horizons.

We are sick unto death of the killing and death-in-life that we witnessed and participated in back in the shadows of Spookistan. We are ready to risk the entire quasi-criminal enterprise on a new way of being that Pop would not have liked one little bit.

Pop would cap us both, on the spot, for making such explorations.

Well.

That said, we return to the question of Gentle Ben.

He said, she said, we said, etc.
|01September08|

We had the tape recorder going for our interview with Gentle Ben.

Transcript (largely intact) follows --

Jeanne: Tribe, this is Ben. whom you know, with affection, as **Gentle Ben**. Ben, this is the Tribe.

[Jeanne makes introductions. Those present were Jeanne, Goose, Eve, David, my brothers Jim and OhJim, Mister Ed, Mr. Red, and Wild Billy, the bookshop cat, who jumped onto Ben's lap and stayed there.]

Ben: Wow, I didn't know that I rated a nickname. I don't know whether to be pleased, or scared. Or more scared than I already am. And I don't know why there are so many of you here. I only met with Miss Eve and Mister Ed last time. Who are you-all, anyway?

Eve: Scared, Dear? Let's start with that. We can deal with your other questions in a moment. These are our trusted colleagues. You can speak as candidly as you did last time, and I know you will.

Ben: Ok. Yes, scared. Scared about this body in the dumpster. The crime scene is essentially the alley behind the sleazy bar where I met that drunk who put me onto you-all.

Jeanne: You mean the **Roll In and Crawl Out**?

Ben: The same -- scene of many an after-work beer with you and others, including this man I wish now that I had never met.

Eve: What is your plan, Dear?

Ben: I feel like I should go and talk to the detectives. The juxtaposition of my stranger and that body ... . I need to say that based on the drawing I think that that dead guy was in the bar when we were talking about secret societies and such. And he seemed to be very interested in our murmurs, though I doubt that he could have heard anything. And it might have been someone else ... .

Goose: Ben, I understand why you might be feeling like you should be talking to the detectives, but I would caution you to hold up on that. Lay down until the feeling goes away.

Eve: We are active in our own investigation, Dear, and you can rest assured that we know what we are doing, and in time you will understand that we are far more competent at this than the locals. We would like you to trust in us, and wait. We will keep you safe.

Ben: This is a lot all at once, but the promise of protection is strong for me, all the same. I'm not thinking straight right now.

Jeanne: This is a good place, Ben. David and I have thrown our lot in with these folks and have not regretted the decision. They have depths and abilities that will amaze you. When they offer protection, it means that they can deliver what they offer.

Mister Ed: I know from our previous discussion, Son, that you are not happy with your current career path. Journalism is not for everyone.

Goose: In fact, Ben, if you will consider joining the Tribe, as we call ourselves, your needs and vocation will be taken care of as a matter of course. Like joining the Army, to see the world and get a free college education.

Ben: Wow, my head is spinning. Who_are_you_people?"

David: You can trust your feelings, Luke. Use the force.

Ben: You make a strong argument, friend, but haven't added any details.

Jeanne: I know this is overwhelming, and there are a lot of us here talking to you at once ... .

Ben: Yes, but I'm not really surprised at the direction we're going in. My last interview, with Miss Eve and Mister Ed, was proof I had stumbled upon something intense. I've been going over what we talked about in the days since, and I realized that I was in over my head as far as writing about this.

Eve: You saw clearly, Ben, and I am pleased. This is our offer: You join the Tribe, and we will mentor you in the ways of the Tribe, and we provide your living -- and good and intense work to do for the Good People.

Goose: Why don't you and Wild Billy go up front for a while and sit. We will come and get you when we discuss a few things. You can think over our offer.

Jeanne: I'll go with Ben and answer questions.

[The sight of the big youngster carrying the cat and walking beside our pretty Punk Princess was priceless.]

Goose: Are we still agreed that the plan is to recruit Gentle Ben?

Jim: Yes, Mister Chair Sir, it is the plan, the man, the canal.

OhJim: Yeah. Panama?

Jim: The same.

Mister Ed: The boy is sound, and it is to his credit that he does not like the ways of the media. I never did, either, and that has a lot to do with why I was covert in the media for most of my time in play.

Eve: I agree, Ed. He is sensitive and fearful, which has its problems, but he is also smart and seems to have some courage to work with. Jeanne says he is a computer hacker supreme. We could use one of those, for sure. Coming here alone, and encountering a full room of strangers, had to be a challenge, but he rose to it well. He has what many might call **balls.**

Mr. Red: I bleeping second to the motion to recruit this boy. Wild Billy likes him, and Eveie does. That is being enough for me.

Tipping our friend the black spot
|02September08|

"This meeting of the **F-Troupe-A** will be in disorder," I said.

"Sniff," Jim said. "What odor? Or do you mean **alphabetical**?"

"Yeah, **sniff, sniff**," OhJim said. "What does **dis odor** smell like, Goose?"

"David," I said, "if you please, go fetch Ben and Jeanne. We have work."
When Ben walked in, we all gave him hugs and handshakes.
David gave Ben one of those lean-in-and-touch-shoulders handshakes.
It actually looked quite cool.

"Ben," I said, "we voted to induct you into the Tribe. What say you?"

"I accept," Ben said. "Jeanne has been explaining things to me, and I accept. OMG. WTF. I had no idea. Well ... ."

"Good," I said. "The alternative would have been difficult, as you might expect and soon will understand. You will be working part time here in the bookshop as your cover and will continue your studies, I am assuming, which is also good for cover."

"Mr. Chair Dear," Eve said. "I move that you, Jeanne, and I quickly convene the subcommittee for the care and feeding of our new tribalist."

"Second," David said. "Always second."

"All in favor, vote by the usual sign," I said.
Everyone did the **F-Troop salute** -- two thumbs up and two middle digits touching, nose to nose. It looked a lot like an up-side down version of the milkman's handshake. (I'll draw you a picture sometime.)

Ben looked amused and puzzled.

"Ben," I said, "take notes. We will answer questions in subcommittee."
Ben nodded.

"We have to come up," I said, "with a strategy to bring Mr. Black in from the cold. Three bodies are enough."

"If it is Mr. Black," Jeanne said.

"You mean to leave the backroom?" Jim said.

"Yeah," OhJim said, "that would be something different. I was beginning to think that we all were suffering from that **angoraphobia** -- itching all over at the thought of entering the marketplace."

"Ben," I said, "my brother means **agoraphobia**, and he knows that he does. It's just that he loves to pun, as do we all."

"I'm another such a pun," Ben said. "I love to quibble and dribble."

"Could it be anyone else than Mr. Black, Jeanne?" I said. "Of course it could, to ask and answer my own question. We need to bring in, or bring down, whoever is out there killing people. And we will not discriminate as to color."

"I'm assuming," Jeanne said, "that our zeal has a lot to do with the perception that we were invited to have concerning the first victim, that he was Mr. Black. Otherwise, it would not be our fight."

"Right," I said.

"And if it is our old friend Mr. Black, we'll tip him the black spot just like in **Treasure Island**," Mister Ed said.

"Black for Black," Jim said. "There's balance there. Be on the lookout, young Jim, for a sea-faring man with one leg."

"Yeah," OhJim said. "Argh! Black, black, no trades back. Let it ride."

"Jeanne," I said, "to the flip chart in your Naomi face, if you will."

"Who's winning the flipping competition?" Jim said.

"Yeah," OhJim said, "but around here, it's the **bleeping** competition."

A worthy opponent - one of us
| 03September08 |

Jeanne, gladdening the hearts of all in the room, rose on peep-toe heels to assume the Naomi position at the flip chart.

"We face," I said, "a worthy opponent -- one of our own (with the caveat that he may not be who we are seeking)."

"Yes, Dears," Eve said, "Mr. Black will be hard to find. That is the bad news. The good news is that we learned from the same teachers as Mr. Black did about how to stay unfound if that is what we want."

"Sounds like a draw," Jim said.

"Yeah," OhJim said, "or an arroyo."

"I'm standing by," Jeanne said, smiling sideways, "ready to draw on this big flipping/bleeping chart, with this big red marker pen."

"Write this, then," I said. "Things to remember about Mr. Black. Item: He can change his appearance effortlessly, so look for the **tells** -- his dark complexion, his age (looks 50 to 60), and his size -- six feet tall."

"Here," Eve said, "is another item: He will not be in the same place twice, unless he is."

"Yes," I said. "I was sure that we saw him in the dark in the park when we went to see some Shakespeare. And we will not see him at the **Roll In and Crawl Out**, unless we do."

"Here," Eve said, "is another item: He is not armed but is dangerous. None of us ever carry guns. We don't have to. He can kill you in so many ways that it would be a shame to miss all the others. You will, however, only get one chance. This is assuming that he has gone off the Rez and is against us. We have to court the idea that he is in his right mind and is protecting us, but we just don't know, at this point, so assume the worst and watch over one other to and past the point of paranoia."

"This," I said, "is why you must live and work in pairs. Eve and I, and the other old guys of color, need not worry so much, because of the level of our training and experience. Our training matches his. The rest of you must watch one another at all times. Carry only such weapons as you can keep and conceal. Your weapon in the enemy's hand is a deadly development."

"And so, effective immediately," Eve said, "the boys and girl must move in together."

There were three surprised faces.

"Wow," Jeanne said. "Room-maties."

"Chicks!" David said. He seemed pleased.

Ben got all goggle-eyed.

"Until we are satisfied," I said, "that you can take care of yourselves, you must stay close to one another. That means working together, playing together, and sleeping in reasonable proximity. Ben will need to work with the two of you on how to deal with his classes."

"What about us?" Jim said.

"Yeah," OhJim said. "We're kids, too, at heart. Boys, like."

"You already live together," I said, "and it may be that you can take some turns watching Ben's back at school. Jeanne and David are more known, though they might stick out less than you would. Blending in, in a hostile environment, such as academia, will be good practice."

"The challenge of Mr. Black brings an opportunity to school the five of you in the arts of the shadows," Eve said. "Nothing works better than the real world, when it comes to learning how to skulk and deceive."

"And," I said, "this is your first challenge. Eve and I will be taking a short vacation, and you will be in charge of the bookshop and of one another. We will stay in touch by email, encrypted, of course, and will be back by Sunday. Mister Ed will be the go-to guy while we are gone."

Mister Ed nodded like a wise, talkative horse, raising and lowering his big head with a majestic sweeping motion. He all but said, **Yes, WWWIIIIIILLLLBBBEEERRR.**

"Wow," David said. "The cats are going away."

"And the mice will play," Jeanne said, smiling at us, to the side, with her signature lemon look.

"Vacating, are you? "Jim said.

"Yeah," OhJim said. "Vacant stares all around."

"When Eve and I return," I said, "we will add to the list. So far, we have given you tips on survival. Next we will plan a trap."

"Enjoy, Dears," Eve said. "We will."

What Naomi wrote on the flip chart --

- Things to remember about Mr. Black --
- He changes his appearance at will, so look for the **tells** ...
  - His dark complexion.
  - His age (looks 50).
  - His size - 6 feet tall.
- He will not appear in the same place twice, unless he does.
- He is not armed and is very dangerous.
- You have one chance to survive if you encounter him in anger.
- Watch out for one another at all times. Carry weapons of choice.

Having a wonderful time ...
|04September08|

Email from Eve to the Tribe --

Hi Dears:

Goose and I are having a good time, doing nothing except the essentials --
eating, sleeping, and things like that.

Goose is adjusting to the pace, as well as he can.

He is such a man of action.

Love, Dears
Eve

... wish you were here ...
|05September08|

Email from Goose to the Tribe --

Hi, all:

We miss you, more than you might imagine. We were orphans in life for so long
that it is hard, but probably good, too, to be away from our family.

That's you.

Tolerate my brothers' puns, and add **a few of urine**.

Love
Goose

For training porpoises only
|06September08|

I gave David one of those shoulder-touching handshakes.
"You show promise, Goose," David said, "but for **training porpoises** I'll
give you the slow-mo version. It goes something like this."
David repeated the ritual at single-frames-per-second speed.
Everyone was laughing.
David is serious. And we liked that about him when we recruited him, and
we are indeed delighted that he feels the freedom to explore other aspects
of being himself. A good spook has a number of persons to pick from for
under-the-white-sheet work. Don't, however, confuse **under the sheet** with
Pop's thing -- **under-the-sheets** work.
To look at Pop, you would have said that only God can make a cockscomb

or a coxswain or cocksman. But that is a different story.

Ben, another serious youngster, was watching everyone with interest.

I wondered how the living arrangement was going, but that could wait.

We were pledged to pick up the narrative of our plan to trap Mr. Black and bring him in (or whoever it was who was killing and dumping bodies in our fair city).

"As we said, Dears, the first part of the list," Eve said, "was meant to give you a crash-course in survival vis-à-vis Mr. Black, who can be a murderous opponent, as we are seeing, or so we presume."

"Now," I said, "we will sketch out a plan to catch him. So. Your thoughts?"

"Well," Mister Ed said, "old friend Black had no obvious faults. Few persons knew how to get to him. That is why he is alive and out there now."

"Yes, Dear," Eve said. "Mr. Black lacks cracks in any of his facades."

"However," I said, "Mr. Black was my very, very special friend, and I know some things about him that he would rather that I did not know."

"For example?" David said.

"For example," I said, "every spook has a bad habit or three. Mine was keeping a journal. A big boo-boo for a boo-spook."

"What," Jeanne said, "were Mr. Black's?"

"That's funny," I said. "I was just about to tell you."

Mr. Black in black and white and read all over
|07September08|

How could I best talk about my old friend Mr. Black to the Tribe?

Some things that would be good to share would be hard to say.

What would be the outcome of our hunt for our lost friend if I withheld the subtext and only shared the obvious?

Isn't it King Lear's Fool who sez **truth is a cur that must be whipped**?

I sat there, musing, while the others watched my thoughts flash across the screen of my well-worn face -- Black thoughts against my White whiskers.

"Well," I said, "I realize that if I am to effect the change that I seek, I will need to be candid about what I know about our old friend Mr. Black. This is not easy for me, because I am privy to the depths of his soul, so to speak, and I will not lightly reveal what I know, except that the crossroads that we find ourselves at demands that I reveal things -- as you need to know -- so that we can bring him in from the cold."

"That's cryptic," David said. "Can you decode it?"

"Certainly he can, David Dear," Eve said, "but will he? Remember that Mr. Black is Mr. Black only in contrast to his old friend Mr. White -- AKA our own dear Goose. The two went together in **Operation Beloved**, and to do the work that they did, and to reap the rewards that they did, and to be caught and convicted in the fields of the Lord as they were, required them to be like two peas in a pod, or two tones in a song, or two trains running."

"That's cryptic, too," Jeanne said. "Decode?"

"**De code, Boss, de code!**" Jim said.

"Yeah," OhJim said, "in plane words, please."

"We can decode, but at our pace," Eve said. "Allow our words to lead you. Don't try so hard to understand what is only meant to be suggestive."

Which drew two leers from my brothers.

"Yes," I said, "and realize that this story has a lot to do with Pop, too. Everything here has a lot to do with Pop. If, as Eve says, Mr. Black and I were like two trains running, like smokestack lightning, then Pop was the trainmaster and Pop also was the match that set us on fire."

"And Pop," Eve said, "deserves his own spot in the light, prior to the full story of Goose of the white feathers and his very good friend Mr. Black."

"So gather around, children," I said, "and we will tell you some stories that will instruct and delight. Stories than could be true."

"And then we will tuck you in," Eve said, "because you will need your rest for the work ahead."

Email from Tommy re: Pop
|08September08|

Dear Brother Goose:

Here are some notes (a lot of notes!) that I've made, based on the emailing that we have done lately in discussing the Story that you want to tell to the Tribe, and the things that you want to be sure to cover.

Things you have told me re: Pop

Your Pop saw clearly how a spook's life depended on who was covering him, in the usual sense of the shoot 'em up movies (**Cover me!**) and also in the sense that the word is used in Pentecostal circles to denote who it is that has vouched for you, by ordaining or licensing you by the laying on of hands. Your Pop was disturbed by the fact that he could not cover himself; he wanted to be his own cover and indeed his own bishop.

He saw the situation as a matter of knowledge, where knowledge is power and power is insurance against all threats. He ruled out relationships because he saw relationships as subject to change (cf. Saul Alinsky's phrase **there are no permanent friends and no permanent enemies**.)

Your Pop also held to another of Alinsky's chestnuts -- **we are the people that we have been waiting for**.

Pop's version, though, was **I am the person that I have been waiting for**.

The Question, as he saw it, was, **What sorts of knowledge created the most power?**

His answer had two parts -- dirty little secrets and dirty big secrets.

The Equation that had meaning for him was this --

Secrets + Documentation = Power.

Your Pop could see that he needed secrets and proofs, and a safe place to store these things (The Vault). He also saw that he needed accurate information on the targets that he acquired, and that he needed accurate information on new data that altered his understand of the targets and associated threats. To his deep and abiding sorrow, your Pop decided that in the end he could not do all of these things by himself, no matter how intensely he wished it possible, so he decided to create The Vault and to share its care and feeding with what he called the Tribe (in contrast to his three families/wives).

Pop's One Rule: Trust your Tribe and all its members, consistently and inclusively. If a Tribalist lets down the Tribe, raising the level of threat, remove him/her with extreme prejudice.

An aside: Mr. Black, if the Tribe's assessment is accurate, is the first Tribalist to cause an increase in the level of threat.

Therefore, the path is clear at the near end of things.

Problem is, no one can predict where that path will lead.

Tommy

Email from Tommy, ad-1: Mr. Black
|09September08|

Dear Goosey Guy:

We move from my **notes and comments on Pop** to those **re: Mr. Black** --

Goose and Eve, sick to death of the ways of Spookistan, are committed to finding more compassionate ways to execute the power and safety needs of the Tribe.

They know that even if they find new ways, some things will endure --

• The quasi-criminal quality and climate that the Tribe creates and inhabits.
• The need for perpetual paranoia.
• The Vault and the delivery of threats.
• The need to stay clear of TLAs and any others who would roll up the network like a carpet to roll out in their own living room for their own comfort and use.

Mr. Black's story

Mr. Black was a minister-under-cover, **the Rev. Mr. Black**, as was Goose, as **the Rev. Mr. White**. They worked, under the cloth in **Operation Beloved**.

At a critical point, as they lurked in the fields of the Lord, they were grabbed and shaken by the One Whom they pretended to serve. Pretense became pre-science and cynicism gave way to **conviction**, which led to **justification** and opened the door to their journey toward **sanctification**, to use churchy language to describe what the two were likely to describe as ...

Holy *bleep*, what a ride!

Shock and awe only begin to describe how the two ministers-under-the-cloth felt. The experience of each intensified the experience of the other, in an upward (downward?) spiral. They became as yin and yang, and they could not extricate themselves from this fresh intertwining of souls and stories.

They became doubles of one another.

They became twins, with a growing sense of cognition that twins often share -- but they were opposites, too, always.

The progression of their mutual, mirrored conviction and conversion meant that they knew one another at feelings levels deeper than speech or thought.

A side-effect for Mr. Black was a surface-level antipathy toward his twin, the Rev. Mr. White. Goose felt the shallowness of this antipathy and could feel it as a longing on Mr. Black's part for a sort of freedom that he would not regain. Perhaps this is why Goose does not press harder for an answer to the questions surrounding Mr. Black, because Goose can feel the truth of the working assumption that Mr. Black is out there, and not dead, not crazy.

Goose saw, and felt, the identity of the shadowy figure that fled from the Tribe on the night of their field trip to see **Shakespeare in the Dark**, in the Park. Perhaps it was this subcutaneous longing for old freedoms that has put Mr. Black out there, for reasons yet to be known.

The following parts of the Story have implications for the Tribe's plan of intervention with Mr. Black --
• Mr. Black will not be found until and unless he decides to be found (because of the level of his training). Therefore, it makes sense to find out something about why he is acting as he is.
• Is he sane?
• Is he impaired?
• Is he under some malign influence (cf. the man who stood frozen in the path of the bus, in the dark near the park).
• Is he for the Tribe or against the Tribe or indifferent to the Tribe?

Tommy

Email from Tommy, ad-2: Modifications
| 10September08 |

We turn to **Goose's (and Eve's) modifications of Pop's Vision.**

The experience of conversion at the hands of the **One Whom** Goose and Mr.

Black served in cynicism, leading to conviction and conversion, made Goose see Pop's constructs of the Vault and Tribe in new ways he shared first with Eve. Goose sees the Church's metaphors and rituals of succession -- the Pentecostal sense of Covering and the general sense of Apostolic Succession through the laying on of hands – as having similarities with Pop's conception of the Tribe and its perpetuation through recruiting and training, or by picking up the discards of the Shadowland system of generating, using, and discarding of Spooks like so many pieces of dirty, worn bedding with holes poked for the eyes.

It is mercy, compassion, and acceptance that have led Goose, and by his invitation and lead, Eve, to seek ways to stop **all** of the killing and **some** of the threat-making. Jesus Christ and Robin Hood have become the exemplars for the Tribe, all but replacing the General -- Wild Bill Donovan himself.

Goose and Eve continue, in fear and trembling, to work out these modifications to Pop's Vision. They know that Pop, if he were alive, would take them out, with extreme prejudice, for the things that they are contemplating.

Tommy

Goose tells a tale to the Tribe
| 11September08 |

My Brother in Christ:

I presented the Story to the Tribe, using your notes as a guide, and actually sharing printed copies of same to each Tribalist. I attach notes that Jeanne took, with her comments, on our proceedings.

BTW, Jeanne sez you are a big fan. Tell me more.

Goose

Jeanne's notes

In the end, after Goose told the Story and the stories that the main narrative contained, concerning Pop and Mr. Black, the Tribe decided to reach out to others, starting with the young and small Tribe, or Band, of Baldi and Luce and their gun-packing assistant Jo-Joe. This is pleasing to Ben, who is bent on the girl who carries the Glock.

Goose and Eve said that they were aware of some ironies --

• To let a lapsed, dangerous Tribalist, Mr. Black, live and go away, rather than removing him with extreme prejudice, would require them to scare the Tribalist to death, anyway.
• Mr. Black would not be amenable to such treatment. Only the young ones might be scared in this matter, by this treatment.

So, to be blunt, there is not nor can there be, a plan regarding Mr. Black. Still, there are some points that apply to him --

- The Tribe must seek him, even though they may not find him.
- The Tribe must maintain its course and its watches.
- Young Tribalists can learn in real time about tradecraft, even if some of their assignments will have no apparent use other than leading them in the ways of Spookistan, v.2.

Jim and OhJim reminded the others of the one thing that is brand-new in the life of the Tribe, post-Mr. Black -- the Bros Grim, P.I.s. Jim and OhJim mused on the things that are possible beyond mere skip-tracing and divorce work, and in their musing the outlines of a plan emerged, like a boat suddenly freeing itself from the mist than had obscured it.

The young ones will engage in training, in real time, in --

- Disguises.
- Traps, honey and other.
- Cut-outs.
- Surveillance.

And --

- The P.I.s will P.I.
- The bookshop will sell books and act as the **holy ground of gathering** for the Tribe.
- Goose will bring Tommy in, in the flesh, to join in the life of the Tribe.

Note this ... a poem to Jeanne
| 12September08 |

"I don't call it a security breach," Jeanne said. "It's more a fan's note."
"I am glad it's not **A Fan's Notes**," I said. "That's different. Novel, even."
Jeanne was telling us about why it was that she knew of Tommy, and we were interested, to say the least.

Our quasi-criminal enterprise requires adherence to basics that ape good sense, for the most part, and Jeanne was telling us why she had filed and all but forgotten an amusing note that Tommy had sent her after reading about her on the blog-over-VPN that she and David had set up for me.

In fact, Tommy is the sole outside reader of my blogged ramblings about the Tribe, suitably laundered and altered to the version that you see here, to protect the innocent, and the quasi-innocent, too.

We have restricted access to invited persons only, and the blog is pass-word-protected, DMZ-protected, DOD-level protected, and additionally protected in ways that no one needs to know.

Tommy is the only outside person that we have invited so far.
So far as we know.

Clearly, the VPN has uses in disinformation, but that is all that I will say on that head, thank you very much. So don't ask.

As a further measure, I have been careful to write the entries as a fiction.

This layer is a source of constant hilarity for the Tribe, who also know the truth, at least in part.

He who laughs last is probably the poster.

Literary types call it **irony** -- the disparity between what the reader knows from a superior position provided by the narrator vs. what the characters in a story know.

And since the narrator, the readers, and the characters are the same persons, my posts are certain to bring smiles and chortles by the mile.

Leave it to an **Onion Man** to create so many layers of irony.

We like a happy ship and crew here at **Caspar's Books and That.**

I guess that I learned a few things about writing down the truth, from losing, and regaining, my verboten journal from my early years with Mr. Black under the cloth as a spook/minister.

You won't see me telling the truth this time. That is a promise.

But close your eyes and I will tell you stories … .

Hidden in plain site/sight.

That is the motto of the Tribe's VPN blog.

David gave the blog the title **The Bros Grim Breakfast Serial**, which I thought was amusing in itself. And, as I said, it is hidden and locked down so well that no one outside the Tribe is actually reading it, save Tommy. Our server stats so far have verified that assumption. The Tribe, of course, is reading the blog, which satisfies my writerly ego.

This is Tommy's note --

Confidential for Jeanne
% Caspar's Books and That

turne on your wanton [sic] fryer
and answer my desire
with mutual eating
pour forth a wee small beer
that onion's 'roma be dearer
with gentle heating
should fat delight when with ginger united
either others herbes with herbes
**   enflavouring,**
heart and gut, nose tipped
to sniff, tongue salivating

"It sounds," Jim said, "like a masher's note."

"Yeah," OhJim said, "a garlic masher, maybe, but is it?"

Eve smiled her **OhJim Appreciation Smile** of Buddha Girl goodness.

"I side with OhJim," Eve said, "though I sleep with my guy Goose. And love Jim like a brudder."

"Me, too," Jeanne said, "as far as everything except sleeping with Goose goes. I was puzzled for a moment when I first read it, but it is actually a parody of a poem by one Thomas Campion, circa 1601, called **Turn Backe You Wanton Flyer.** Tommy also sent me a brush drawing with Chinese brush lettering on one side and a charming note on the obverse side.

We all were glad to hear that our soon-to-be brother in the flesh was as sane, or more so, than we were.

"Look," Jeanne said, "listen to the original. I found it by Googling. Read along. I've made copies."

> Turne backe, you wanton flyer,
> And answere my desire
> With mutuall greeting,
> Yet bende a little neerer,
> True beauty stil shines cleerer
> In closer meeting.
> Harts with harts delighted
> Should strive to be united,
> Either others armes with armes enchayning:
> Harts with a thought,
> Rosie lips with a kisse still entertaining.

"One thing is clear," I said. "Friend Tommy has noticed you."

"We would not trust him if he had not," Mister Ed said. "Our Jeanne demands such attentions, particularly from testicular types."

Mister Ed bowed crane-wise to our Punk Princess, who gave him her best lemony smile, to the side.

"Tommy promised to drop by this afternoon," I said, "so be sure to be near. I want you all to meet him, since he can't hang out with us often, because he has a real job."

"What does he do?" Eve said.

"I think he's some kind of spook," I said.

"This should be interesting," David said.

Eve, who is unable to do the Spock thing, raised both eyebrows.

I just smiled into my chin whiskers and out through my eyes.

Tribe and Tommy, love at first sight, bite
| 13September08 |

The Tribe has had a period of rapid expansion, with David, Jeanne, and Gentle Ben Whick joining our quasi-criminal enterprise in the past year.

But wait. That's not all. If you act now, you can add yet another. See your TV screen for details.

Ok, it's not an infomercial that we're talking about.

No, we're talking about Tommy.

"Tribe," I said, "this is Tommy. And Tribe, Tommy is one of us, already."

"Explain," Tommy said.

"Yeah," Jim said. "Ex-plain is now gaudy."

"And yeah," OhJim said, "former plain, ex-jet, now exotic."

"Explain all that, too," Tommy said.

"I expected a sell job to the Tribe," I said, "but not you. But here goes."

"Yes, Dear," Eve said. "Going on this would be good. Some seem pissed."

"Ok," I said, "here's the deal. I liked and trusted Tommy like a brother from the moment I met him, that night when Mr. Black, or so we thought, bought it on the grille of that bus. In the months since, we have been in close contact, mostly by secure, double-encrypted email, and I have nothing but admiration for him and (turning to Tommy) for you, too."

"If we accept him," David said, "his nickname should be **Him**."

"Don't I get a say in that?" Tommy said. "I've given up on the surprise inclusion in the Tribe, but nicknames are very personal."

"And communal," I said. "We don't get to pick our own. That's axiomatic around here. Be not the Him that haws."

"It's aromatic, anyway," Tommy said. "Tell me it doesn't reek."

"Look," Jeanne said, "this is my biggest fan. I showed you his poem."

Jeanne rose, to general appreciation, and sat on Tommy's lap.

"I told you that you would like the Tribe," I said.

"You did not understate the case," Tommy said, red in the face.

Jeanne kissed him on his nose and licked his ear lobe, and went back to her seat between a crestfallen David and a crestfallen OhJim.

"Oh, Jim," she said, "I have enough love to go around. You, too, David."

The two went from doggone disappointed to puppy happy, just like that.

"Seriously," Tommy said, continuing to be red all over, "I value Goose's offer, and I am not a stranger to the Tribe, by any stretch. And I accept what has been so freely and quickly bestowed. Goose actually prepared me for this moment. We've been having some fun with you."

"Not so fast," David said, "though I am inclined to approve of your inclusion in the Tribe, and not only because you are already the confidant of our Daddy, who BTW sez that he assumes that you are some kind of spook."

David raised one eyebrow.

"Are you?"

Tommy slaps a shot at Puck

| 14September08 |

"A pert question," Tommy said. "What did you say your name was? **Puck**?"

"**Puck yourself** and see how you like it," David said.

"Ok, Huck, let's start over," Tommy said. "**Hello, Huckleberry!**"

"**Hello yourself and see how you like it, Tom Sawyer**," David said.

They smiled at one another, and David approached Tommy.

That worried me a tad, though Tommy was a few inches taller and about 50 pounds heavier than our David.

It was the demands of hospitality that concerned me.

Boys, after all, will be boys.

They did that shoulder-touching handshake thing.

I was relieved. Very relieved.

I love watching two brothers do that shoulder-touchy thing.

"The question from our **Huck 'n' Puck** is a good one," I said, "and my answer is that you are some kind of a spook, Tommy, that much has been obvious to me from the moment I first saw you. I just don't know which sort. And don't much care, frankly (and, as I have told so many persons, so many times, be very careful when I say **frankly.** You might wanna check your wallet)."

"Guilty, guilty, guilty," Tommy said, "but I'd rather not say which TLA or TLAs I'm associated with so I don't make myself feel like I have to report on this dual relationship with the Tribe."

"That doesn't make sense," Jeanne said. "I expect better from my adoring public. And, Goose, why do you trust someone whom you assume to be a spook on nothing better than your warm and fuzzy feelings?"

Jeanne pouted at Tommy, then at me, and her pout, as an inside-out version of her lemony sideways smile, looked nothing like other people's puckers. I kinda liked it. I guess there isn't much about Jeanne that I don't like. She reminds me of a younger version of Eve. Jeanne, like Eve, is like the sun, the moon, and the stars, and a delight to all the senses.

"Look, my Jeanne," Tommy said, "and I will teach you a spookish lesson."

"I'm all ears, and out of my bottle," Jeanne said.

"The hell you say," Jim said. "You have other parts that play, and other orbs than lobes."

"Yeah," OhJim said, "indeed, you dew, like the dew at dawn on a summer's day. Hell's bells, I like your ears, too. And orbs."

"As I was about to say," Tommy said, "a lesson: **The enemy of my enemy is my friend.** That was a lesson that I learned the hard way from a Brother-in-Christ who happened to be **Mossad.** He chose an Arab's word over mine at a critical point, though we had worked together in the past. I was startled, and when I confronted him, he said that he wanted to shore up his relationship with the Arab guy, even at my expense, because the guy was a good guy whom he wanted to encourage. **The enemy of my enemy is my friend**, he said."

"The enemy, then?" Jeanne said. "Who is the enemy. And since when is a Jewish spook a **Brother-in-Christ?**"

"The enemy was the great unknown," I said. "That night, Tommy and I were looking at the same ugly scene and both of us were wondering what really had happened, and both of us were aware that the other was trying to read the subtext of that dark story."

"The subtext, then," Jeanne said. "What was the subtext?"

"The subtext is the obvious intervention of a malevolent force, bringing sudden death to an unwilling victim," Tommy said. "My brother and I stand against such things."

"Look," David said, "I know that you will report this contact."

"Another piece of pertness, Huck," Tommy said.

"Well," Jeanne said. "Your answer?"

Black/white but not Black
|15September08|

"My answer," Tommy said, "is obvious, isn't it?"

"**The enemy of my enemy is my friend,**" Jeanne said.

"Bingo!" Tommy said. "And here is why. Goose and I have been working together because our interests coincide. Goose and you his associates are not a problem for me and so none of you will ever be or become a problem for my Vicar."

"**Vicar?**" Jeanne said.

"My handler, my boss, my ball and chain," Tommy said. "I am his eyes and ears, so I am selective about what he sees and hears. Otherwise he gets nervous, and when he gets nervous he becomes nasty and small-minded."

"Truth, Jeanne," I said, "is a fluid and tricky thing at best. Sometimes handlers need less than they think that they do, and so we control their sense of what is enough and what is withheld. It is like any relationship. People decide, moment to moment, what is most helpful for the health of the connection. Both sides do. It's all need-to-know."

Jeanne gave me her sideways smile.

I gave her mine, the one hidden in my whiskers but echoed in the eyes.

"We of tribal caste have been stymied in our inquiry into Mr. Black's death and/or disappearance by our need for circumspection, Tommy, my friend," I said. "Perhaps, you can help us."

"I certainly can," Tommy said. "I have access to all manner of information as a normal course of events. My toys are the best. What do you need?"

"A mugshot or drawing of the first victim would be a big help," I said. "Can you swing that?"

"I can, like a dead cat in a tight spot," Tommy said." In fact, I have a drawing of the hapless dead person on my person. I thought you might appreciate that."

I found that I was looking at a drawing of a dead man whom I knew in the initial nanosecond was not my old, alive friend, Mr. Black. I was not surprised, nor was I glad, for I had already decided that this was the way of it, and Mr. Black's continued presence among the living had even become vexing for me. Still, I was pleased to have confirmation.

That drawing is the door to new territory, where we might find facts and fictions that help us understand what was going on. The victim, though he looked something like Mr. Black, with the same sort of dark, indeterminate features, was not Mr. Black. I guess that I can be expected to recognize my shadow, my double, my Brother-in-Christ, my brother.

"Thank you, my friend," I said. "What can you tell us about the victim?"

Tommy knows what we know
|16September08|

"The one thing that we know about the victim," Tommy said, "is that, according to you, Goose, who should know, it is not Mr. Black, your associate and very close friend."

"You mean he is really a **John Doe**?" Jeanne said.

"Yes," Tommy said, "he really is."

"And you really don't know squat about him?" David said.

"Yes, **Huck 'n' Puck**," Tommy said, "we really don't know squat about him except for the fact that he is dead, that the county coroner has secured a verdict that he was killed -- deviously -- in anger, and that the recent opinion of an unnamed source close to Mr. Black is that the victim was not the person whom he had suspected that he was."

"And," Jim said, "**John Dough** was the stage name of a big <wink> time male porn actor in the 70s."

"Yeah," OhJim said, "like my brother the porn expert sez. I myself, I don't know from Dough."

Tommy looked at my brothers in a way that promised a retort.

It promised to be a sharp one.

"Tommy, my friend," I said, "my brothers love to make wry comments and, God-help-us-all, puns. And rather than begrudge them their fun, we usually join in, or if we are working, which we do when we have to, we just ignore them. It does not hurt their feelings. Go on. Try it."

Tommy looked at me, and nodded. He looked less pinched and frown-like.

"I can adjust to that reality," Tommy said. "So. Where are we with the **John Cash**?"

"You mean the **John Dough**, don't you? "Jim said.

"Yeah," OhJim said, "the really big porn guy."

"No, my funny friends of pun and porn," Tommy said, "I mean the **John Cash**, to avoid the unfortunate association with your instructional sex films and such. And I say again, Goose, where are we now?"

"If I may," Mister Ed said, "I would like a clarification. Before I tripped on the tangled roots of your antecedents, I thought that I noticed that you had reframed Goose as an anonymous caller or source whose information did not pan out. Correct?"

"Correct," Tommy said.

"Good," Mister Ed said. "I guess that you can walk out under your own power. Any friend of Jeanne's is a friend of mine, unless he poses a threat to Goose, say."

"That is comforting," Tommy said. "A blood bath makes a mess that obviates any possible cleansing effect."

"And," I said, "we are in recovery around here, Ed, about the killing and maiming thing. I guess you didn't read my mind or Eve's mind about that."

"I am happy to hear of this, Goose," Mister Ed said to me while looking at Tommy. "We'll have to do lunch or something."

"Better than doing Tommy," Jeanne said. "I kinda like him."

Unlike David, whose courage outstripped his size and experience, Mister Ed was pound for pound a match for Tommy, and then some. Time had added to his considerable size, like yearly increases in taxes. Their collision would have been a monumental mess and a pyrrhic victory. And as the original pyrrhic general said, **We cannot afford another victory like that.**

Good people caught up in a culture of killing, that was the old way now. I needed to get that word out, and pronto.

We were changing, I hoped, one person at a time.

Would Tommy have killed his way out to the street? Only if he had to.

Would Mister Ed have made good on his threat? If he had seen the need, he would have done his best to execute.

To execute Tommy.

Thank the Dear, it did not come to that.

And if it had, an eye-blink or three would have told the tale.

We have a powerful set of motivations to find another way.

Don't let the glasses fool ya, in any direction, even peaceful ones.

At least one of us would need no convincing that we needed to turn from violence. Gentle Ben, living up to his name, on the **Far Side** of the room, looked like a deer caught in headlights, drawn by Gary Larson. The caption? **Gentle Ben sees a ghost.**

"Look," Tommy said. "I'm growing weary of asking you the same question. And now that it is settled, that I can live, I'm going to leave. I'll email you about the **John Cash**. We're not done with him."

Tommy follows with encrypted clarity
|17September08|

Dear friend Goose:

It was an eye-opener to see you-all in your element, and I don't just mean Jeanne, though her choice of seats (mine) was fundamentally gratifying. I also appreciate being given my life back by Mister Ed, whose age belies his level of threat. Just between you and me, I am very glad that he was satisfied by my answer to his deceptively simple question. Life in the demimonde of Spookdom has its thrills, as you know so well. I was floating for a moment there.

The central question of the time remains, however -- what to do about this **John Cash** in the coroner's freezer. It bothers me that we do not have a name or any other information about this dead guy. Such a scenario points to a Spook vs. Spook scenario, either this guy vs. your guy, or some other guy vs. the dead guy. For sure, as you saw at the scene that dark, wet night, someone did a number on someone, who ended up dead. Bowling buddies gone bad don't settle things this way. Spooks do, on occasion, and the reasons are as numerous as the spooks, never mind the TLAs and other quasi-covert or quasi-criminal groups, such as your Tribe, and their needs and motives.

It is in my interest to see this through, but I think your need may be more pressing. All I have to do is say to my Vicar that I'm drawing a blank on that one, and I can repeat that as necessary.

Everything comes down to need-to-know, beginning with self and going on to all others. Am I right?

You, however, must attend to the fundamental security question posed by the disappearance, and the concomitant and related, or not, odd actions of a killer who is dumping bodies all over the city. Well, two, anyway, which is probably two too many, unless these bodies were persons who meant your crew, er Tribe, harm and Mr. Black, to spin a hypothetical, is staying "out there" to protect you.

Or, as you have said, he may have simply gone off the Rez in body and in mind.

My time and resources are yours for what you decide to do.
Best to all, especially Jeanne.

Warmly <vbg>
Tommy

P.S. The next time we get together, let's talk about the **Afterblatt's** Senior Crime Reporter, who is a friend. She may be able to help us. I'll explain later.

Goose to Tommy - tales of the crypt
| 18September08 |

Email from Goose to Tommy re: **the John Cash** --

Dear Tommy, Tom, Tom:

You hit the nail on the cuticle, my friend, in your email, in general, and in specific, too, now that I think about it. Some of my thoughts run in other directions than the **John Cash**, such as using this as an opportunity to train the youngsters in our craft. David and Jeanne seem to be ready for fieldwork. Ben needs some prelims of the **talking - listening** sort. Eve will be good with Ben, and I can take on the field stuff, with some help from the over-the-hill gang that hangs out at the bookshop.

It was good to see you and to have the others brush up to, and collide, with you. No hard feelings, I assume. David is young and so gets a pass. Mister Ed is old and so gets a pass, though he was the more difficult of the two to read in the moment. And, of course, I need not apologize for Jeanne. You seemed to enjoy her attentions as much as we do.

Sometimes I worry that we have embarked on an impossible journey, what with so many new recruits at once, and you as an associate member, too. Time was, we would simply cap anyone who proved to be a liability, or someone would do the deed for us. Those days, for us, are gone. I don't miss them.

My shadow, my soul mate Mr. Black occupies a part of my heart and my mind day in and day out, but I keep banging up against the same ideas -- that he will be found only if he decides that he wants to be found and that if he has gone mental in some fashion he might never decide to be found because he no longer understands that being found is an option for him. These dead-ends are keeping me from acting, and that can't be good, though a zone of passivity sometimes ends up being the wise course, at least for a while.

I just don't know. Let me think about it some more ... .

I'm all ears about your friend the senior crime reporter.

We will be having a simple meal with our friends Baldi and Luce, and their Jo-Joe. I'll let you know if they bring more than potluck.

Potluck. Gotta love it. And God's people said yeah!

Goose

P.S. Can you secure a drawing or photo of the second vic? And tell me what you know about him?

Our potluck - meetin' ... eatin' - at last
| 19September08 |

At last.
Potluck.
Or, as we used to say in the pews, **No meetin' without eatin'.**
I said that, and Mr. Black said that, and Baldi said that, too.
Baldi, unlike Mr. Black and I, had been a minister in earnest, back there and then. Today he is more like a multimillionaire, but who is counting? Not Baldi. He pays people to do things like that.
But I digress.
The first of the **Baldi-and-Luce Show** to appear in the doorway of the backroom, freshened for the occasion, was Baldi and Luce's bodyguard, **Jo-Joe**, a twenty-something girl worth watching.
Jo-Joe's parents wanted a boy, so they named her **Josephine**.
What they got was a black-haired Punk Warrior dressed in black lace with lithe body, amazing arms, tats all over in pastel blue and pink, and a woman's way with weapons.
Jo-Joe is Punk with a Goth overlay, like Jeanne.
Two perpendicular wires of silver grip her lower lip.
Jo-Joe wore a black lace catsuit complete with this teasy flesh-colored satin backing.
She designed it. Luce paid for its making.
Everyone benefits from the collaboration.
You are sure that staring at the lace will yield titillating results, though in the reality of things, the promise exceeds the product, or produce, depending on your points of view. The bustier top adds to the pleasant illusion. And the mid-range black peep-toe pumps. Her tats, and deep red lipstick, are the only splashes of color. And although the promise is partly illusion, Jo-Joe still is striking, like a pinup librarian in glasses and an archival smile.
When Jo-Joe puts her hands behind her back and rounds on you, you have the terrifying flash that she is going to put a big hole in your chest with the Glock that resides in a holster out back where you cannot see it.

Though it is a bit unorthodox to holster her gun where she cannot see it, Jo-Joe can draw, with dispatch, with either hand. The Glock is in plain sight like a tail light for anyone walking behind her. That is, when she isn't wearing her black leather coat that comes down to her calves.

In defending her holster placement, Jo-Joe says that a lot of professional baseball players with averages above .300 step in the bucket every time they take a swing, which still yields results one-third of the time. **Every kid who steps in the bucket gets yelled at by his coach**, Jo-Joe said. **What do they know?** Jo-Joe is lethal, and her holster is her business. And where she puts it. As is usually the case with the best, Jo-Joe is self-taught. No coach in sight.

Batting a thousand.

No one else in our orbit carries a gun.

We have a different sort of lethality.

Jo-Joe does, too.

"Wow," Jim said, "just another Punk with a gun."

"Yeah," OhJim said, "but I wouldn't tease her about it if I were you. Drop the **Glock-n-spiel**, Bro."

Jo-Joe has eyes, and ears, only for Gentle Ben.

"Bengie!" she said at scream-level and jumped onto his frame, throwing her long, cat-suited legs around his midsection. Though he is a big and healthy boy, Bengie barely kept his footing.

At the top of his long frame, though, he was beaming from ear to ear.

Lucy and Baldi follow the Glock-n-girl
| 20September08 |

After Jo-Joe made such a dramatic entry (how could she do otherwise?) Baldi and Luce Cleanue followed. Jo-Joe's job is to go before them to make sure that they stay safe.

Luce is a crowd-pleaser, but in a different way from Jo-Joe.

Something along the lines of Eve and further on up the line in terms of size. Luce is a big woman in every sense of the word -- big-picture thinker, big and beautiful woman.

When Luce hugs you, you learn a lot about her parts and the whole position she takes toward others.

When Luce hugs you, you know that you have been hugged.

Before she and Baldi struck it rich in the 21st century Gold Rush, she was a pastor's wife, and a good one.

As to what she is now, more in a moment.

The two started a not-for-profit foundation, the **Ibbity-Ibbity-Bye Foundation**, loosely based on a legendary phrase made famous by the **Three Stooges**. The money that the Foundation gives out stays in the community, and to get a grant you have to prove that your idea will be a source of among other things, fun, for the persons to be served.

Luce's mom and dad gave her two things -- the admonition to eat all the food set before her so she could be **big and pretty** and a name with layers of meaning -- Luce for **light** (Latin), and Luce for **Lucy**, as in Lucille Ball, first among comediennes and first lady of Jamestown, New York, which was Luce's hometown, too.

Next in our hearts after our friend Luce is her man, Baldi, who is the only guy in the universe with a comb-over whom I like. **Baldi** -- besides witnessing to the fact that he would be better-served to shave his head -- is short for **Garibaldi.**

I met Baldi and Luce (her nickname is **Loose Luce**, to play on the fact that she is the polar opposite) when Mr. Black and I were doing our undercover work in churches, which brought us to Buffalonya to subvert some liberal congregations during the early years of the Vietnam War.

Baldi embraced us, and later when we revealed our true selves to him, he still embraced us. By then, he was a minister in name only, having found it impossible to continue serving a parish that knew (as everyone knew) that he and his wife were suddenly worth millions upon millions.

Baldi and Luce, who is the younger by several years, still live in the same house on the West Side of Buffalonya where Baldi grew up, but they have found it necessary to use some of their new money to hire the Glock Girl and to install some sophisticated security systems. It only took one door-knocker, looking for a handout from the newly rich minister couple, for Jo-Joe to send a message heard all over the city by the close of the day.

Take yourself somewhere else, and tell all your friends about the girl and the gun that you encountered when this door opened in your face, Jo-Joe said she had told the hapless messenger.

The word spread as quickly as an STD in a low-end knocking shop.

After we eat, we meet
|21September08|

The social reason for our gathering speaks for itself.

The business reasons need some explaining.

Before hitting the big time with the Lottery, Baldi served a middling urban church with a zeal that was the envy of his colleagues. Luce worked in non-profits in Buffalonya, which is a ministry of another sort altogether.

No one envies those who work in urban not-for-profits.

After riches came their way, and kept coming for a multiple of millions, parish ministry was no longer possible for a man who could undergird the usual urban church budget many times over from his pocket change. Baldi tried to stay in the pulpit, but he became embittered by the grasping quality of the interactions that he had with persons whom he had once loved and admired. They were giddy from seeing their shepherd transfigured before them as a Sugar Daddy.

Baldi didn't see himself that way at all, and after bestowing a generous one-time gift of six solid figures on the church, he retired to his home on the West Side and closed the door, and posted a guard with as much metal dangling from various points of her body as was contained by the Glock on her belt. Luce just quit, and it was like no one noticed.

Baldi had always wanted to be a Spook like me, and like Mr. Black, and we had egged him on some, just to pass the time, after he learned what it was that we really did.

Baldi and Luce embraced the covert life as a stimulating avocation after the loss of their vocation.

Baldi and Luce had developed excellent connections with the various local minions of the TLAs (there are many, many more of such persons than you would ever dream). Baldi and Luce had done a thing similar to what my brothers and I had done, by hiding their covert activities behind a Private Investigations front.

Beware the small-time operator.

They say they like the idea that they are on their way to becoming the **Tommy and Tuppence** of our time.

Our agenda was to discuss Mr. Black with them.

Their agenda was to steal Gentle Ben from us.

Ben gets a very sweet deal
| 22September08 |

"Well," Baldi said, "I see that our Jo-Joe and your Ben have something more than a nodding acquaintance."

"More like a snogging acquaintance," Jim said.

"Yeah," OhJim said, "and maybe even a spooning one, too."

The kids, who had their heads together, didn't react.

No surprise, that.

"I love your brothers, Goose!" Luce said, laughing in the glass-shattering way that she does. "Do they ever make any sense?"

Luce went over to Jim and jerked him to his feet and gave him a big hug.

After pushing him back into his chair, she did the same to OhJim.

My brothers looked like they had been mugged by **a good-looking dame in a pretty frock that stuck out to *there*, Officer.**

Because they had.

"Yes, Dear," Eve said, "the brothers Jim Grim are capable but just not motivated to prove anything. They say it has something to do with their golden years as opposed to the life they led. I think they like to b.s. the brass, and everyone else, as often as they can."

"There's ambition for you, and focus, too," I said. "Pop would be proud."

My brothers continued in a semi-dazed condition that they needed to move on from unless they wanted to get mugged again.

Come to think of it, they probably were sandbagging in just such hopes.

Like I said, when Luce hugs you, you know that you have been hugged.

"We have a pressing need for a tech guy," Baldi said. "Maybe Ben would like to take a stab at the job. Our last one moved on to warmer places. He and Jo-Joe had some rough spots, so it was better that he go before we had to ask him how we could ever miss him if he didn't go away."

"Sure!" Ben said. "I promise nothing but soft spots for Jo-Joe."

"Watch it, Kid, she's got a gun!" Jim said. "And wait a minute, **Bucko Ben**. We need to negotiate some before we yield. We want to miss you only a little because we have received a lot."

"Yeah," OhJim said, "we are holding out for a future draft choice and hoping for Jeanne's twin sister. Or just the prospect of some good will."

He grinned at Luce.

Luce laughed.

The windows rattled.

"Well," Baldi said, "we can agree to those terms."

"Yes, Luce said, "we are good to our assistants. For us, It's like a **WWJD** thing. They obviously will be good to one another."

"**Who wants Jack Daniels?**" Jim said. "I think that's what **WWJD** means."

"Yeah" OhJim said, "but the proper pastiche is **What Would Jesus Drive?** Answer: an Accord. Everyone knows that -- **they were all in one Accord.** I think it's in the Good Book somewhere. Unlike **WWJD**, which ain't anywhere to be found except dangling from necklaces and bracelets."

Luce laughed, and the windows rattled in their channels. Being double-hung, the windows were no match for Luce's high-spirited laugh, which was like the rush of a mighty wind.

Luce leads us by her light to darkness
| 23September08 |

"Enough about us," Luce said. "What about your Mr. Black?"

"In a word," I said, "we don't think that he is dead."

"I counted a phrase there," Jim said.

"Yeah," OhJim said. "In a phrase, brother, **yes.**"

Luce laughed that laugh.

My brothers were getting spoiled and were loving it.

"Refresh me," Baldi said, "on which of your circle is Mr. Black."

"Oh, you know, Baldi," Luce said, "the one with the foul mouth."

"There are two such, darlin'," Baldi said.

"The good-looking one with all the hair," Luce said, "meaning no offense to Mr. Red, who is actually a dear if you can get to know him, I'm sure."

"That was refreshing -- and regressing," Jim said. "A new read on Red."

"Yeah," OhJim said, "or redressing. And we didn't have to lift a finger."

Luce laughed.

"What we ask," I said, "is that you take Ben under your care and teach him the shadow craft."

"We aim to please," Luce said.

"And so does Louise," Jim said.

"Yeah," OhJim said, "please and thank you."

"Don't mention it," Baldi said.

"There goes my future draft choice," Jim said. "We sold the farm."

"You still have a draught choice," OhJim said. "The Pabst is past, but we presently have Coors right and Bud left."

Luce laughed the windows into a nervous condition.

Love that laugh. Paneless.

"Email us the particulars about Mr. Black, in secure mode, of course," Baldi said, "and we will make some discreet inquiries with the TLA types on our virtual, thrice-encrypted Rolodex. And since we are very discreet, that will take some time, but you don't seem to be in a twist over this, frankly."

"Probably true," I said, "since the rules of engagement that we live by offer us our best protection. We are mostly concerned that someone, and possibly or probably our friend Mr. Black, is killing people and dumping them in full public view. Call it curiosity, then. Cat scratch fever."

"Which killed the cat," Jim said.

"Yeah," OhJim said, "and fur nuttin'."

"Call it an intense curiosity," Eve said. "We are concerned but not panicked. We want to say a benediction over this one, in a timely way."

"Amen to that," Baldi said."

Luce, smiling like Texas, made the Sign of the Cross.

Jeanne and we get some new roomies
| 24September08 |

"There goes a good roomie," Jeanne said.

"Well, Dear," Eve said, "we may be able to double the recompense for your loss with double the roomies."

"How so?" Jeanne said. "And, perhaps, why so?"

"What say you to these?" I said. "They have room enough and to spare."

My brothers could only grin in Grim fashion and bobble their shiny heads.

First Luce and now this.

They **were** getting spoiled.

"Yes," Jim said, "we have a **pied-a-terre** over near Goose and Eve. Upstairs, to be exact."

"Yes, Dear," Eve said. "We thought it would be fun, and functional, to move in together, so to speak."

"That gives us three places to sit around, tell stories, and make up one-liners," I said. "Upstairs, downstairs, and out back at the bookshop, here."

"Sounds like a plan," Jeanne said. "Otherwise, David and I would get to be like an old married couple in no time what with our Bengie launched so well from the nestie."

"Old and married without ever being the fun kind," David said, "the young and married kind."

"I don't think that Jeanne is the marryin' kind, **Podna**," Jim said. "And keep your hands where I can see 'em."

"Yeah," OhJim said. "Smile when you say that, **Stranger**."

OhJim slapped at his butt, groping for guns.

"I can see that you will be watching some Westerns if the old guys corner the remote," I said.

"I resemble that comment," Jim said.

"Yeah," OhJim said. **"Me, too."**

"AOL?" David said.

"Sounds like," Jeanne said, "which brings up some questions, such as Internet access and bedroom space."

"The house," I said, "is on the large side and has been set up with separate everything per floor, like a duplex, plus high-speed Internet access. We live on the ground floor, and the boys live on the second floor, and there is an attic room, presently empty, that you can fight over."

"How far are you from Bengie and his new parents and live-in squeeze?" Jeanne said. "And I'll take the attic, BTW."

"Five minutes max," I said. "You can sleep over with Ben and Jo-Joe anytime you want."

"To sweeten the deal, and just because," Eve said, "-- we are changing our wills so you and David will share with the brothers Jim in the ownership of the home, and the bookshop, in the unlikely event of our death."

David gave his bug-eyed smile through his round glasses.

Jeanne smiled to the one side and to the other.

"That's right," I said "We plan to live forever, at least as memories. We have no kids and won't leave our assets to Wild Billy. We'd hate to bankroll a litter of lawyers rolling in kitty litter over the prospect of a puss in bucks."

Jeanne and David look at one another, in a sly way.

"Deal," David said.

"Sold," Jeanne said, "as long as we get to keep your brothers in the event of your untimely demise."

"Knock, knock," Jim said.

"Who's there?" OhJim said.

"Tick, tock *Tribe*," Jim said.

"Tick, tock *Tribe* who?" OhJim said.

"Tick, tock, the clock says. It's *Tribe* to move in together," Jim said. "Film at eleven."

A house is a home if you wish
| 25September08 |

We live on a corner in a neighborhood that mixes refugee families, Native American families, black families, Hispanic families, and white-bread families of sometimes Italian extraction, or -- more often -- just plain old white bread. And us, a tribal offshoot of multiple hues and views.

In view of our history, aspirations, and education, Eve and I notice a disparity between ourselves and our neighbors (who keep mostly to themselves).

We have cars, and cash, and can come and go as we please.

Many of our neighbors go on foot, to the bus stop, and can go as far as the buses do, including, I suppose, train, ship, and plane connections.

Our home, a typical working-class duplex of the vertical variety, known locally as a **Double**, has two of everything.

It is traditional for the landlord to live on the ground floor and rent out the second floor.

Many of the homes in our neighborhood were built with wood salvaged from the 1901 Pan-American Exhibition. The site is within walking distance.

This house is where we brought Jeanne and David to join in our home life. In true tribal fashion, we treat our home as **Holy Ground**, a place of amity and harmony, as best as we are able. Maybe we do not promise to avoid negative thoughts, negative speech, or violence, even, but we do strive for a place of blessing for ourselves and those whom we invited inside.

Who, really, is more idealistic than one who has been salivated upon by the roaring lion?

We knew the roaring of the lion from what it sounds like from inside the distended jaws.

And we sensed that our youngsters, despite their tender years, had had such experiences, as well.

Jeanne has alluded to a past of horrific edges.

David has said nothing, but one cannot **not** communicate, even in silence.

David, AKA **David X. X.**, does not have a middle or a last name he has ever shared with us.

Well, Eve knows but is not saying. Eve writes the checks.

There will be time for all stories.

Email to Tommy re: recent decisions
| 26September08 |

Hello, my brother:

Time for an update.

We had a pleasant evening with Baldi and Luce, whom you have met in other contexts, and Jo-Joe, their Punk Girl with a gun. We gained some fine recipes from Luce for seasonal vegetables but lost our Gentle Ben, who is on loan to our friends to fill their needs for a computer/security systems person.

In return, Baldi and Luce are going to take on Ben's training in the craft that we know so well.

On my list of things to follow up on is the second victim, the hanger-on around local media types, and getting a pic or drawing and more details. Baldi and Luce are going to make some inquiries, too, so we shall see what we shall see.

We are waiting for Mr. Black to get better or worse. If he stays the same, not much will happen, though every day does seem to have its little surprises.

On another front, Ben's leaving for the friends' house left a situation where David and Jeanne would be rooming together, for security reasons, but now without the addition of Ben to their sub-tribe. Eve and I decided to bring them into our home and have them share the upstairs with my two brothers Grim. They like one another enough without having a living situation that begs them to get in over their heads emotionally. I know, I know, they will do as they will do, and I for one hope that they do do, but it seems better somehow to bring us all in under the same roof. Slow and sure beats **wham bam thank ya ma'am**.

Eve and I are not acting exactly like bear handlers, or as match makers, either. We're looking for a middle way that shows some actual respect for the persons involved as well as acting for their safety. Time will tell.

I get this funny feeling that with the new and expanded Tribe we are trying to set up something that will endure, while knowing that nothing endures forever. After recovery from the work and life of the shadows, I for one am noticing a heightened need for stasis and safety, feelings that I rigorously murdered in their sleep when I was under orders, cloth, and cover. This is different from the open-ended, need-to-know based reality -- those in possession of secrets must not, on pain of punishment, usually fatal, divulge those secrets. That is a separate issue and an important one that we are working on. We can have secrecy, but we may not be able to keep the Tribe intact, for so many reasons.

In personalities, alone, we have tremendous challenges, and always have had, though we did reach an understanding with the other color-coded old guys around our common goal of providing safety for Eve. The addition of the three youngsters, to a large extent, and the addition of you into our circle of secrets, to a far lesser extent, provides fresh problems, opportunities, excitement, and terror for me. I've never done this. Recruiting was always someone else's job.

And there's more. I've never been a former spook, currently operating in quasi-legal ways, who recently has started crawling in the footsteps of Gandhi in hopes of one day walking in them. I've never done any of these things before, either serially or in relation, except the spook part. That is the thread, the white sheet with the eye holes, that ties all this together and provides its cover. Except for the new spirit of nonviolence. That is inside-out.

Your brother
Goose

Violence spins off emails on same
|27September08|

Dear Goose:

I only have a minute, so this will be quick. What the hell are you talking about when you say that you are taking a look at avoiding the violence that shadows the shadowland? Can't be done, my friend.

Tommy

Dear Tommy:

Eve and I want to find a way to create safety without resort to killing, and we pray that it is possible. And if we find Mr. Black, we will be put to the test. I fear that he may need to be taken out of circulation in one way or another.

Violence is life, in a way, and I'm thinking about what Wild Billy does when he catches a mouse, tortures it, kills it, and leaves it in our way so we can praise the little meowing murderer.

I'm thinking of Coyote -- patron saint and resident trickster of all spooks. Coyote kills and eats. Coyote would kill Wild Billy in an eye-blink of violence and stroll away after, violence forgotten.

Coyote does not know from violence. Neither does Wild Billy.

When Eve and I were working in the shadows, killing was the ultimate solution, just like it was for Hitler's minions.

We didn't kill, but we knew the killers, and we set them on persons who were seriously in the way of the aims and goals of our handlers. And our hand-to-hand training has led us to maim and harm others in instants of reaction. Then one day I walked away, hoping that the nightmares would not come. And I woke up screaming. Still do.

We still use the potential for violence to help us evaluate persons and situations -- if we err, they lose. It has not come to violence, but I could not come to that conclusion with the innocents whom we have brought into our fold.

I sicken of what keeps me, and more important, my lovely Eve, alive.

Goose

Pop the roof, reach for the sky!
| 28September08 |

Eve and I have lived in the tribal house for all the years we have been partners. At first, we just treated the second floor like a walk-up walk-in closet, but when my brothers appeared, back from their travels, we all jumped in and made the second floor a home for them.

And now for the youngsters.

We have privacy in the measure that we need.

The house began its life as a **semi-shotgun bungalow** -- the narrow sort of dwelling that has the distinction of being famous for the fanciful assertion that a shotgun blast fired from the front door would hit all the walls -- to the sides and at the other end.

Our house is only semi-shotgun.

The space has been partitioned into two rows of rooms, with the kitchen across the back, next to the stairwell. A true shotgun bungalow has no hallways or internal walls. Our variant has no hallways. Someone long, long ago popped off the roof and added a second story, and a stairwell, and an attic with standing headroom at the center. It is working class all the way.

And comfortable. And durable. And big enough for an urban ur-tribe.

And cheap, too. Our house cost about the same as a mid-size SUV.

In Buffalonya, houses like ours with two of everything are called **doubles**, not duplexes. There are two of everything, right down to separate lights in the stairwell and the basement, and two furnaces, two hot water heaters, two electrical panels ... like that.

The idea is to rent out the second floor and live on the first, but Eve and I had had no intention of bringing strangers into our covert existence.

Let them watch from across the street.

The blessing and curse of urban living means that we can bring in my brothers, and the others, and no one will think to ask us what is going on, and in many cases our so-called neighbors, the ones who have not moved on to the next rental, probably will not notice the change.

They will, I wager, notice Jeanne but not beyond appreciating the view. Our street dead-ends short of **community**. Can't get there from here.

Good fits and bad news
|29September08|

Email from Goose and Tommy -- **re: That reporter** --

Hi my brother:

Just a note to remind you that you had said that we should talk about your friend the senior crime reporter. This idea seems to have fallen on hard times and can't get a break at any cost.

Goose

Black/white and read all over
|30September08|

This editorial ran in the **Lake Effect edition** of the **Daily Afterblatt**.

Poker rules
Discard all but one -- anyone -- and put him on probation

Bodies are good, if for no other reason than to be a vehicle for one's mind.

And then there are all the pleasures that the body presides over.

These are good things, you and we probably would agree.

Bodies in the street, dumped in dumpsters, peeled from bus grilles -- these give no one of sound mind, and body, any pleasure.

No one, save the murderer still loose, wants this sort of thing for the body. This, too, we can agree on.

But our elected officials, and those law enforcement persons charged, and paid -- and paid well, we might add -- to serve and protect the public good, can't agree on anything, except for one thing.

It's someone else's fault.

The Coroner is to blame, say the Detectives.

The Detectives are to blame, says the Coroner.

No one, except perhaps the media, is blaming the person or persons unknown who are killing and discarding bodies in our city.

And this is not drug stuff -- the ugly testosterone-driven drive-by shootings that confine the violence to the population that gets and receives violence coming from the forgetful smoke of a bong or the infectious point of a dirty needle.

Sometimes the innocent, or less culpable, anyway, catch bullets meant for others who, if they don't deserve those bullets, certainly were the intended targets.

No, three bodies, and a murderer, or two, or three -- this is not acceptable in our city. Neither, we hasten to add, are drive-by shootings.

Who can fathom the hormonal antics of kids with guns and no impulse control?

Let us confine ourselves to what we understand.

We understand bodies bereft of soul and life, cut off by malevolence.

We have ways to respond, beginning with the police and continuing in the courts, with the Coroner and his ilk lurking around every corner of the process from murder to detection to detention to conviction to the electric chair.

That's right, death for death, and not a minute too soon.

These things, we understand.

The infighting of officials and police?

This, too, we understand.

So stop the crap, and all the carping, and get on with the process, youse guys.

We're watching, and we do not like what we see.

We vote, and we have thousands of friends.

-- the editors

The following was the lead story on Page 1 in the same day's edition of the **Daily Afterblatt**.

Why Bother?
Coroner has that to say of homicide detectives

By Jane Carlotto
Senior Crime Reporter

The Eerie County coroner had just two words and a question mark to spare for detectives who are investigating three unsolved homicides in a case widely known as the "Mystery Man Murders."

"Why bother?" Dr. Bruce Backstaff said when asked if he has taken steps to further the investigation into three deaths police began linking a month ago.

When pressed for additional comment, Backstaff said, "Talk to Blucote and Schmidt. You'll find them at their desks, unless they are on a donut run."

Backstaff was referring, and none too kindly, to lead Det. Joe Blucote and his partner, Det. Bill "Joe Bob" Schmidt. And contrary to the coroner's tongue-in-cheek statement, the detectives were not available and have not responded to repeated follow-up phone calls and messages.

The Police Commissioner's Office and the police press liaison referred all queries to the two detectives, Blucote and Schmidt.

Sources at City Hall and in the police department say that the coroner and the detectives have such a frosty relationship that it is no wonder that nothing has developed in the seemingly frozen investigation into three murders:

• Late last March, police were called to the scene of a bus vs. pedestrian accident in the dark, on a rainy night, near President's Park. The coroner later asked for and received, from a Coroner's Jury, a finding that the death was by misadventure, by a person or persons unknown. In other words, a homicide. The name of the victim has not been discovered despite the detectives' assurances, recorded in previous stories in this newspaper, that they were pressing their investigation.

• In early summer, the body of Bill Zeohn, a freelance photographer known to government insiders downtown, was found in the middle of a street on Buffalonya's East Side. The coroner has yet to release a cause of death. What little is known about Zeohn has come from media representatives who worked alongside him in covering city government.

• Last month, a man's body was found in a dumpster in an alley downtown. This third body was linked to the other two by the discovery of a symbol drawn on the side of the dumpster with indelible ink. And authorities have released a drawing of the victim, a John Doe like the first victim.

No official who would be expected to know about the third homicide has been forthcoming with details. The equivalent of "no comment/off the record" has been the only sound to arise from such quarters.

This has led insiders to speculate endlessly over the reason for the silence.

Some say that it must be a matter of national security of the first magnitude. No other matter could enforce such a news blackout, these persons are saying.

Attempts to gain comment on such speculations, which have been repeated, and in some cases originated by local bloggers, have gained this and other reporters nothing for publication.

One media insider said that it is as though officials have taken over media keyboards and written, ***End of Story***.

F-Troupe-A meets, greets, schemes
|01October08|

"This meeting of the **F-Troupe-A**, formerly known as the **F-Troop**, less formerly and formally known as the **F-Troop-A**, will be in orbit," I said.

"You mean **in odor**, don't you, Mister Chair Sir?" Jim said.

"Yeah," OhJim said, "or in **hors d'ourves**, perhaps."

"Whatever," I said. "Greet our friend Tommy, at this his first meeting of the F-Troop and its various permutations and nicknames."

"Glad to be here," Tommy said, "and I have absolutely no idea what you are talking about."

"Me, either," Jim said. "I was hoping that a smart man like you might shine a light on our darkness."

"Yeah," OhJim said, "or at least curse it. Anything would be helpful at this point in time."

"We don't worry overmuch about making sense at these meetings, Tommy Dear," Eve said. "You will get used to it, I'm sure. I did."

"Yes," I said, "when we came to our senses in that dark wood where the straight way was lost, in the journey of the middle of our lives, we decided to weep as we walked. At first, anyway."

"After such experiences, and such ways of making sense of our experience," Eve said, "we have found that playful celebration makes our present and pleasant estate sweeter."

"Speaking of estates," Jeanne said, "and not meaning to foreshorten this pleasing display of literary allusion and illusion, did you-all read the editorial and follow-up crime story in the **Daily Afterblatt**?"

"One could do worse than be a swinger of birches," David said.

We all looked at him with dropped jaws. The boy was full of surprises.

"I am still in the dark, in that dark wood," Tommy said. "Maybe it's because I work for a living. But your odd ways are affecting, nonetheless."

"But you have miles to go before you sleep, don't you, Dear," Eve said. "I know the feeling."

"We did have a frost the other morning," Jim said.

"Yeah," OhJim said, "and today we have been channeling Robert Frost."

"Mister Chair Sir," Mister Ed said. "I rise as parliamentarian of this august body, meeting in October, to point out some regular, and irregular, aspects of the discourse so far. To wit --

• "You called the meeting **in orbit**, **in odor**, and as **hors d'ourves**. None of these three, though amusing, were decent or in order. Meetings come **to order**, or they come to nothing at all.

• "As an aside, thank goodness that you did not attest to there being a **quorum**. One shudders to imagine the puns that that bit of **Robert's Rules** would elicit.

• "You were correct to greet and welcome the guest, but you have yet to call a vote on whether to seat him (hold your puns, dammit) or to give him voice, or voice and vote, or nothing.

• "The various allusions, to Dante and to Robert Frost, were apt and well-done, but stick a fork in it. That turkey is done.

• "The lovely Miss Jeanne (love the heels, as usual, by the way) came close to actually making a motion (and let us not revisit the hilarity on that score again, please) but veered off. As a result, Mister Chair Sir, we are nowhere and everywhere we want to be, all at the same time.

"That is all."

We sat, in awe, of Mister Ed. Having a parliamentarian was a source of great pride for all of us. Regardless of whether we understood him.

"Mister Chair Sir," Jeanne said, "I move we discuss the article and editorial in the **Daily Afterblatt**. If I get a second, I will speak to my motion."

Mister Ed gave Jeanne a wink and a crane-like nod, decent and in order.

We go back to the good old F-Troop
| 02October08 |

"There is a motion on the floor," I said. "Can someone pick it up? Dust it off? Take it for a spin? Like that?"

"But first," David said, "I would like to suggest that we go back to the good old **F-Troop**, unless anyone can say why we ended up with the exotic, and unwieldy, **F-Troupe-A.**"

No one could, and we all nodded. Mister Ed, the pinnacle of parliamentary procedure and prudence, did not raise an objection that there was a prior motion on the floor. We even gave David the **F-Troop** salute -- thumbs up, middle fingers in.

Maybe it was because David was clearly going to a rant if we did not agree. Any fool with the floor knows that Robert in his **Rules** does not address rants, rats, or raffles.

"I rise in second," Jim said, "to sister Jeanne's motion, Mister Chair Sir, that we discuss the recent machinations of the Fifth Estate, particularly the **Daily Afterblatt (Lake Effect edition!** we all shouted, except Tommy, of course) as they devolve upon the Tribe here gathered."

"Yeah," OhJim said, "and I vie for that distinguishment, though I cannot match the elocution of my eclectic elder brother."

"To no avail do you vie," I said. "Your brother is going ahead before you."

"Well," Jeanne said, "every duelist needs a second, so thank you, Jimmy, and this is the deal. I think that Jane Carlotto has hit the jackpot, the big casino, the trifecta, the hat trick, **and** the grand slam in her article. **Not!**"

"How **not** so, Jeanne Dear?" Eve said. "She found sources and info in every direction."

"One suspects," Mister Ed said, "if I may add my oar to Jeanne's troubled waters, that **the Carlotto** is on autopilot where some of her sources are concerned, if you know what I mean and if you will allow me to mix my metaphors into a thin gruel(and please disregard the redundancy)."

"Autopilot?" I said. "I guess I had a reaction like Eve's."

"Yes, autopilot," Mister Ed said. "She is the captain of her own ship when it comes to her insider sources. She has looked into her mirror and said, **Mirror, mirror on the wall, who's the fairest of them all?** And the mirror has answered her, **No one, so make some stuff up and attribute it to insiders, wags, city hall hangers-on, what you will. And by the way, you** *are* **looking marvelous.** Or words to that effect."

"In other words," I said, "she has woven her story from hairs plucked from her own head."

"Thank God, "Jim said, "that you said head, not beard."

"Yeah," OhJim said. "Who is **beered**? Is that anything like **pie-eyed**?"

"I don't understand you people at all," Tommy said, "but I like you. Don't know why, but I do. Not enough to go into spook exile, mind you, but this is all attractive in a bizarre sort of way. You remind me of **family.**"

Jeanne gave Tommy her sideways smile.

Tommy went all pink, like most of us did the first time.

"And," Jeanne said, "that joke of an editorial. What a study in urban white racism. They all but said that the druggies can **eat bleep and die** for all they care, since they confine their killing to their own kind. And that's just for starters."

"Granted, Dear," Eve said, "-- white fear AKA racism in the urban sphere, but what about clues and directions specific to our inquiries?"

"Two things," Jeanne said, without batting a kohl-rimmed eye. "Number One: Why do we lack a photo or drawing of the second victim, Zeohn? And Number Two: Is there a TLA-type fix in with the hapless local detectives, or is dear Jane just blowing smoke? What say you, Tarzan?"

Jeanne turned to Tommy.

This time she was not smiling.

Tommy returned her gaze and their eyes locked.

Tommy blinked.

And smiled.

Tommy switches to need-to-know
|03October08|

Tommy continued to smile at Jeanne, who continued to not.

"This is what we are dealing with," Tommy said. "And need-to-know."

"Is that why you didn't tell us until we asked?" Jeanne said.

"You are beginning to be wise, Dear," Eve said. "It's a lot like **Twenty Questions**, only you better get it right the first time."

"Do you want to hear the answer to your question," Tommy said, "or do you want to ask **Why Questions**?"

"**Why Questions**," I said, "are generally unhelpful in the shadow places where Spookistan still holds sway."

"Why of course," Jeanne said, "and like Tommy here I have no idea what you are talking about. So, I guess I'd like to hear the answer."

"Good," Tommy said. "Focus on what is possible."

"I'm focused," Jeanne said, "and waiting."

Jeanne walked over to Tommy and grabbed him by the nose and shook it. Tommy just took it.

He didn't even seem to notice, but when he was set free again, he spoke.

"Ok, then," Tommy said. "Need-to-know. The fix is in on Mr. Black, and the locals are muzzled so tightly that they have to take their kibble through a straw after a run through a blender with a little water added. Needless to say, they do not like it, but it is not the first time they have been told to back off and leave the bookshop crew alone. They caught it hot after they came here to the bookshop for an innocent visit right after the bus vs. man thing came down."

"**Who** are you, Masked Man? "Jim said.

"Yeah," OhJim said, "and **whose** are you, I would like to know."

"That," Tommy said, "you definitely do not need to know."

Who, who, who?
|04October08|

This is my list of questions and thoughts after hearing Tommy's story about the de facto gag order on local law enforcement --

- Who ordered the gag on the locals?
- What does Pop have to do with this?
- What else can Tommy tell us about the three murders?
- ... and, yeah, just for yucks, **Who are you**?

Jeanne didn't make a list, but she went right at Tommy with questions.

"What can you tell us about who it was that ordered the gag on local law enforcement?" Jeanne said.

"Not much that you need to know," Tommy said.

"I'm assuming," I said, "that it is people whom we have been in touch with, over the years, to remind them of the Vault and its secrets."

"Bingo," Tommy said.

"Ok," Jeanne said, "and what about the way that local law enforcement resents the hell out of gag orders from TLAs and always finds a way to get word out in the media?"

"Yes," Tommy said, "that is an issue, always, in such matters, and if you think back, the locals who go public discredit themselves and are easy to discredit further by their supervisors, who are laughably easy to scare."

"So we can expect that dance to commence soon?" Jeanne said.

"It may be in train already," Tommy said, "depending on who were the sources for Jane Carlotto's latest follow-up on the **Mystery Man Murders**."

"One last question," Jeanne said. "Who are you, anyway?"

"Tommy," Tommy said, "-- tribalist at large, enemy of your enemies."

"Beyond that, Jeanne," I said, "you and I don't need to know. The future is always open. Pragmatism in the here-and-now, taking into account the there-and-then, is the essence of what we do and who we are."

"Bingo," Tommy said.

"Oh what the hey," Jeanne said, "here's another question. What else can you tell us, today, about the murder victims and possible suspects?"

"I can tell you that I have nothing to add, today," Tommy said. "Tomorrow's outa sight but soon will be in our sights. Who knows what tomorrow will bring."

"Something tells me that you know," Jeanne said.

"Bingo," Tommy said. "That is a good working hypothesis. Just remember this. The enemy of your enemy is well-connected."

"And just a touch arrogant," Jeanne said, "but then who isn't?"

Tomorrow brings ... today
|05October08|

When we gathered as was our custom, on the next day, we noticed that nothing had transpired. We were relieved, I guess, though some bouts of noise and confusion do have their place in a well-paced and varied life.

At least that is what Mark Twain wrote.

On a hot day in a Mississippi River town, in the heat and dust, a dog fight or the arrival of a stern-wheeler was always welcome.

Everyone, Twain wrote, was **grateful for the noise and confusion**.

When I shared this with the others, they had various reactions --
- **Eve**: "Yes, Dear, that is amusing but not practical."
- **Jeanne**: "Works well for Huck Finn but not for real life."
- **David**: "I like the scene with Huck and Jim in the thunderstorm, seen and heard from the cave on the island."
- **Jim**: "There is a pun in there somewhere, but I can't retrieve it."
- **OhJim**: "Yeah, me either. Or is it **neither**?"
- **Mister Ed**: "Satire has its moments, and Twain had more than most."
- **Mr. Red** (shouting from the front desk): "Bleep you and Twain, too."
- **Wild Billy**: "Meow."
- **Tommy** (via email): "Bingo, Brother Goose."

Detectives go off the Rez
| 06October08 |

We were talking about everything and nothing when Mr. Red came back.

"A couple of bleeping detectives wanna talk at youse," Mr. Red said.

"Show them in," I said, "and bar the door."

Detectives Blucote and Schmidt came in, chips on shoulders.

This should be interesting, I thought. **Dumb and Dumber in the flesh.**

"Is there someplace where we can go and be alone, Grim?" Blucote said.

"No, Sport, there isn't," I said. "Grab a seat or leave."

"Listen here, Grim," Blucote said, "you can't be taking an attitude with us. It just makes us angry."

"That's right," Schmidt said. "In words of one syllable -- angry."

"Ok," I said, "I'll pretend we're equals. How can I do-you, gentlemen?"

"You can quit hiding behind your mama's skirts," Blucote said.

"Which one?" Jim said.

"Yeah," OhJim said, "we have three. Which one?"

"Gentlemen," I said, "turn that around. Does your mama know that you're here, harassing me and my sisters and brothers?"

Blucote jumped up, but before he got any further, Mister Ed was towering over him, inches from his slightly protruding belly. They glared at one another for a long time before Blucote took his seat again.

Blucote took out a notebook and pen.

"Give me your names, all of youse," he said.

"**Mickey Mouse**," David said.

"**Salome**," Jeanne said.

"**Seymour Butts**," Jim said.

"**Ivan Yackinoff**," OhJim said. "With two effs."

"**Howard Hughes**," Mister Ed said.

"**Eve**," Eve said. "We've met. That's **E-V-E**, Dear."

"**I. P. Freely**," I said. "We've met, too, and I was pissed."

Blucote was a bright shade of red when he walked in.

Now he was a lurid shade of purple, and a throbbing vein over his left temple was about to blow.

Schmidt, after breaking his silence, had not said another word. His face was like a blank slate the color of old chewing tobacco. Schmidt was not going to change his affect just because a roomful of scofflaws had just told his partner to **bleeping bleep off.**

That's when Tommy walked in.

"Detectives," Tommy said, "you seem to be a long way from the Rez. Does the Big Chief know you're here?"

"Agent," Blucote said. "We didn't expect to see you here."

"And I didn't think that I had to tell you my feeling about you coming here," Tommy said.

"We were just leaving," Blucote said. "Miss Eve, a pleasure, as always. And the rest of youse, well, I have nothing to say, just now."

"You were leaving," Tommy said, "and then you were talking. Which will it be, Detective?"

"Leaving," Blucote said, "and my partner as well."

When we heard the little bells on the front door tinkle as the detectives departed the premises, Tommy said, "Sorry about that. They aren't taking their orders well, and who can blame them. But I will, and as soon as I leave. A gag is a gag, and that ain't funny."

"We sorta gave them the old run-around," I said, "and a bunch of creative names when Blucote demanded to know who-all he was talking to."

"I haven't had that much fun since the pig bit my little brother," Jim said.

"Yeah," OhJim said. "I resemble that comment, brother."

"So," I said, "my friend, what's new in the Mr. Black file?"

"Funny you should ask," Tommy said.

And smiled that shark smile.

Tommy comes bearing gifts of art
|07October08|

Tommy reached into his blazer and pulled out a small notebook and tore out two pages. One was a drawing of a man, portly but young, and not too bright by the look of him. He had a funny thing on his forehead and the drawing made him seem to be looking up at what was, or was not, there. One was a drawing of a woman of a certain age, with wavy hair, glasses, and enough -- if not prettiness -- then at least distinction to put her in other places than the company of a portly young dullard cursed for all time with a weird knot in the middle of a very high forehead.

"That's Zeohn. **The Twilight Zeohn,**" Jeanne said. "I'd know that male-pattern baldness anywhere. And that looks like Jane Carlotto, too."

"Bingo," Tommy said, "twice. The man is Bill Zeohn, 37, the second victim in the **Mystery Man Murders** and the only one of the three whom we have a name and a story for. And yes, the other drawing is of Jane Carlotto, Senior Crime Reporter of the **Daily Afterblatt.**"

Lake Effect edition! we all shouted, with high fives all around.

"I did the drawings myself from photos in Zeohn's file," Tommy said. "I want to keep you on the back channel, and I was in a bit of a hurry. This is why I didn't just get copies of the photos. You need to stay off the books. The drawing of Zeohn is post-autopsy. They cut off his lid to take a look inside, I guess. That isn't his bald spot. That's his brain. Sorry. I faked in the bald spot from memory. Everyone knew Zeohn."

"You better keep your day job, whatever it is," Jim said.

"Yeah, **Agent Whoever**," OhJim said, "**Agent Picasso** you ain't."

"If you were looking at coroner's files, did you see any new data on the first victim?" I said.

"Yeah," Tommy said, "but that's not a bingo. DNA samples have come back with no hits in the registry. They still don't have a clue about this guy, and they don't even know that he isn't Mr. Black, your old friend. I figure what they don't know won't hurt them."

"My question," Jeanne said, "is this. Why was Jane's photo in Zeohn's file? Zeohn was always around at photo opps, taking pictures of his own, but we really didn't know why he showed up or who was ever buying his stuff."

"Good questions," Tommy said, "and Jane may be able to tell me why her picture was in that file. There is a sticky note in the file that says Jane denies any knowledge of why a photo of her would have been found in Zeohn's effects. A note on the note says **R/O stalker**."

"He was creepy, I'll say that about Zeohn," Jeanne said.

"Well," Tommy said, "give me some time and I'll see what Jane says, in a more private way. Jane and I have what you might call an understanding."

"Time? Yeah, we got that," I said. "Loads of time, in any denomination that you might want, from minutes right on up to eons. Let's spend some time right now updating our list. Miss Naomi, if you will."

"Naomi?" Tommy said.

"Present," Jeanne said.

Jeanne clicked over to Tommy and sat in his lap. She licked his ear and dangled one of her black pumps from a very cute big toenail painted deep red. Tommy went all pink again. He really does need to work on that.

Jeanne is just that way, sometimes -- a 100-proof licker.

We do not want her to change anything.

Beaudreau vs. *Budrow*
| 08October08 |

Jeanne slipped her pump back on and tapped over to the flip chart.

"Where are we, Toto?" she wrote.

"Cans/ass," Jim said.

"Yeah," OhJim said, but that's redundant, too, **Beaudreau**."

"How do you spell that?" Jeanne said.

"**B-U-D-R-O-W**," OhJim said. "It's French, I think, but Southern, too."

"What were they like as boys?" Tommy said, with a look of wonder.

"Little twerps, just like me," I said, "but smart. Smart-ass smart."

"We always liked **Smarties**," Jim said.

"Yeah," OhJim said, "and **Bazooka** bubble gum."

"Focus," Jeanne said. "I want all eyeballs on this paper."

She didn't have to ask twice.

Tommy in particular, newly flesh-colored rather than brightest pink, was particularly rapid in compliance.

Jeanne drew in a big red dot and turned to us.

"Questions," I said.

"Questions," Jeanne wrote.

"The connection between the victim Zeohn and the reporter Jane Carlotto," Eve said and Jeanne wrote.

"The nature of Zeohn's fatal injuries," I said and Jeanne wrote.

"Any connections between Zeohn and the other two victims," I said and Jeanne wrote.

"More info on Zeohn's effects, from his clothes and from his apartment (can we get in there?)," David said and Jeanne wrote.

"Any stories out there about Zeohn as a stalker?" Jeanne said and wrote.

"Who, if anyone, was Zeohn selling his photos to, and can we see what was in his camera when he died, and his photo files?" OhJim said, to a beaming Buddha Girl smile from Eve, and Jeanne writing.

"Who were his parents, and did he have any siblings or friends," Jim said and Jeanne wrote.

"Why did the killer allow one of his victims to be identified but not the other two," Mister Ed said and Jeanne wrote.

"Based on the information we now have, what picture of the killer -- or killers -- is emerging?" I said and Jeanne wrote.

"Killer vs. killers, qv," Jeanne said and wrote.

"Which of the facts that we know or think that we know are meant to confuse and mislead us?" Eve said and Jeanne wrote, smiling to the side.

Jeanne loads our bullets
|09October08|

We divided the questions into **Field trips**, **Things that Tommy could answer**, **Wish list**, and **Questions to ponder** --

Field trips

- Getting into Zeohn's apartment (Tommy and David).
- Zeohn as stalker/connection with Jane Carlotto (David and Jeanne).
- Zeohn's camera and photo files (Jim and OhJim).

Things that Tommy can answer

- Zeohn's fatal injuries (copy of coroner's report?).
- Zeohn's friends and family (Tommy asks Jane Carlotto to do a story?).
- Any connection between Zeohn and Jane Carlotto?

Wish list

- Any connections between Zeohn and the other two victims?
- Killer vs. killers, qv.
- A lot more information on the first and third victims.

Questions to ponder

- What picture of the killer -- or killers -- is emerging?
- Which of the facts are meant to confuse and mislead us?
- Under single-killer theory: Why did the killer allow one victim's identity to be known but not the other two?

Tommy shares his *cans*
| 10October08 |

"Tommy," I said, "there are some questions that you probably can share answers for right here, right now."

"I'll start, Dear," Eve said. "What was the cause of death for Zeohn?"

"Blunt-force trauma to the head," Tommy said. "That is why they cut the top of his head off, to see what they could see."

"Yep, dead," Jim said. "They could tell that before they tapped his brain bucket. I see, said the blind coroner as he picked up his hammer and saw."

"Yep," OhJim said, "he sure is. Dead, that is. Sure glad we cut him a jack-o'- lantern lid. Might come in handy on Halloween."

"Blunt-force narrows the field to anyone, male or female, who can wield a baseball bat to the blind side," I said. "Still, it is a piece of information."

"Bingo," Tommy said. "This stuff should have been in the newspaper weeks ago, but no one seems to care about poor Billy Zeohn. A field trip to his apartment might be more fruitful, even if the locals have gotten there before us, which they have. Like I said, no one really cares about this guy. They pretty much phoned in that bit of investigation."

"I've never done a black-bag job," David said. "This will be interesting."

"Have you ever done a black-bag anything?" Jim said.

"Yeah," OhJim said, "or maybe something in a plaid?"

"Next question," Eve said. "Will your friend Jane do a story about Zeohn's family and friends, and are there any data out-front about a connection between the two?"

"Question No. 1: Yes, Jane will do a story," Tommy said. "I will salt the mine with some fool's gold flakes to excite the journalistic magpie reflex."

"**Magpie reflex**?" Eve said.

"Right. Reporters can't resist shiny little bits of information," Tommy said. "Jane is no exception."

"And question No. 2?" Eve said. "Any connection?"

"Jane told the locals **no**," Tommy said, "and she usually stays reasonably close to the truth in dealing with her sources in the Cop Shop. But I can go deeper on that when I talk with her. I'm betting that Zeohn was a stalker of the **look-but-don't-touch** type."

"When do we break and enter?" David said.

"Now," Tommy said. "I have the key. It was laying in an unquiet way in the evidence box, like a nervous hen, so I liberated it, Huck."

Adventures in apartment living
| 11October08 |

"It was so messy," David said, "that we had no idea where to start or when to stop. We finally just left. We were walking on compressed paper the whole time. It was weird, like being in the tall grass and not knowing when some rodent or snake would dart up your pants leg."

"Well," Eve said, "take it from the top, Dear."

"We walked up to the apartment building and went in the side door and up to the second floor," David said. "Tommy had the key, so we just walked right in. The stench was unbelievable, and not just because the place had been shut up for weeks. Zeohn was a little porky piggy when it came to being a housekeeper."

"Why do you think that no one has cleaned out the place?" I said.

"The building is a real dive," David said. "The kind of place where some burnout is in charge of collecting rent, unplugging toilets, changing light bulbs, and getting apartments ready to rent. Judging from the lack of attention to all those details, I'm betting that things happen only when someone from the rental agency screams bloody murder."

"Did you find anything interesting?" Eve said. "Any photos?"

"We did come away with this Bible," David said, "but that's about it. There may be all kinds of stuff under the paper and trash that was strewn everywhere. The cops had a go and we had a go, but the Hope Diamond could be in there and no one would ever find it."

"Continue," I said. "You're doing just fine."

"I think I know why our killer let us know this victim's name," David said. "It doesn't make a bleep's bit of difference one way or the other. This was a shadow of a person at best."

I took the Bible -- a black pasteboard model, King James Version -- and opened it to the presentation page.

It said, **Given to Billy Zeohn for perfect attendance, Zion Community Church, Easter 1982**. It was signed, **Pastor Joseph Gazilot**.

Not much, but something.

Something that the detectives missed. I walked over to Eve's computer and typed in the church name. No hits. The pastor's name. No hits. For yucks, I typed in **Zeohn Bill Buffalonya**. Nothing conclusive beyond those Web sites that offer to trace persons for a fee while teasing you with a bunch of names that resemble but don't match the one you are looking for.

"Where's Tommy?" I said.

"Home taking a shower, which," David said, "I soon will do."

News from the Tribal Home front

| 12October08 |

When David said that he was going home to take a shower, he meant that he was going to the Tribal House.

Things have been interesting on the home front, to say the least.

David has taken the unused bedroom on the second floor, where my brothers have been living. Jeanne has moved into the attic, which features a dry, snug room the length of the house, with the requisite garret-style ceiling. The boys on the second floor have behaved themselves, as far as Jeanne is concerned, as has she. For that matter, so have Eve and I.

That-there is some full disclosure for you.

Since the house is big, we don't trip over one another, which is a good thing. And since we do like one another -- and some of us have even stronger ties, of blood or relationship-rising-to-the-commitment-level-of-marriage, it does not surprise me we get along (with the occasional spat).

Each floor has its own door to the stairwell, which was added when the second story and attic were added to the original single-story house. We come and go without disturbing one another any more than we wish to.

As I predicted, the neighbors are gob-smacked when it comes to our Punk Princess and her comings and goings, and the amazing and gratifying results she gets from a wardrobe of well-fitting black items and red accents.

Why should the 'hood be any different from anywhere else?

Jeanne has had a rough life, with many terrible and terrifying episodes, at far too early an age, mainly with men who should have been indicted, but she has come out the other side a mature and beautiful young woman with only a few tics and quirks and quarks.

Tommy has been the butt of that, lately, but he is not complaining.

Jeanne is proof that it is not what happens to you that counts as much as your decisions about what has happened and your chosen responses.

The men in my orbit are coming to love her as much as they do Eve, with the same promise for anyone who evens speaks, let alone acts, to the contrary.

Jeanne says it is a lot like dorm life except the boys are men (whom she likes and trusts). My brothers only pretend, for comic effect, to wish for more than that from Jeanne.

And David?

He is an open book.

The situation on the grounds

| 13October08 |

Email from Gentle Ben --

Dear friends and family:

I am enjoying my stay with "Clan Cleanue" very much. Baldi and Luce are wonderful, and I think that you know how I feel about Jo-Joe.

I'm upgrading security and doing maintenance on their computer systems.

We have had many conversations about the dark arts that you wanted them to teach me, and I am in awe of the world that their instruction represents. Baldi says that I'm almost ready for field work. A trip to cyberspace maybe.

You were right when you said that this little tribe is hidden in plain sight. Their house is nothing much to look at on the outside, but inside it is marvelous and reflects the riches that have come their way. I don't understand why they insist on staying in a moldering neighborhood, but no one is asking my opinion and I have not forced it on them.

Waiting for orders
Yr friend and crafty hacker ... Ben, gently

A no-knock knock-knock
| 14October08 |

I'm taking a few days off with Eve, so Jim and OhJim will be posting some jokes and stuff.

Here begins the time of posting, by Jim and his idiot brother, OhJim (don't stare at him; it makes him crazy). Hi, you are reading Jim's post, standing in for his brother Goose, who gets to go away with Eve, like the spoon running away with the dish. That's our Eve.

Here is a knock-knock joke that I kyped from someone. I can't remember who it was, though. It goes like this:

Knock-Knock
Who's there?
Control Freak ... and now <u>you</u> say, "Control Freak who?"

I like that and so does my idiot brother, who BTW will be posting tomorrow.

In the meantime, here is another joke:

(I suppose it isn't politically correct to call my brother an idiot.

(If I meant it, it would be a terrible thing.

(As it is, you can judge for yourself. Tomorrow.)

What did **Delaware**?
New Jersey.

And **the sand was hot to Molly**.

One joke that you'll never hear from me is any variation of **Pop goes the weasel**.

Pop was adamant about the **Pop/weasel thing**.

He didn't want to hear anything about that particular pairing, and he didn't want to even talk about why he didn't.

Message received. No **Pop goes the weasel** from this corner.

Over and out
Jim

OhJim takes the High Road low
| 15October08 |

Hello, strangers all. OhJim here. AKA OtherJim.

If you have read my brother Goose, you know from his posts that I have had a lot of nicknames, from the early days with our Pop (he called me **OtherJim**), and continuing onward.

I've settled on **OhJim**, though, because Jeanne gave me that one, and Jeanne is very important to me, and my other brother Jim. And let me just say, my brother Jim is the idiot in the family, not me. How do I know this? Because the blackbird is involved in what I know, and because among twenty snowy mountains the only thing moving is the eye of the blackbird; because of those petals on a wet, black bough; because one could do worse than be a swinger of birches; because anybody lives in a pretty how-town.

I know a lot of things, at least in part or pieces.

Actually, my brother and I are like two pees in a pod -- we're both mad as hatters, and joyfully so. He usually takes the lead, and I usually follow, because life is way too short to argue over who gets to be first. The way we do things, either position has its advantages, and either position can deliver the giggles.

We're like basketball players who can pivot off either foot and go to the basket with the ball in either hand.

You may wonder why we crack wise so often, and you may assume that we aren't all that serious about things.

We aren't, er, are. Let's just say that we take being **lite** very seriously, and we care deeply about **not** making a lot of sense. And we used to tell the truth, all the time, with no exceptions. And things are different now. We're much happier now.

You can't believe a word that I say. And Jim, the same.

With a grain of salt? More like a bag of peanuts or a pot of peenuts.

Good luck with this.

We're pulling for you.

I mean it!
OhJim

It was good to get away
| 16October08 |

As much as I love my new life, my redeemed life, my life with colors and feelings, I also enjoy a few days away, once in a while.
That is a new thing for Eve and me.
Time off.
Because Spookistan stands apart from time, as a side effect of a general, pervasive suspension of all rules as we know them, **taking time off** was not an option when we lived there. Time itself was in a warp. Time was a suspended thing that one remembered but did not miss. Much.
The time of exile that we entered, kicking and screaming, when we were thrown from the train, was a hard bounce in the dust that restarted our clocks. Suddenly, we once again knew Time, and we suddenly knew that we were lost in Space. And like those who learn that they must either forgive or forget, and move on, or be destroyed by bitterness and rage, we slowly came to savor Time -- its seconds, minutes, hours, and days -- as Time worked its healing in us.
And by re-acquainting ourselves with Time, we also drew near -- for some, for the first time -- to the knowledge that we were going to die.
Not now, but soon, or later.
You might think that death is the spook's constant companion.
The reality is that in the shadows you become a wraith, and you walk in a fog, and you do things that later will be one of the many reasons why you find yourself screaming yourself awake from dreams that you know are yours but not how or why. This is part of what waits to greet you if you are lucky enough to be born again in the tossing aside that happens to those who find the one way out of Spookistan, life intact and ticking once more.
Sound dramatic?
You better believe it.
When the big and little hands too strong for me grabbed me by the back of the neck and the seat of the pants, and cast me back into the light, it was the God I had mocked in my covert work who caught me on the first bounce, like a fuzz-free tennis ball, the kind dogs gnaw smooth and slimy.
I was as one thrown against a brick wall in an alley of broken dreams.
God was waiting there, oddly aloof and gently focused, offering to guide me in the ways of Life with a capital **ell**.
God waits in the kind of place where bodies show up in dumpsters.
I don't know why. I just know. Ok?

≈ ≈ ≈

Pop tried, with some success, to inhabit both the shadow world and the **bright-lights, big-city** world of wine, women, and song. He fathered the three of us, the **Bros Grim**, and he imparted to us stern lessons that made Tough Love look like sissy stuff. Out of his desire to serve two ravenous masters who had their hooks in him so deep that he finally was pulled apart to satisfy their rival claims, Pop created a life in death and a death in life, where he was never happy and only partly alive.

Pop had something of the zombie monster about him. Still, we loved him, and he loved us.

Pop's wives, our mothers, fared less well, at Pop's hands, because he had no ability to love them but only an intense desire to use them. The blessing for our moms was that Pop struck like Zeus in swan's feathers covering Leda, and flew on just as quickly. Perhaps they recovered, and survived. Just perhaps. We have never seen them, and we assume that they are dead, and we have always deemed it best to allow this vital connection to languish.

You might expect us to be monsters. We **were** cursed, each of us in his own way, to take on shadowy work that demanded a surrender of the soul in exchange for a changeless grin, a free ride, and an empty soul. We sleep-walked our way through most of adult life in a nightmare without feeling. When we found one another again, we felt whole again, for the first time since diapers.

My story, you know in part.

My brothers' stories you will hear when they are ready to tell you.

≈ ≈ ≈

Pop's desire to inhabit both worlds destroyed him, but not before he collected, and safely stored, critical information and issued specific threats based on his cunning cache of information -- the **Vault**.

Someday I'll tell you about how Pop died.

As Pop's chosen one to follow in his work in the shadows, I had this critical information that Pop had collected firmly in hand and when I was thrown from that train and had bounced like a ball into the arms of a loving God, I took steps to renew the threats and secure anew the proofs of the Vault.

Thus, I suppose, does a Spook show the love of God to a hurting world.

I was slow to come to a sense of the demands God's love laid on my life.

Gratitude was one of many foreign feelings that I reclaimed one at a time, and sometimes for the first time. In the time since being tossed back into life, I have been following a path that is well-trodden, with a trail marker that says **The Way of Fear and Trembling**.

In the shadows, I could not feel my feelings and survive.

I could not have a moral sense of what it was I was doing, and survive.

I could not have desires, and survive.

I could not live my life, and survive.

In the light of exile, I learned to feel, and to think and feel at the same time, and to have a sense of self again, like a man waking up from an induced coma meant to save his life by giving his mind and body time to heal without the self's meddling and muddling.

The greatest of the things that I got back, for the first time, was the ability to love. That, as I have told you, was Eve's doing.

When you have nothing, you have nothing to lose.

When you are a spook, you might as well be a zombie.

When you come to your senses in the dark wood where the straight way is lost, you experience a lifetime's worth of fear and trembling in an instant. If you survive, you come back to life for good, and you know in that moment how precious life is and how fragile your life has always been.

There are many frightening things in this life --

- A Calvinist convinced that she is doing the will of God.
- A spook come back from hell.

The straight way was the spook's way. The straight way was the way of no choices, no feelings, and no fear. The crooked way is my way, now, with fear and trembling, an aching love of life, and a powerful desire to love, to bless, and not to possess, my self and my loved ones, and my life itself.

I hold my life lightly now, and well.

And that is my hope for you, too.

I guess that you might say I have come back for good.

Bouncing quirky stuff off Tommy

|17October08|

Email from Goose to Tommy -- **The operational merry-go-round** --

My dear friend:

I couldn't sleep last night, so I made a list of operational assumptions concerning my very good and missing friend Mr. Black. Here they are in the order in which they floated to the top of the cesspool that I call my mind -- damned if I know whether they are ranked, or just rank --

- Mr. Black is worth more out in the open than he is dead or detained, or otherwise neutralized.
- We do not need to know all the **whys** in order to make positive use of Mr. Black's puzzling actions and his decision to disappear. The quark does have his quirks, which no one knows better than I do.
- Mr. Black can uncover networks and plots aimed at the Tribe, if we allow him to move as he wishes and if we can chart his moves at any level of accuracy, like positing the existence and movement of quarks.
- Mr. Black can be allowed to continue on in any way that he wishes without endangering the Tribe and its aims or those of its friends, such as yourself.
- Mr. Black should be causing our foes to make sympathetic and noticeable movements that we can pick up on, and probably with more success than we can chart our quark.

Forgive any appearance of discounting your abilities or understanding of trade-craft.

I find it best to spell out what I believe to be common goals and approaches.

To that end, do you quibble with any of my points, or have any to add, or would you delete any?

Yours in secrecy
Goose

The F-Troop rides again, again
| 18October08 |

I got an email from Tommy.
He acknowledged my midnight musings.
His quibbles were small enough to be called by some other name, he said.
"This meeting of the F-Troop will come to rue or ruin," I said.
"Be more positive with your feedback, Mister Chair Sir," Jim said.
"Yeah," OhJim said, "feedback is hard on your amplifier, your speakers, and your screaming fans' ears."
"I call," I said, "on lovely Naomi to read the minutes of the last meeting."
"I rise to that occasion, Mister Chair Sir," Jeanne said, "and I offer the following for your consideration and commiseration."
"And remember," Jim said, "as the Bard himself was wont to say, **Forewarned is forsworn.**"
"Yeah," OhJim said, "and **forewarmed is pre-heated.**"
"Googling over here, Mister Chair Sir," David said, punching his thumbs at the small wireless internet phone device in his lap. "I find no references despite an excellent concordance of Shakespeare to the phrase **forewarned is forsworn,** by any spelling."
"This is passing strange," Jim said.
"Yeah," OhJim said. "This thing of darkness, mine."
"Mister Chair Sir!" Mister Ed said -- thundered, is more like it. "I propose, as parliamentarian of this varied and checkered assemblage, that the question concerning the words **forsworn** and **forewarned**, and the likely, or indeed the probable, nay, the exact source of said words, is extraneous to these proceedings, which I might add have not proceeded far at all. In fine, Mister Chair Sir, I propose that you rule one and all out of order and return to the request that you made to our fair scribe, Jeanne of Goth and Princess of Punks."

The minutes are ours when we clutch at them ...
| 19October08 |

"Mister Chair Sir," Jeanne said, "my minutes look more like something bigger -- hours, maybe. I refer you to this flip chart from the last meeting."
"Yours, mine, and ours?" Jim said.
"Yeah," OhJim said. "**Hours,** brother, and not **ours.** Hers."
Jeanne rose, turned on a slender heel (dark red pumps today).
She walked to the wall where the flip chart resided.

Jeanne knows how to make a point. And I don't mean just with her choice of heels. We were ready to cede that.

Or stipulate that.

Or both.

"This," Jeanne said, "is the list of field trips flowing from of our wide-ranging discussion on a spectrum of topics with a mutually satisfying conclusion."

"I like your conclusion," Jim said. "I'm satisfied."

"Yeah," OhJim said, "and your foregone preclusion, too. I like you coming and/or going."

Jeanne gave my brothers her best sideways smile, some bitter and a lot sweet.

Jeanne was one of the few who acknowledged their pun-ishments.

Come to think of it, her **I-just-sucked-on-a-lemon** smile was the perfect counterpoint to my brothers' puns. The rest of us usually just took the pun-ishments in silence. A silence broken by the occasional groan, mind you.

My brothers did not mind the silence.

Nay, keeping silence is like pouring gas on their fire.

"We are moving forward," I said. "Tommy and David visited the apartment that Bill Zeohn lived in, when he was among the living, and David has written the brief that you have in your hand, or hands, as the case may be."

"I always use two hands," Jim said. "No way I want to drop the ball."

"Yeah," OhJim said. "Me, too. Coach goes ballistic if we don't, and do."

"Mister Chair Sir," Jeanne said, "I propose that we schedule the rest of the field trips mentioned on the list."

"Yes," I said, "and I also want to talk about a meta-exercise that will include all of us and the other Tribe, too."

"The other tribe?" David said. "Isn't one quasi-criminal enterprise enough for one city on the edge of the **Abyss of Greatness**?"

"Yes, Dear," Eve said, "the other Tribe -- Baldi, Luce, Jo-Joe, and Ben."

"How soon I forgot," David said. "The **Tribe** and the **OhTribe**."

"Mister Chair Sir," Jim said, "I move that we so call the Other Tribe."

"Yeah," OhJim said, "as the son and recipient of the maker of the moniker, I second the motion."

When I called the vote, everyone voted by the usual sign -- two thumbs up and two middle fingers touching. Mister Ed joined in the fun, and he refrained from flagging the fact that there was a proposal, from Naomi, on the floor, gathering dust.

David's essay on breaking/entering
| 20October08 |

What I did this summer

By David the GreenGuy*

These are some additional notes I made to go with the oral debriefing that Goose and Eve conducted with me after I returned from going through the apartment of second **Mystery Man** victim Bill Zeohn.

I summarize the debriefing at the end of this piece.

The first thing to say about the apartment, which was on the second floor of a three-story apartment building on one of the side streets not too far from the bookshop (Gazetteer Street) is this: It was a mess, mostly from paper of all sorts and many varieties -- newspapers, magazines, junk mail, pizza boxes.

The second thing to say about the apartment is that the stench was something that you almost, but not quite, could put out of mind. Part of that was the fact that the place had been sealed with police tape and the windows were closed. The rest is a testament to the way this man lived.

He lived like an oinker.

The locals, in the form of our old friends Dets. Blucote and Schmidt, had gone over the place with a one-tooth comb, like a couple of dorks. I doubt that they found anything of note, because they clearly had upended the contents of boxes and drawers to do a drive-by on the contents.

Problem is, they added to the depth of the detritus on the floor, which added to the enormity (and I mean **enormity**) of the job ahead for anyone who thought that the paper carpet held any buried treasures.

I learned in my anthro class and my archaeology field class that a kitchen midden takes centuries to reach a height of a few inches. Bill Zeohn, with the ham-fisted help of Blucote and Schmidt, had created a paper-based midden in every room in the house -- in a single lifetime.

Like the detectives before us, we did a sampling of the midden. Partly because it was just too daunting a task to do properly and partly because Zeohn truly was a guy that no one, including us, as it turned out, cared much about.

He made his mess and lived in it, and any hope of learning about him died in it, as far as investigative excellence goes.

Tommy explained to me that one develops a sense about these things, and he judged that based on the quality and quantity of the midden in the apartment that there was nothing of value to be had by diligent application of several days of work by a team of forensic types.

Tommy pointed out that the papers were compressed. He pulled at the edge of the stuff in the front room. It had utility bills from the 80s and newspapers as old or older. Tommy said that anyone who had hidden anything in that mess would have disturbed the uniform crust and compacted interior. He likened it to a mole's trail through a lawn.

No one had disturbed the midden, except to kick at it around the edges.

We decided that we would not go any further with the floor coating.

"There might be a treasure in there somewhere," Tommy told me, "but no one wants to pay the bill to seek it, especially if no one finds anything."

So we sampled the mess, mostly by applying a judicious kick-and-peek method.

Tommy also taught me about the obvious places to look for important things that people hide.

We looked in the closets.

We overturned the couch and easy chair, and felt for bumps and bulges.

All we found was the odor of old furniture.

All we found was lint, pennies, and more lint.

We looked in the medicine cabinet, and we looked under the bed and behind the chest that once had had a padlock on it but no longer, thanks to the detectives who had gone before us.

We went through the pockets in the few coats and pants in the bedroom. Nothing.

We tumbled what was left in the freezer and took a look, very quickly, at the contents of the fridge.

That was nasty.

Shortly after, we left, having found nothing of interest except a pasteboard Bible like kids get in Sunday School. The Bible had been left in the chest in the bedroom.

We vowed to take showers ASAP, and did.

These are points I covered in my debriefing with Goose and Eve:

• No one has cleaned out the apartment, we assumed, because it is the sort of low-rent place that has some burnout in charge of collecting rent, fixing problems such as burned-out light bulbs or dripping faucets, and cleaning up the empties for the next renter. Judging from the lack of attention to lighting in the halls and the fact that every faucet in Zeohn's apartment was dripping, we figured that the **go-to guy** only responded to loud threats from the rental agency. A **go-to-hell guy**, I'd say.

• The killer is playing with us by choosing a victim such as Zeohn that no one cares about. We will not find much solid but Zeohn's name.

• The Bible may warrant some footwork. It is a Sunday School presentation Bible that cost a dollar or two. The inscription reads, **Given to Billy Zeohn for perfect attendance, Zion Community Church, Easter 1982. -- Pastor Joseph Gazilot**. Googling the church and pastor yielded no hits. Maybe Baldi knew this guy Gazilot.

---

* Those of you who have forgotten why I'm the GreenGuy may recall my undercover trip to the coroner's office and my quick exit after getting a peek at the morgue mugshot of the battered and faceless victim whom we once thought was Mr. Black.

Youse go here ... and here
| 21October08 |

"Ok," I said, "thank you, David. You learned at the feet of a master."

David smiled and nodded, aping Jeanne's signature sideways smile.

That brought a chuckle from us all.

Jeanne rewarded David with the real thing. Sideways. Bitter and sweet.

"I'll add **call Baldi about Zeohn's pastor from the 80s**," Jeanne said, "to the list of things to do. I also will add **Jeanne will start a Murder Book**."

"A murder book is long overdue," I said.

"Yes, Jeanne Dear," Eve said with a Buddha Girl smile. "A plan, ma'am."

The Murder Book, Intro
| 22October08 |

Jeanne took off a black pump with a long and lethal-looking spike and rapped smartly on the floor.

"Now that I have your attention," Jeanne said, "I'll pass out the first part of the murder investigation chronology that I'm working up."

"This looks good, Dear," Eve said. "I like your understanding that how you begin has everything to do with how you continue and where you go."

"I like the way you have with shoes myself," Jim said.

"Yeah," OhJim said, "me, too. **AOL. LOL. YMMV. ROTFL. RTFM.**"

"What is he talking about?" Tommy, who was able to make the tail-end of the meeting, said.

"Ever heard of Google?" David said. "Use it. It's all there, even most of OhJim's obscurities. **GIYF.** Translation: **Google Is Your Friend.**"

"**BTW**," I said, "I like this approach, too, Jeanne. Clear as a bell."

"Yeah," OhJim said, "and colder than hell. Google that and see how you like it, Tommy whoever-you-are."

"A word on these words," Jeanne said. "I can see that I will be doing a synopsis of Goose's daily posts, then I will be doing a more traditional, and separate, chronology of the three murders themselves. And I won't slay trees left and right. The rest I'll post to the network."

This was what Jeanne gave us:

Murder Book - Style Sheet

Compiled by Jeanne Wheenin (former reporter, current bookshop clerk).

Some thoughts out front about how this book will be constructed –

• The book will be chronological in general, with the understanding that some entries will be the result of later work and will be out of sequence.
• This book will be kept in a searchable form on my computer, with a copy posted to Eve's computer as the book is updated.
• I will interview Goose and others as needed to reconstruct the initial time-line before I came on board after quitting my job at the Daily Afterblatt, Lake Effect edition. Attribution will be assumed from the context.
• I also will draw upon the writing that Goose has done concerning the case of Mr. Black, subsequent developments, and the blog posting that he has been doing on our private network.
• The usual steps to secure the data will be in force including encryption of all emails but also the contents of local boxes and blog posts to our private network, and firewalls, VPN tunneling, and the security-augmented blog software that David and I have developed for Goose's posting project with mucho help from Resident Hacker Ben Whick.

Note: It is our common opinion that we have taken all necessary steps to secure our data from prying eyes by using a Virtual Private Network protocol with additional security features from Gentle Ben that you do not need to know.

A briefing on Zeohn's photo files
| 23October08 |

"Take one down," Jim said.

"Yeah," OhJim said, "and pass it around."

"This is a briefing paper on our attempts to track down Bill Zeohn's photo files," Jim said. "We'll give you the executive summary, which is the same, almost, as the report. In short, we have zip. Well, we have one crazy idea."

In fact, the paper that they handed out was a fair drawing of a goose egg.

"Yeah," OhJim said. "So far we can't prove to our satisfaction that this guy ever put film in his camera."

"He seems," Jim said, "to have been a shadowy presence at most photo opps downtown, but we are actually being serious when we speculate that this guy was shooting blanks."

"Yeah," OhJim said. "There is the problem of who we are -- guys with no standing to be asking questions about a murder victim, even if we use the P.I. pose, so we have been passing ourselves off as old friends who wonder what happened to all those wonderful photos that Bill used to take. We've talked with photo department people at the **Daily Afterblatt**, over the phone, and made very general inquiries about Zeohn, but they say that they have never bought anything from him because, for one thing, he never offered them anything."

"Thus," Jim said, "my brother's seemingly whimsical assumption that our dead guy would show up and only pretend to shoot photos. We did establish that he used an old print camera, not a digital one, so the possibility stands that he was just fooling around, and there are, on the other hand, no computer files to track down, since he was **Old School** all the way."

"Stranger things have happened," I said. "We will go with that assumption, for now, that Zeohn for reasons we do not know was shooting blanks with an empty print film camera."

"Yes, Dears," Eve said, "we have no motive for his murder, and it seems that his freelance presence may have been fatal for him. Otherwise, we have no clue, so ruling out what we can imagine is the place to start. Very good work, my little Grimlins."

My brothers beamed.

"I don't know," Mister Ed said, "if Zeohn was dull in the head and only pretended to be taking pictures, but I certainly have heard stories from photo-journalist friends who thought they were shooting with film in but learned later, on their way out the door, pink slip in hand, that they had forgotten to load film before shooting. Editors go off their rails when photogs pull dumb tricks like that. It would be like a press crew running several miles of newsprint through a press with no ink on the rollers."

"I bet you only do that once -- shoot with no film," David said, "-- unless you are only out to amuse yourself and get off on the subterfuge of making people think that you are taking photographs. Maybe it made him feel better about himself, somehow, some way."

"And our victim Zeohn," Jeanne said, "certainly was quirky, what with the compacted-paper rug that you found in his apartment and all the rest. That kind of decorating taste comes at a high personal price. I remember him as a very creepy presence in the background at various media events.

His camera flash certainly worked, and he would stalk around and shoot up a storm. It could very well be that his grip on sanity was an off-and-on sort of thing. This might strengthen the stalker hypothesis, too."

"I once," David said, "was asked to shoot pictures at a family event, and I realized halfway through that I had only brought one roll of film, so I did begin to pretend to take pictures of people, and tell them to say **cheese** and all that bleep. It actually was rather amusing, and because I had a few shots to show for my efforts, no one was the wiser and I never had to come clean about my error. But that is still a long way from what we are thinking Zeohn was doing."

"And," Eve said, "whether he was shooting with film or only pretending to, if he was in the wrong place at the wrong time, taking photos, or so it seemed, he might have been killed for nothing except an assumption. The killer could have gone to his apartment, looking for prints and negatives, found none, but have been surprised by a returning Zeohn. A blow to the base of the skull would not have registered much trace material in that pig pen environment."

"Yes," I said, "we do not know where he was killed and we do not know why he was killed, except we do know that where he was dumped was done after he was killed at some other location. The locals seemingly have no idea about where, and I'm betting that they don't really care."

Newsies put their noses together
| 24October08 |

"Jane Carlotto," Jeanne said, "stands for the bull-bitch bottle-blond style of getting on in a man's world."

"That doesn't sound politically correct, Dear," Eve said. "I like that."

"No," Jim said, "it sounds like Jeanne."

"Yeah," OhJim said, "our fair sister."

"This is very interesting," I said, "but a briefing on the aspects of your inquiries that shed light on Bill Zeohn would be even more interesting."

"Well," David said, "we had a talk with Jane Carlotto at that scruffy bar downtown near the **Afterblatt** building and sorry, Grimlin Guys, Jeanne introduced me as her boyfriend. Jane seemed pleased. Said so, anyway."

"Jane is a lot like you are, Eve," Jeanne said, "but she has a hard edge that one does not find with you. And a portly book-selling boyfriend she calls **Hudso**n who she says does not get out much."

"More," I said.

"Well," Jeanne said, "we set it up so that we could tell Jane that I was showing David some of the sights from my old life and we just happened to run into her at the bar."

"Good, Dear," Eve said.

"Newsies love to gossip," Jeanne said, "so it was child's play to lead Jane to a discussion of Bill Zeohn as soon as the pleasantries were done. All I did was make a general comment about how no one, even a creepy person like

Zeohn, deserved to be dumped in the street."

"Jane," David said, "had some choice words to say about Zeohn. We were right in thinking that he was a creepy stalker type. She said he was always sticking his camera in her face and taking pictures of her. Staring at her. Following her around when she was on assignment."

"But she said Zeohn never rose to the level of scary stalker," Jeanne said. "Jane said he was always just a creepy type of gawker."

"Jeanne tried out the idea that Zeohn was running around with a camera but no film," David said. "Jane just laughed at that and said **why bother**. She didn't have any information one way or another, though."

"She didn't have any new details about him," Jeanne said, "so I think that we have gone just about as far as we can on Bill Zeohn."

"On to the next thing, then," I said. "And remember that we still don't know why her picture was in Zeohn's file."

"That could be everything and nothing," Jeanne said. "Who knows why things end up in police files. Half the time the police have no clue about half of the clues that they collect."

"We have so little right now," I said, "that we can just assume that there was a reason that we don't know yet for Jane Carlotto's picture being in Zeohn's file. And that is after I give a huge margin to the fact that Blucote and Schmidt would not know a clue even if it could dance and sing its way into their little hearts."

Goose lives up to his name
| 25October08 |

Email from Goose to Tommy -- **A little poke** --

Dear sole mate:

How's tricks?

We're moving along on several fronts and have been checking on Bill Zeohn, as you know so well (David briefed us on your visit to the apartment). David also went with Jeanne to talk with Jane Carlotto, who basically said that Zeohn was a creepy gawker but not much as a stalker. I suspect that we're spending too much time on this poor dead loser because we don't have anyone else to pick on at this moment in time.

Thus the email. And since it is not advisable to bleep with a streak, we're sticking with Zeohn -- for one last question. Do you know anything about where Zeohn was actually killed? Or to put it to you another way -- do the locals give a rip about Zeohn and are they putting any energy into pinning down those details? We are going with massive head trauma from a heavy blunt object. Correct?

Goose

I hit the button to send the email and had just started a serious petting session with Wild Billy when I got a reply from Tommy --

Dear flower wasting its scent on the desert air:

I actually like being your sole reader, for a couple of reasons --

- If you had more, your pinhead would grow to alarming proportions.
- Wider circulation would be a security nightmare.
- Adversity builds character.
- _____ [fill in the blank].

If you get tired of the lack of notoriety, Jeanne could take over.

I have no answers to your excellent questions, but give me a day or two and I will have something. My suspicion is that the locals aren't spending any time on any aspect of the case and its three victims. Still, I will check and see what they say. Double-blind for you, of course.

Your friend and shadow named Tommy

Who we worked for in the shadows
| 26October08 |

Email from Goose to Tommy -- **Who is The Man? --**

My covert brother:

I have been thinking about cabbages and kings, or presidents, really. And I have been thinking about my work in the shadows of Spookistan.

Well you might ask yourself, **Why is Goose linking himself with presidential matters**?

Here is the crop --

I begin with the realization that no matter who is in power -- be he a he or a she, and a liberal, a conservative, or a mugwump -- the President will make use of spooks and the work that only they can do.

In my bitterness, I once thought that Spookistan was the creation of rightist elements of the ugliest caricature of conservative privilege, because to my horror, when I came to myself in that dark wood on the way to the light, I knew that **The Man** whom I had been working so hard for did not share any of the ideals that I was discovering in myself -- a sense of justice rather than privilege, a sense of the love of God rather than the manipulation of the masses, and on and on.

Now I know better. Power attracts, spawns, and utilizes covert activities. All types and stripes of power. The more things change, the more this will stay the same. In any case, I do not expect the dismantling of any spy agencies. Whoever is chosen as President next month will demand security briefings.

When I was a card-carrying citizen of Spookistan, I was charged with doing the bidding of others, beginning with my handler and continuing on up the food chain to the top, one would assume.

At the time, I didn't think about such things. In fact, I tried, with significant success, as underscored by my frequent wake-up-screaming fits in the middle of the night, to this day, to not think, or feel, anything that was not connected with my cover. I was a well-lubricated machine, and I did my work with lubricious zeal. I did not gaze at my navel, and I did not cry for the victims of the plots and counter plots that I took part in. The shadow world was a stage, and I was but one of the many players upon that stage. I stuck to my lines, which others wrote for me.

I was my father's son, and as the son of a spook I was determined to be better, last longer, and gain a more substantial reputation than Pop had among the shadow ministers of the parliaments and places of power in the underworld that I had chosen to live in and that was living into me in ways that almost killed me.

I ruined small careers for reasons I never asked for or would have understood. I participated in cleansing actions that purged our own ranks of persons deemed to be unfit for the quasi-police state that I was helping maintain.

I acted against citizens of my own country, for reasons I did not have any interest in at the time.

A hint of dissatisfaction has crept in to my discourse. Now. But then, I was not aware of any political, moral, or spiritual aspects of anything, particularly those aspects of my work that these days make my soul shrivel in the small hours when my guard is pinned down by the seductive arms of sleep.

The first crack in the boilerplate of my facade came when my under-the-cloth work in churches, **Operation Beloved**, where I subverted good people left and right, but particularly of the left, backfired. The public prayers that I prayed to maintain cover, and the other things that I did to create the illusion of a man of God, serving God's people, were mere words to me, until like Paul on the road to Damascus, I had a shattering and life-saving conversion experience, complete with fire and smoke, and **the Voice of God**. I no longer could stay blind to **who** I was and **whose** I was.

I did not know it at the time, but this was the beginning of the end of my time as a happy citizen of a place that dealt unhappiness to perceived internal enemies of the state.

My friend the Rev. Mr. Black, beside me in the fields of the Lord, mouthing the same platitudes and playing at the same illusions, at the same time had a similar experience. Call it **God's Economy**.

Two for One.

It took a while, but sooner than we expected, or could see coming, we were tossed from the floating world of spooks and told to fly away and never, ever look back.

Now, some years later, I know what a blessing it was that I had done my ugly work so well that it took what amounted to a **Deus ex machina** to stop me. The same can be said of Mr. Black. At first, upon reaching the borders of the real world, and seeing in my mind the motto that Dante places over the doorway to Hell -- **abandon hope, all you who enter here** -- I came in time, and with the help of Eve, to see that what I had feared would kill me was what saved my life and put me in a world of colors that I had not known since childhood.

Now I look to a future that certainly, and in a reasonable amount of time, will not include me, or my precious Eve. Eve and I spend hours talking about how to be who we are, and how to protect the Tribe that means more to us than anything except our own connection, while walking away from violence as the ultimate protection of what we hold most dear.

And if I solve this tangle, I probably will move on to **atonement**.

Goose

Goose, you ignorant slut
| 27October08 |

Email from Tommy -- **re: Who we work for in the shadows** --

Dear Brother Goose:

Or, **Goose, Goose, Goose** ... .

Or as Dan Aykroyd, aping James J. Kilpatrick, was fond of saying, "**Jane, you ignorant slut**."

Mind you, although I misquote from a parody of Kilpatrick, I did not quote my favorite phrase of Kilpatrick's, that he used when he found himself in agreement with his **Counterpoint** foe Shana Alexander --

**"If you lie down with dogs,
you end up with fleas ...
and I'm itching all over**."

Seriously. And honestly. Being younger, and of an arrogant cast, or caste, I can relate to your musings about **The Man**, but I cannot replicate your experience or feelings, or thoughts, for that matter, on the matter.

As one who, in your view, must be seen as inhabiting two worlds, one real and one floating in shadows, I can only acknowledge the pain and wisdom of your last post. No one knows better than you do that a convergence of two persons' self-interest can easily become, or begin, as a collision of self-interest. We have been blessed with a convergence rather than a collision, and I for one am mighty glad.

The work that I do, and the buffering work that you and your Tribe do, and have done, does not tolerate mistakes, though we make mistakes every day. Perhaps it is the willing blindness of my handler (who runs, and who runs me, true to type), and the notable absence of your handlers (who have treated you like Caliban ["**this thing of darkness**"]), that makes all the difference.

Know that I am glad that you were thrown from the train, but not under the bus, and all your mates, too, and your mate, Eve. Know that I understand that what happens to one can happen to all, and I spend a bit of my focus on such questions, but only a bit. You know why.

I, too, hear stories such as yours and say to myself, "It will be different for me." And it will, if only because no one steps into the same river twice, and no one can step into another person's puddle even once.

Your friendly shadow
Brother Tommy

Reach out and touch Baldi
| 28October08 |

I called Baldi about the pastor listed on the presentation page of Bill Zeohn's kid Bible -- **Zion Community Church ... Easter 1982 -- Pastor Joseph Gazilot.**
I was glad that I called, for several reasons --
- I like being close to Luce, and talking to Baldi is closer than talking to the wall.
- I like being close to Baldi, for he is a blessing-strewing guy.
- I like getting answers that do not start with ... **No, I don't know** ... .
Baldi said that Joseph "Gaz" Gazilot (**GAZ - ah - lot**, not **GAZ - ah - low**, which must have been a curse for the Rev. Mr. G. as a child) is long dead and was indeed pastor of Zion Community Church, on the East Side of the city, in the 60s through the 80s. Baldi said that Gazilot, who claimed, as did just about everyone else, that he marched with the Rev. Dr. Martin Luther King, was a dynamic preacher with a largely black congregation of middling size. Baldi had no idea why a white boy like Billy Zeohn would have attended the church (also, why not?). Baldi said that his recollection was that Gazilot died on Easter, in the 80s, but he could not be more specific. He suggested that I go microfiching at the Public Library (sort of a nice man's way of saying **RTFM**).
And that is what Baldi is, was, and ever more shall be, a **nice man** in the best sense of that tricky, turned-inside-out word. **Sweet** is closer to the point, perhaps. Baldi lives to be a blessing even in his wealthy exile.
And so does Luce, which makes her a joy to be near, as well as Baldi. Bet you thought that I was going to say something instead about her voluptuous allure or her safe-cracking laugh.
Just did.
Happy now?
Thought so.

Compiled by Jeanne Wheenin (former reporter, current bookshop clerk).

Chronology

On the night of April 1, 2008, Goose Grim happened upon an accident scene near President's Park near downtown Buffalonya. A man had been killed by a metro bus. The bus driver did not see the victim until it was too late. The driver and others told police investigators that the man was standing in the traffic lane with his arms outstretched, "as still as a statue."

By all reports, it was a dark and stormy night.

Goose assumed the identity of a Private Investigator doing some ambulance chasing. It was at the scene of the death that he first met a man that he first referred to as the **Stranger**, then as **Tommy** (no last name given). The two sized one another up as members of a fraternity of shadowy persons commonly known as spooks.

After hanging around to see what they could find out (nothing much), they had coffee and cemented an acquaintance that has grown in the weeks and months since that first death. There is a **BOMFOG** thing going on here.

The local press did not show interest in the story until a week later, when a staff-written (no byline) follow-up story gave the few details that the police said that they had. The lead detective, Joe Blucote, and his partner, Bill "Joe Bob" Schmidt, appealed to the public to come forward with any details that they might have. No one did, or has, come forward. The authorities still do not know who the victim was. He has been described as a business man in a well-made, dark suit, and dark-complected or well-tanned. His body yielded no wallet or identifying papers.

Blucote refused to talk about press speculation that the man had no wedding ring or other jewelry

The story quotes Dr. Bruce Backstaff, the county coroner, as saying an autopsy had been performed and toxicology tests were being done in the state forensics lab.

Initially, that was all that was known about the victim. Almost nothing.

Privately, however, Goose was beginning to realize that victim bore some resemblance to Mr. Black, a longtime associate from the shadows and later at the bookshop whom Goose (whose case name was **the Rev. Mr. White**) had known as **the Rev. Mr. Black** a long time ago in **Operation Beloved**. Goose decided that he would keep this to himself, and didn't even share it with his brothers. As Goose was to reveal, he had kept many things from his brothers.

Eve heard the whole story.

Goose has alluded to but has never disclosed what he referred to as a **single fact** about the victim that made him initially certain that the victim was Mr. Black, whom he initially gave the case name of **Parke Eno Darke**. In time, he settled on **Mr. Black**, after his knowledge was in wider circulation among his immediate circle – his partner, Eve, and his brothers, Jim and OtherJim now OhJim.

Goose knew that the man, if it was his associate Mr. Black, represented a life in the shadows, what he routinely calls **Spookistan**. Goose knew that news about that shadow life must not and never would be described in any way to the authorities, and the local authorities in particular. For a time, Goose kept his speculations to himself. In mourning the loss of his close associate, Goose vowed to himself that he would find out what had happened. In time he added the very real concern that the covert community built around the bookshop **Caspar's Books and That**, owned by Eve, was in danger because of what had happened to Mr. Black.

At this time, Goose was having some contact with Tommy but was being indirect about the true nature of their relationship. Goose referred, at first, to the **Stranger**, who was a faceless ear that Goose said he was whispering into -- telling about his relationship with Mr. Black and his initial conviction that to tell his brothers about his own shadow life would put them in a dangerous place. Increasingly, Goose found that he could not with any zeal continue to play at P.I. with his brothers and the little agency they started, and nested, in the backroom of the bookshop.

Real play would be more helpful, but how to begin?

A package in the mail

About two weeks after the man was killed by the bus, Goose received in the mail a journal that he had kept in spite of strict rules to the contrary during the years that he and Mr. Black had been undercover as ministers. Goose said that such journals were a common, if forbidden, tool for men and women who could talk to no one about their "true" work. They talked to the empty page, and it seemed to help with the isolation and loneliness.

The package did not have a return address, and there was no note inside, just his old journal that he didn't even know that he had mislaid. Goose has never found out who the sender was, but his first reaction was to decide that "someone has me in their sights."

At first, he read the journal with mild interest.

He did not recognize it as his own until he had sampled it at random. He said that he felt a rush of horror when he finally put together the echoes from the pages and remembered them as his own. In time, he decided, based on the fact that nothing catastrophic occurred, that the sender had been a friend. This alteration in his thinking seems to have put the matter on his back burner. He stopped thinking about the journal's return and moved on to more pressing matters. As he put it later, "I realized, as quickly as I went on **Code-Oh-Crap**, that an enemy would not have sent me the original of so shortsighted a thing as a written record of my covert life."

One wonders, though. One does.

As an aside, I would venture the guess that Mr. Black himself had sent the journal back to Goose, as a kind of code or warning. Goose refuses to speculate on or discuss this, beyond agreeing that that might have been the case, and I have to respect that, but my mind is not easy that we have totally mined the ore from that particular vein.

In April of this year, Goose began to write new journal entries based on entries from his old journal. He wrote about Mr. Black in particular but also about himself. He said that he and Mr. Black were like the black and white of a photographic negative because together they made a picture that could be understood. Goose posted to a VPN-based blog on the Tribe's private network, **for eyes only**.

Goose described how he had been ejected from the only life that he knew, Spookistan, and how he had wandered in a daze until stumbling one day on the bookshop, and Eve.

About three weeks after the man vs. bus death, the **Daily Afterblatt**, in its **Lake Effect edition**, ran a follow-up story that gave no new details, that said toxicology reports were still weeks from being done, and that repeated the appeal to the public to come forward with details, any details.

Goose and his brothers were moving their business into the backroom at the bookshop. This was a matter of great joy for the boys, and they enjoyed getting to know the place and its people. Goose still had not revealed anything about his life in the shadows of Spookistan beyond a bare outline of some of the facts to the Stranger.

A month later ...

About a month after the man vs. bus accident, the Bros Grim and Eve received a visit from Dets. Blucote and Schmidt. The detectives didn't really say why they were there, though they did know and admire Eve, and no one really asked them what they were looking for. Jim and OtherJim managed, almost without trying, to create a good deal of tension by teasing Blucote about how to say his name and speculating on where the name came from and what it might mean.

I get the impression that the detectives had been in the habit of making periodic visits to the bookshop when they were dealing with murky cases of the sort that the Mr. Black matter represented.

After alluding to that history, and begging for a call with any information possible, Blucote took himself and his partner away and did not return for a long time. However, in the course of the conversation, Blucote made veiled references to the sort of life that Goose had led -- and Eve had led, come to that.

The brothers Jim demanded an explanation.

Eve told Jim and OtherJim that Goose had an interesting and important story to tell them. She basically **outed** him to his brothers. She told the brothers that Goose had been recruited by their father to follow him into the shadow work that Pop had done all his life. She also **outed** their dead father, who they had not known was a spook just like their brother.

Eve insisted that it was time to be on the same page and to get serious about who had killed their old friend Mr. Black.

Jim and OtherJim had the insight that this very important matter concerning Mr. Black's life status should be the first, and only, case that the young detective agency should be working.

After being forced to do the right and the smart thing with his brothers, by Eve, Goose on his own decided to tell the Stranger, AKA Tommy, about his history. And as he had to that point, Goose continued to mask from the rest of us the true nature of both who Tommy was and what his relationship with Tommy was.

Eve as time went on became comfortable with a family theme that the Bros Grim had learned from Pop – laugh at what would otherwise destroy you and do not take things seriously if you can joke about them. Eve was more prone to bless and nurture those whom she met, but she began to loosen up a bit, too, and at least laugh at the jokes and puns that flowed like a rain-swollen storm drain. She did, however, maintain the focus on solving the demise of Mr. Black.

For example, was it murder?

Making a list ...

Where once there was one former spook in possession of information, now there were four crafty persons in possession of that knowledge.

So they made a list (an old, and current, pastime).

Goose wrote out the list in his journal that I and others turned into the private network blog that he continues to post to daily (note that he still was calling Mr. Black by the initial case name of **Darke**):

The four agreed that --

• Someone, singular or plural, was behind Mr. Darke's death (making it murder).

• Someone nice, perhaps Mr. Darke, sent me my old black-book journal. A foe would have withheld the thing for evil uses later on.

• Our lives depended on identifying the person or persons involved in Stipulation No. One.

• The identity of the friend in Stipulation No. Two might be of assistance. If it was Mr. Darke, it possibly spoke to his state of mind. At the least, it was a provocative detail to pin down, one of the few butterflies that we could see to chase at this point.

• We were on our own, and we could trust no one, friend or foe: Friends would be put in danger and foes would become more dangerous if we took anyone else into our circle of intention.

The four made a list of the things that they knew so far:

• Mr. Darke, AKA the Rev. Mr. Black, was dead, by misadventure.

• We knew what Dets. Blucote and Schmidt knew, and more.

• There would be weekly updates in the **Daily AfterBlatt** for a while yet. That could help us.

• We could trust the bookshop cadre of color-coded old men in narrow roles, with Eve as liaison.

• The brothers would work together, carefully, with ears open and mouths shut. They would be back to back at all times, like a parody of the **two-backed beast**, when it came to watching out for one another.

• Eve and I would work solo. That was our way and the safer option for us.

• We all would be carrying -- cell phones and otherwise. Licenses? Oh, please. Ask the drug dealer on your street if he has a weapon permit. His answer will be priceless.

• I would start with my memories of Mr. Darke, beginning with the most recent, and write a memo to brief the others.

At this point, Goose and the others were focused on the journal's return, but they quickly were distracted by other events. Notice, too, that Goose alludes to the fact, or fiction, that they would be **carrying**. He subsequently has made it clear that the elders of the Tribe have never relied on guns for protection.

NB: This is an example of his way with words and truth. You never really know where you are with Goose, except for what you need to know.

Another thing that Eve and the boys realized, about this time, was that the usual sources of information were suddenly made suspect by what they assumed had happened to Mr. Black. This proved to have an effect on the pace and scope of their investigation. They went even more slowly than before. And after that, they kicked back a little more.

In fact, until I came along, they did next to nothing.

Another follow-up story ...

Two months after the murder in the dark, near the park, the **Daily Afterblatt** ran a second follow-up story in the **Lake Effect edition**, still using staff reports. No hack wanted to touch the story. It hadn't budged in two months. There was a renewal of the plea for information, and the introduction of speculation among insiders that the death had been a murder. The story introduced the phrase, which has stuck, "The Mystery Man Murder." There was also insider speculation that the coroner was about to convene a Coroner's Jury in the matter. Turns out, that was right.

The Coroner's Jury was the first interesting thing in the case, and as an **Afterblatt** cop reporter, I was given the assignment to cover the proceeding, which I did. Along the way, I noticed a man (Mr. Red) outside the jury room who aroused my suspicions to the point that I followed him back to the bookshop. The jury quickly returned the verdict that the coroner sought -- "death by suspicious circumstances by a person or persons unknown."

As my story made clear, the coroner had no idea what had happened to the victim but he was convinced that someone had forced, coerced, or hypnotized him to stand there and take it from that bus.

My story stirred up the crew back at the bookshop, because I had written about the mystery man outside the courtroom door. Mr. Red.

I followed up my story with an sudden, unannounced visit to the bookshop, a favorite haunt of my younger days (I even knew Mr. Black by sight from that time). You might say that I did not know the danger that I was putting myself into when I walked into that backroom and made a proposal that they either had to accept, or kill me. I got lucky, and much more lucky than I realized, but I was working out of an existential nausea that I had not surfaced to consciousness at that point.

My proposal was this: Hire me as anything or I'll follow through on being a reporter and blow your Pop-stand to bits, in print.

Their decision?

They said "Ok." Their rationale, I did not know until they had abandoned it as an option and had welcomed me in full: If I work out, and prove to be who I say I am, I live. Otherwise, they know what to do and how to do it.

I wrote a long and somewhat naïve memo to my new colleagues to explain my motives and to reveal that I had had a conversation with one of the Cop Shop veteran reporters who had filled my head with stories about the bookshop and the shadowy characters who inhabited it.

(**Note to all the others**: Could this Deep Throat character have been the same one who talked later to Ben Whick and told him a similar story? Indeed, could it have been Mr. Black himself? He would have to be a master of disguises, manners, and voices, but apparently he was.)

That was back in May, and in the five months since I have been more happy, less hard-edged, and more hopeful than I ever have been at any time in my life.

It was the right move, and the elders made the right decision, to give me a life-or-death chance to show who I really wanted to become.

My coming onto the scene elevated David's status, since the elders of the Tribe wanted to bring us along together, so we could help one another.

They also hope to breed us, I think, but no one is talking about that, including me. Or David. **LOL**.

David had been hanging around the bookshop, after being recruited, but he had not gotten much training.

That began to change, and David started hanging out in the backroom with us, and Mr. Red, after a grand Old World hissy fit, grumped his way to the front desk and mostly has stayed there except for when Goose calls him back for specific reasons.

Compiled by Jeanne Wheenin (former reporter and current bookshop clerk).

The second victim

On June 5, the day after I quit my reporter job at the **Daily Afterblatt**, a story on the front page of the A section, written by intern Ben Whick, told of a body being found overnight in the middle of a busy intersection on the East Side of Buffalonya. Ben wrote that initial details were few except that the victim had been killed elsewhere, then dumped in the street.

The elders of the Tribe, on a hint from Mr. Red, began to court the idea that the second murder sounded a lot like Mr. Black's signature laugh line, with a twist. Mr. Black, who taught Mr. Red the many uses and meanings of the word **bleep**, would say little else, even to his friends. For example:

"Hello, my friend."

"**Bleep-**you" (one word with the accent heavily on the first syllable, according to his old and dear friend Goose).

The second murder was tantamount to the killer saying, ***Bleep you* in the middle of the street**, the elders decided.

My asking the simple question – **did anyone see the body of the first victim** – got a major project up and going. David and I went down to scam the coroner's crew so that we could see the body. David claimed to be a worried neighbor. When they showed him a photo of the victim's battered face, David turned green and ran from there, and promptly got sick.

We had a stern briefing from Goose on the need to go and come in pairs, at least the younger ones among us, and Jim and OhJim. The color-coded types could go as they wished, drawing upon their superior tradecraft and many years of experiences in shadow work.

Goose reported that just as they were pleased with my abilities, they also were pleased to see David step up to his new duties, which was a source of satisfaction for them. They recruited David for such things, and he was validating their instincts about him. Goose said that David's initial job had been to augment the aging zeal with which the color-coded guys protected Eve. A young hand was welcome here, Goose said, and he stressed that Eve did not need these attentions but that giving her these attentions helped one and all focus on what was most important to them.

The preparations for David's and my trip down to the Coroner's Office took a lot more time than might seem warranted, but we were getting to know one another and we were learning the tradecraft from our elders, David and I. But, still ... **WTF!**

That made the outcome – more questions and no new answers – an acceptable development in the right direction. That's not exactly accurate, however. It was on this trip that I found out, from an old source, the name of the second murder victim in the "Mystery Man Murders." Bill Zeohn.

The man that time forgot

A story in the **Daily Afterblatt, Lake Effect edition**, on June 23, under the byline of Ben Whick, summed up what the local authorities knew about the latest, and the first, murders in the case now known as the "Mystery Man Murders." A few things were known about Zeohn, but as time went on it became clear that no one really knew or seemed to care about Zeohn.

Here is an interesting quote from Ben's story -- attributed to a media person: "He was always in on the action, always around the ball, and always taking picture after picture with that annoying flash, flash, flash."

Ben's story also mentioned an unidentified young man who came to the Coroner's Office to see if the first victim was his missing neighbor. The story, however, did not blow David's cover, or ours.

We met to debrief on the trip to the Coroner's Office, but beyond a bunch of excellent puns, and a discussion of hair tints and dyes, we did not get anywhere in particular. In the days that followed, we entered what can only be described as a season of list-making. We brain-stormed on what we knew, which was not much, and what we wanted to know, which was a lot.

We were aware of the irony of sitting in a circle, away from the world, talking about the developments that were causing us stress, but we also understood that we had to use what we had, our brains, to make our actions speak louder. As part of this process, Goose and Eve told us, bit by bit, as we needed to know, about the underpinnings of the Tribe – the Vault that Pop had designed and the powerful secrets that he and others have put into the Vault, for the Tribe's basic protection. Goose explained that the Vault and what it contained, and the persons who knew what the Vault contained, were the reasons that the Tribe was able to conduct its quasi-criminal activities with impunity.

We began to get a fuller picture of the shadowy figure that Goose called the **Stranger**. We found out that the Stranger had been present with Goose on that dark night near the park when Goose was hanging out around the edges of the investigation into the death of Mystery Man No. One, who had been killed by the metro bus. Goose finally shared with us the Stranger's name, **Tommy**, and we began to get some details about him. Later, we met him in the flesh. Bingo.

Gentle Ben interrupts our idylls

Our huddles in the backroom came to a conclusion when Gentle Ben Whick, still working out his summer internship at the **Daily Afterblatt**, called me for beers and confronted me about wild stories that some guy on a barstool had told him about some secret society with a coyote symbol and some sort of connection, allegedly, with the bookshop where I was working.

The Tribe decided that the best way to deal with this threat was for Ben to come and talk with Eve and a color-coded regular, Mister Ed AKA Mr. Blue.

There was a time of confrontation and surprise when Goose explained to us, on pain of death, that there indeed was a secret society and that we could either join or face the consequences.

We joined. I did, David did, Jim did, and OhJim did. Each of us, in our own ways, said that the Tribe was more important to us than anything we had ever experienced. Goose was pleased, as was Eve, since they were trying to find ways to protect the Tribe that did not revolve around killing and other forms of extreme violence.

While planning the pivotal meeting with Gentle Ben, we took a tribal trip down to President's Park to see some Shakespeare and ended up on the local nightly news and in print, because Goose, with the rest of us in his wake, made a monumental scene in the middle of the play when Goose saw and pursued a man whom he said looked and moved like Mr. Black. From this time, we began to wonder if the first victim was Mr. Black, or Mr. Black's victim.

Ben helped us some by giving me a doodle drawing of the guy whom he had talked with concerning the secret society.

It looked a lot like Mr. Black.

When we returned to the matter of Gentle Ben, we all hid, listening in with wires, while Mister Ed and Eve were interviewed by Ben and Ben was all but recruited by them. We were glad, because Ben was a valuable asset and because we did not relish prosecuting the alternative if he had refused to join the Tribe.

Fade to Black – and a third body

Cementing our relationship with Ben allowed us, with the addition of his briefing on the Mr. Black-like man who told him all about the secret society and his drawing of the man, to move forward on the question of whether Mr. Black was dead or alive.

A story in the Aug. 29 **Daily Afterblatt, Lake Effect edition**, under the byline of Jane Carlotto, senior crime reporter, announced the finding of a third body, in a dumpster, with a symbol scrawled on the outside of the dumpster that tied the murder to the other two, after the coroner and the detectives reviewed their evidence boxes and found that the symbol was present in physical effects from the other cases.

The advent of stories by the senior crime reporter signaled an increase in interest and attention to the "Mystery Man Murders."

A follow story added a drawing of the victim and a drawing of the symbol.

Ben's fears were kicked up by this murder, and he requested a second meeting with Mister Ed and Eve that led to his full recruitment, made easier by his transition from summer intern to college student.

Another follow story by Jane Carlotto linked the second victim, Bill Zeohn, to the other two victims.

The successful recruiting of Gentle Ben was a long and careful process that gave newer members of the Tribe a larger window into what they had joined. The culmination of the process allowed us to focus on our new assumption that Mr. Black was alive, not dead, and was being good, bad, or ugly. We strategized on how to proceed.

Perhaps it was the gentle nature of young Ben, but Goose and Eve began to muse at length to one another about changing from a strict adherence to the eye-for-eye justice that Pop taught them. They report that they were sick of violence and wanted desperately to find a new center. They realized that Pop would have whacked them himself if he had heard such heretical talk.

Perhaps, too, it was the increasing focus on their old and dear friend Mr. Black and his seemingly strange behavior choices that intensified their musings. What would they do if Mr. Black had simply jumped the rails and gone out to kill innocents?

They did not know how they would respond even though they knew that Mr. Black in such a case would have to be stopped, permanently, and no one could do that except his friends. No one else would ever be able to catch him. And this, as much as anything, was the reason that we went so slowly into that dark night. We did not know what we would find, and we did not know what we would do, and we did not know if we could keep one another from harm.

Tommy, meet your sibs

It was into this morass of questions but not answers that Tommy and Goose decided that it was time to bring Tommy in, in the flesh, to meet the Tribe. At first, it did not look promising, because Tommy was clearly some kind of TLA wallah, which spooked most of us, except for the elders, and because Tommy has an abrasive and arrogant style that takes some getting used to.

Everyone says as much, anyway.

I found that he was no match for a lick on the ear and a nip on the earlobe. I have to say that I laid it on a bit thick, but I have tradecraft in survival, too, that I learned in dark places of my own, so I did what I do best, when confronted with a powerful man. I brought him to his knees with a well-placed series of teasing moves. The others rubbed up against Tommy in their own ways, and rather than a bloodbath with no one left standing or breathing, we had an alliance based on Goose's and Tommy's maxims of keeping your friends close and your enemies closer and trusting those whom you want to trust until such time as they prove themselves untrustworthy.

Tommy has been beyond valuable, and we have learned that he will answer specific questions with what generally sounds like factual answers. What more could we ask for? His access is vast compared to ours, and if he is watching us, it is for our own good as well as his.

I've had friends that I trusted far less.

And Tommy, though he has not sat in my lap or twisted my nose, did send me an amusing and touching poem that I shared, somewhat to his surprise, with the others. He had sent the poem to me after reading a profile that Goose had written on his blog that we keep private to the VPN. Early on.

Tommy showed us drawings of the first victim in the "Mystery Man Murders," and though there was a vague similarity to Mr. Black, Goose was adamant that the vic was someone else. We decided to call this vic the **John Cash**, after rejecting **John Doe** as too trite and **John Dough** as being already taken by a porn actor from the 70s. And Tommy had nothing to add to the nothing that we knew about the John Cash. The drawing was a huge increase in knowledge for us, since nothing will get you nothing but the same thing, over and over and over again.

After meeting Tommy, we had a potluck and met Baldi and Luce, old friends of Goose and Eve, recipients of a huge Lotto hit and now former ministers (him) and non-profit direct-service execs (her). Now they give away money to people who have some whimsy in their plans to address the needs of the poor. Baldi and Luce, and their girl guard with a Glock, Jo-Joe (Gentle Ben's heart-throb) met and ate with us, and Ben went home with them, to his delight and that of the other three, too, especially Jo-Joe. Ben has been sitting at the feet of Baldi and learning tradecraft while providing techy things like maintenance and security for their computer systems.

Knock knock

To the strains of a pretty good knock-knock joke that includes a pun on **tribe/time**, we all moved in together. Ben's leaving for the sub-tribe left David and I all alone in the apartment that we had been sharing, for safety's sake, with Ben. Goose and Eve decided that we would all be better-served to move in with them. So David got a room on the bachelor floor, the second, and I have a snug room in the attic.

I know that nothing is forever, but I like my life right now and this crazy urban Tribe that I'm part of.

David and I, and Ben, even, and certainly Jim and OhJim, have led lives of subterfuge, in so many ways. And in our own ways, we have felt vulnerable and not-safe, too often and too long. Our stories go to every point of the compass, it is true, but it is also true that we have a common experience of fear and trembling at the center. **YMMV.**

I will tell you my story, but not just yet. Not because I am ashamed of my story or because I have dissociated on parts of my story, but because it just is not time yet. But **fear and trembling**, I will say that much.

Living in community is the latest thing in the wider culture, according to Ben, who has looked into some of the new and strange ways of doing that, such as **New Monastic Communities** (I'll have nun of that!). Ben sez that these intentional communities are better than they sound, and I guess he may have something there, because the Tribe, with the presumptive exception of those love birds Goose and Eve, seems to be living a monkish existence focused on work.

Goose can be as coy as he wants about David and me, but I still plan a monkish existence for myself and the men in the Tribe, who seem to wish, in their differing ways, for a more libidinous picture. I reference my story, which I know that you have not heard. Anticipation holds reader interest. Any community college creative writing teacher will tell you that.

I'm leaving Tommy out of this, for reasons that should be apparent, or maybe not. Again, see my story (when it comes out).

Don't get me pissed off

Goose and Tommy exchanged emails about Goose and Eve's growing aversion to the use of violence, particularly murder, to enforce the safety of the Tribe.

Tommy's take – it can't be done any other way.

Goose's take – we will keep trying to imagine another way.

Goose says he is only too aware of the problem of violence, because he knows that he would use whatever level of violence necessary to keep Eve -- and me (ain't that sweet?) -- safe. He vows to keep trying to find that other way, because he says he is sick of all the killing and wants to stop that bottle and keep that Genie from causing misery. This Jeanne -- me -- he isn't worried about.

(**Note**: Goose alluded to some work that Eve has done on the question, but he did not share her work with me. I think that it would be instructive to hear her stuff and to have a general discussion.)

An editorial in the Sept. 30 **Lake Effect edition** of the **Daily Afterblatt** added more heat than light to the public discourse concerning the "Mystery Man Murders." The same can be said for a front page story that ran in the same edition, by Jane Carlotto, giving the monthly update and focusing on infighting between the detectives on the case, Blucote and Schmidt, and the coroner, Dr. Bruce Backstaff.

And no new details, of course, except some new speculation by unnamed insiders about the possibility that a gag order of a highly informal but extremely effective tone has been applied to the murder investigation from a very high and lofty place.

At a meeting of the F-Troop a day or so later, Tommy confirmed that the fix was in concerning Mr. Black and the rest of the "Mystery Man Murders" case.

We don't ask and Tommy does not tell where he gets his information.

A few days later, we had a visit, brought to a sudden end by Tommy's arrival, from the two detectives. They called Tommy "Agent." Just "Agent," noun of direct address. Again, we do not ask, etc. **WTF**.

Tommy had dropped by to give us two drawings that he had made while looking at the locals' file on the second victim. One was a drawing of Zeohn, with the top of his head cut off as part of the autopsy, and the other was what I immediately saw was a drawing of my old colleague, that Queen Bee Jane Carlotto, senior crime reporter of the **Afterblatt**.

What has ensued is a series of inquiries into Bill Zeohn's life, partly as training and partly to further our own investigation, and partly because there is not anything else shaking.

We have worked Zeohn over pretty good and have very little to show for it.

Note to all: This ends the first effort to create a chronological history of the investigation into the three murders, to date. The idea is to update with any and all actions, as they occur. This, I will do.

List lacks Jeanne's *certain something*
|31October08|

We wanted to list on the flip chart Jeanne's asides from her **Mystery Man Murders** chronology, so David volunteered to give Naomi a break.

"Not very sexy," Jim said.

"Yeah," OhJim said, "maybe it's the messenger."

"I resemble that comment," David said.

"But not the original," Jim said. "Neither Jeanne nor Naomi."

"Yeah," OhJim said, "that's the problem, in a nutshell."

"Or a nut case," I said, "or even a nut sack."

"Spell that, brother," Jim said.

"Yeah," OhJim said, "give it a break."

"I wasn't talking about the Strategic Air Command," I said.

"Meow," Wild Billy said, from the lap of Mister Ed, who said nothing.

"Let us let all this pass," Eve said, "and quickly."

This was the to-do list that David pulled from Jeanne's summary --

• The man in the bar.

• Eve's musings re: violence.

"Well," Jeanne said, "thanks from Naomi and me for the sincerest form of flattery, David. Let's discuss what we wrote."

Jeanne gave David a sideways smile with just a little less of the lemon than is her practice.

Maybe it was her wink.

David went all pink.

"First up," I said, "is the question of just who it was who spoke to Gentle Ben in that bar and told him fairly accurate stories about who we are here and what we do. I think that we go with the drawing that Ben gave us and assume that it is indeed Mr. Black who was speaking to him."

I took a blow-up of Ben's drawing and stuck it next to the flip-chart.

"That is my thinking, too," Eve said. The resemblance is strong, and our old friend Black can pull that sort of thing off and always has."

"Well," Jeanne said, "I think you both are right and I also think that this merely intensifies our confusion and gets us no closer to an answer -- why is Mr. Black doing some or all of the killing and other provocative acts such as putting a coyote in Ben's ear?"

"Yes," David said, "I agree it was Mr. Black. It's like we won't know anything until we talk with him or he deigns to talk or communicate with us, in ways more specific than leaving bodies as metaphors in the street and tidying up with dumpsters. It's all or nothing, it seems."

Next on Jeanne's list

"That leaves just one question," Jeanne said. "Eve on violence."

"I can state the case in brief," Eve said. "Goose can honk on as he will."
Eve gave me her very best Buddha Girl smile.

"This is the question," Eve said. "How can we make the Tribe and all it
stands for, and all that we have done, will do, and are doing, safe and
secret? The answer to that question, going back to the first Q and A by Pop
was that we trust everyone until or unless they show themselves to be
otherwise, then we kill them or cause them to be so served. I no longer can
subscribe to that simple formula, and I am deeply and even desperately
thankful that we have not had as of yet to apply the ultimate solution to
any problems that have come along. I am restive about the Vault, and the
need to make threats and keep dossiers and renew threats, but that seems
to be a lesser, and more workable, sort of evil."

"That's right," I said, "we cannot simply trust in the kindness of strangers
to leave us alone and to indemnify us universally and for all time, in either
directions on the time line."

"The color corps understands that they keep faith or bad things happen all
around," Eve said, "because this is the nature of covert work and play."

"The sudden increase in our ranks, of talented but young and unseasoned
persons such as yourselves," I said, "has challenged the elders of the Tribe
to choose wisely and has challenged the elders to be very, very clear on the
consequences and responses to any breaking of faith."

"And our deep, and quick-growing love for you, Dears," Eve said, "has
made what has always been a cut-and-dried rattling of sabers a matter of
intense uneasiness for us. And that does not touch on blood ties Grim."

No longer smiling, I nodded and look at my brothers.

They for once were silent.

"It is easy to kill a rat," I said, "but not so easy to kill a mouse. And to kill
a child ... . Go ask Abraham how hard it was to lay the wood for a fire and
to put his son Isaac on top. For that matter, ask God how hard that was.
Notice how quickly God sent an angel to say **Stop!** when Abraham showed
the depths of his resolve. I do not have those depths, not anymore."

"We know," Eve said, "how vulnerable that makes us all, now. As Goose
has said, again and again to me, **Pop would kill us for even saying these
things, if he were not already dead himself.**"

"It seems that we have intervened just in time," Jeanne said, "to keep
you from spinning another revolution of questions and fears before ending
up at the same place. You are right. We are young, dumb, and full of
hormonal liquidity. And as ones who are young, we do not have the long
view except as an idea advanced with some frequency by our elders. We
seem to prefer to think with our hormones instead of our brains."

"I see it this way," David said. "We may be young and untried, compared
to the color corps, certainly, but you did choose well, and where you chose

best was in judging rightly that we have no place else to go where we would feel either safe or stimulated. As far as the future, I can't say. As for today, I am where I have always longed to be."

"If we are to continue as a quasi-criminal enterprise," Jeanne said, "we will need to follow the form. Name me one such enterprise that does not use the threat of violence to enforce silence."

"The Boy Scouts, "Jim said.

"Yeah," OhJim said, "and maybe the Church."

"May I speak, Mister Chair Sir?" Mister Ed said.

Mister Ed - a wise old horse
|02November08|

Just an aside before I tell you what Mister Ed said.

Mister Ed AKA **Mr. Blue**, the editor among us, showed once again that his nickname is apt. He is not just a plodding and slow and maddening old horse, albeit a talking one; Mister Ed is also wise and concise, and without fear. He took our texts of fear and trembling, cut out the extraneous words, and gave us a headline that summed up all that we were saying -- **Wake up!**

"Here," Mister Ed said, "is my sense of the group --
- "You have done, are doing, and will do unlawful acts ...
- "You see yourselves as Robin Hoods ...
- "You want to develop leaders as good as yourselves for the future ...
- "You have made choices on who to recruit ...
- "You fear the application of the ultimate penalty for breaking faith ...

"Am I right so far?"

Yes, we all said, either out loud or by slowly nodding our heads like the **Talking Horse** himself.

"I'll take things a little further," Mister Ed said. "You are engaging in what amounts to a circle jerk because you are terrified of what you will find if you ever can bring Mr. Black into this backroom and ask him what has been driving him to make the choices that he is making. Sick of the killing? It's right under your noses. Afraid of retaliating in kind? What other choice would you have? I see your real choices as these -- either find our man Black and stop him, or stop pretending to be scared about what might happen to the new recruits and just watch what he does without intervening. You seem so far to have made that second choice."

We sat in silence, around the circle, looking at the lovingly varnished floor boards, hoping to find down there an answer other than the one that Mister Ed was insisting on.

After a long time, like baby chicks, we looked up. I could see, from our faces, that no one had found any new answer that went against the grain.

"Thank you, my friend," I said. "When Eve and I say we are sick of the killing, we are looking back to the shadows, and ignoring the bodies that are as you say piling up under our noses. The killing that we enabled in the shadows had a kind of self-sealing justification. Anyway, it's over and we're in exile from all that, and thank God, etc. I cannot say that about the three victims we might thank Mr. Black for, if we could but find him. These are not justified."

Mister Ed nodded like a sky crane on the job.

"I'm beginning to think," Eve said, "that if we can resolve this pressing issue concerning Mr. Black the background questions of a cosmic sort will

sort themselves out according to the choices we make and are forced to make concerning Mr. Black. That is a breath of fresh air for me. I realize that I have been holding my breath for a long, long time. Whew!"

"Now that you're making some sense," Mister Ed said, "take another look at that enlarged copy of the Ben's drawing up there on the wall and tell me what you see."

Close your eyes and see
|03November08|

"I once wrote a headline," Mister Ed said, "to go with a story about a roadtrip that a reporter took from the east coast to the west coast -- **From sea to sea, to see**." I'm proud of that one, and it gives us an avenue to walk down in starting over with our investigation into the **Mystery Man Murders**, Mister Chair Sir."

"So ordered," I said, "and be in order, all of youse."

"Well-yoused here, Mister Chair Sir," Jim said.

"Yeah," OhJim said, "well-done here, like a hotdog with no fleas, thanks to the judicious application of boiling water. Works well, but has side effects. Boils, actually, Mister Chair Sir."

"Mister Ed Sir, you were saying," I said.

"I submit to you this drawing, done by young Ben and given less than its due, at the time and in the days since he shared it, in my humble opinion," Mister Ed said. "If you will, and by your leave, Mister Chair Sir, I purpose to lead us in an exercise in seeing in the way that the animals do."

"I'm game," Jim said.

"Yeah," OhJim said, holding his nose, "and I'm gamey."

"I'm in," Jeanne said.

"I'm out but in," David said.

"I pass, Dears, and am in," Eve said.

"And I'm named after a talking horse," Mister Ed said. "Close your eyes, pick an animal to emulate, and hold that in reserve."

"I bear responsibility," I said. "Nicknames are my specialty. I am as proud of your nickname as you are of that headline -- **From sea to sea, to see**."

"Exactly," Mister Ed said. "Your penchant for nicking names is another avenue to walk down. Any avenue will do, actually, as long as it is one that you think you know well."

"Streetwalkers, all," Jim said.

"Yeah," OhJim said, "or men named the same. To wit, Johns."

"To begin," Mister Ed said, "I want you to look at this drawing and tell me what you see. Here, I'll put it right in front of you. What do you see?"

"A guy in hoodie and baseball cap," Jeanne said. "Nice smile. Disarming."

"And he looks like he doesn't usually wear hoodies," David said. "He looks like a cop in a hoodie and cap. Sharp dresser, dressing down."

"His mustache is wrong," Eve said. "Too busy, too bushy. Looks fake."

"What else," Mister Ed said.

"He looks like Mr. Black in disguise," I said, "but not up to his usual standards. I agree, too fake. Mr. Black has his hair in hand and at all times."

"Why do you say it's **Black**?" Mister Ed said.

"Because of the nose and eyes," I said, "and the overall sense of elegance already mentioned."

"But why Black?" Mister Ed said. "Why not someone else with a great tan and good looks?"

"There is a quality," I said, "that that man has that he can't hide from his friends and that he can't hide from strangers like Ben, either. Ben's drawing has captured that essence without Ben's knowing what it is, because Mr. Black's presence is that powerful. He is a force of nature. You feel him when he is in the room. I feel him in that drawing."

"It's our friend Mr. Black," Eve said. "I agree, Dear. He cannot hide such light under a bushel -- or a baseball cap. Or behind a fake mustache."

"It's Mr. Black," I said, "because I would know him in a cave with no flashlight, or dressed in black against a black background, or if my eyes had been plucked out. I know him as well as I know myself. The two of us make one picture, with highlights and shadows. We complete one another in ways that once terrified me. Should I go on?"

"This," Mister Ed said, "is a good start, but we are barely scratching the surface. We have not set the context. What else do you see?"

Talk to your animals, people
|04November08|

"I thought that you were a talking horse," Jim said, "but all you can say is, **What_do_you_see**. I'm beginning to see a zombie."

"Yeah," OhJim said, "your eyeball is up in a tree. Call the fire department for a hook and ladder. Call the cops to the copse."

"Still," Mister Ed said, "the question stands. What do you see?"

"I see," David said, "the symbol that was drawn on the dumpster that played host to the body of the third victim."

"I see," Jeanne said, "an arrow from Mr. Black to the symbol and three little dots leading to the other figures."

"I see," I said, "a star of David with the bottom point clipped."

"I see," Eve said, "two characters as one, and a question mark beside them."

"I see," Jim said, "the logo of the bar -- **The Roll In and Crawl Out.**"

"I see," OhJim said, "a light socket surrounded by a thicket of triangles."

"Ok, Mister Ed said, "now what do you see?"

Mister Ed turned the drawing on its side.

"I see that I missed the arrow above the drawing of Mr. Black," I said.

"And," Jeanne said, "I know that the drawing, and the arrows and dots and question mark, were part of the message that Ben's brain was receiving and transmitting through this drawing and all the random doodles there."

"Come to that," David said, "we have not mentioned the exclamation point next to Mr. Black's head."

"And," Jim said, "it strikes me that we have not commented, not one little bit, on the two human figures over there at the right of the drawing, at all."

"Yeah," OhJim said. "Sure glad you didn't, then, brother."

"What do you see now?" Mister Ed said.

Mister Ed turned the drawing upside-down.

"Some things stay the same," I said, "and some things change."

"The question mark shows its true character," Eve said, "-- a fish hook."

"There are," Jeanne said, "not one but two sets of three little dots -- ellipses, not ellipsis."

"There is a border around the main drawing, of Mr. Black, but not around the other two, or around the whole drawing," David said.

"Now what do you see?" Mister Ed said.

Mister Ed taped pieces of paper over part of the drawing.

"I see a man who lives and sleeps on the street," Jeanne said.

"And I am aware that I had ignored that obvious fact," David said.

"I see a man who looks like the drawing of Mr. Black," Eve said.

"I think it is another drawing of Mr. Black from another occasion," I said.

"That is arresting in itself, Dears," Eve said. "Goose, you see, is always sure about what is and is not Mr. Black."

"I see," Jim said, "a comment on the closeness of the two characters."

"And I see," OhJim said, "that the character in front of the other is wearing some kind of hat that blends into the poncho or whatever that the figure behind is wearing."

"It's not Mr. Black," I said, "because the eyes are too close together and the glasses are squarish instead of round. And the figure is wearing an expensive-looking shirt or overshirt, or melton jacket, in contrast to the figure behind, who looks homeless and scruffy. I don't think that they are together in any sense."

"What else do you see?" Mister Ed said.

"I see a man and his familiar," Jim said. "A deep connection."

"Now," Mister Ed said, "reveal your animal and give the drawing a message and a title."

"Meow," said the furry animal among us.

Inner animal, message, title

|05November08|

"Does everyone understand the assignment?" Mister Ed said.

"Inner animal?" Jim said.

"Yeah," OhJim said, "or outer. In your case a well-worn werewolf."

"Where?' Jim said.

"Wolf," OhJim said.

"I'll go first," I said. "Animal -- goose. Message: The guy on the left is very important, and is related to the symbol of the light socket and to the two guys on the right. Title: **Left, Right, Left.**"

"Me next," Jeanne said. "My inner animal is a feline, and the message that I get from the drawing is this: Everything is related in the drawing, nothing is optional. Title: **Go Round the Circle; Repeat as Necessary.**"

"Ok," David said, "here goes. My inner animal is a canine. The message that I get from the drawing: Talk to Ben about what he drew and why. Title: **Ring Ben's Chimes.**"

"My inner animal," Eve said, "is the mockingbird. The message that I get from the drawing is to separate the mockers from those who are helpful. My title: **Bar None at the Roll In and Crawl Out.**"

"My brother has already revealed my inner animal, and when the moon rises, he will catch it hot," Jim said. "The message in the drawing? Chew each bite to get all its essence. Title? **Bite me.**"

"And last but not least," OhJim said, "-- yeah, is me. My inner animal is the frog, the message in the drawing is to remember how the prince got there. My title is, **Kiss Me, You Fool!**"

"What about you, Ed?" I said. "You have led well. How would you follow the rest of us?"

"My role is to pull from you what you know and didn't know that you knew," Mister Ed said. "That makes my inner animal the owl -- with the refrain of **who, who, who,** for **what, what, what do you see?** The message that I get is this: A drawing is a closed system with its own rules and stories to tell. My title: **Do You Know These Men and Memes?**"

"Amazing, Mister Ed Sir," I said. "Simply amazing. I'd say that the next step is to get our young and gentle friend Ben back here for a chat, ASAP. The question for Ben? **What_did_you_see?**"

Goose muses on spooky stuff

|06November08|

Email to Tommy -- **We're like ghosts, we spooks --**

Dear sole reader:

How you been?

We just finished an exercise that Mister Ed led us through, in looking at the full page of drawings and doodles that Gentle Ben did after meeting a mysterious man whom we think was Mr. Black in that bar downtown, **The Roll In and Crawl Out**, where the third **Mystery Man Murders** body was found out behind in the alley, in a dumpster. Mister Ed had us standing on our heads and all sorts of stuff, and along the way we began to see things more clearly. That got me to thinking about the experience that I and the other elders of the Tribe had when we were cast from the roll of covert folk and ended up in a very overt existence not of our choosing. I just am not ready to let that go, I guess. Can you listen while I worry away at this **one_more_time**?

≈ ≈ ≈

We were like ghosts, we spooks, because we had experienced the death-in-life that is exile. We were shadows of our former selves, which once were murky by design. Once exiled, we became like ghosts who could only suggest their true selves. At first, in the glaring light of the overt realm, we thought our protection was that people could not see us, and because they could not see us they were not afraid of us, because a ghost is only a threat if one can see the ghost.

By the time the bodies began to pile up, we had long left behind ghostly things.

When we activated the Vault that Pop had so carefully constructed, and saw the fear and trembling in our enemies, who were also the ones who would find it in their interest to protect us, no matter what we did, we went from ghosts to spooks, and we knew that we had turned a corner, from darkness to light, and from fear and trembling to a watchful ease. First, though, came the shock of judgment, from the ones who had raised us and trained us, and used us until we could no longer perform to their satisfaction, one by one. We were weighed in the balance, each of us, and found to be so light as to not register any longer on their fine-tuned scale of utility. That is, we were judged to be all used up and no longer of use in the shadows where covert operations are carried out by substantial persons with specific gifts and a general level of lethal training.

Go away, they told us, because you are used up and cannot do us either good or ill. Go where you will, and do as you will, for you cannot harm us. Just go, beyond the borders of what is covert, into the realm of the overt. Go where people will see you, and not see you, at the same time. You are, and will be from now on, ghosts who leave little in the way of what is real. You have become, on our scale, slightly less than zero. Time to go, and no you do not need to sign any papers, because we cannot see you. **Go**.

And go, we went.

And we found that the overt realm had plenty of pitfalls for us, in our new and naked condition. But we learned, in time, that we had been conditioned to see our condition as other than what was true. That is, we were only as light and insubstantial as we assumed that we were. Our training, judged to be no longer of use, had saved us, and we set about to stub the toe that had kicked us so hard when we were down. We had introjected the projection of those who threw us away like feathers in the wind. We were spit out because we were neither hot nor cold. And our lukewarm self-image was an inherited thing from the wolves that had raised us to do their bidding. Once the shame of exile eased, as we validated for ourselves that in the overt realm we had substance and could wield considerable power, thanks to the **rough raisin'** that we had had, it was only a matter of time before one of us went rogue and started laying people out, if only to show the others that it was possible, blow by blow, to go from projection to introjection to rejection.

I pray that the three deaths that we are investigating have more meaning than that, but no one as yet can say why there has been so much killing. And who better than Mr. Black, whose answer to any question, from friend or foe, was **Bleep**-you. Who better to show us that we were real and had substance, and could become powerful again. And who had enemies who could hurt us, if we didn't learn that we could have substance in the overt.

For Mr. Black, the path to power in the overt realm was to use his training to kill, or (just maybe) to protect those whom he loved. Eve and I chose another mode, in the joining together of our lives and stories. Love drove us, too, but love drove us to create more love. This has been a second exile, but once you are on the road, in the magic bus, the horizon looks about the same. We do not know what is driving Mr. Black, and our love makes us terrified of colliding with such an alien force with such a precious and familiar face. What will we find, learn, decide, and create, when we finally see Mr. Black, face to face?

≈ ≈ ≈

Our chat with Gentle Ben is set for tomorrow morning. I hope you can make it.

Yours in fear and trembling
Goose

We gently draw out Ben
|07November08|

"No one wants to harm you, Ben," Jim said. "Believe me."

"Yeah," OhJim said. "Probably because, at least partly, no one else has a girlfriend who packs a Glock."

"Weird, huh?" Ben said, smiling at Jo-Joe, who smiled back while patting her behind, out where the heater in question sits. It was good to see our gentle Ben, who come to think of it would someday be a lot like our older giant, Mister Ed, who was also in the house.

The backroom was bulging, but since we all liked one another, it was a cozy meeting nonetheless.

"Seriously," I said. "Well, somewhat seriously. Welcome back to the motherhouse. And you mothers, too. I trust our Ben is giving satisfaction?"

"Smile when you say that, Partner," Baldi said. "There's fathers here, too. Ben's my boy."

"I resemble that comment somewhat," Luce said.

Luce gave Ben a dazzling smile of Luce-light.

If you had seen it, you might have wanted to be Ben. Ben sure did. It was good to see our youngest, and perhaps most vulnerable tribalist, in such loving hands and bathed in such a loving light.

Ben had a long way to go, but he was moving on a good path.

"Really," Eve said, "welcome, Dears, and well-met. Ben, we have started over, essentially, in our inquiry into all the murders of late. We fished out your drawing of the guy you talked with at the **Roll In and Crawl Out**."

"Love that name," David said. "It's even better than the **Dew Drop Inn**."

David and Ben went through a series of gyrations with handshakes, twisty brother handshakes, and that shoulder-touching thing that I think is so cool.

"Right," Ben said. "The drawing."

"Walk us through the drawing," I said. "We spent a while looking at it from every angle, including upside down, and we realized that we hadn't given it more than scant attention."

"Well," Ben said, "I drew the main guy at the top right with a **bang** and the other two with a **question mark**. He was the one who told me about the coyote logo and the secret society and stuff about **Caspar's**. Going counter-clockwise, I drew a version of the light socket logo that the guy drew for me on a bar napkin, then I drew these two guys who were hanging around at the bar, and I ended with the bar logo at top right."

"Good, Dear," Eve said. "What do the exclamation mark, the arrow, the question mark, and the two sets of dots refer to? Only you know that."

"I wanted," Ben said, "to mark the main guy with the exclamation mark, and the arrow was to connect him with the logo and establish the flow. The two sets of dots were meant to show that the two guys were equally of interest -- by their being there, mostly. That was the import of the question mark -- were they just there, or were they with the guy, or somehow trying to listen in?"

"Great questions," Eve said. "Answers?"

"Well," Ben said, "I got the impression the two guys knew each other. They seemed to be pretending they weren't together, but their body language was saying the opposite in spite of their difference."

"Difference?" Jeanne said. "You're doing great, Bengie, BTW."

"Thanks, **Gee**," Ben said. "I mean that the younger guy, in the cape, smelled bad and was some kind of homeless guy or burnout. The other guy was older and much better dressed."

"Did the main guy seem to know them?" Jeanne said.

"Not at all," Ben said. "He never really looked at them. He kept his gaze on me, and that was a bit spooky, because he was very intense. And more than a little drunk, as was I. Everyone was, including the bald, youngish bartender, come to think of it."

"Tans," I said. "Who had tans?"

Ben's story draws, quarters our theory
|08November08|

"I'll repeat my question, Ben," I said. "I don't mean to be confusing. Did any of the men in the bar have what you might describe as a deep tan?"

"Well," Ben said, "if I'm hearing you right, the two older guys both were either dark-complected or well-tanned. In that dive, it was hard to see at that level of detail. But the homeless guy definitely was lighter in skin tone.

Basically a WASP."

"Here's the deal," Mister Ed said. "When Eve and I talked with you, there were a few subscripts that had to do with deciding whether you were open to an approach, and if you were, were you someone that we felt we could trust. As you can appreciate, these were vulnerabilities that took most of our attention, so we didn't debrief you the way we are now, now that you are one of us and seconded to a sister Tribe, so to speak."

Mister Ed bowed to Luce and Jo-Joe, which reminded me of a tall ship dipping its main mast to go under a well-built bridge.

I don't know how Jo-Joe and Luce would describe his bend, but they seemed to appreciate it.

"So," I said, "as my friend Ed says, this is the deal -- we believe that the main guy in your photo is Mr. Black, an AWOL elder of our Tribe and long-time associate, and we further fear that he alone is responsible for the three murders that the press is calling the **Mystery Man Murders**, and we believe that the two other guys are Victim No. Three (the younger) and some other guy who will be lucky to see next month, if Mr. Black continues on the path that we have charted as his. I'm making this last bit up in response to your story."

"Yes, Dear," Eve said. "I agree that the third man is a person of interest for us and a person who as you say will be lucky to see next month. Nay, next week."

"Well," Ben said, "all I can say is that he had a vague sense of African-American or maybe Arab-American, or just a guy with a great tan. This is what I could say about the other guy, too."

"Wow," Jeanne said. "That is both interesting and confusing, because that is what others around here say about Mr. Black. We may have to go on the assumption that either of these characters could be Mr. Black, and that the one who spoke to you was given his lines by the other. Off the top of my head, responding to the new info."

"The mustache," I said. "Ben, was it, in your opinion, real?"

"Well," Ben said, "I had my doubts. It was a lot more black than his hair was, although that could be the result of male beauty products."

"Frankly," I said, "I am beginning to lean toward Mr. Black being the guy on the left, rather than the guy on the right. And I would love you to say something like, **Oh, yeah, that's two drawings of the same guy.**"

"Well, Dear," Eve said, "it seems that we have a significant amount of new detail, and that we may have to spin out some additional scenarios."

"And this may be," David said, "the first time that I have heard you say **frankly**, Goose, and probably mean it."

Once our four friends had departed, we turned to one another.

"Well," Mister Ed said, "Mister Chair Sir, that certainly was an eye-opener."

"Yes," I said. "This calls for the full powers of the F-Troop. Circle the wagons. And grab your red marker pen, Gee, if I may call you so."

"**Gee**? Jim said."

"Gee, Jim-wiz," Jeanne said. "Like Naomi, only shorter."

"I'm confused," Jim said. "Has Jeanne been hitting the bottle barefoot?"

"Yeah," OhJim said, "hitting and missing, and I'm all confused and it feels fine. I think there's more than just Jeanne in that bottle. Goodie!"

Jeanne just smiled her lemon-thing smile.

And we all looked at one another, our faces showing various shades of **bewildered** and **blank**, because when we had said that we were starting over we did not expect to see all our theories self-destruct.

Who you gonna call? The F-Troop!
|09November08|

"Did I miss anything?" Tommy said, as he walked into the backroom.

"Yes, Mister Agent Sir," Jim said.

"Yeah," OhJim said, "and maybe it's just as well. One clear mind would be good about now."

"Well," Tommy said, "glad to oblige."

"You, my friend, are just in time for a timely meeting of the F-Troop," I said. "Friends, we will be in a circle, and hiding under our wagons."

"It can't be that bad," Tommy said.

"Oh, but it is," I said, "and better. Who wants to brief our brother?"

"If I may, Mister Chair Sir," Mister Ed said, "I will flag some things."

"Say on," I said.

"First thing," Mister Ed said, "is to set the scene. With us, until a moment ago, were member-of-our-Tribe Ben Whick and the three members of the Band that he is staying with, Baldi and Luce Cleanue and their girl guard, the Glock-packing Jo-Joe, rumored to be Ben's, well, you know ... ."

"**Main squeeze**, or simply **squeeze**," I said, "would get at it, I think, Ed. So far so good."

"Second thing," Mister Ed said. "Mister Chair Sir, since I will not be giving an exhaustive summary of the exhausting interview just ended but will give only a few impressions in the rough order of their impressiveness, on me personally, I move that David be commissioned to write a verbatim account of the conversation itself and that we re-gather to spin out new scenarios and revise old ones, based on that record."

"Ok," I said, "and let us clean up as we go along. Those in favor?"

F-Troop salutes all around -- two thumbs up, two middle fingers touching.

"Congrats, David," Jeanne said.

She followed with her sideways smile full of bitter, sweet promise.

David smiled a more rueful smile than his usual bug-eyed grin.

"Not to worry, Dear," Eve said. "I got the whole thing on tape. I knew no one would mind."

"And," I said, "you can refer to my posts on the VPN."

David's smile broadened. The job was in the mail. Done.

"Back to you, Mister Ed Sir," I said.

"Third thing," Mister Ed said, "is this. Ben told us a lot of things about the meeting in the **Roll In and Crawl Out** that we had not heard before. And subject to the more rigorous summary by friend David, I will say that it would be helpful to re-examine the drawings closely, remember Ben's take on the situation, and realize that we have a few new scenarios to consider."

Mister Ed put up Ben's drawing for us, once again.

"Frankly and honestly, Mister Chair Sir," Mister Ed said, "I like the scenario that says the guy on the left and the guy on the right, at the bottom, are the same guy. Or maybe twins. Otherwise, I don't know what to say."

"I was struck," Jeanne said, "by the possibility that the three of them were a team, which makes no sense in terms of what Goose has been saying all along about Mr. Black."

"Well," Tommy said, "being here would have made a big difference."

Tommy slipped me two envelopes on the sly and left.

What was in those envelopes
| 10November08 |

Faith on the Radio

Jeanne get out, get out, run away
Caspar's is not a place you should stay
For tomorrow you meet Mr Kurtz
His answers three shall all be
"It wasn't them -- it was we."
Run away Jeanne, for should you meet Kurtz,
Come you two face-to-face
What then? What if ...
Could it be the great I AM
Is all this time sitting backwards in his skiff
And Pogo has our thumbs caught in the gimbals?
Would you have the secret of life?
Not at Caspar's.
Books, yes, but they don't got that.
Run away Jeanne for in that vault lies
Wuz it we couldn't or wuz it we didn't,
Referring, in the oblique, to Flight Ninety- ...
Flee Jeanne. Get out.
Caspar's is not a place you should be.
And the secret?
It's just as Faith says on the radio:
There ain't no secret. And it ain't free.

When I got a moment to myself, I took a look at the envelopes that Tommy had slipped me -- the human dead-drop. You would not believe how seldom I get any time alone. There was a poem called **Faith on the Radio** and a note in an envelope that was addressed to me. The other envelope was addressed to Jeanne.

I put on my sweater and hat and made noises resembling speech. No one seemed to care, one way or the other. I walked on out the back door and down to the next corner, reading as I went.

A few comments from me --

- v. **The Secret of Life**, a song by country singer Faith Hill.
- Seldom repeated but usually true disclaimer -- Google it (**JFGI**), which applies to anything I or anyone I quote says, implies, creates, mangles, or steals.
- What makes male bonding sweet are the women we love and admire.
- The fact that you and all the Tribe are reading this, now, is my comment on what **private** means.

Tommy's note w/the poem --

My friend:

You said that I could simply show up as an answer to your last email, and you seemed to be at pains to distance anyone, including yourself, from what you were saying in that email re: the question of violence.

Maybe your pain embarrasses you, my brother, but what else do you have?

Why exile yourself from your exile?

Who will care, really, if you do or don't? You will.

What else can you point to and say, **God and I know what is going on here, and one of us has forgotten.** Please, rearrange your position on yourself, and celebrate not only the gift tucked into the snowball that smacked you in the face but also the gift of being able to share with friends, enemies, and strangers something about what that means and can mean in a cold and well-nigh heartless world of quietly desperate strangers.

It's your choice. Either you are the only one who can say, after hearing the story, **Holy Bleep, What a ride!** or you can empower others to have the same sleigh ride, too.

Now where is the pain?

And what is the gain?

End of proclamation.

That is your wheelhouse, anyway, not mine. My "proc" is a **.doc.**

I just tend the big, fat mooring lines and sit on the bollards.

I have given you a copy of what was also meant for Jeanne for her to do with as she will, and I carbon you to acknowledge that your Tribe can only exist on a footing of constant revelation, one to another -- where there can be secrets, but only until someone asks, and then it is need-to-know, and the Tribe will always need to know enough to be satisfied that the walls are intact and that the watchers are standing in the gaps. I will leave it to Jeanne to share her note, or not.

Tommy

Jeanne catches us alone
|11November08|

Eve and I were enjoying a moment alone in the backroom.
Jeanne stuck her pretty head around the corner and smiled like she does.
You know the smile. The one that leaves a hint of lemons on the air.
"Can I talk to youse guys a minute?" Jeanne said.
"Certainly, Dear," Eve said. "Just let me put on my **guy-guise.**"
Eve gave Jeanne her Buddha Girl smile.
The one that leaves a hint of roses on the air.
Jeanne clicked in and sat. She handed me the envelope from Tommy.
"I don't get this," she said. "Should I be worried?"
"Can I look?" I said.
"Sure," she said, "but it is like **Geek to me!**"
That didn't sound right.
I was expecting Jeanne to have from Tommy what I had, so I was surprised but unlike her I was also pleased.
"Here," I said, "this is what I got. It is the translation of what you got -- in Chinese ideographs. Read it and then we can talk. Eve has seen this already, so she will be of assistance, too."
"That's right, Dear," Eve said. "I have the blood-shot eyes to prove it. Goose was at this thing for a long time last night."
Jeanne read the translation of Tommy's poem that Tommy had given me, and me alone, I was relieved to find out.
Let me tell you.
Because as confused as Jeanne was -- by getting Tommy's beautiful rendering of his poem into Chinese ideographs, by his own hand -- she was bound to be puzzled even more by the English transliteration of his poem that Tommy gave me. And alarmed, even. Now that she was with Eve and me, I felt Ok about showing her my version.
I was particularly thinking about the refrain -- **flee Jeanne**, and variations, repeated three times at least.
I had lost some sleep the night before and had made sure that Eve lost about as much, in discussing how to deal with Tommy's poem.
"Listen, Dear," Eve had said well after midnight, "this is all good. It tells us a lot about Tommy, and his intentions, and it will tell us a lot about Jeanne, too. Listen, and learn."
Eve was right.
And I was all ears.
"Well, Dear," Eve said, "that's some poem, isn't it? And his brush work is superb, too."

Exegesis vs. eisegesis
| 12November08 |

"Here's how this will go," I said. "We will have a chat about **exegesis** vs. **eisegesis** of texts of an evocative and ultimate nature, just the three of us, and later we will share with the Tribe as we see fit, as in **need-to-know**. And since I will be posting about this conversation as soon as we have it, it is all rather academic, anyway, since we all read my posts with the greatest attention, and Tommy does, too."

"Goose and I will decide the need-to-know part, Dear," Eve said, "and you will have a chance to make suggestions on that. Goose's posts could all be labeled **need-to-know**. It's easy to forget that. Not everything gets into the VPN and not everything that does is in fact, fact, as you know."

"Good words," Jeanne said. "Let's talk, because this translation of the poem confuses me even more than the ideographs did. I mean, I like Tommy, and I actually like his poem, a lot, but I'm having trouble seeing it as a poem and not as a mysterious message from the handsome figure in the cape, waiting at the back door with a second horse held by the halter while the young niece of the lord and lady of the castle, who thought that she was in line for the throne, is being told by her maid to flee into the dark and away from the light."

"Good start," I said, "but first a few terms -- **exegesis** (pulling meaning **from** a text) versus **eisegesis** (the evil pastime of pouring your favorite meaning **into** a text). We want to emulate the one and sneer at the other."

"Goose is just having his fun with words, Dear," Eve said. "I doubt that the terms matter as much as the concept, which is sound."

"Figure out what the poem and the poet intend under the level of the language?" Jeanne said.

"Very good," I said. "And what do we know about the poet?"

"He likes to ring my chimes and bust David's chops?" Jeanne said. "And he turns as pink as any of you do when I tongue-tease him?"

"What else, Dear?" Eve said. "What about this specific poem?"

"Well," Jeanne said, "he did give me the Chinese version, which was a flirty and sweet gesture. And he gave the translated version to Goose, which was challenging and maybe even alarming."

"Challenging, certainly," I said, "but why do I not say **alarming**?"

"Because by giving you the translation, he put you in the driver's seat," Jeanne said. "You had the choice of giving me the words that go with the pictures that I got, or you could have simply filed them where no one would ever find them."

"Exactly, Dear," Eve said.

"I agree," I said. "Tommy could have given us both a copy of both versions of the poem, rather than giving you the puzzle and me the solution to the puzzle. That version of Tommy would be someone to watch carefully and to keep either at a far distance or very close. The Tommy that we know did a friendly thing."

"That leaves the text itself," Jeanne said, "and the dire warnings to me about dangers to come from the Heart of Darkness."

English majors all, more or less
|13November08|

Jeanne continued to frown at Tommy's poem.

"The funny thing," Jeanne said, "is that I was an English Lit major in college. The **Daily Afterblatt** was a way to put a fire under the pot and keep it boiling. I really didn't give a rip about the Fifth Estate. Literature was more to my liking. But I'm stumped here."

"English Lit ... me, too, sort of," I said. "I have used English Lit, professorial tweeds, and a supercilious smile more than once in my covert work."

"Me, too, Dear," Eve said. "I look good in tweed, and I even bought a bookshop once."

"That means we should be able to parse this poem, and pronto," Jeanne said. "I'll be glad when we do. This is starting to hurt my self-concept."

"I think, Dear, that the problem is not in the critical competence of your reading but in how you feel about what you have read," Eve said.

Jeanne nodded, slowly, thrown into thought.

Eve nailed that one. You could see it on Jeanne's face.

Tens for Eve's mental gymnastics, even from the Eastern European judges.

"Let me just say," I said, "I reread Joseph Conrad's **Heart of Darkness** yesterday. Just 62 pages printed from the Internet. Took 90 minutes to read while underlining. Great, great, great stuff. Darkness, darkness. Conrad is Tommy's exemplar, here."

"**Mistah Kurtz**," Jeanne said, "**he dead**. I always liked the wild and beautiful native woman with her naked arms raised in the air. And the guy who dressed in his dazzling white European clothes -- damn the heat and bless the local woman who did his laundry."

"The river into the soul," Eve said. "The darkness inside darkness. Night on the Thames, waiting for the tide to turn, telling stories to the void."

"And Faith Hill," I said. "-- a beautiful woman who sings so sweetly."

That earned me a faint smile of grace and a well-drawn lemony one, too.

"The title, **Faith on the Radio**, with a nice quibble on **faith**," I said, "and Faith's song **The Secret of Life**. Chosen by Tommy. Sung by Faith Hill. When you get to the top of the mountain, keep climbing."

"Let's jump right in," Jeanne said. "What about the first couplet?"

"It rhymes but does not offend," Eve said. "Not like Rap, though I don't enjoy rapping Rap, if you know what I mean. To each her own."

"The first couplet speaks in the imperative voice and does not lie," I said.

"It seems," Jeanne said, "to warn me away from **here**, conditioned on meeting Mr. Kurtz **tomorrow**, whenever that is, and whoever he is and wherever **here** is. I'm NOT leaving this-here backroom, BTW. I live here now. That is what has me so upset, I guess."

"**Heart of Darkness**," I said. "AKA Mr. Black, in my view. The two are seen here as roughly equal, and after rereading the Conrad I certainly would offer that at full price. No discount."

"Bingo," Jeanne said." That fits. **Mr. 'Kurtz' Black.**"

"What else, Dear?" Eve said. "Is the threat/warning -- **get out, get away** -- referring to something that is **imminent** or **transcendent**, to borrow some more of Goose's theological twaddle?"

"More transcendent than imminent, I would say," Jeanne said, "and so more of a possibility, or a what-if, than a probability."

"So," I said, "what does Tommy want to convey here? Leave what you love? Or can it be a simple invitation to get out and get some fresh air -- to get away."

"I choose to believe that he is saying that **It is right to fear Mr. Black**, because Black/Kurtz is showing us **answers three** -- three bodies -- that prove he is armed and dangerous and should not be approached alone. Think **Hannibal Lecter**," Jeanne said. "The kat that got your tongue, by force."

"Such is the first warning," I said. "It's like a briefing or the rehearsal of a warning. Dire in tone, distant in execution. Histrionic, even. Overdrawn?"

"That covers the first warning, but we have not yet accounted for the first rationale," Eve said, "-- the phrase **it wasn't them -- it was we.**"

"That seems," Jeanne said, "to go with the Pogo reference (**we have met the enemy and he is us**). It speaks of our complicity in the three murders, and not only by keeping information to ourselves but also the possibility that Mr. Black is acting for our protection rather than simply channeling the Hannibal L."

We looked at one another, almost too tired to smile.

The work of parsing Tommy's poem felt like heavy lifting.

Finally, Eve managed a Buddha Girl smile.

Jeanne, as ever, was squeezing lemons to the side.

Further into the darkness

|14November08|

"I agree," I said. "Jeanne, you are talking sense about Pogo, the Tribe's complicity, and the dangers of Hannibal L."

"Me, too, Dear," Eve said. "Agreed. Well-said and -done."

"The next section," I said, "although it has merit as poetry, is less alarming as personal communication."

Run away Jeannie, for should you meet Kurtz,
Come you two face-to-face
What then? What if ...
Could it be the great I AM
Is all this time sitting backwards in his skiff
And Pogo has our thumbs caught in the gimbals?

"Why less alarming?" Jeanne said. "It's as scary as the first iteration."

"The language," Eve said. "It's all conditional -- **what if ... could it be.**

Nothing emphatic here. He's zooming out. Taking a longer and lazy or at least deliberate look at the question."

"The message," I said, "is **relax but be focused, Grasshopper.**"

"Jeanne Dear, what echo do you get from the **great I AM?**" Eve said.

"I hear Popeye the Sailor Man -- **I yam who I yam; I cannot be another,**" Jeanne said.

"Me, too, Dear," Eve said. "And a shout out to **Olive Oyl**, of course."

"Beautiful image of the great I AM -- God -- sitting backwards to lead the cosmos into the future," Jeanne said.

"I often feel that sort of backward burden in leading the Tribe," I said.

"I'm sure you do, Dear," Eve said. "I'm certain of it."

Jeanne actually laughed with delight. Her unbridled smile plucked the sting of Eve's irony.

"Ouch," I said. "I guess I had that coming, or going. Next time I'll row facing forward, like they do Down East."

"Then maybe you know what **gimbals** are," Jeanne said, "since you're such a salty dog."

"Oh, he really is, Dear," Eve said, "but mum's the word and Bob's your uncle, and so on."

Eve should have, and I did, blush.

Jeanne laughed even harder.

Eve assumed her smiling Buddha Girl pose.

"Didn't have a clue, I'll level with you on that," I said, "but I Googled **gimbals.** Has to do with two spheres that make a compass stay level no matter what the ship is doing in the waves and troughs."

"I like the phrase **wuz it we couldn't or wuz it we didn't,**" Jeanne said. "Sounds something like Pogo again."

"So," I said, "by the third repetition of the admonition to **flee Jeanne flee**, I say that **the container has become the thing contained** and alarm has been swallowed up in the rhetorical backwash of an excellent poem."

"We should send Tommy some flowers," Jeanne said, "but I may just bite his earlobe the next time I see him. He would like that better, I think."

"I think so, too, Dear," Eve said.

"Another reason for taking the long view of the warning that Tommy is giving you," I said, "is this. I assume that he wrote the Chinese version first, then found as close a transliteration as he could into English. The English is fluid, but the Chinese would be a word string such as **young girl ... danger ... running ... cave ... opportunity ... loud box-without-wires ... song ... that-which-has-its-breath-in-it.** Like that. Sometimes you win, sometimes you lose, and sometimes it rains."

The boys take a turn
| 15November08 |

"This meeting of the F-Troop will be in order," I said.

"In **ode-r**, too, Mister Chair Sir," Jim said.

"Yeah," OhJim said, "and in iambic pentameter."

"I see," I said, "that the news of Tommy's poem has gone before us."

"That would be a function of reading your daily posts, brother," Jim said.

"Yeah," OhJim said, "we secrete secrets like a faucet -- a drip feed."

"That's right," David said, "it's all there on the VPN blog-- a free flow from a secure spring."

"Well," Jeanne said, "that greatly simplifies a lot of things, doesn't it."

"Yes, Dear," Eve said. "Goose and his posts are indeed the post-haste way to stay in touch in the Tribe."

"I like the part," David said, "where we pretend to need elucidation."

"Elucidation? Sounds like some sort of laxative," Jim said.

"Yeah," OhJim said, "which is an oxy for the jackass, moron, because there is nothing lax about a laxative. It brings enlightenment in a hurry. Post-haste."

"More like a pile driver?" David said.

We groaned, and grinned, and got down to business.

"Mister Ed Sir," I said, "have you any thoughts on the poem that Tommy has graced us with?"

"Yes, Mister Chair Sir," Mister Ed said, "I do have some thoughts, beginning with an alternative phrasing for **graced us with**. It seems more like a **shot across the bow**. More like **grazed** than **graced**.

"Say some more, Dear," Eve said.

"Well," Mister Ed said, "I have followed the parsing of the poem to this point with a preponderant precognition that peace yields place to petard."

"Well-said," I said, "but what are you poking at with all those Pees?"

"Just this," Mister Ed said. "I think, Mister Chair Sir, that we still do not understand why Tommy, who seemingly should know better, is telling Jeanne to flee the one place where she ...

- "Has ever been happy ...
- "Has ever felt safe ...
- "Has ever been valued for her mind rather than what lies south -- above and below the equator."

Jeanne gave Mister Ed a sideways smile and would have done more, clearly, but Ed and awe go together, so she stayed where she was.

Mister Ed's smile was the width of a pencil line. Thin, friendly. He did not go all pink. We love that about Ed.

He is as steady as a draft horse and twice as smart (at least).

"Yeah," OhJim said, "it's like Tommy doesn't get that. If this is just a poem or an exercise in teasing the hot chick, it is ill-winded from the start."

Tommy's foot work, plain and fancy
| 16November08 |

Jeanne was sitting on Tommy's lap, licking the lobe that she had but moments before bit.

Tommy was pink, the ear lobe was red (lipstick/trauma).

Jeanne got up, slowly, and clicked on her kitten heels to a neutral corner.

"I second that motion, Mister Chair Sir," Jim said.

"Yeah," OhJim said, "I like to see that motion as often as I can."

Jeanne gave the boys their lemony treat.

"Well, Mister Chair Goose," Tommy said, "I see, from the posts of late, and the bite marks on my ear, that my poem caused a commotion."

"Right," I said. "We are still puzzled about a few things, and I hope you can help us put the sky together. That's always the hardest part. You have to go by the shapes of the pieces rather than any variation in color."

"A good image," Tommy said, "for what I was doing."

"Constructing a jig-saw puzzle?" David said.

"In a way," Tommy said. "More like the posing of a problem."

"I'm hearing here, Dear," Eve said, "that you were taking us through an experience, but I'm not sure what your goals were."

"You have a piece of it," Tommy said. "I wanted to find a way to tease the Tribe into a place where you-all could look with new eyes at what has been ticking in your ears for so long."

Tommy bowed to Mister Ed, the **what_do_U_C** man.

Mister Ed, ever the crane, bowed from the waist in reply.

"Thus the tone of danger and warning," I said.

"I should bite your other ear," Jeanne said, making to rise, which totally wrong-footed the poet, turning his elegant iambs toward dopey dactyls.

Tommy got his groove back when he realized that Jeanne was bluffing.

"Look," Tommy said, "I don't care if Jeanne sleeps in a subway station. That isn't the point. The point is that all of you need to begin assessing the threats more accurately and actually doing things in response, and even taking the initiative. I chose the poem, and the calligraphy, because those are open forms that I enjoy. The aim was to goose you into some action, in some direction, and to say that in multiple voices."

"I see your point," I said. "We have chosen an enlightened sort of passivity in response to the **Mystery Man's** machinations."

"You are," Tommy said, "reaching the limits of passivity in this matter."

"Do you have any specific information that leads you to say that?" Jeanne said. "Anything we need to know?"

"Not anything specific," Tommy said, "just the ticking clock and the vague feeling that someone new to you-all is going to wash up on the shore of Mr. Black's interior landscape of perceived pain."

"I have to be honest with you, my friend," I said. "(And watch it when I say that I'm going to be **honest**.) I still feel uneasy about action of any active sort. I still do not know what is motivating my old friend Mr. Black, and I am content to keep the Tribe safe while we wait for his next move."

"Someone will die for that," Tommy said. "I fear that."

"Someone other than those in this room, Dear," Eve said. "I, sir, am sure of that. And I have squared that with what you say about your innocents."

"If I could stop Mr. Black now, I would," I said, "but I have nothing to go on, and I will have nothing to go on until he acts."

"Ok. Fine," Tommy said, "so tether a goat and watch from hiding places. Catch him in the act."

"An ancient gambit," I said, "and sometimes a good one, but we are talking about a trained and lethal weapon here. No one of us has more skills, and of the elders no one of us has much less, than what Mr. Black has. You are critical of our balance."

"There is no discernible disparity between Mr. Black and the others in the color corps," Eve said. "Any victory would be pyrrhic. We cannot afford any more of such victories."

"Then make me the goat," Tommy said. "I can tip the balance your way."

Thanks go to the goat
| 17November08 |

Email from Goose to Tommy -- **We like sheep, have gone astray** --

My dear friend Billie:

This is the crux -- is a tethered-goat trap the right thing to do, and if it is, are you the best goat to tie down, and if you are, why are you, and if it is a good plan, how will we proceed?

You are right, I will admit. We have been our own enemy, by making ourselves stay put, watching and waiting. If this were a story, I might be open to criticism for prizing passivity over action and allowing the narrative to falter, but since we are dealing with very live ammo here, it is better to keep our heads down, and our heads together, and to work on the problem in the best way possible.

I am grateful that you have found a way to shake me and the others into at least considering a firm plan, and your generous offer of your own skin to bait the trap is beyond my ability to praise in words. You are offering, and insisting, to do what I have been loathe to ask any of the others to do. It was risky enough to send Mr. Red downtown, though we did gain Jeanne as a result. That was about the last active thing that we have done, except for a few fieldtrips.

And you are right.

You can tip the balance toward us and away from Mr. Black.

Did you catch the reference in my email heading? It's a variation on Handel's wording from the **Messiah** that an old friend of mine would sing out. Imagine, the friend would say, a headline concerning a titillating public confession of a bestial nature --

We like sheep,
have gone astray.

It gives the old text a new meaning. And is a way for me to admit that we have been a lot like sheep who have gone astray and wandered in passivity. But for your offer we would continue to bleat and to pull up grass by the roots, and chew our way across the meadow, with no other goal in mind.

I fear the attempt, but I am willing to make it since you are willing, too.

Goose

No news is good news (and gospel)
| 18November08 |

It feels so wrong to drag my feet and hope for no new news. Such an approach was never seen as viable in Spookistan. But in my happy exile, I have gone east of that place and found that I have abilities in the direction of inaction that I never knew that I had.

Until Tommy insisted ...
- That we had to act ...
- And that his poem was a way to smack us into action ...
- And that he was willing to be the tethered goat in a sting aimed at Mr. Black.

I have been content to watch and wait, and to work on the skill set of the young ones, for the future.

That, at least, shows that I see a life for the Tribe beyond the matter of Mr. Black.

We can win, but I can't see how.

Maybe, now, Tommy does.

With Tommy's offer to be the tethered goat, we are breaking out of the passivity that we have been exploring for a very, very long time.

I must admit that I am still ambivalent about becoming active in regard to Mr. Black, but I cannot disagree that Tommy's entering the mix will tip the balance in our favor. Tommy is younger, and smart, and strong. His training is a match, at least, for that of the elders of color in the Tribe. This is significant. The balance of power will shift to the Tribe, and away from Mr. Black. Perhaps Mr. Black's perception of the difference, alone, will modify his behaviors (unless Mr. Black is working on our behalf, only).

I have become womanish, frankly, in my feelings about this matter, and I know that to lead the Tribe I must be strong and resolute. Godlike, even.

Still, I am uneasy. And all puffed up like a toad. The trick will be to enter into the planning with a will. A good plan will go a long way toward meeting my goals of keeping those whom I love safe.

And yet, for one last time, I remember the words that the balky pitcher tells his angry catcher -- **If I don't throw it, they cain't hit it!**

Going deeper - all (?) about Eve (!)
| 19November08 |

In preparing for a **come-to-Jesus** meeting with Tommy around his challenge to make him the tethered goat in a sting operation designed to catch and not release Mr. Black, I am thinking about specific covert skills that Eve has that no one else in the Tribe has.

For me, the fairly specific skill, currently unique in the Tribe, is my time as a resident theologian and pastor (and concurrent spook called to spy on my own people, my own flock, in the one-time, longtime op called **Operation Beloved**).

This skill, which I shared with Mr. Black, as a brother under the cloth in covert intention, keeps me in constant need of heaven's mercy and assistance, in my exiled life. I am constantly looking back on sins against my brothers and sisters, and against my God, too, come to that.

I for one cannot say that **I am a man more sinned against than sinning**.

Suffice it to say, I make myself sick when I think about it -- and most of the time when I look in the mirror. It was only the God whom I once mocked who saved me, when I stopped mouthing the promise that there is no sin so heinous that God cannot forgive and started believing my own once-cynical, covert-led preaching that God forgives the broken and broken-hearted person who cannot bear to look in the mirror most days.

In words of orthodox faith -- **the Lord is near to the broken-hearted and helps those who are crushed in spirit.**

If those words repel you, I am deeply sorry.

≈ ≈ ≈

Eve, with her saintly Buddha Girl smile, beautiful soul, and winning ways, has her secrets, too, and as she **outed me** to my brothers, a few months back, in forcing me to tell them the truth about myself and our Pop, I now take upon myself the task of **outing her.**

She will thank me for this, in time … .

Seriously, friends, I have her concurrence in telling this part of her story.

For once, I am speaking as honestly as I know how.

Enjoy it while you can. If you have eyes to see and ears to hear.

I do this with her approval and coaching.

As in **I am Eve and I approve this message.**

That sort of thing.

For Eve, the agony of recovery from the shadows, and the turning of painful exile into blessed days in the happy isles of those-hoping-to-be-redeemed, has similar but different aspects when compared to my time as a self-damned pastor-and-spook.

Eve was a therapist-as-cover, which was her personal contribution to the long-standing (and still ongoing) domestic effort to spy on the home team. Think **Patriot Act**. Think George **Dubya** Bush. Think, and fear, **NSA**.

Like that.

Operation Shrink-Wrap. That was Eve's op.

Sure, it is illegal as hell and punishable to the extreme (in God's eyes?), but try to prove that elements of our covert structure do not spy on our own citizens at will, right now, with no remorse. And little or no oversight.

By law.

I can't prove or disprove that, and neither can you. Only the spies can. Such spying was true before the Patriot Act and is true, and legal, since the Patriot Act.

Ask any geek about the Clipper Chip, or muse on the NSA's ability to read your email. All of your email. Wave to the satellite, honey.

Mind you, I'm not talking about conspiracy theories.

Lord deliver us from such.

When you have been in the dark places that I have been in and done the dark acts that I have done, and Eve as well, in **Operation Shrink-Wrap**, you laugh at conspiracy theories, in the same way that those who have seen God, felt God, and heard God will laugh at the gyrations of self-styled atheists and others who pull on simple reason until it goes out of true like salt water taffy -- tasty enough, it is true, but watch out for your fillings.

These folk do not have a clue. God is not reasonable, or nice. Just loving.

If conspiracy theorists did have a clue, their conspiracy theories would go so much further than they ever do. I'm saying that what goes on, and what the Vault reflects, is so much more than you could ask for or imagine or make any sense of using the categories that **The Man** has sold you, at deep discount. We are not talking about conspiracy but the simple and ugly truth.

Am I ranting?

Well, excuse me.

≈ ≈ ≈

To return to Eve's contribution to **Amerika**. Eve was asked to use her considerable charm and innate goodness to subvert confused and hurting persons who came to her for mental healing. Sure, she healed them; a relationship with Eve cannot but be healing.

I am not the only person who owes his life to Eve's goodness and skill. You have seen and heard enough to believe me when I say that. That much, taken alone, would be the cornerstone of her self-esteem, but the overlay of covert aims makes this same God-given gift of interpersonal healing a source of deep and abiding pain, and shame, for her. Rightly so, I am pained to say, as you who know the denied, projected feelings that go with betraying one's own brothers and sisters, for The Man and The Man's goals and aims, know. Eve and I, and the other elders of the Tribe, have, like Pogo, met the enemy **and he is us.**

To survive this cesspool of other-driven evil and distortion is to spend the balance of one's days, in happy exile, in a search for redemption based on a renewed and cleansed use of one's God-given gifts.

For covert reasons that can only be described as demonic and ugly, Eve received extensive training in the Transactional Analysis techniques of Dr. Eric Berne.

Berne's system of explaining and understanding the human personality, and the human personality particularly in social interaction, has few rivals. Berne is the one who first wrote about **the games people play.**

Why **TA**, and not some other system such as Freud's? you might ask.

Two reasons --

• Transactional Analysis, or TA for short, is elegant and accessible, and portable, as a way of understanding, talking of, and predicting the behavior of persons who stand in social relation.

• Berne developed TA partly as a reaction to his own personal rejection by the traditional Freudian community.

Am I an expert?

Not at all, but I do sleep with one and I do listen to what she says.

And just as I seek to be the blessing-strewing person I am at times and parson that I once pretended to be, in the way I approach myself and others, post-Spookistan, so too does Eve desire, with all her heart and soul and mind and strength, to visit healing where she once visited a cynical sort of healing that generated, as a side effect, a damned goldmine of damning information used to subvert causes and persons who did not deserve such treatment. No one deserves such treatment, and nations have always felt some level of need to do such things in the dark, be it from fear or dogma, or some disgusting combination that always seems to generate a rationale that catches and enslaves otherwise fine minds and good-intending persons.

Such as Eve.

Eve no longer offers therapy.

Tommy takes a positive charge
| 20November08 |

"The F-Troop will be in order," I said.

"Out of order, Mister Chair Sir," Jim said.

"Yeah," OhJim said, "as in back-ordered."

"Order in the court," I said. "The judge is eating beans. His wife is in the bathtub, shooting submarines."

"You are so weird sometimes, Mr. Chair Sir," Jim said.

"Yeah," OhJim said. "Good job!"

"Be that as it may," I said," we do have work to do, we **do be do be do**."

"I'm just glad that Tommy is late," Eve said." He doesn't get this part of the Tribe's protocol yet."

"Who doesn't?" Tommy said, striding into the room and sitting between David and Jeanne. "I understand that these Grim gentlemen fart in a bag and no one pays any attention or turns up the nose or takes offense. What's to understand?"

"You," I said. "You don't get the **laughing at doom** thing yet, according to Miss Eve, who knows such things. Maybe you do not yet value the principle."

"I understand that Eve knows a lot that I didn't understand before reading your last post, Goose Man," Tommy said. "I think we're getting somewhere."

"If it don't get dark," Jim said.

"Yeah," OhJim said, "and if the horses don't forget the way home."

"I'm referring," Tommy said, "to the potential of Miss Eve's training in human behaviors and triggers."

"**Drivers**," Eve said. "In TA, we call triggers **drivers**."

"Well," Tommy said, "I'm happy to sit in the sidecar and let you drive. I'm thinking that we need a profile on Mr. Black. Can you do that?"

"Certainly, Dear," Eve said.

"Perhaps," I said, "Miss Naomi could step to the flipchart, marker in hand, to the rapt attention of a grateful nation, or at least the men in this room."

Jeanne smiled to the side, and to the other side, and clicked on her spike heels to the easel. She struck a pose in red and black.

"I think," Tommy said, "that we need to set some goals concerning Mr. Black and the tethered goat approach that I'm advocating for. First thing that I think of is this. Do we want to catch Mr. Black?"

Jeanne wrote and underlined: **Do we want to catch Mr. Black?**

"I'll go through a decision tree with my choices apparent," Tommy said, "so the next thing is this: **If yes, why do we want to catch Mr. Black? ...** and **How do we plan to catch Mr. Black?** And after that, this: **What will we do with Mr. Black when we catch him?**"

Jeanne wrote down Tommy's tree to the root.

"And if I may, Mister Chair Goose, I would like to lead the discussion of these points," Tommy said.

"Take your turn, my friend," I said.

"First question," Tommy said. "**Do we want to catch Mr. Black?** Do you?"

"Yes," Eve said, "I do want to catch our old friend Mr. Black."

"Why?" Tommy said.

"Because," I said, "he is -- as far as we can tell -- killing people and we do not know why and because no one else is going to be able to catch him because no one else knows that he exists."

"Why, then," Tommy said, "have you not yet caught him?"

"Because," Jeanne said, "we are afraid of what we will have to do when we do catch him, and the elders seem to be afraid for the safety of the youngsters before, during, and after capture."

"Fair enough, Goose?" Tommy said.

"Fair enough, Tommy," I said.

"So," Tommy said, "why do you **now** say you want to catch Mr. Black?"

"Because," Eve said, "we are getting nervous about another body, and because we fear that the three to date might have been innocents whose blood is on our heads. And although I can square that with myself, I would rather cut off the count at three."

"My answer to your **why now** question," I said, "is that once we pull the trigger on this, we will lose control of the outcome. I know that sounds silly, but I do feel that. And wanting to maintain control has kept me from acting. Which definitely sounds strange."

"And so," Tommy said, "a generous measure of control would be good?"

"Very good," I said. "I would add that your willingness to be the bait in the trap --the **tethered goat** -- has given me some hope that I did not have before. Without something like that, we are looking at a blood bath among lethal equals. I can take out Mr. Black, and he will take me out, in the same stroke. Same goes for any of the elders. Zeroed out. And I didn't want to sacrifice anyone. You, now, that is a different story --."

General laughter kept me from finishing.

"I think I know what you mean," Tommy said. "And I am willing to try myself against your Mr. Black, as long as you-all have my back. Let's just say it is in my professional interest to see this matter closed."

"**It is in my professional interest to see this matter closed,**" Jim and OhJim said in monotone/unison.

"With any outcome?" Eve said.

"With any outcome," Tommy said.

"I want to discuss outcomes that stop short of killing our old friend," Eve said. "I am no longer willing, nor is Goose, to simply erase those who threaten us. That was then."

"This is now," I said. "We want outcomes that affirm life, and until we understand Mr. Black's motives, we need your assurances that **dead or alive** is shortened to **alive** ... alive but under restraint, certainly."

"If we can catch him, we can hogtie him long enough to assess his state of mind," Eve said, "and that is one place my training will come into play."

"I will play by those rules," Tommy said, "with the understanding, and agreement, that I and you will escalate if necessary to protect ourselves. I see myself and the Tribe as of greater utility than Mr. Black, and I want an iron-clad agreement that he loses if he forces the issue with any one of us."

"Agreed," I said, and noticing a thicket of F-Troop salutes, added "-- and so say you all."

My assertion drew the usual smiles, headbobbles, and silence.

We were like that. To a fault.

"That covers the questions of **If** and **Why**, Tommy said.

"Next question is **How.**"

Tommy plugs his meter with quarter notes
|21November08|

"Oh," Tommy said, "you pretty much missed the point of my poem."

"Creative misunderstandings are the best kind," Jim said.

"Yeah," OhJim said. "Someone had to be creative. You may be an agent, but you need one, too."

"Ouch," Tommy said. "But also, you had some good insights. It's just that you missed the **Big Casino.**"

"Ok," Jeanne said, "I'll bite (and I do, BTW). What did we miss?"

"Well," Tommy said, "I misspoke. You got it half-right. When I said **get out, Jeanne, get away**, I was talking about doing something other than sitting in this room, in a circle, **thunder-mugging** -- pulling puns out of the air like potshots."

"Oh," I said, "I see what you mean. And our current conversation, with the current topic, that of how to go about tethering you as a sacrificial goat, to trap Mr. Black, will get us out of the house."

"Unless," Eve said, "we decide to spring the trap right here, in our own backroom sandbox."

"Well," Tommy said, "for so many reasons I hope that you do not decide to foul your own sandbox. Pick someone else's. My view, that."

"Seems like we have been, once again, successful in thwarting action," David said, "but we may be half again the distance from here and there."

"Any kid knows," Jim said, "that you can divide a line in half endlessly."

"Yeah," OhJim said, "we're just getting started."

"Tommy," Eve said, "press ahead. Ask the **how** question."

"**How**," Tommy said, smiling with hand up, palm forward at my brothers. "How will we set up the sting -- **where** and **when**, too.

"I thought you would never ask," Eve said. "To catch Mr. Black, we need to have a sense of who he is, what his **Life Script** is, what his **Script issues** are, and what are the **social games** he prefers to play. By your leave, Tommy, and by your leave, Mister Chair Dear, I'll take the lead for a while."

We nodded.

"First," Eve said, "is the question of who Mr. Black is. Any takers?"

"Well," I said, "he is brilliant, he is volatile, he is relentlessly foul-mouthed, and he is as deep a believer as I am, having mocked his way to sudden and life-shaking conversion like I did."

"Ok," Eve said, "a good start. Now, about his Life Script. That means the life story that he is living out on the stage of life (complete with Script issues). A Life Script can be either **heroic** or **banal**. I'm guessing that Mr. Black's Script, which like all life scripts is inherited from one's significant others, particularly parents, is heroic."

"Why not banal?" Jeanne said.

"Well," Eve said, "on the surface -- the **overt** level -- he is heroic in the extreme, a trait he shares with the general run of spooks. But at the **covert** level, he could be working in a counter-direction, like you are implying by your question, Dear. Things are seldom what they seem, with persons, and no two do the same with a similar set of traits and such."

"I experience my old friend as bigger than life, and twice as smart as most folk," I said. "And prone to arrogance, another trait of the generality of spooks, I guess. Covert self-sabotage."

"So, Eve said, "we will need to figure out his favorite **Social Game** to set a devious but obvious trap. A word about social games. They are always meant to be a way to avoid intimacy but still gather in **strokes**, positive or negative -- it does not matter, as long as the strokes are strong -- powerful enough to create a sense of liveliness and excitement. And yes, Dear, covert self-sabotage. The payoff in a social game is always negative and all players end up feeling yucky."

"I don't know the name of the game," I said, "but Mr. Black simply refused to take me seriously, ever. Any conversation began with a comment or question from me and a **bleep**-you and additional insult from him. I never liked that about him, and I couldn't see how he could like it himself, though he did it every time we talked. Intimacy is not his strong suit."

"That reminds me of two games that Berne identified," Eve said, "-- **Kick Me** and **Now I Gotcha, You SOB**. The two go together like a hand and a glove. A **Kick Me** player knows how to get others to give him a good, strong kick in the pants. This person has a big bull's eye painted on his behind. He needs to be kicked in order to feel validated by others. A person who plays **Now I Gotcha** is the one who needs to kick others. He excels at enticing **Kick Me** behaviors even from persons who do not normally play **Kick Me**. In TA-Speak, a **NIGYSOBer**."

"So," Jeanne said, "the trap is to offer Mr. Black a chance to play his favorite game - **Now I Gotcha**."

"Another variation," Eve said, "is for the **Now I Gotcha** player to pretend to play **Kick Me**, but when he is kicked, he counter-kicks with exponentially greater intensity. Like he is saying, **How dare you kick me, you SOB. Now I gotcha!** And delivers a thundering kick."

"Sounds like we have the beginnings of a plan," Tommy said. "Well-done, Couch Potatoes."

"Ain't no couches here," Jim said.

"Yeah," OhJim said, "and no potatoes either. The body metabolizes potatoes just like sugar, Sugar Daddy."

"You had to be there," Tommy said. "I can see that you were not."

"It is clear," I said, "that we have a modality. Now we need a place. All I can think of is a bar. He was using a bar -- the **Roll In and Crawl Out** -- to make contact, according to Ben, and he might try that again."

"I thought the same thing," Tommy said, "and I think the **Roll In and Crawl Out** is as good a place as any to try out this sting. I could use a beer after all this talk. And just about now, in fact."

Tommy does the old bait and switch
| 22November08 |

Tommy looked at me with intensity.

"What?" I said.

"We're going at this backwards, brother," Tommy said. "I have no problem with being the bait, but Mr. Black does not know me like he does you-all. That fact, which is our ace in the hole, demands another approach. Mr. Black will bite if the bait is some tasty thing he knows. Like you, Goose."

"What?" I said. "Me?"

"Exactly," Tommy said. "It makes perfect sense for you to be the bait and for me to have your back." That way, we can both be in the bar. If I'm the bait, who could be the other? Doesn't work. He knows all of you-all. And this makes the best use of my abilities and yours."

"While we're at it," David said, "do we think that it is possible that someone unknown to us has Mr. Black's back?"

"As likely as not," Tommy said, "so a few of you will lurk in the alley."

"I'm thinking that you might have something there, Tommy, and I also," I said, "think that David is onto something, too."

"Something can come of something," Jim said.

"Yeah," OhJim said, "but **nothing will come of nothing, Fool**."

"If I may, Mister Chair Sir," Mister Ed said. "I would like to volunteer to be one of the persons lurking nearby. And I would suggest that we lurkers go in on a code-word signal. I suggest **riposte** as the code word."

"I'm in, in the alley," David said.

"And," Jeanne said, "I want to take David in my car and sit outside the bar tonight to see who comes and goes. We should have long ago."

"I'll go with you," I said, "provided you don't embarrass me by smashing face or anything like that, except to maintain cover. I'll be your bodyguard. It would make me feel a whole lot better."

"If there is bare-assing, I'm in," Jim said.

"Yeah," OhJim said, "me, too. Butt barely."

"So," Tommy said, "this is the plan. Goose, Jeanne, and David go to watch the bar tonight in Jeanne's car (I hope it's a beater). Tomorrow we gather again to hear their report. Tomorrow night, Goose and I go into the bar and see if Mr. Black shows. Mister Ed will be in the alley, and Eve will be in a car parked right outside. We will hit Mr. Black with an eye spray that I have access to that will make him all but comatose. He will be alert enough to appear drunk. We don't want the bartender or any other patrons intervening or calling the cops. The worst would be if the newspaper got hold of a story like that."

"Tell me more about the eye spray," I said.

"It's fool-proof," Tommy said. "I've used it before, and it is quick-acting and accurate in a tight pattern from a few feet. That means I won't hit you or anyone but Mr. Black. Leave the details of approach to me."

"A backup plan for apprehension would be good," Eve said.

"How about this," I said. "The backup plan is to hand him a cell phone with Eve on the other end. She tells him that there are several weapons menacing him as they speak and he should come out and get in the car parked at the door. I want Mr. Red in the backseat, to protect Eve and to help with getting Mr. Black safely in the backseat. Eve can talk to Mr. Red. He will say yes to her. Eve can reason with our old friend Mr. Black and get him to comply."

"It is important to make things up as we go along, if need be," Tommy said. "We need to be confident that we can prevail. I will be the one to decide if we must abort or cut our losses and run. Agreed? My code phrase for abort will be **Cheese it, the cops!**"

"Agreed," I said. "And the op is **Operation Blackout**."

"One refinement," Jeanne said. "We can use throw-down cell phones to coordinate backup. David and I can set this up in the morning."

"One last question," David said. "Will we know him in a fresh disguise?"

"I will," I said. "Mr. Black cannot fool me. Don't worry about that."

"Agreed," Tommy said. "Get going, and we'll meet in the morning."

It sounded simple, which had me very worried.

Even so, I did trust our ability to envision an operation.

Sit and watch, sit and wait

| 23November08|

"Let's go," Jeanne said. "It's Happy Hour."

Ms. Punk Princess clicked her way toward the front of the bookshop.

David and I stomped along behind.

"Don't wait up for us, Red," I said.

"Bleeps to you, Consort Man," Mr. Red said.

"Meow," Wild Billy said from Mr. Red's lap.

It's probably a good thing that most cats don't speak English.

It is bad enough that most cats understand English.

The little bells on the plate-glass front door of the bookshop warned of our departure. We stepped into the cold and wind and dark. Jeanne buttoned her coat -- red nails against black wool -- over her deep red dress that tickled at her black nylon-clad, high-heel toned calves. Jeanne let us into her indifferent Buick -- not too old and certainly not too new -- a perfect car for the work.

Jeanne had inherited the Buick from her auntie or some such kin, and it was old enough to have bench seats, front and back. So much the better for our needs. The Buick was that shade of ho-hum tan usually called **taupe**. Or **snuff**, in some lower life circles. No one would give it a second glance. The collection of dings and creases, plus the slightly round-heels character of the wheel covers, completed a picture of such barfly banality that one would almost forget it while still having it in the field of view. You could argue that the mind would not bother to store such a banal image as Jeanne's Buick. Jeanne's ride was nothing like Jeanne.

David got in the passenger side up front, and I got in the back. Jeanne bounced behind the wheel and turned on the wipers to get rid of the dusting of snow that had fallen throughout the evening. We headed downtown.

"It's a bit early for the club crowd," Jeanne said, "but we are not going to a club, are we. The time is probably just about right for a serious drinker on a beer budget. Or a newsy bent on pickling a few brain cells after a bored-bleepless evening on the barricades."

"The **Roll In and Crawl Out**?" David said. "Perfect timing for that."

"You guys will sit up, close to one another," I said, "and do some nose-rubbing. Think shadow-show. I'll hunker down. Pick a spot across the street, Jeanne, away from street lights if you can. We shall see what we shall see."

"We'll play **Photography**," David said.

"What's that?" Jeanne said.

"**Turn out the lights and see what develops**," David said, smiling his bug-eyed smile with lots of teeth and round glasses.

Jeanne pulled up on the block-long side street, across from the **Roll In**'s narrow and recessed door. She had no problem meeting my requirements. There were street lights at the corners but that was it.

The bar itself, at mid-block, surrounded by warehouses and abandoned little storefronts, had some neon in the long window next to the door but not enough to read by. The buildings nearby, in tones of brown and sun-faded tans and whites, were a match for the Buick. The storefronts along the street were common-wall. At the bar you would have a view out the long, low window. Approaching the **Roll In** was like riding into Box Canyon. Anyone approaching the bar would be on the sidewalk, unless they snuck in from the alley behind the bar that ran parallel to the street. That was the alley that held the dumpster that had held the body and that bore the coyote symbol on its side. Watching the alley was beyond our budget, in terms of both person power and degree of exposure, on this occasion. We settled in for a long wait.

Every so often, a time or two per hour, a well-bundled figure, almost always male, would go in or come out of the bar. It would be a neat trick to pick out Mr. Black, but I knew his walk, his profile, and his freaking vibrations, even. If Mr. Black was in the Zip Code, I would get a twinge. Of that I was certain.

Auto traffic was light, and foot traffic was minimal, and no one else parked along the street while we were there. A few cars and a van or two were scattered about. It was a bad night to be a stray dog. The snow had eddied into scant piles against the buildings, but the streets were clear. It was cold enough, but serious snows were a few weeks away.

David slipped over next to Jeanne on the Buick's bench seat, like two on a couch. I went with that, instead of having them switch, because a man sitting close to a woman in the driver's seat sent the right sort of sleazy overtone that we were trying to project.

Some guy trying to get lucky.

No second glance.

Except for someone like Mr. Black, who has more feelers than an alley cat has whiskers. I know, because I am like that, too. One is like that, in Spookistan and after Spookistan -- effortlessly, relentlessly para-paranoid.

You might say that we were coat-dragging as much as we were watching from a static post. I was Ok with that, since we had the cover of the car and the kids had me to watch their back. I spent half my time looking out the window to each side. And behind, always, mostly by feel. Our breath fogged us in and added a lacy sheen of ice to the windows all around.

A few hours had gone by and we had each made tiny holes in the steamed windows to peer through. Jeanne and David kept up the nose-rubbing to sell the shadow show. They had a knack. And it didn't look like an act, either.

Neither one was complaining.

"Heard any good jokes lately?" Jeanne said.

"I saw a random blog post this morning," David said, "that claimed that Sarah Palin's recent political gyrations were greater than one might think because she did them with only half a brain."

We laughed softly.

Time passed. The kids moved closer together, and I hugged myself. It was cold and getting colder. The wind had come up and was juddering against the Buick. The bit of snow had scattered. The pace of drinkers was quicker, in and out of the bar, but the numbers had dwindled.

"What if he doesn't show?" Jeanne said. "Plan B?"

"Plan B is to come back tomorrow night and just waltz in, Tommy and me, and start drinking," I said. "All coat-dragging and no concealment."

"What if," David said, "he doesn't hang here?"

"Don't know," I said. "Plan C is a further escalation of higher-profile parading of one or more of us who are known to our old friend. He will become aware of us. Mr. Black has to be watchful if he is doing what we think he is doing."

We sat tight, and cold, until after midnight.

The wannabe lovers in dumb show didn't seem to mind their assigned places. In fact, from where I was sitting, they seemed to enter into their roles with a zeal of generous and genuine proportions.

"Let's try an experiment," David said, "and then maybe we can go home. I can slide out and go in the bar and have a beer or two. If I see someone who looks like Mr. Black, I'll speed dial Jeanne on the sly and leave. If you hear my ring, Jeanne, you start the car and swing around to pick me up. On the other hand, if I see no one I like, I come on out and get back in, and youse can see if I grow a late-night shadow or an untimely tail."

David bugged out his eyes and smiled.

"Ok," I said, "but no close shaves. And don't try any cowboy stuff. Just a beer or two, and back, Good Knight. And no jousting."

David's gambit - a knight to remember
| 24November08 |

David pulled his baseball cap down tight and slipped from the Buick, triggering the dome light. I made a mental note to teach them how to make sure that did not happen the next time.

On a night like this, light was not our friend.

David walked across the street and into the **Roll In and Crawl Out.**

I looked at Jeanne. She looked at me. We waited. And watched.

In the silence, I noticed my own aroma of sweat and unease, and Jeanne's usual mixture of various faint perfumes. She smelled, I'm sure, the way that the inside of her handbag smelled.

Women are like that, at least the ones that I know.

It is an odd sort of intimacy, being led by the nose.

But I am a push-over for the ladies.

David had left little behind in the way of scent, just a whiff of deodorant, but he was heavy on our minds while we waited for him to call or come back out of the bar.

"I'm getting too old for this," I said, "but not entirely. Just almost."

"Thanks," Jeanne said. "We're not ready to go it alone, Master."

"I know," I said, "but I'm hopeful, very hopeful. Doing this shows a lot of heart, both of you. I am pleased with David's initiative, though I do admit that I'll be very glad to see him again, and soon."

"Me, too," Jeanne said. "I've grown accustomed to his funny face."

She smiled, like that, and poked the corner of her mouth with her tongue.

"How long does a beer or two take?" Jeanne said.

Five minutes had passed.

"More than this," I said, "if he does it right -- not rushed, not laid back."

More silence and scent, hanging in the air of the darkened Buick.

We made our peep holes just a bit bigger and kept watching.

I was thinking about David's idea that he was playing out, and I was trying not to call it a **gambit**. Gambits, and lost pawns, are business as usual in Spookistan. I wanted David to fail at his gambit and get his narrow patoot back in the Buick so I could say, **Good job. Nice try. Let's call it a knight**.

About the time that I was deciding that I am not as hard-edged, or as funny, as I thought I was, and a lot older in both **soul** and **soma** time than I was giving myself credit for, Jeanne's cell rang.

"That's David's ring," Jeanne said. She started the Buick and did a quick U-turn to pull up in front of the bar.

David got in. His face was giving nothing away.

David appeared at the curb at the same time that Jeanne had put on the brakes, on the bar side of the street, and unlocked the passenger door with her master button. It took all of 10 seconds. All of it to the opening bars of **Hey, hey, we're the Monkeys!** on Jeanne's cell.

"Jeanne," I said, "douse your phone, turn on your headlights, and pull away, now, but slowly. Drive normally."

I looked back to see if David had grown a bushy black tail.

Nothing.

I turned my attention to David. Jeanne drove.

"What gives?" I said. "You used the rainy-day signal."

"I was sitting, and drinking my second beer," David said, "when I noticed that a man in a baseball cap and hoodie had come out of the door from the **Ladies** and the **Gents**. He looked like the man in the drawing that Ben gave us, so I hit my speed dial, got up slowly, and walked out. I didn't look back."

"Good," I said. "Jeanne, drive around the block and go by the bar again."

When we pulled into the side street, I could see a man standing outside, with his back to us. Bingo. Mr. Black.

As we drove by, he looked at the car, and I looked through my peephole in the Buick's tinted and frosted window at my old friend.

"Take us home, Jeanne," I said, "and do a few right-hand turns after we get about halfway there."

"Checking for tails?" David said.

"Yeah," I said. "Yours is so short I almost missed it. Oh, and good job, by the way, my friend."

David smiled a jumpish smile.

"I was doing fine at first," he said, "and enjoying my beer. I was about to leave anyway when he came in from the back. Turning my back on him was one of the hardest things that I've ever done, and walking instead of running, and saying **Good night** to the bartender -- that was hard, too. Very,

very hard. Can't say that enough."

David would be prattling for a while. That was the usual way of it. I wanted him to know that he had been in danger and that he had done well, but I did not want him to forget that wide feeling of fear and control.

"Who else was in there?" I said.

Jeanne started her series of right-hand turns, and I watched out the back while David answered.

Nothing.

"It's a nasty little place," David said, "and there was only one other guy at the bar, an old guy in an overcoat he probably got from some thrift shop. There are a few small tables, and a very large man and a very sexy gypsy-looking woman were in one of them, away from the door. They were very interested in themselves, and the guy at the bar was very interested in his half-empty glass. The sort who would not see the glass, ever, as half-full."

"Good, Jeanne," I said. "I saw nothing. Head for the bookshop. Park, and turn off the lights."

"Roger, Goose," Jeanne said, with a sweet and sour smile -- that smile. Jeanne was doing fine.

"David," I said, "was there an unattended beer glass at the bar or on any of the tables?"

"I didn't notice any," David said, "though I couldn't see to the far side of the guy to my right."

"And you didn't want to wait long enough for Mr. Black or any of the others to get between you and the door," I said. "All things considered, you did the best thing that you could have done. This was a recon effort, not a suicide mission. You done good, my friend."

David smiled again, and his smile was more like the one that I wanted to see, with a bit of bug-eyes through his round glasses and lots of teeth. Much better than the one he gave us a few minutes and miles back.

I thought about the timing of Mr. Black's entry.

And I wondered whether he had been in the bar all night, or had come in from the alley.

I decided that David had gotten lucky with Mr. Black's decision to go see a man about a horse at that particular time.

I was pretty sure there had not been enough time for the bartender to alert Mr. Black. A lert, and Mr. Black would have one or more, is always a problem. Lerts. We need those not. Dealing with a lert is no joking matter.

The guy at the far end of the bar, away from the door, had the best spot in the house for watching all the comings and goings.

That is where I would have wanted to be, on a stool to that man's right.

The last stool on the right, in fact.

The fact that the man had sold David on the idea that he was only interested in his beer didn't mean that much to me one way or the other.

"Give me a little more detail about the serious drinker," I said.

"He was middle-aged, or slightly more," David said, "and kind of slumped over, like he was tired or a bit drunk. He had on a sock cap, dark blue or black. No facial hair, a few days of stubble. Like I said, a serious drinker."

"By the look of him anyway," Jeanne said.

I nodded.

Jeanne pulled up just down the street from the bookshop.

"Turn off the headlights. Now we sit," I said, "and see who comes by, if anyone. We'll give it 15 minutes, then head home. Breathe deep and wait."

"**S.O.P?**" Jeanne said.

"**S.O.P**," I said.

Tomorrow night was looming already in my mind.

What are the odds, even?
| 25November08>

The next morning, bright and early, we were all in the backroom at **Caspar's Books and That**, hot coffee in hand -- which is not nearly as painful as it sounds.

"Do you think he made you?" Tommy said.

"Only if he is interested enough in the latter day changes at the bookshop and knows Jeanne's car," I said, "and that would not surprise me."

"Did anything surprise you?" Tommy said.

"Yeah," I said." I didn't expect to see friend Black at the same place where he had been seen before. That does not fit or sit well with me."

"I know, Dear," Eve said. "What are the odds? He must be a regular at the **Roll In**, or he has ESP that you wouldn't believe, or a network of henchmen and henchwomen to watch our comings and goings. And that would surprise me in the extreme. It would not be like our old friend Mr. Black to confide in anyone. And the payroll would be staggering. He can't have access to that much cash or **quid pro quo**, can he?"

"You wouldn't," Tommy said, "suspect the guy at the bar, or the couple in the corner, or the bartender, to be anyone but who they seemed to be?"

David, our man on the ground in the bar last night, shrugged one shoulder and arched the opposite eyebrow above his wire-frame glasses.

"Yes, Dear," Eve said. "Mr. Black does not mix well, and he has never been one to work with anyone else. He always said, didn't he, Goose Dear, that he had his own bleeping back."

"Yep," I said. "That was his mantra, and most of his religion, and all of his trust -- what he saw in the mirror. **Mirrors don't mumble or blab** -- that was another of his chestnuts."

"Leaving open the possibility that mirrors do talk," Jim said.

"Yeah," OhJim said. "**Mirror, Mirror on the wall, who's the spookiest of them all?**"

"Ok," Tommy said, "that was then, but what about now? Is there any evidence, or any profile data, Miss Eve, to indicate that your old friend has learned any new tricks?"

"I would say no, Dear," Eve said. "Provisionally, of course."

"Me, too," I said. "Mr. Black has the juice to do what he has been doing.

And what he has been doing is not any more complex than what he has done in the past. He is a man competent in violence and misdirection, and he has complete and utter trust in himself, and no one else. Being his friend was like trying to share a log in the middle of a river with a scorpion."

"It is in the scorpion's nature to sting," Jim said.

"Yeah," OhJim said, "and to not say he's sorry."

The little bells at the front door rang.

"To return to the bar, and your disquiet about that," Tommy said. "What are the odds that Mr. Black is just waiting for us to come in and talk with him, maybe have a beer?"

Tommy got an immediate and lively answer to his idle question.

Summon all the dust to rise,
Till it stirre, and rubbe the eyes;
While this member jogs the other,
Each one whispring, *Live you brother?*
    -- from **Dooms-day** by George Herbert

Part Three

A few awkward moments
| 26November08 |

The little bells.
The silence of the Red.
The **presence of an absence** (to repeat an apt phrase).
I looked up to see a darker version of myself, staring back at me and smiling a certain mocking sort of upside down smile with raised eyebrows.
A smile rising like mist from a hot, wet highway.
"Odds are good," Mr. Black said, standing in the doorway.
Baseball cap and hoodie. Mustache. Just like the drawing.
He had a sputtering Mr. Red in a friendly hug or headlock against his side. It was hard to tell which.
Tommy jumped up, David jumped back, Jeanne and Eve sat like statues.
My brothers looked like they were about to crack a few jokes.
Mister Ed was already two inches from Mr. Black, looking down at him like a very pissed-off Zeus on a thundercloud.
Red, released, blocked the doorway.
And I? I took the road less traveled by.
I was busy assessing all of these reactions.
That made all the difference.
  "Relax, friends," I said, fielding a quick wink and nod from Eve. "At ease. The Prodigal has returned. Let us rejoice, for this our brother had been lost and now is found."
Mister Ed took three reluctant steps back, and I could see my old friend's face once more.
  "**Bleep**-you, Goose Man," Mr. Black said -- one word, with the accent strongly on the first syllable, just like he always did. "And hello to you, Miss Eve. Long time no see."

Mr. Black's smile for Eve was as straight as a highway in the desert.

Mister Ed stepped forward again, bumping Mr. Black, like a knight defending his Lord's Lady. Mr. Black slapped Ed's face, back and forth and back, three times in as many nanoseconds. They stood nose to nose, panting, with not even room for a cigarette paper between them, but nothing like Jeanne and David last night on the front couch of the Buick.

"Bleep," Mr. Red said, "bleeping bleep."

Snaking his way between his old friend's legs, Wild Billy said, "Meow."

Billy once again had the last word.

Thank the Dear for the comic timing of a cat.

"Meow," Billy said to manic laughter, "meow, meow, meow."

Keeping one eye on the truculent Mister Ed, Mr. Black said, "Tell me, are youse guys and gals ever going to get up off your butts and go outside?"

"Nice to see you, Dear," Eve said. "We thought that you were dead, and then we thought that you might be alive, and then we wondered if you had a tumor pressing on your brain or something like that. Like a serial killer."

"We decided, in the end," I said, "that you might have been on a three-man killing jag, spaced over the past six or eight months. Or not."

"I see," Mr. Black said. "We have a few things to talk about. May I enter?"

I nodded to Ed.

"You always were a freaky old bastard, Ed," Mr. Black said. He smiled, like a guy-wire, and gave Ed a squeeze on the shoulder.

"What would you do if we said no?" Tommy said, rising.

"Relax, TLA," Mr. Black said. "Some of these good people might even vouch for me."

Tommy stopped just inches from our old friend, looking like a pissed off sibling eye to eye with our Prodigal.

"Tommy, my friend," I said, "no one is doubting your ability to harm friend Black. Step back and let him in. I do vouch for him, as a matter of fact, now that I've heard him speak and watched how he holds himself."

Tommy stepped back to his chair and sat like a coiled snake.

All this stepping up and stepping back made it look like we had taken up line dancing, to the tune of the **Black Swamp Stomp**.

Mister Ed, down from Olympus, moved up a chair for Mr. Black, who sat down between Mister Ed and Tommy.

"I'll talk with you, but I want you to promise that you won't just sit here and rot," Mr. Black said. "I've been watching you for a long time, and sometimes I wondered if you were still breathing."

David wandered back to his chair. Jeanne, long legs crossed, bounced one of her high heels, slowly, on her pretty big toe.

Eve settled in with a beatific smile on her Buddha Girl face.

"I'd ask for some introductions," Mr. Black said, "but I know you, by sight, from the youngest to the oldest, and this fine fellow as well."

Mr. Black petted Wild Billy.

"And," Mr. Black said, "I have no doubts that you know me. I just wonder what sorts of lies old Goose Man has been telling you about me. He never did like the truth much. You really should see someone about that, G-Man."

I smiled into my whiskers and out through my eyes.

"Good to have you back, old friend," I said. "And just to tie up things and clean up as we go along, this is Jeanne, next to her is David, and the two guys with half-smiles and my nose and nose hair are my brothers Jim and OhJim. Tommy and your old friend Mister Ed, you have already met, up close and personal. And Mr. Red, you know only too well, it seems."

"Bleep you, Consort Man," Mr. Red said from the doorway. "I am always betting on the Black. I'm never thinking is that stuff true."

"Well, Dear," Eve said, "we have a million and one questions."

Eve smiled at our old friend with extra-special Buddha Girl warmth.

"Meow," Wild Billy said. "Meow, meow. Meow."

No questions, please, no questions
| 27November08 |

I looked at my old friend whom I had been so unwilling to see, and I realized that my worst fears had been all fear no fact. Having Mr. Black back in the arms of the Tribe was a big enough adjustment for all of us without any concurrent need to tie him up and call for massive amounts of backup.

Not that we would ever have done that. Call for backup.

I had a short list of questions -- **who** died in the dark that night near the park, and **who** has been killing all those guys, and **why**. And **why** stay out in the cold for so long, and **what** was he planning to do now. I wanted all those answers already, so I really didn't know where to start, but I knew Mr. Black. He hated questions more than anything else, which is saying a lot for an angry man such as Mr. Black.

Asking Mr. Black questions was not an option.

Mr. Black would set the tone, the pace, and the sequence of his story, and no one would force him to do anything that he didn't want to do.

I was relieved that he had come in on his own, because Tommy and I vs. Mr. Black and any unknown associates, in a beer-soaked bar on a downtown side street from hell -- that was not a movie that I was sorry to miss.

Tommy, however, was ready to roll. He hadn't come down much from being two beats away from delivering a cupped hand to the throat of Mr. Black, who certainly would have had a bloody response, on his way down and out. But two more bodies, one barely alive and the other bleeding all over the floor, was not an outcome that I intended to see.

"Tommy, my friend," I said. "Stand down, man. Uncoil."

Tommy growled something I couldn't catch, but he eased up.

You could see it in his eyes, and then in his shoulders, and lastly in his uncurling hands.

"Thank you," I said. "I am grateful."

Tommy gave me a half-smile, but only just, like a cobra's eye-blink.

"Friends," I said, "I propose that we give the Prodigal his head and simply drape the best robe over his shoulders, slip the family jewel onto his ring finger, and send out for a fatted lamb. As for his story, it is his to tell, in his own way. Let's be like the overjoyed father instead of the angry older brother, Ok?"

"Wow," Mr. Black said, "who died and made you the **Wise One and Only Prophet**? Where did the Goose Man fly off to? Pop would be pleased, though he would want the witness of two or three before he would believe me."

"I also," Tommy said.

Mr. Black glared at Tommy.

"I don't like **Agent TLA** being here, G-Man," Mr. Black said. "Not one tiny little bit. He doesn't need to hear my story. No way can he keep a secret."

"Well," I said, "you will have to accept my guarantees to you, about him, just as he had to, about you. I don't care if you like one another or not, but I insist that you get along, at least avoiding blows, and that you trust me."

The trick of leadership is where you sit.

Right in the middle was working fine for me.

And as Wild Billy jumped into my lap, I saw, too, the importance of allies.

The Tribe was ready to listen.

Time for some stories that could be true.

Truth-time? Not the same, my view.

Ambling pace suits our storyteller
|28November08|

"You are probably wondering why I called this meeting," Mr. Black said, "and I intend to tell you, and I hope that my account of the past eight months will be shorter than eight months, or weeks, or days, or hours, even, in the telling."

"Take your time," Jeanne said. "We don't like to rush around here."

"I have seen that," Mr. Black said, "and craft my preamble so."

"Did he just say that he was going to amble?" Jim said.

"Yeah," OhJim said. "I got that he was in a hurry. Maybe you should ask him. Or lay down until the feeling goes away."

"Reverend," I said, "just ignore them. They will not mind, and the rest of us will thank you for it."

"Ok, Goose Man," Mr. Black said, "fair enough."

Mr. Black lined out that highway smile.

"Where to begin," Mr. Black said, "and how to continue, and when to say enough. Ah, the storyteller's dilemma."

"Two horns," Jim said. "**Toot** and **patoot**."

"Yeah," OhJim said, "and caught on both. Pity."

"Well," Eve said, "you are a storyteller, Dear, and I for one know that you have a plan and will stick to it, and if you deviate, to either side of the path, no one but you will know that you have. And just let me say, you are one of my favorite storytellers."

Eve got up and walked over to Mr. Black, who stood in some trepidation.

After all, previous greetings had come on a high tide of violent intentions that had dissipated like waves breaking against the hard cob of the shore.

Eve hugged Mr. Black for a long time.

She sat down, fiddling at her eyes with her fingers and blinking rapidly.

"Now I understand," Mr. Black said, "the reference to the Prodigal."

"Thought you would, Reverend," I said. "Tell us about the far country to which you fled, and why."

"I will, Goose Man, I will, but in good time," Mr. Black said. "First, though, I want to switch to another metaphor, that of the dark path through the forest where the straight way has been lost."

"In the middle of the journey of our life, **dot dot dot**," Jim said.

"Yeah," OhJim said, "**dot dot dot** I came to myself in a place where the straight way had been lost."

"The Reverend tells a good tale," Jim said.

"Yeah," OhJim said. "Dante, though."

Mr. Black laughed.

"Brothers," he said, "you clearly have the brains in the family."

"Pop didn't pick me for the shadows because of my erudition, strong though it be," I said, "but for my restless and broad interests. These two hombres have most of the gray follicles. Mine are more white. Same goes for the division of brain cells. Or, this: They like the ride; I like arriving."

"And I like a well-told story, soon finished," Mister Ed said.

"Another brother!" Mr. Black said. "I am double-parked, in terms of my life as I currently know it, so I will just tell you what you need to know and then I will be on my way."

Mr. Black brings diatribe to the Tribe
|29November08|

"Look," I said, "the story is important, and if you have to run, then you can email it to us in pieces, or come back every once in a while, or post to the blog on our VPN -- which I swear is a secure network. But one way or another, we need to hear what you have to say."

"Patience, Goose Man," Mr. Black said. "Don't go leaving for the sunny south and taking the flock with you."

"It's **Tribe**," I said, "not **Flock**."

"But **Let's get the** Flock **out of here** is a lot more amusing than **Let's get the** Tribe **out of here**," Mr. Black said, "but I do digress. It must be the company that I keep."

"Manifestly, Dear," Eve said.

"Well," Mr. Black said, "I will get started and you-all can catch up with me as you are able."

"Fair enough," I said. "Start your diatribe, for the Tribe is waiting."

"For your diacritical remarks," Jim said.

"Yeah," OhJim said, "or the diacritical skid marks on your shorts."

"The most important thing to say," Mr. Black said, after groaning, "is that I have been, by my own choice, outriding like a monk for the past several months, and giving the Tribe, as you call it, protection from a forward position. I'm sure that you can guess at the precipitating factors that led me to decide to do this."

"And why," I said, "you allowed one and all to be in the dark in the park about the first murder."

"That was a clear-cut case of self-defense," Mr. Black said, "plain and simple. The more devious one was the one who prevailed. You'll get the whole story in good time, but that is the banner headline -- **The Quick and the Dead, in the Dark.**"

"The quick and devious one would be you," Jeanne said, "by process of elimination. You are the feisty one."

"Look it up," Jim said. "Fundament is fundamental."

"Yeah," OhJim said, "and be ready for a surprise. Nuff said on that head, if you know what I mean."

"I like these brothers, Goose Man," Mr. Black said. "I'm beginning to see a little of the lure of sitting here and chasing the tail with the head until one becomes dizzy, but my lot was otherwise, and I have witnessed more punishment than puns in the places where I have been lately."

My brothers were beaming. They didn't go pink, however.

Only Jeanne could pluck that tone from them.

"I am curious," I said, "as to the identity of the one who lost the contest in the dark, near the park."

"Ah," Mr. Black said, "me, too."

Everyone started talking at once. Mr. Black raised his hand.

"Take turns," Mr. Black said, "and I get to go first."

We nodded.

Some of us chuckled.

"I wish I knew who he was," Mr. Black said, "but covert necessity plus the imposition of silence as the best defense for all concerned has made it impossible for me to find out any answer to that question."

"And the answer to that question," I said, "is taking on even more importance than it has had to this point. And the level of interest was already off the scale. the chart, or any other measured image you wish."

"We have tried," David said, "as have the police and the press."

"We have been lazy," Jeanne said, "and I more than most. Mea culpa."

Jeanne gave her always evident chest a ritual beating, three times, with a crossing right fist. This ancient gesture garnered more attention around the circle than it deserved, in a generic sense.

"Now would be a good time to develop the **Mystery Man** cases, all three," Mr. Black said, "now that I can tell you my part of the story. For I am convinced that the entire story hinges on that first victim's identification, and those hinges hold up the door of knowledge through which we must pass. To be succinct, someone is trying to kill us -- each one of us here in this room -- and we must find out who and why."

Once again, everyone started talking at once.

And Mr. Black, once more, held up his hand.

Mr. Black parcels out the prizes
| 30November08 |

"Order," I said, "ladies and gentlemen."

"Hobos," Jim said, "and tramps."

"Cross-eyed mosquitoes," OhJim said, "yeah, and bow-legged ants."

Mr. Black smiled an arid, straight highway smile.

"To continue," Mr. Black said. "Everyone in this room, and everyone connected with **Caspar's**, is a target, and none of us knows who has his finger on the trigger and our foreheads in the cross-hairs."

"Someone has us by the short-hairs," Jim said.

"Yeah," OhJim said, "and by the beard as well."

"Yes, Oh Dear," Eve said, "and the less said the better."

"Thank you," Mr. Black said. "This is the problem -- I cannot ride out to be the off-site spotter and protector and look into the central question at the same time. I need some help in here and out there, so one of you will be riding out with me, to watch my back while I watch yours, while this **posse comitatus** uncircles the wagons and thunders off in the direction of the enemy, or at least in the direction of where one might find out a hell of a lot more about who our enemy is."

"We prefer the phrase **quasi-criminal enterprise**," I said, "though **Tribe** is best. **Posse comitatus** is a bit stiff in the saddle and long in the tooth."

That highway smile again from Mr. Black.

"I would recommend that you take David with you," I said. "He has high potential, and he learns quickly."

"I second that," Tommy said. "David in my view is the first choice for your second, Black."

Tommy and Mr. Black locked on, but only for a moment.

After all, **the enemy of my enemy is my friend**, and Tommy was beginning to hear what he needed to hear.

"The second and third victims," Mr. Black said, "in what the press is calling the **Mystery Man Murders**, I assume were the work of unknown soldiers from the army that is arrayed against us. Here, too, I cannot both protect you and investigate them. I will say that the deaths seem to be meant to embarrass, discredit, and expose the Tribe, as you call it, to unwanted attention in public, populist places such as the press and in private, privileged places, too."

"Noted," I said.

"Yes, Dear," Eve said. "Noted and underlined."

"Jeanne," I said, "we favor David for this phase of the work with Mr. Black because an ugly pup like him would not be much of a loss compared to yourself. And, even more to the point, you surpass even David in ease and pace of learning. If the work calls for the distaff side, you will be there, but in general Mr. Black's cover is being a man in a poor man's world of beer and fortified white bread. Not your sort of cover."

Jeanne nodded, tongue in the **bleep**-you position, distorting her cheek.

"I agree," Jim said. "You would look much better in silk and pearls than boots and spurs."

"Yeah," OhJim said, "and don't forget the heels. Those are very important. Some guys do like boots, and spurs, but I'm partial to pumps, I guess."

Jeanne gave the boys her sideways smile, bitter and sweet.

They went all pink.

Mr. Black just shook his head and smiled that guy wire-tight smile of his.

"I love these natives, Goose Man," he said. "Love 'em. And I do accept the offer of David as having more utility than someone like Jeanne, say, in the places where I've been lurking. You better like fizzy 'merican beer, Boy!"

David just smiled, all teeth and bug eyes through round glasses.

"And," I said, "I will join you when you need a third in those places."

"Just like old times," Mr. Black said. "Lord have mercy."

"Christ have mercy," I said.

"Lord have mercy," Tommy said. "I don't understand how you-all can spout such drivel and still end up with a viable plan."

"TLAs, with their manuals of operation, have their pluses," Mr. Black said, "and perhaps some day we will understand what those pluses are. Until then, we prefer to make light, move fast, and mix it up **mano-a-mano** in the dark."

"More drivel," Tommy said, "but Lord help me, you begin to make sense. Here I am **mano-a-mano** with my operations manual in hand -- musing, by heart, on some nuance -- and you are already done. **Make light, move fast, mix it up mano-a-mano in the dark.** I like. First the F-Troop, now this."

"Well," Jim said, "don't quit your day job, Mister Agent Sir."

"Yeah," OhJim said, "we need your sources."

A kiss or two before parting
|01December08|

"Well," Mr. Black said. "A question. What the bleep is the **F-Troop?**"

"An old thing from a Grim childhood, like the tribal emphasis," I said, "that my brothers and I dusted off when they came to live with me, about the time you went off and got yourself killed."

"Ok, Goose Man," Mr. Black said, "but what is it?"

"We hold meetings," I said, "under **Robert's Rules of Order**, with me as the Chair, and we make motions and second those same motions, and debate, and vote. We did this as kids, the three of us, and it's a game that you and I used to play all the time, in our churches. It has worked surprisingly well as a way to shepherd the Tribe. I didn't suggest that format for this discussion, however, because I could not see you wanting to address me as **Mister Chair Sir** like the others do in such evident glee."

"You got that one right, Goose Man," Mr. Black said, "though I have always found it convenient to let you fan your feathers, and Miss Eve has, too, from what I can see and what I remember."

"It is in the Goose Man's nature to honk, Dear," Eve said.

Mr. Black smiled like Death Valley in winter. Miss Eve gave me her very best Buddha Girl smile.

"Once one can get it past the nose that you didn't kill anyone, Reverend, except in self-defense," I said, "the need for discussion is greatly reduced, to the point that we have the same focus -- find out who wants to hurt us, and why. Or simply **how**, as in **how do we stop them**. However, it would be good for all if you could brief us on what happened in your contest with the man who was killed by the bus."

"Agreed," Mr. Black said, "and well-put. However, the dictates of my present role, as outrider, are that I must go back out there quickly and maintain vigilance and presence. However, I will tell the story to David and ask that he write it down and deliver it to you, as soon as he can. I can come back for further discussion after that. Agreed?"

We agreed.

"And," I said, "you don't need to be a stranger."

"Yeah," Mr. Black said, "but a spook does not deal well with flesh. I need to come here on the sly, like a shade, to maintain my apparent demise."

"Look," David said, "I can carry messages back and forth. If I maintain a presence here and assume a disguise for the new work with **the Rev.**, I can liaise with the best of them."

"And better than most," Jim said.

"Yeah," OhJim said, "though the language might suffer some. I did know a sweet little girl name Liaise once ... ."

"Well," Mr. Black said, "as your Pop, the **Father of Us All**, would say, **Let's do and then chat**."

"Good words, Reverend," I said. "But first, I am curious. You made several references to knowing us all and things like that."

"That's right," Mr. Black said. "I've been crashing across the street in that tall apartment building, and I have kept an eye on you as often as I could, mainly during the non-drinking hours of the day. I saw Jeanne following Mr. Red, and I saw her come in the first time. And I've seen your two brothers coming and going like critically opposed pistons. And with the collusion of my good friend Mr. Red, I have gotten frequent reports on your thinking. I had considered bugging this room, but Red would not hear of it. That was one double deal too many."

We gawped at Mr. Red. Who knew?

"**Bleep**-youse," Red said, "I am doing this for Eveie, and I am doing this for my old friend of dark who I am always trusting with the life."

"That explains a lot, raises some dust, and goes a long way toward explaining the Reverend's advanced state of understanding," I said. "If you were going to double one of us, Red was your best choice. Of all the knights around the table, no one has more color-blind zeal for Miss Eveie than Red."

"Bleeping right," Mr. Red said. "I even will be always putting up with you, Consort Man, for Eveie."

"I could say a word of prayer here," Mr. Black said, smiling like a straight-line highway in the night, "but instead I'll just say **amen**."

"I know what you mean, old friend," I said. "The less said the better. What counts is who you count on."

"One thing puzzles me," Jeanne said. "I am not understanding why you did not communicate with us. It's been months."

"It was because of the threat that I assessed from the first **Mystery Man** murder," Mr. Black said. "I decided that it was clear and certain that I had been targeted by a professional, and everyone knows that a professional does not act on his own hook for personal reasons, and after I factored out any personal matters that would attract such a foe, I decided that the threat was general to all of us as well as already specific to me. As specific as could be, in fact."

"So you went away to draw away the pursuit," Jeanne said. "The **mother-bird-with-broken-wing** thing."

"Something like that," Mr. Black said. "And after I teach David a thing or two about having my back, we may learn more about who these foes (and I believe it is plural) are. I can't draw them and follow them, too. And they have been spotty and sporadic in their follow-up, so a friend can help me stay sharp in waiting for the foe to return."

"The Vault," I said.

"Exactly," Tommy said.

"I agree," Mr. Black said.

"Mum's the word, then, Dear," Eve said.

"Good-bye, for now," Mr. Black said. "Come, Young Tonto. Away."

Emails to/from Tommy/Goose
|02December08|

From Goose to Tommy --

Dear friend in high places:

How was that for drama? Mr. Black, back, instead of **Mr. Black, he dead**.

And I trust that your self-interest coincides with that of the Tribe in its present bloated condition with the return of Mr. Black.

When Mr. Black appeared over the transom, I had expected the debriefing to take a very long time, but our assessment that our old friend was in his right mind moved things along more quickly than other scenarios we have been dreading. I'm sure many questions will arise. We will be able to find out the answers now.

David has sent word that he will have a verbatim for us by tomorrow, concerning the first death in the **Mystery Man Murders**. I'll alert you when young David's paper is in hand.

Goose Man

From Tommy to Goose --

Greetings, Goose Man:

I should write another poem. Perhaps I will. After all, things could not be any more confusing. Until then, I think my previous stands -- get the bleep (as you would say) out of the bookshop and find out some things that you need to know.

Although it pains me to say so, as one who far more prefers a briefing, or de-briefing, to move according to generally held and effective tradecraft principles, it seems that a meeting of the F-Troop, at your earliest convenience, might be good at this juncture, when David delivers his verbatim. Call it, and I'll be there.

Tommy

The quick and the dead, in the dark
|03December08|

David's verbatim re: Mr. Black --

Friends:

It has been both exciting and unnerving to be out in the shadows of our own community with Mr. Black. The story he has told me, about the first murder victim, is more than half of the burden I'm feeling.

To tell the story correctly, we have to go back to that wet and windy night in the dark, when someone, no one knows who, was struck and killed by a bus near President's Park.

Mr. Black, who admits that he would rather be alone than just about anywhere he can think of, except **Caspar's Books and That**, was alone in the bookshop on an evening in the spring. He had just locked up the bookshop and turned out the lights when a man drove up to the storefront next door, got out of his car, a brand-new Crown Vic, and opened the trunk.

When the man pulled out a chopped shotgun and shielded it from the street under his gangster-length coat, Mr. Black ran out the back and around to the front of the store, timing his arrival so that he was looking at the man's back.

The man was looking into the bookshop and shielding the shotgun from any passing cars or walkers -- of which there were none.

Mr. Black eased back into the shadows at the side of our building.

The man walked quickly back to his car and drove off.

Mr. Black jumped into his pickup truck and followed the car down Delaware.

Mr. Black was uneasy, in the extreme, and he wanted some answers, but he also did not want to tip his hand, so he followed at a comfortable distance.

The man in the Crown Vic seemed content to just drive, with no evasive moves to see if he had picked up a tail.

Mr. Black, noticing this, decided that he was either dealing with an amateur or the man was slick enough to set a trap for anyone who might be following.

When the two got closer to downtown, coming in from the north, where the bookshop is, the man pulled to the side.

Mr. Black pulled up in shadows a reasonable distance back, and waited.

The man sat for a long time in the car, then got out.

He walked across the street and into the dark park.

Mr. Black got out and went quickly, and carefully, into the park.

≈ ≈ ≈

Mr. Black decided the man clearly did not know the park but that the man was trying to double back in such a way as to vector with anyone following. Mr. Black turned the tables, and came up behind the man.

Mr. Black stuck a stick into the man's back.

"Don't move," Mr. Black said, "or I'll blow a hole in you."

"Not with that, you won't," the man said, and he whipped around, elbows up, hoping to connect with nose or chin or chest. Mr. Black sidestepped and hit the man as hard as he could with the flat of the palm in the chest, driving his blow like a piston.

The man staggered a step, feinted a counter-punch, and ran.

Mr. Black saw that the man, unsure of his surroundings, was going to run at full speed out of the park and into the rain-darkened street.

A bus was coming.

The man ran into the street while looking back to see where Mr. Black was. When the man heard the bus honk, he threw out his hands, as if to stop the bus by embracing it in welcoming arms.

Or, perhaps, Mr. Black told me, the man was accepting the consequences of failing to kill Mr. Black. The Hit Code.

That would account for the bus driver's report that the man whom the bus hit was standing with his arms out, like a statue.

Punch my ticket for failing, he seemed to be saying, by his arms-wide gesture, Mr. Black said. **I embrace my fate and punishment.**

Miss a hit, and you are out of business.

Permanently.

Choosing death might reflect a default stance of **tie a millstone around my neck and cast me into the sea if ever I fail to deliver a corpse**.

Or, Mr. Black said, the man was simply unable to reverse his momentum.

The bus and the man were frozen in the bus's headlights for one heartbeat.

That was the man's last heartbeat.

"The impact was sickening to see and to hear," Mr. Black said. "I would not wish such an end on even an enemy."

Mr. Black, watching from the dark edge of the park, decided -- in a New York minute -- that he had to stay away from his apartment, the bookshop, and his usual haunts, until he found out what was going on.

"Paranoia happens when you rocket to the top of the Hit Parade," he said.

Mr. Black went to his old apartment, packed a few things, like he was going away for a trip. He got his passports and rainy day money, and left a note for the building super that he was off for an emergency trip to visit his favorite aunt out on the West Coast and did not know when he would be back. He promised to send post-dated rent checks, which he did in a few days, paying nine months ahead and asking the super to watch for his mail and keep it for him.

Mr. Black, the next day, after sleeping in his truck and wondering over and over again what was up, went to the building across the street from the bookshop and rented an apartment on the top floor, on the street side of the building. He has been able to come and go out the back, on the parking lot side, so we have had friendly surveillance but have been none the wiser. He sold the truck and got a sedan.

Mr. Black decided on that first night that he could not and would not be in contact with the bookshop crowd, that he would not, ever, talk to the local police, and that he would not use any of his usual sources, local or otherwise, until he had a much better idea about what was going on.

One question that he had no answer to was this: Was the man intending to kill Mr. Black, or was he going to grease whoever was at the front desk alone at closing time? Mr. Black had no idea at that point whether the contract was on him, or on one, or all, of us.

≈ ≈ ≈

To end the night, however, Mr. Black had driven back to the top end of the park and walked, in hastily adopted disguise of hoodie and baseball cap (to which he added a droopy mustache as soon as it grew), down to where all the red and blue flashing lights were still marking the accident scene.

He loitered on the outer edge of the crowd, well away from Goose and Tommy, who were right in the middle of the cops and other emergency responders. He pulled his cap down over his eyes.

He had only a vague idea of who Tommy was. He figured, correctly as it turned out, that the cops did not think that the accident was anything but the tragic end of a clearly crazy guy who had ran into the path of a bus and flung out his arms **like Jesus Christ, fer Christ-sake!** That was the kind of talk he was hearing from the cops and ambulance people, and the distraught bus driver and the few persons who had been on the bus.

Mr. Black waited until everyone left, to see if anyone figured out that the guy had arrived in the car still parked across the street from the accident spot.

There were a few cars parked here and there on the street, so the victim's car did not stand out.

Mr. Black noticed, now, that the car had Pennsylvania plates that started with an **E**, which meant that the car was a rental. A shiny Crown Vic.

An old Crown Vic would have had **cop** written all over it, but a brand-new one was another matter. Only higher-ups would be driving a brand-new Crown Vic, but not a rental model.

He decided that it would be less of a risk to steal the car and tumble it somewhere else than to break into and tumble it where it was, so he waited until the cops and such left, and the traffic dwindled. The guy had left the keys in the ignition and had not locked the door, when he ran into the park to try and trap Mr. Black.

(Mr. Black appeals to his peers on this; it's part of the training, he said, to leave the keys in the ignition in a case like that, to make it that much easier to start the car and give fresh pursuit, if necessary, upon returning.)

Mr. Black points out that crime professionals and cops alike are generally arrogant about their autos.

He drove the vic's Vic to the other side of the park and chose a dark side street. He searched the car, as quickly as he could. He wore a pair of calf leather driving gloves that he found on the front seat. He found nothing. Not one piece of personal stuff, such as the packet of important-looking papers that the car rental places give you.

Mr. Black continued to assume that the man, now dead, was a professional.

He felt more focused than ever about staying away from the persons and places that he was known to like the most.

The last thing that he did with the car was to drive it to the closest drop-off for that particular rental agency, whose logo was easy to find on the driver's side door channel up there where the oil-change places like to put your reminder of when to come in for your next oil change and bait-switch comedy.

He wore the gloves the whole time, and he put the keys in the drop-off slot at the rental agency. He wiped the door.

He figured, rightly, it seems, that the rental people would call up the car on the computer and process the paperwork, without any suspicions. A lot of people drop off cars and forget to leave the paperwork.

The rental agency, for the information of those who will follow up, was the **Cars R Us** outlet toward downtown on Delaware.

That catches everyone up on what went down that night, and I'll write you again with details about the months since, as soon as I hear the stories from Mr. Black and can write them down.

Davey Jones, drinker

The F-Troop has questions and quips
|04December08|

"Let us be indelicate," I said. "F-Troop, circle the wagons."

"And," Jim said, "break out the flagons."

"Yeah," OhJim said, "and break in the brogans."

"Or something like that," Eve said. "Shoo, shoes! Go away!"

"Or not," Jeanne said. "Especially if you are cute ones with little bows."

"Mister Chair Sir," Mister Ed said, "I rise in support of whatever the ladies are supporting, hands down."

"Don't go there," Jim said.

"Yeah," OhJim said, "**stays** out of it."

"That," Jeanne said, "sounded like a reference to the over-the-shoulder-boulder-holder, Ya Big Boob."

"I think, Dear," Eve said, "that we have lost sight of land."

"To heel, then," I said, "and come about."

"I have an idea," Jeanne said. "We could discuss David's verbatim concerning Mr. Black."

"And, dare I say, Dear," Eve said, "we could discuss Mr. Black himself."

"Who wants to start?" I said.

"I will," Jeanne said, "and this is my take on the whole thing. It is in the form of a question. If we are all in danger, why has nothing happened in the eight months since the first death in the **Mystery Man Murders**? What was Mr. Black doing that took the focus off of us, and what did he do to avoid a repeat visit upon himself?"

"One explanation," I said, "would be that whoever sent the first guy went passive when he never reported back. And whoever **whoever** was, they may have decided that their man was the victim in the bus vs. person smashup."

"And," Eve said, "as for our man Black himself, I am certain that he is dealing with a full deck, that he is not one brick shy of a load. David may be able to tell us more after he is with Mr. Black for a while. Sometimes older persons -- and friend Black despite appearances, is such a one -- present symptoms randomly and infrequently. Watch and wait, I say, and until such time as we become worried press ahead on the fronts that Mr. Black has opened for us."

"Such as my work on the final sections of the blank, blankety, blank, blank Murder Book. I seem to have a block," Jeanne said. "I do miss David. A girl like me needs more than just a couple of hangers-on."

Jeanne smiled, sideways, at my brothers.

"Brothers," I said, "how about you following up on the car rental angle?"

"Sure," Jim said. "I, P.I."

"Yeah," OhJim said, "me, too -- **P. Me**. And **P. You**."

Tommy walked in late, but not too late, since we were revolving slowly around the usual issues.

Wild Billy was weaving his way in and out between Tommy's feet, as Tommy walked to a chair.

Billy jumped into Tommy's lap and rotated.

"Still huddled in the backroom, I see," Tommy said, "and waiting for Jesus to walk through the wall."

"We're reading and discussing David's verbatim," I said.

"David emailed me a copy," Tommy said. "It makes for interesting reading, but are we any further along?"

"Not really," I said, "though we can follow up on the auto rental agency."

"And the Murder Book," Jeanne said.

"And with Mr. Black himself," Tommy said. "Goose, can you arrange for you and I to meet him and David at the **Roll In** tonight?"

A few beers with friends
|05December08|

When Tommy and I walked into the **Roll In and Crawl Out**, Mr. Black and David were waiting, and by the looks of things, they had been waiting for a long time.

Empty beer bottles, like captured pawns, stood at attention.

David had captured three. Mr. Black had captured three.

Stalemate, stale beer.

I shook David's hand, and he did that shoulder-touchy thing with me.

Mr. Black handed out nods all around.

David and Mr. Black were in hoodies and baseball caps.

Tommy and I had chosen ratty tweeds and jeans.

We presented a generally low-rent profile.

"Your meeting, TLA Tommy," Mr. Black said, "so I guess you're buying."

Tommy smiled like a thirsty shark.

The bartender, a young guy with an ear ring and humpty dumpty-bald head, came over with beers.

All around.

It was a typical night at the **Roll In**, with one of the tables occupied by a couple of **Touch-Me's** who looked like they were a grope or two away from just getting a room.

Down at the far end of the bar, a guy in jumble sale clothes was drinking his beer, his one beer, in slow motion and staring out the dirty window into the lost-planet landscape of dull, abandoned storefronts and warehouses.

The snow was filling the street up to the top of the curb, and the snow was still coming down, as evidenced by the rapidly falling flakes back-lighted by the street lights at the ends of the block.

There wasn't any traffic to speak of, and our tire tracks were the first to deface the evening's accumulation of snow.

No one was thirsty enough to walk in, either.

Yeah, it was a typical night at the **Roll In**, and it made you flash, fleetingly, on jumping off a cliff.

The **Roll In** took you to the edge.

The **Roll In** was best in very small doses, but Mr. Black seemed to have made it his home away from home.

"Good verbatim, David," Tommy said. "What did you leave out?"

David gave Tommy his bug-eyed smile through his round glasses.

Tommy waited.

"What?" David said. "You mean like the kitchen sink? I put in everything that I remembered, which was all that I heard. I have a photographic ear."

Mr. Black squared around. Tommy glared back.

Here we go again, I said to myself.

I figured that they were not going to do that touchy-shoulder thing, but they did surprise me.

They laughed and bumped fists.

"Do you want to tell them, or should I?" Tommy said.

"Go ahead," Mr. Black said. "Your dead-pan delivery is indicated here."

Dead-pan would have described David and I. Or **shocked**.

"Mr. Black and I went on a trip a while back," Tommy said, "and he made me promise that I wouldn't tell anyone until he gave me the green light, which I have adhered to, with a few embellishments of a bellicose cast that seem to have tricked the Tribe, one and all."

"I'll say," I said. "I had the two of you down for 15 rounds, main event, Vegas, even odds."

"Me, too," David said.

"Where did you **Blood Buds** go?" I said.

"We visited the lovely city of Pittsburgh," Tommy said. "We rented a shiny new Crown Vic from that rental agency, **Cars R Us**. Mr. Black wanted to trace the trail of the **John Cash** -- the first victim in the **Mystery Man Murders**. We were gone only for a day, because of the demands of my work and the desire I have to keep the Tribe and its dead and/or missing elder off the books and in the back channel. My handler just would not understand."

Tommy gave us his shark's smile.

"We did not get a name for the John Cash," Tommy said, "but we did a lot of trying, including some contact with sources who know how to forget names and faces. We left these forgetful fellows with some cash and a few tips on how to spend their money, and then we came home. Pittsburgh is lovely in the latter days of fall. Perfect for a round of coat-dragging."

"Lovely is right," Mr. Black said, "but tight as a terse tick when it comes to relevant information. Not even an urban legend."

"But we did do our bit of coat-dragging," Tommy said, "and the cash in hand and those forgetful fellows will do a little more, now and again. We hope to hear something sooner or later. We can always go back."

"Well, hell," I said, "I don't know whether to shoot myself or go bowlin'. Who would have thought that the two of you could work together."

"**The enemy of my enemy is my friend,** Mister Goose Man Sir," David said, and drained his bottle.

Cheeky monkey.

Jeanne sez her assignment wuz murder
|06December08|

"Here's the deal," Jeanne said. "I thought that I could light a fire under myself, by promising to finish the **Murder Book** work by this morning, but the truth is, I have not."

"Oh," I said. "And why is that?"

"There is a lot of stuff to chart, Mister Uppity Man," Jeanne said, "and also a few problems with your numbering and dating of VPN posts. I've put in hours and hours, and still I'm not finished. Tomorrow, though. I promise."

"It's Ok, Dear," Eve said," because part of what you will be publishing is a list of how the rest of us have not lived up to what we said we would do."

"Well," Jeanne said, "you are right on that head, Eve, and I'm glad that I didn't have to say it. There will be a few other forgotten factoids along the way, I promise you that."

Jeanne returned to her corner, sat to the side, and started going though pages and pages of notes and print-outs. She would look up, every once in a while, at her computer, with a fixed stare -- body language that was unknown to humanity before the coming of the P.C.

We watched Jeanne bounce her heel on the tip of her big black-clad toe, for a while, before silently realizing, one after another, that such were the things that made us go off the rails when we had work to do.

"Where shall I start?" Jim said. "Lighting a fire under myself or being right on the head like Jeanne said?"

"Yeah," OhJim said, "the mind cannot hold two such ideas at the same time without deep confusion."

"The images alone," Jim said, "never mind the ideas. I'm speechless."

"Yeah, me, too," OhJim said, "with these few exceptions."

"Well," I said," I didn't think that I would ever see this -- the **Bros Mum.**"

"And their sib, **Mister Uppity Man,** Dear," Eve said.

Eve gave me her Buddha Girl smile.

I gave Eve my best **Mister Uppity Man** smile.

My first, in fact.

Over in the corner, Jeanne continued to bounce her way -- heel and toe -- through the relevant records.

Murder Book - Investigative Notes

"Listen to hear," Jeanne said, passing out papers to one and all. "This is the **Murder Book** that I've been promising to finish for weeks and weeks and weeks on end."

"Good work, Dear," Eve said.

"Thank you, I guess," Jeanne said. "It has not been easy. The dates on early blog posts to the VPN are still a mess, though I have tried to key the correct dates to my entries as I went along. And then there is the caveat that we can and do change details all the time, at our whim and for the demands of the service. It is not true but it is chronological, at least in a superficial sense."

"I'm easy to please," Jim said.

"Yeah," OhJim said, "me, too. So please."

Jeanne gave the boys her sideways smile, bitter and sweet.

The Murder Book, Part Two
-- Investigative Notes - Part 1 of 2

(Note: **Part One** was the **General Chronology**.)
Compiled by Jeanne Wheenin (ex-reporter, current bookshop clerk).

Victim No. One
• **Evening of 01April08.** First news story, **Daily Afterblatt, Lake Effect edition**. Headline: **Police in a pickle: Details elusive in suspicious death in the dark downtown**. No byline on news story. Tagline: -- **compiled from staff reports**. Police detectives (lead Det. is Joe Blucote, Buffalonya Police) have no leads, no i.d. of victim, and no reason for victim's apparent suicide. Victim was wearing dark suit of good quality -- Blucote. No wallet or jewelry. Quote: "(victim) had all the appearances of a successful business executive." Bus driver and four passengers on board bus. Blucote refused to i.d. them. Autopsy completed - "cause of death was obvious, but there may have been contributing factors, such as drugs or alcohol" - coroner. Toxicology tests requested - will take weeks.

[**Note from Jeanne** - Get names from Tommy, esp. bus driver.]

• **03April08 ff. VPN posts**. Goose mentions but does not reveal the "one detail" from news story that convinces him of the victim's i.d. - Mr. Black AKA Mr. Darke. Initial i.d. by Goose, who makes up case name - **Parke Eno Darke**. Goose says he won't go to the police ever. Goose initially vows to keep the truth to himself, to protect his brothers (and others TBA).

[**Note from Jeanne** - Follow up with Goose on the "one detail".]

• **VPN blog posts beginning 10April08**. Goose tells of receiving, in the mail, from an anonymous source, a journal he had kept during the time he worked covertly with Mr. Darke, AKA and henceforth in this document, Mr.

Black (cf. Goose AKA Mr. White).

• **Second news story (17April08) Daily Afterblatt, Lake Effect edition.** Headline: **Unclaimed, unnamed: Police remain in the dark in death-by-bus.** No byline - compiled from staff reports. No new info - police. Toxicology test results still pending - coroner. Location update - downtown on Delaware, near McKinley Park, better known as Presidents Park. Renewed plea for public's assistance - Blucote.

• **Visit to bookshop from Det. Blucote (24April08):** Present: Blucote and Tribalists Goose, Eve, Jim, and OhJim. Det. Bill "Joe Bob" Schmidt, Blucote's partner, appears at the end of the interview. Blucote makes some puzzling comments that lead Eve to tell Jim and OhJim about Goose's covert past. When Goose gets outed, by Eve, the four of them agree to get serious about the death of Mr. Black.

[**Note from Jeanne** - Why didn't anyone check on Mr. Black's apartment? The answer that I got from Goose is that no one knew where he lived (secretive loner).]

• **Third newspaper story (Daily Afterblatt, Lake Effect edition, 03May08).** Headline: **Habeas corpus: Police have body but little else.** No byline - compiled from staff reports. Story comes a month after the event. Blucote and Schmidt brief press, ask for help. Toxicology tests finally come back, are negative - coroner. First mention of "Mystery Man Murder" - insiders' tag. Unconfirmed report of a pending Coroner's Inquest.

• **Fourth newspaper story (Daily Afterblatt, Lake Effect edition, 16May08).** Headline: **It's murder for sure: Coroner's jury concurs in Mystery Man case.** Byline: Jeanne Wheenin, Afterblatt staff writer. NB: verdict by coroner's jury: Death by suspicious circumstances by person or persons unknown. Case to remain open until coroner releases body for burial - open for the time being.

[**Aside from Jeanne** - One could say that the coroner wants to keep a lot of pressure on the detectives.]

Victim No. Two
• **Initial news story (06June08) Daily Afterblatt, Lake Effect edition.** Headline: **Bumped body: Bus hits pedestrian on busy street; man already dead.** Location: East Side, Michigan and Blaine streets. Byline - Ben Whick, Afterblatt reporter - AKA Wacko Whick. Body dumped overnight 4-5 June (wet night of thunderstorms). Cars and a bus run over body. Blucote - man was already dead.

[**Note from Jeanne** - Ask Tommy how man was killed.]

• **VPN blog post 04June08** - "Bleep, bleep, bleep goes the beat": Mr. Black's signature? (**Bleep-**you **in the middle of the street**).

• **VPN blog post 10June08** - "Jeanne dreams up some questions": Jeanne's question - did anyone see the body? re: Mr. Black. Answer is No.

Jeanne urges visit to the Coroner's Office. David and Jeanne visit, 17June08, with slender results - David sees a photo of a badly battered man's face. No i.d. possible. Side effect of the visit - Jeanne gains i.d. of the second victim, Bill Zeohn.

• **VPN blog post 18June08 - "Take this down and check it"**: Goose refutes any idea that DNA will be a factor in i.d. of first victim, Mr. Black. He says spooks don't end up on any such databases.

• **News story (first follow) on second victim, Bill Zeohn (Daily Afterblatt, Lake Effect edition) 25June08**. Headline: **Busy streets: Two murder mysteries stretch into future; police stumped**. Byline - Ben Whick, Afterblatt reporter. No i.d. in first case yet. Second victim, according to sources, is Bill Zeohn, 37, a freelance photographer. No local relatives. No one answers at Zeohn's address - phone calls, loud knocking. Quote: "He was always in on the action, always around the ball, and always taking picture after picture with that annoying flash, flash, flash" - media person. Blucote/Schmidt - no comment on motive for Zeohn killing.

[**Aside from Jeanne** - Zeohn clearly was in the way, making himself a target, or worrying whoever is after the Tribe. Also, was he shooting with film all the time, or shooting blanks, as we later learn from newspaper sources?]

• **VPN blog post 27June08 - "Something else is bothering me"** - Goose, in the course of a **trust-your-feelings-Luke** pep talk to himself voices, for first time, vague doubts about just who the first victim is.

[**Aside from Jeanne** - re: Mr. Black/first victim: In debriefing David, we discover that first victim had brown hair with gray mixed in, based on the photo that David saw at the Coroner's Office. Others are quick to point out that Mr. Black's jet black hair was probably tinted.]

[**Aside on the aside** - This is more conclusive than we thought at the time.]

• **VPN blog post 24July08 - "A cub's obsession with Coyote"**: Post relates a conversation that Ben Whick says he had with "some burnout in a bar" - NB - **The Roll In and Crawl Out**. Ben hears about a secret society from this source.

[**Aside from Jeanne** - Ask Mr. Black if he was the guy who talked with Ben. And if so, why did he!]

• **News story (Daily Afterblatt, Lake Effect edition, 29July08)**. Headline: **Ruckus on Play Knoll - 'noises off': Costumed group upstages the Bard, exits stage left**. Byline - Ben Whick, Afterblatt reporter. Ben tells the story of the Tribe's excellent adventure in the park in the dark. We may have set a record for number of 911 calls flooding a switchboard for one incident.

Victim No. Three
• **Initial newspaper story (26August08) Daily Afterblatt, Lake Effect edition**. Headline: **Trash crew finds body in dumpster downtown**.

Byline - Jane Carlotto, senior crime reporter. Drawings promised next day. Unconfirmed reports - young adult male, slight build, curly hair, full beard. Location - alley between Fillmore and Bush streets, downtown district. Quote - "A bar of the seedy, hard-life sort empties out the back into the alley."

• **Second-day story (27August08) Daily Afterblatt, Lake Effect edition**. Headline: **Dumpster death - another Mystery Man: Buffalonya detectives release drawings in murder case**. Byline - Jane Carlotto, senior crime reporter. Detectives making a lot of mistakes the press is slow in noticing - they say that their investigation of the third victim and the finding of the symbol of Coyote sent them back to look at evidence in the first incident, back in March. But it isn't until another two days that they will announce that the death of Bill Zeohn in June was the second of three murders in the investigation, known now as the **Mystery Man Murders**. Two drawings released - mug shot drawing of dead man and drawing of symbol scrawled on dumpster where body was found. No i.d. on the body. Victim was clothed. Symbol drawn with marker pen.

[**Aside from Jeanne** - What about fingerprints!!! Ask Tommy. Everyone has fingerprints. Is this like DNA for spooks? They probably don't land in fingerprint databases, either. Well, ask, anyway. Also, ask Tommy the color of the ink.]

• **Second follow-up story on third victim (29August08) Daily Afterblatt, Lake Effect edition**. Headline: **Middle 'Man' makes three: Police link another body to "Mystery Man Murders'**. Detectives follow up their announcement of a second **Mystery Man Murder**, in a dumpster, with an announcement that a murder in June, of Bill Zeohn, is also the same work, making three **Mystery Man Murders**. Detectives claim that confusion in each case led to initial treatment that did not have the rigor of a homicide investigation. They want to shift that blame onto the coroner and his assistants and workers. When the dust cleared, and the effects of each victim were researched, the coroner found that pieces of paper bearing drawings of the symbol were in the jackets of victims one and two. For victim three, the symbol was drawn on the dumpster in which the body was found.

[**Aside from Jeanne** - We must rule out the implication that Mr. Black alone may have opportunity and means to put those symbols in the jackets of victims one and two, and on the dumpster where victim three was found. Who else would have been able to do that?]

An end to the Murder Book
| 08December08 |

The Murder Book, Part Two
-- Investigative Notes - Part 2 of 2

Compiled by Jeanne Wheenin (ex-reporter, current bookshop clerk).

• **VPN blog post 03September08 - "A worthy opponent - one of us":**

The Tribe goes forward on the assumption that Mr. Black, not dead, is a serial killer x3. Mr. Black is a worthy opponent, indeed. To answer the threat implied in this assessment of Mr. Black, David, Ben, and Jeanne move in together.

- **VPN blog post 13September08 - "Tribe and Tommy - love at first sight"**. Tommy's reason for befriending Goose and the Tribe - the enemy of my enemy is my friend. Ground rules from Tommy - he will answer specific questions only. Tribe and Tommy pick the name **John Cash** to describe first victim.

- **Editorial, Daily Afterblatt, Lake Effect edition (30September08)**. Headline: **Poker rules: Discard all but one -- any one -- and put him on probation**. Tag at end of editorial: **the editors**. The gist: Enough blaming between detectives and the Coroner. We want results.

- **Follow-up news story on the Mystery Man Murders (30September08) Daily Afterblatt, Lake Effect edition**. Headline: **Why bother: Coroner has that to say of detectives on the case of homicides**. Byline - Jane Carlotto, senior crime reporter. Insiders speculate that a gag order has been imposed on the investigation from TLAs on up the food chain.

- **VPN blog post 03October08 - "Tommy switches to need-to-know"**: Tommy affirms that the fix is in on the locals, concerning Mr. Black, the bookshop, and the **Mystery Man Murders**. Tommy affirms that the fix comes from persons who fear what the Vault holds. Tommy brings the Tribe a drawing of Bill Zeohn and a drawing that Jeanne recognizes as Jane Carlotto (whose photo is among Zeohn's personal effects).

- **VPN blog post (11October08) - "Adventures in Apartment Living"** - Tommy and David tumble second victim Bill Zeohn's apartment. Papers litter all the rooms to a thickness of several inches depending on the room. They find a Bible given to Zeohn in 1982 - "Given to Billy Zeohn for perfect attendance, Zion Community Church, Easter 1982. (Signed by) -- Pastor Joseph Gazilot."
[**Aside from Jeanne** - Still waiting for Goose to follow up on this .... When, Goose, oh when?]

- **VPN blog post (20October08) - "David's essay on breaking and entering"**. David writes up his experience with Tommy at Zeohn's apartment - "What I did this summer". It was fall, but let that pass (**Jeanne**). David speculates that the killer lets the Tribe know the second victim's i.d. because Zeohn is someone that no one cares about: "We will not easily find anything but his name, I'm sure."

[**Aside from Jeanne** - The gag order on the **Mystery Man Murders** has silenced the media and probably has encouraged the detectives to put up their feet, eat donuts, and move on to other cases. There have been no newspaper stories since 30September08, and it is now December. A chat with Jane Carlotto (Tommy?) would be interesting. We can urge her to write a story about the gag order. That would be amusing.]

- **VPN blog post (23October08) - "A briefing on Zeohn's photo files"**: Jim and OhJim report that Zeohn left no photo files behind, from what they were able to find out. The boys speculate that Zeohn was not using film in his old print camera, just the flash.

• **VPN blog post (24October08) - "Newsies put their noses together"**: Jeanne and David meet with Jane Carlotto re: Bill Zeohn. Jane says Zeohn was creepy. Always taking her photo. She scoffs at the idea that Zeohn was not using film in his camera.

[**Aside from Jeanne** - We met Jane at the **Roll In and Crawl Out**. A lot of newsies go there. It is near the **Afterblatt** offices. There is a backroom there, too. No one has mentioned that yet .... There is more than meets the eye in that dive.]

• **VPN blog post (28October08) - "Reach out and touch Baldi"**: Goose (finally) reports on a call to Baldi about Bill Zeohn's pastor, Joseph Gazilot. Baldi suggests that Goose go microfiching at the Library for more about the pastor and the church, and about the Zeohn family, too.

[**Aside from Jeanne** - Amen! And maybe a call to that guy Parmgartner would be possible too, Goose Man.]

• **VPN blog post (29October08 f.) - "Murder Book"**: Jeanne posts Murder Book chronology in two parts.

• **VPN blog post (02November08 f.) - "Mister Ed - a wise old horse"**: Mister Ed leads the Tribe through an exercise of looking closely at the drawing that Ben did after meeting in the **Roll In** with the man who told him all about the secret society and what goes on at the bookshop. The Tribe invites Ben to come back from his new digs for a chat about that conversation that he had at the **Roll In and Crawl Out**.

• **VPN blog post (10November08) - "What Tommy's envelopes envelop"**: Tommy writes Jeanne another poem, **Faith on the Radio**. After exhaustive analysis, the Tribe asks Tommy for his take on his poem. **Get off your butts, get out there, and do something. Anything.** That is Tommy's message, Tommy tells us. Tommy offers himself as a tethered goat in a sting at the **Roll In and Crawl Out** to try catching Mr. Black (if he ever comes back there).

• **VPN blog post (23November08) - "Sit and watch, sit and wait"**: Jeanne, David, and Goose go down to the **Roll In** to stake out the place to see if Mr. Black still goes there. He does.

• **VPN blog post (25November08) - "The presence of an absence"**: While the Tribe is huddling over the news that Mr. Black is alive and drinking nightly, it appears, at the **Roll in**, Mr. Black suddenly appears in the doorway. After a certain amount of testosterone-driven circling of virtual fire hydrants by various of the men, Goose assures us, and Eve agrees, that his old friend is in his right mind and is telling the truth when he says that he is not the killer in the **Mystery Man Murders**. After briefing us, Mr. Black takes David with him and returns to his forward post at the **Roll In**. Our job is to investigate; their job is to provide security for us all by keeping attention away from us and on them. David gives us a verbatim (03December08) of Mr. Black's story of what happened that night in the dark in the park, with the first victim, the John Cash.

[**Aside from Jeanne** - This catches up the **Murder Book**, both chronology and investigative notes, to 08December08. Somebody say **amen!**]

Always remember and never forget
|09December08|

We sat for a long time, reading Jeanne's investigative notes. Most of us were making notes of our own.

"We really suck at this," Jeanne said, "and we are better than this. There are so many things that we have not followed up on."

"Well, Dear," Eve said, "that is true in a sense. However, we did choose to sit here and be deliberate rather than rash."

"Which has finally given me a rash," Jeanne said. "I'm ready to roll."

"Me, too," Jim said, "but squares don't roll."

"Yeah," OhJim said, "and my itch is in a place that I can't scratch, no matter how rash I feel."

"I'm getting more in the mood for activity," I said, "now that Mr. Black, who before only talked about resurrection, has now come back from what we thought was the grave."

"**O Grave, where is thy victory?**" Jim said.

"**O Death**, yeah, **where is thy sting?**" OhJim said.

"Face it, friends, we like to talk," Eve said, "and make obscure little jokes, and there are few places on **God's Green Earth** where even such simple conversation is safe or mutual. I for one am happy with our choices of the past eight months or so."

"Yes," I said, "we are all in one piece, which cannot be said for victims two and three, who seem to have been hapless hangers-on in life who were picked on because of their vulnerability."

"Yes, Dear," Eve said. "I think we have a sacred duty to make sure that their stories are told, because they may have died, in a sense, because of who we are and what we hold in the Vault that others are afraid of. I'm not saying that we could have shielded them, but we do have a powerful, open-ended connection with them that deserves our best attention."

"Amen," Jeanne said, "and someday I will tell you how hard a word that is for me to say. So let's get going on finding out the stories."

While we talked, the snow was coming down, as it had all day.

The wide streets were beginning to look like narrow lanes, as drivers parked more and more into the traffic lanes as plows went by and piled up the snow at the margins. A foot had fallen like the other shoe dropping. It was the first big snow of the season, and we were warm and toasty in the backroom.

That was about to change.

Wild Billy burst into the backroom and jumped onto Jeanne's lap, which he never had done before. The little bells on the front door rang with violent agitation, and a voice of strong, feminine tone said, "Red, you bleeping bleeper! Spread 'em and be showing me some identification, you **Old Rake**! Don't make me introduce you to your telephone, because I'm likely to demonstrate its abilities way down south where things are getting embarrassing."

Her name is *Meme* as in *Shiva*
| 10December08 |

I looked at the others. Eve raised an eyebrow, as did Jeanne. Mister Ed began to smile. He seemed to know exactly what was going on.

"Red's flame," Mister Ed said. "Hotter than blazes, and guttering like a Zippo in need of a new flint, from the sound of it. We are all in for a treat. Red's flame sets the place on fire."

"**Red's ... flame ...** ," I said in a hopeless and strained sort of way. "Who knew he even had a wick?"

"Now, Dear," Eve said, "Red is a sexy man in an aged-in-peat sort of way that I would not expect you to really understand. Right, Dear?"

"Right," Jeanne said. "Sexy in a **Sneaky Pete** sort of way is good. Men really don't know from sexy."

My Buddha Girl and her bitter lemony protégé shared a snickety little smile of secret glee.

"Officer!" Mister Ed said, in a voice pitched to the top of the mainmast. "Come back here, and bring that sputtering miscreant with you."

"**Bleep**-you," Mr. Red said from afar.

"Put the **Back in 10 minutes** sign up, Red," Mister Ed said, "and get back here, already now."

We looked in some amusement and alarm at one another, and each of us made a quick scan to make sure that nothing provocative, especially the lovely Naomi's flip chart, was on display.

Red appeared in the doorway.

He looked like the **Mask of Reluctance** with bow legs.

Wild Billy greeted him, male to man, from the warmth of his new crib.

Behind Red was a tiny woman of perfect proportions and sky-high appeal.

She had a bouff of black hair and a wide, full, and friendly mouth.

The red dot in the center of her forehead was different.

She was dressed in a simple red silk dress that created complexities with the light. The dress cleaved to her like a flirty younger sister, giving her an air of youth surrounded by maturity.

When I say tiny, I mean short, I guess, because otherwise she had something of the fertility doll about her. The other noticeable feature was her strong presence of a nose, which kept her from being perfectly beautiful but not from being extremely pleasing. Frankly, with a smaller nose, she would have been less dangerous.

She kept trying to see around Red, when she wasn't poking him in the side or flicking at his ear. I have to admit that I never had Red down as an object of such ferocious sexuality.

"Hi", the woman said, elbowing her way past Red into the room. "I'm Officer Shiva; you can be calling me **Shi**. Red does, or at least he did until his telephone stopped working. He used to call me **Buffalonya's finest.**"

Office Shiva pivoted on her spike heels and poked Red, hard. It was clear that she liked him, in a school playground sort of way, but how Red felt about her, I could not tell. Red was living up to his name. The bulging vein over his left temple was throbbing.

Officer Shi was making the rounds of our circle, shaking hands and making little comments.

"I am knowing you," she said to Jeanne.

"I know," Jeanne said. "I know you, too."

"And you, you **Big Gorilla**, I certainly am knowing you, but softly, softly," she said to Ed. "Mustn't get Red jealous."

"Why not," Mister Ed said. "Or do you want to **don't** and say we **did**? Let's do **something** ... ."

Officer Shi laughed, which put me in mind of a herd of little glass figurines colliding against one another, as if shaken in a box by a child. The effect was startling but not at all unpleasant.

"The rest of you," Officer Shi said, "I may have seen, but certainly will see in the future. I'm the beat cop in this district, and walking the streets is my stocking and trading."

"**Stock and trade**," Mr. Red said in a prim, pedantic stage prompter's voice I had not heard before. Officer Shi winked at us and wagged her head.

Office Shi's voice sounded like it had arrived in Buffalonya by way of Mumbai with a stopover in London.

Three forms of Queen's English jostled in her speech.

Officer Shi laughed like expendable but expensive glass and hugged Red, who was moving from red toward purple.

"Beat cop, Dear?" Eve said. "I did not know we had one. Love the uniform, by the way." Eve raised both eyebrows. "Lace not leather ... ."

"Oh, but we do have a beat cop," Jeanne said, "and if you-all were the fans of my journalistic output that you really should be, you would know Office Shi in amusing detail thanks to the story I wrote about her."

"Oh, yes," Officer Shi said, "-- knowing me just like my **Ever-Reddi Red.**"

"Well," I said, "I certainly can endorse your uniform. No cuffs, though."

"You smartie without the hair on top," Officer Shi said. "This is my troll's outfit. And where would cuffs go on a sleeveless little dress?"

"I think you are meaning **trolling outfit**," Mr. Red said, "and I am thinking you don't knowing what you say or trying to say are."

Again, the prompter's **sotto voce**.

Helping with the words by example.

At once helpful but also reproachful. The sounds of Mr. Red giving anyone **Engleesh** lessons gave us a bad case of the giggles.

"I am trolling for you, **Mister Phone Up My Chute**," Officer Shi said.

She smiled like a sleek mink with very sharp teeth and heels.

Black/white and read all over

Reprinted from the 15March08 **Daily Afterblatt, Lake Effect edition.**

Officer Shi
Lady cop walks to the beat with purposeful steps

By Jeanne Wheenin
Afterblatt Staff Writer

Once in a while, you encounter someone who seems to change before your eyes with the light, like a diamond. Hard. Lovely. Brilliant. Durable.

Such is the case with Meme Shiva, or Officer Shi (pronounced **Shy**) to her friends and colleagues.

It sounds like **Shy** -- but the lady is anything but.

She is Officer Shi to the scores of persons she meets on the street every day. So who is this person?

Funny you should ask, for you need to get in line, to talk with her, and it is a very long line indeed.

Officer Shi is one of a kind, and as such has garnered a lot of attention.

Let's just cut across, using a bit of the fabled power of the press. Getting an interview with this special police person is hard but not impossible, because Buffalonya's Finest are proud of a new development.

Beat cops.

Not "beat" as in Beat Bard Jack Kerouac, mind you. More like walking-the-beat cops, an old idea that has been dusted off for a new program, funded by federal Title Nine funds -- in other words, giving the girls a chance just like the boys have had.

Why *that* girl?

Well, Marlo Thomas she ain't, and no one is complaining about that, but who is Officer Shi?

Part Indian, from Mumbai; part English, from London; and part U.S. of A., from Buffalonya.

"We're excited about hiring a very special person for our Title Nine-funded beat cop position, and we think that the northern reaches of the city, where Officer Shi will be walking, will benefit from this personal approach to police work," said Commissioner Tom Tonolody, head of the Buffalonya Police force.

"I'm a walker," says Office Shi, "and I like to meet the people, and I believe in this approach. I've seen it work well in places like Mumbai, where I was born, and London, where my family moved when I was a teen. Buffalonya deserves this kind of success, too."

Law enforcement wisdom is coming around to the idea that beat cops make sense, and save dollars and cents, according to Tonolody, who fought long and hard for the program.

The 34-year-old member of the Buffalonya force has been in Blue, here, for seven years, in the traditional patrol division.

Look, Ma, no ring!

When asked if she is in a relationship, Officer Shi said, "Private is private, but you don't see any ring on my left or right hand, do you?"

Since the interview was conducted during the officer's personal time, there was not a single ring on either of her hands.

More like four rings on each -- or, one ring per finger.

And beautiful arm bangles, made of silver, and a perfume that makes one think of hot nights in crowded markets and tangled crowds, of half-naked bathers greeting the dusty, dusky dawn in the River Ganges.

"I've come a long way, in my life, and the further I go the closer I come to myself," Officer Shi said. "I miss my family, but I relish these opportunities that I have grabbed for myself."

Her parents live in the United Kingdom and two siblings live in New York City. She has extended family in Buffalonya, which she points out is good but not the best.

Sometimes a girl needs her mom and her dad.

"I landed somewhere between Slackers and Clubbers, and I find that boys and girls of similar age to myself are trying to find new ways to be in a world that seems cold and walled off," Officer Shi says. "My beat work comes from my heart, from a place that says someone in uniform needs to make connections in the community."

And arrests, if need be.

Office Shi, walking the beat by herself, in line with single-car patrols in the city, as per union contract, has the skills and training, and packs the usual lethal weapons and adult toys of the police professional -- gun, cuffs, billy club, and lots and lots of squeaky leather.

"I am preoccupied with the community," Officer Shi says, "and I will do whatever is necessary for the safety of those whom I serve. Sometimes the needs and demands collide, but police work is always like that. I just get the bonus of fresh air, good company, and lots of exercise."

Mentors to die for

She was first in her class at the police academy, and her mentors have the sort of names that turn some very traditional heads in law enforcement circles.

Perhaps only in New York state, with its myriad hues and tones, could a Hindu woman expect to get a serious hearing and a real chance to prove herself -- and where better than in a polyglot community that has countless minorities and street-wise pockets of refugees from every imaginable corner of the globe.

"Gotta love it," Officer Shi says. "Not everyone gets a shot at things like this."

On the job, Officer Shi is firm and friendly, and has an enviable record of service, according to the chief.

Off the job, Officer Shi is likely to be seen in the clubs, in her favored costume of spike heels, sheath dresses, and, sometimes, a red dot on her forehead.

What about traditional roles?

"The Title Nine aspect," Officer Shi says, "is a two-edged thing. It means that other beat cops will follow me, and that those who follow will also be female cops. The funding stream makes moot any debate about women being more relational than men and thus more suited to this sort of police work."

Chief Tonolody is quick to back up his favorite walker cop.

"We deal with persons, not genders. We don't do profiling on anyone, cop, citizen, or con. Officer Shi is the right person for the job, and she beat all comers. In time, if we find that beat cops are making better use of our resources, and giving us more bang for our buck, we will hire male beat officers, too," the chief said.

"Until then, we are well-served. And more."

Clearly, you can see, the officer is destined for the top floor, and along the way she will be setting new stones in the pavements of our city.

And taking the stairs.

Walking.

Named after a god

The multi-limbed Hindu god Shiva, often called the **Destroyer**, may seem to be an odd family name, but Office Shi says that "it's like Lord or Cohen, or a dog named Diablo, or a Russian-borne hockey player named 'Satan'."

"Besides," she continues, "my religion is more of a way of life and a way of seeing and understanding the world. Fundamentally, I'm no fundamentalist. And 'Hindu' touches every part of me."

The black-maned officer has been walking the streets of her north district for a week now, and she is convinced that walking the streets, rather than driving the streets, will suit the police force of the future.

"If citizens are ever to 'trust the force, Luke,' it will be because we get out of our patrol cars, and stay out," the officer says.

"If you see me walking down the street ... walk on by," says an old pop song.

Office Shi says, "If you see me on the street, stop and say hi. I don't bite. I bend over backwards to see the best in each person. I hope to see you soon."

And you saw her here first.

Editor's note: Reporter Jeanne Wheenin, a hometown person who attended local schools and secured a bachelor of arts degree in journalism and an internship at the **Daily Afterblatt**, has been a full-time staff reporter for three months. She drives everywhere she goes, she says. This is her first profile for the **Afterblatt** Sunday magazine, **The Lake Effect**. It might be fitting, Wheenin says, that her first effort will be printed on the Ides of March. Why that is so, she did not say. "God knows, but I've forgotten," she said, "and God so often speaks in silence." Her comments came in a recent email to the magazine copy staff.

Here's hoping she remembers in good time!

Jeanne explains her life change
| 12December08 |

"I'm glad to be meeting of you all," Officer Shi said.

She sat next to Red, who was not black and white but red all over.

"Well, Dear," Eve said, "I didn't know that you had met our Red."

"Yes," I said, "he seems to get around more and better than we knew."

Red was on his best behavior. He had been provoked so far beyond his usual tolerance that I looked for signs of possession. It was refreshing to see, and hear, the difference in Red, but I was concerned about his close-ness with a member of the local constabulary.

"How did you meet Red, Dear?" Eve said.

Officer Shi laughed like tinkling glass and made a grab at Red's earlobe with her red-tipped fingers.

"Ouch!" Red said.

I think he meant to say **bleep!**

"Oh," Officer Shi said, "Red isn't fast. He's really, really old. But I like him fine. He used to like me, but one day no calls, no flowers, no smiles."

Red continued to ape the beet.

"Actually," Officer Shi said, "I am making up the jokes. Red is my friend on the beat, and I enjoy teasing him. He really is a lovely man, and I love the bookshop. I usually am stopping by early, so I have managed to be missing you except for that fine young man David, who is absent, I see."

"Well," I said, "we're delighted to make your acquaintance."

My mouth and my thoughts were keeping to neutral corners and as far away from one another as they could get.

This was a cop, after all, and cops are inimical by nature to quasi-criminal enterprises, especially friendly cops -- oxymorons for sure.

"Yes, Dear," Eve said, "I remember Jeanne's profile and I was glad to see community policing make a comeback in our fair city."

Like me, Eve seemed to be casting about to get the range on this thing.

"Why are you leaving the newspaper, Jeanne?" Officer Shi said. "You have such of the gift."

"I'm much happier here," Jeanne said.

"Why, though?" Officer Shi said. "You are a writer and there are so few."

"Maybe, yes," Jeanne said, "and I thank you for the compliment, but newspaper writing, and writing, are only similar. They actually are in separate Zip Codes and there is little communication between the two."

"But my profile! I am loving it!" Officer Shi said.

"And I quickly got to the point where I was cranking out crap in my sleep and no longer agonizing over word choices or looking for fresh images," Jeanne said. "When that point comes, it feels like some kind of a generic, banal sin to continue, especially if you respect your readers."

"I am beginning to understand," Officer Shi said, "but why, forgive me, a bookshop? You are a star, my girl, not a clerk."

Jeanne blushed, and she looked at Eve and at me.

"This is family, Shiva. This is my mother and my father," Jeanne said, "and my brothers and my sisters. I never had family the way that you did, and this relative obscurity means more to me, now, than anything I have ever done."

Just then, my brothers walked in, did a triple take, and stood in the doorway with slack looks on their bobbling bobblehead faces.

No surprises in this.

I had seen this movie before.

Starting all over again.

My brothers do their *Shoe-Bop* thing

| 13December08 |

"Who is this mirage?" Jim said. "Nice heel spikes, BTW."

"Yeah," OhJim said, "does anyone know who she is? And I agree. Great crampons. Let's blow this sandbox and get glacial."

Shiva looked like a wary child checking both ways before crossing.

"These," Jeanne said, "are Goose's two brothers, Jim and OhJim. Boys, Officer Meme Shiva."

"Officer Shiva?" Jim said." You're arresting, too."

"Yeah," OhJim said, "as in **Anon, da Shiva?**"

"No," Officer Shi said, "Shiva as in **Worship me, Little Piggies!**"

"And **blimey me beads**," Jim said.

"Yeah," OhJim said, "and where wallow these worshipful piglets?"

Eve smiled her Buddha Girl smile.

"Jim and OhJim, Dear, were born to boogie," Eve said, "and they just can't quit. Boys, Officer Shiva likes to be called **Shi**, which is short for what Jeanne gets to call her -- **Shiva** -- for reasons we have not yet discussed. Officer Shi is the beat cop in our neighborhood, and she dropped by to tease Red into a catatonic state. Poke him, and you'll see."

Jim walked over and poked Red in the chest.

Red didn't react.

OhJim did the same.

Red didn't react.

Officer Shi walked over to Jim and poked him in the chest.

She did the same to OhJim.

"How much for the pair?" Officer Shi said. "They might be the amusing pets, these brothers of the Goose."

"If there is to be any petting around here," Jeanne said, "these Toms will be purring for me. And they know what I mean by that."

Jeanne gave the brothers her sideways smile.

Jim and OhJim went as pink as Wild Billy's tongue.

Officer Shi broke some expensive glass with her laugh.

"No sale, then?" Officer Shi said. "Pity, that. Still, I am looking for companions for the evening, since Red is way past his bedtime and not likely to be recovering before the dawn."

"Why don't I take you to the **Roll In** for a Christmas beer," Jeanne said, "and Goose can go with us. Ok, Goose Man?"

"At your service," I said, "as long as Eve goes. too. What say you, Ed?"

"You bet your beatific boots," Ed said. "At your service, My Lady. Pour the beer, **head to come**. Right, Jeanne?"

"**HTK**," Jeanne said. "Got it."

"Let's be going," Officer Shi said. "My dancing shoes are getting thirsty."

My brothers began to get that gleam.

Jeanne, to the side, was talking softly into her cell.

Holiday hoisting at the Roll In

| 14December08 |

We walked into the **Roll In and Crawl Out** with our new friend Officer Shi.
Only Jeanne knew what to expect from Mr. Black and his five o'clock shadow David.

Jeanne had called to warn David that we were coming with company.

Mr. Black looked straight ahead. We took our cue from his indifference.

The entire time that we were in the back, Mr. Black maintained his post in the front bar, as he had done night after night for months now.

David gave Jeanne a big hug and a kiss. She rubbed his stubble.

"Surprise!" David said.

"Come home with me," Jeanne said. "I can't live without you."

"I never disappoint a lady," David said.

He had a newly sprouted mustache.

"Well, then," Officer Shi said, "I must meet this shaveless man."

Officer Shi didn't recognize David in his new look of beer-soaked hoodie and cap, and we didn't let on. His rough stubble look was working.

"There will be time for such things in their season, Shiva," Jeanne said, "but first we go to the back."

That was news to most of us, that the place even had a backroom.

We followed Jeanne's clicking heels.

In the backroom, there were plenty of tables, and not too many competitors for the space. We pushed a few (tables, not patrons) together and sat.

The room was big on space and small on windows -- none, in fact.

The floor was original and it had that retro look that old linoleum takes on. The walls were a nondescript tone of something neutral in a tan, and by the looks of the walls, the paint was as pre-war as the flooring.

The ceiling was clad in embossed sheets of tin that someone had painted, long, long ago, in a cool white that had faded and chalked into interesting tones, like old bones.

The other patrons faded away, and we had the space to ourselves.

Officer Shi continued her flashy ways, and Jeanne had little trouble isolating David. She used the expedient of sitting in his lap to good effect. His ears got a good chewing, and he didn't complain once.

In fact, he had a very silly grin on his well-lubricated, stubbly face.

My brothers flanked the elegant officer and explored with her the limits of gender and political correctness. No one of the three of them was any good at any sort of political correctness, so they managed to have an uproarious good time.

Eve and I took a small table to the side and drank in companionable silence. Eve's Buddha Girl smile sat well on her beautiful face.

A good time was had by all, especially David and Jeanne, who were playing up the **Fancy meeting you here** thing.

When we left, Mister Ed quietly stayed behind to take David's post.

F-Troop rides again, and again

|15December08|

"This meeting of the F-Troop will be in Dresden, or in session, whichever is closer," I said.

"**Jawohl**, Herr Chair Herr," Jim said.

"Yeah," OhJim said. "Unlike my Jim-bro, I don't know any French, so I got nothing to add, Mister Chair Sir."

[Present were: Goose, Eve, Jim, OhJim, Jeanne, and Mister Ed. Mister Red and Wild Billy were out at the front of the bookshop.]

"Well," I said, "who wants to go first."

"I'm Ok, Dear, if the meeting doesn't go too long," Eve said.

"Me, too," Jeanne said, "but don't make me laugh."

That was one Buddha Girl smile and one sideways smile, full of bitter lemons and a scant teaspoon of sugar.

My brothers and I sat like three bald bobbleheads in shock. Chicks making jakes jokes about the mystery of the sphincter. You gotta love that.

"We must be in heaven, Man," I said.

"Pinch me," Jim said.

"Yeah," OhJim said. "Pinch me and I'll deck you, **Number One Son**."

"Mr. Chair Sir," Mister Ed said, "I rise in some lugubriousness, mainly because otherwise I might feel left out, and also because the frivolity seems to be waning rather than waxing. And (he glared at the bros Jim) no jokes about waxing, please. And thank you. Very much."

Another jaw-dropping moment.

Mister Ed making a joke. Waxing his wit.

It was easy to see that we were worried about something.

"The Chair recognizes the **Great State of Ed**," I said.

"We circle like settlers in their wagons to consider matters of police excellence, and other efforts that fall just short of that particular accolade," Ed said. "I refer, of course, to Officer Meme Shiva and what may or may not have been an innocent visit."

"I agree, Dear," Eve said.

"And what a hoot," Jeanne said. "If Shiva only knew the covertness of our recent dealings with certain information of interest to the locals."

"Yes, Dear," Eve said, "I was reminded, once again, of what the word **irony** means -- a disparity of information between one person and another, as appreciated by observers who know the minds of both parties."

"Close enough," Mister Ed said, "and fresh, too. Stick with **disparity**, and **irony** will not be far off. And as some say -- **here's to our wives and sweethearts, and may the two never meet!** I say **here's to the irony that we enjoy; may others never join us in our glee!**

"That's ironic," Jim said.

"No, dummy, you weren't listening," OhJim said. "You mean **that's amusing**. Not the same."

Eve gave everyone her best Buddha Girl smile.

"So," I said, "speaking of the long and attractive arms of the law ... ."

"Not really, Dear," Eve said. "After all, we aren't even in jail yet. And Tommy would probably go our bail anyway."

"I take that to mean," Mister Ed said, "that you favor continuing our inquiry into the three murders, or whatever they were, Mister Chair Sir."

"Bingo," I said. "When murder **isn't**, it **is**, indeed, **most foul.**"

"Jingo," Jim said.

"Yeah," OhJim said, "and isms of that ilk."

Meow, Wild Billy said, from the doorway.

"Where did my lap blanket go," Mr. Red said, in strident tones, up front.

In a manner that seemed to some of us to be the heart of irony, Wild Billy said from Eve's lap, once again, **Meow**.

For when our Wild Billy speaks, there is always a disparity.

Stuck in/on the Vault
| 16December08 |

Email from Goose to Tommy --

Dear sole reader and friend:

I'm thinking about the Vault. Partly because the main chamber of the Vault is in my frontal lobe. Partly because I am more and more convinced that whatever is happening, is an attempt on the Vault. An attempt on the physical Vault, I assume, with a glancing blow at the cerebral Vault.

Any vault of secrets begins with the brain cells.

This has to be the lowest, most vulnerable level of the Vault -- the human memory. Death would end the threat that this sort of vault holds, unless an heir, with proofs, should appear. Thus, the task of maintenance has two aspects -- imparting an oral tradition and providing security for the human repositories.

The maintenance of what might be called relics (those proofs that an heir must possess) is a separate but equal matter. To produce a bit of bone or cloth at the pregnant hour keeps the line alive and thrusts the threat into the future and under the long noses of the outwardly upright -- those who fit the Vault's purposes like a hand in a glove.

The physical Vault, with its primary objects that cannot be duplicated (but which can be photographed or copied), has need of a physical space or spaces. The rise of digital proofs makes the physical Vault more potent, and far less vulnerable, since disks and hard drives and CDs and DVDs and other storage media can be endlessly duplicated with a damning digital signature or checksum always intact. Who knows what evil lurks in the heart of digital data?

Most folks, by now, do know.

From the inception of the photographic negative, and on to the rise of the personal computer, this strain of the Vault has gone from secondary, and vulnerable, to primary and ubiquitous.

Although the Vault must have mass, it can have mass anywhere, and the mass can be binary. This threat carries a nuclear charge. Where once the safety deposit box or the wall safe were the choke-points, they now serve little use beyond those of big, locked boxes with long-forgotten baubles inside. These vaults serve everyday needs, but **The Vault** resides elsewhere, and -- **Oh my God** -- is apt to be anywhere and to have been copied endlessly. Words will walk, and fly.

A safety deposit box in a bank is a stalking horse rather than the real animal. Such a thing as a safety box, any more, is the equivalent of the fire that Huck Finn lit on the island that he had been hiding on with runaway slave Jim. Huck knew that the fire would draw those who would want to catch them while he and Jim fled in the other direction. Or like the DMZ approach to computer network security, where hackers are lured to attack a digital position that will occupy them but will yield nothing but a warning bell for those inside.

Another image is the **tethered goat**.

The drill now is to share stories, secure relics, copy digital data, memorize locations, groom heirs. The recent attempts to throw suspicion on the Tribe are aimed, I am certain, at the Vault. We must get to the bottom of these murders, or quasi-murders, in the **Mystery Man** matter.

As time goes by, and I muse on Mr. Black's last briefing, I am convinced that murders No. Two and Three are anything but. Murder No. One, we know to be self-defense. We still need to know who is behind all this and who has been compromised. And how they were compromised. Nothing is gained and no one we care about is served by leaving these ends dangling. That is something up with which I shall not put.

Your friend Sir Goose at the Sign of the Dangling Modifier

P.S. Let's get together.

Jumping jack flash
| 17December08 |

Email from Tommy to Goose --

Dear Brother Goose Man:

I see that you are exercising on the Vault again. Nice lecture, BTW.

I certainly agree that that Vault is also the **Point**, the **Pivot**, and the **Fulcrum**, and any other image that might come to mind of a primary nature. I think of the vanity of human wishes when we talk about the Vault. And I think of all the persons who want stasis and even achieve it, for a season.

Don't get me wrong. I want the Tribe to be fat and sassy, for as long as the

Tribe's members endure and for as long as you find others to take your places. Our interests coincide, permanently, Bro. For once, I will not say **no permanent friends, no permanent enemies**. Our interests will endure, as will our alliance. Trust, certainly, has a lot to do with this, but also there is affection and respect. As long as there are persons who choose the shadows, we will align like a family of planets revolving around that dark sun of covert necessity.

The vanity of human wishes. The dreams of a ridiculous man.

The price of life is vigilance, for people like us, and to have one another's back doubles the chances of survival -- something like making the two-backed beast but without the sexual bits, of course. Sorry to poke a hole in a fine metaphor. It looks like a donut now. Watch the donut, not the hole ... . Oh, well ... .

I, too, have times of difficulty with the life, and I look to you and Eve, and the others, for confirmation that the work is important. I do a lot of things and hear much, and I have seen more than I can remember. The weight of all that makes me tired, sometimes, and it gives me strength to know that if I cannot in every moment understand all that I do, hear, and see, at least I know exactly why I stand in the gap for you and yours. Some shreds of meaning can go a long way, Bro.

I would apologize for my apparent lapse in manly rigidity, but you will know and understand the Zip Code I find myself in at times.

Do let us meet, and soon, to talk about the push to wrap up the **Mystery Man Murders**, at least for ourselves and our adversaries. The public will never know much of the real story, of that I am sure. It is like a family matter.

I have my ear to the ground, and as you might imagine, there have been some rumbles of a covert nature -- rumbles that sound a lot like indigestion at being forced to eat some things that should, in others' opinion, never have ended up on the menu. Well, **bleep 'em if they can't take a joke**, as my sainted mother used to say. Together, we are strong, like brothers. Like family.

Brother Tommy from the back pew

It must have been that barbiturate ...
|18December08|

Back to the backroom at the **Roll In and Crawl Out** I went, for a meeting with Tommy and Mr. Black.

Getting there, in the dark, in the 9 degree F. temperature, with subzero wind chill, was just under half the fun. I bundled up, borrowed Jeanne's Buick beater, and layered on the warm clothes. I told Eve not to wait up.

The streets were bare of snow, and largely without patches of ice. Snow was piled high in the gutters. This pressed the parked cars into the edges of the travel lanes. Winter in Buffalonya, in other words.

Snow had fallen, snow on snow, in our bleak midwinter.

It was, in a word, **a bad night to be a stray dog** (which I realized that I have said before, but when I like a phrase, particularly when I have stolen it, I try to use it frequently).

Upon arriving, I checked the usual -- lines of sight, probable sniper positions, suspicious autos, and who was or was not on the street. I dived into the bar, and stood there shivering. From the cold.

Mr. Black gave a slight nod and headed for the back.

David stayed at the bar. It looked like he was taking his beer seriously.

Scruffy David did not nod.

Good boy.

My spyboy.

Your spyboy.

Tommy was already in the backroom, alone, with beers for himself and for me. Mr. Black brought his own.

The bottle in Mr. Black's hand looked like part of his arm. You might think that that was good cover, what with having all the beer you can drink and discharge, and all the time in the world to occupy a barstool (**I claim this stinking barstool for the queen!**) but there really is no good cover. And, yes, Virginia, beer will kill you just as dead as whiskey will. Or wine.

Mr. Black seemed to be bearing up, but he also looked like a beer-soaked homeless guy, and he smelled like one, too.

His mind was intact, however. The one-liners came as quickly as ever.

"Goose Man," he said, "long time no pee."

"What else is there to do here?" I said. "So hit the can already."

"Yeah," Tommy said, "pea soup from behind the bar, and all that."

"Heard any good ones lately," I said, "speaking of the woman who walked into the bar, smelled the pea soup, and said -- **I haven't had a pea for ages!**"

"Well," Mr. Black said, "here's one -- lion walks into a bar, sits next to a barfly, asks the bartender for a glass of water, and takes a little white pill. After a while lion leans over and bites the barfly's head off. A while later, lion says to the bartender -- **I don't feel so good.** Bartender says to lion -- **Doesn't surprise me. It must have been that** bar-bitch-you-ate."

"That's a blast from a piggy past," Tommy said.

"Yep," Mr. Black said. "Once you get it past your nose, you got it licked."

"That's another," Tommy said. "If this were church, I would brace myself for a third, because they always do things in threes, in church."

"You mean," Mr. Black said, "like -- **walk this way and you won't need to use powder?**"

"I know," I said, "that this titillating trinity is mild compared to the patter that you trot out with your drinking buddies, but let us move on to less hilarious but perhaps more pressing issues."

"Such as what?" Mr. Black said. "What's more pressing than pissing?"

"Such as," I said, "who is planting evidence, and swiping bodies and leaving them in dumpsters?"

"I don't know any or all of the answers," Mr. Black said, "but I appreciate those questions, and those questions have a lot to do with my present bad company here at the **Roll In**."

"Perhaps," Tommy said, "I can provide some facts for us to chew on."

"Dish them up," I said. "I have a sweet tooth for stuff like that."

"Just remember the ground rules," Tommy said. "Specific questions, and no fishing expeditions. Got it?"

"Ok," Mr. Black said, "I'll start. **How long have you been a poofter**?"

Tommy glared at Mr. Black, nose to nose. They burst into buddy-laughter.

"You know how politically incorrect that was, right?" Tommy said.

"Answer the question," Mr. Black said, with his white-line highway smile. "The question is in bounds. Besides, some of my best friends are poofters."

We get down to cases and managers
|19December08|

"Ok," I said, "moving on to matters of actual import."

"Import or export, taxing or not, I'm with you," Mr. Black said. "Actually. In the flesh. Up-front and personal. As you were. Continue, already. Smoke 'em if you got 'em."

Tommy and I looked at Mr. Black.

Tommy felt Mr. Black's forehead. Tommy shook his head.

I just looked grave. Dead-pan, in fact.

"The bodies," Tommy said. "Numbers Two and Three."

"Right," Mr. Black said. "Number One is accounted for, as far as what happened, but we still need to know who, in what high place, crossed the vic's palm with silver. Who his primary target was. And if he had secondary targets. Things like that. Was he after me or was he told to grease whoever he found in the shop? These spooky questions will have spooky answers."

"Right," Tommy said, "but there is nothing to report."

"So," I said, "Victim Number Two, Bill Zeohn."

"Hapless shmoo," Tommy said. "Truly a guy who no one cares about. No kin, no friends, no lovers, no enemies. He was just a half-witted crazy who hung around and got in the way at crime scenes and press conferences."

"We wondered," I said, "whether there was some sort of motive in his killing that had to do with his getting in the way of the person or persons who are trying to get in our way."

"Nothing conclusive on that," Tommy said, "but it would explain why a less-than-zero sort of guy attracted anyone's ire. Odds are, he simply was the victim of a faceless crime of the moment for reasons we will never know. Or his body was diverted for this other use. Falling dead drunk out of bed onto one's head can cause blunt-force trauma from natural causes."

"What we do know," Mr. Black said, "is that he got dead, possibly by violence, and that he was the recipient of a piece of paper with the dreaded coyote symbol on it, said paper probably being placed in his clothing after it landed in an evidence box."

"Or," Tommy said, "as the coroner claims, a prior placing that was at first not noticed by the coroner and his crew because there was a slight delay in naming Zeohn a murder victim."

"Ok," I said, "which leads us to Victim Number Three, probably a plant."

"Yeah," Tommy said, "a homeless guy. Cause of death was never published, because of the gag order that came down like rocks from a roadcut."

"So," I said, "I am betting that we will find that both victims died of natural and accidental causes."

"I'm on it," Tommy said. "Let's meet again tomorrow night. All of us. Same place, clean glasses. And, sadly, more beer."

The Tribe circles up at the Roll In
| 20December08 |

Two nights out in a row?

That's what I said.

On a night tailor-made for designer PJs, we stumbled from the ice and snow and wind into the **Roll In and Crawl Out**.

David slid, and I do mean slid, from his bar stool at the front bar and followed the crowd into the backroom. We would leave it to the bartender to watch our backs. And since it was a night made and meant for PJs, we had the **Roll In**'s backroom to ourselves.

"Well," Mr. Black said, "welcome to my humble abode away from my other humble abode. Who is up for beer?"

Hands shot up, here and there.

"Good answer," Mr. Black said, "since you can have anything you want from the bar, as long as it comes to a head."

"Won't touch that," Jim said. "I'll just have a beer."

"Yeah," OhJim said, "to say any more would be indelicate."

Jeanne just smiled, to the side.

Eve smiled her Buddha Girl smile.

I grinned into my chin whiskers and out my eyes.

Mister Ed and Mr. Red, over in the corner, seemed to be asleep.

Except for Tommy, that was the crop.

"While we wait for the one who works for a living to show up," I said, "here is the place where we find ourselves."

"You are **here**," Jim said.

"No," OhJim said, "I am **here**. **You** are **there**."

"Be that as it may," I said, "the question is a deep and existential one, I must admit. However, we are in a particular place, together, and the way out will be a common effort."

"Say more, Partner Dear," Eve said. "I didn't realize that we were at the far end of Box Canyon."

"We have been grappling, mostly in slow motion, and only when forced to, for the past several months --" I said.

"-- since last spring and the first **Mystery Man Murder**," Jeanne said.

"As I was saying," I said, "before I lost the floor, we have been wandering for months now, and the first murder case, in time, took on two more."

"And," David said, "we are of the opinion that the second and third murders were probably not murders, **per se**."

"Or," Jim said, "**per quo**."

"Yeah," OhJim said, "possibly **per annum**."

"And," I said, "to bring this groping exercise in groupspeak to a close, we are beginning to court the idea that murders two and three were cooked up by someone from either the Coroner's Office or the Cop Shop. The inescapable impression that I have is someone wants to embarrass us, or worse."

Tommy walked in.

"Who wants to embarrass you?" Tommy said. "How could you slip any lower than you already have?"

"Just kidding, Dear?" Eve said. "Go ahead and say it out loud. It will do you good, especially in this crowd, which as others are fond of saying, resembles your comment."

"Just kidding," Tommy said. "Any reference to persons either living or dead is not intended."

"And what say you, my friend," I said, "about the coroner's reports on victims two and three. What lies behind **Doors Number Two and Three**?"

"It is like you said," Tommy said. "Natural causes, essentially."

Eyebrows -- either single or double, depending on the adroitness of the raiser -- were raised all around.

"I'm already missing the murders," Jeanne said. "I guess we'll just have to talk about the **Mystery Men**."

"And talk we will," I said. "Tommy, my friend, let us start with No. Two, Bill Zeohn."

"Ok," Tommy said. "Bill Zeohn, who we assumed from the fact that the coroner sliced off the top of his head, during the autopsy, was murdered by some blunt-force trauma, was a victim of nothing more, the coroner's report says, than time and chance. He slipped in a drunken state and broke his noggin on some icy stone stairs, or so they speculate. Nobody's fault but his own, and looking a lot like blunt-force trauma all the same."

"But I thought that he had been battered," David said.

"All we had, when the gag order came down on the cases, was prelims," Tommy said. "Now you know the final stuff. And there was the provocative fact that someone threw the body in the middle of the street in the middle of the night for cars to run over, which they did. The coroner's report says that was post-death. My sources believe that was done on the spur of the moment by someone who shot out the street lights with a bb gun."

"The implication is there," I said, "that those unknown persons were causing mischief for someone, and I say they were taking a fling at us, trying to link up the first murder with a second body, to intensify the pressure."

"Ok," David said, "I agree. And I'm also curious about Vic No. Three."

"Victim No. Three," Tommy said, "is a classic John Doe, or as we started saying with Victim No. One, a **John Cash**."

"Classic?" Eve said.

"Yes," Tommy said. "No identification on the body, no next of kin filing a missing persons report, no wife, girlfriend, or drinking buddy looking for him. And also, of equal interest, no signs of foul play, according to the Coroner's report, other than the fact that someone drew the coyote symbol in marker pen on the side of a dumpster and threw the body into the dumpster that just happened to be close to the back door of this fine establishment, which by that time had our own Mr. Black as **Drunk in Residence**."

"Same spiel," I said. "Someone is trying to bleep with us."

"You'll get no arguments on that, Dear," Eve said.

Re: the hit guy
| 21December08 |

Email from Tommy --

From: Tommy
To: Goose
Subject: Mystery Man Murder Victim No. 1 (the **John Cash**)

Eyes Only - Need to Know - etc. , etc., blah, blah, blah, noting usual penalties and strictures.

I have been working, working, working, and have attached information that has finally surfaced about the hit guy who tried to introduce Mr. Black to a blunt-cut shotgun that night at **Caspar's Books and That**. I speak of the guy whom Mr. Black ran to ground in the park, in the dark --

• The man's name may have been **Charles James "Chuck Jim" Reivers**. "May have been" because this sort of citizen rarely is on the books as who he is.
• A man named **Charles James Reivers** died in 1958 and was buried in a location known to the databases referenced in this report. Whoever has assumed the identity of Charles James Reivers, a dead man, is probably the man whom Mr. Black lured to his death in the street alongside President's Park.
• Obvious implication: **One cannot kill a dead person**. Therefore, there is no need to plead self-defense or anything else.
• Assuming the identity of a dead man was an old and often-used ruse in former days. Its relative success in this case is due to the infrequent use in latter days of this ruse. No one would think to look for such a lame old trick.
• Obvious downside: If you die in anger, no one gets the blame but you, for using a cooked identity. Others such as Goose can muse on the moral implications. The legal implications start here: **There are no legal implications**.
• A database search and comparison of missing-persons reports yields the supposition that Charles James Reivers, hereafter referred to as "Chuck Jim," is the man we are speaking of.

Double-blind inquiries yield these facts --

• The family of Chuck Jim reported him as missing in early summer of this year, and light inquiry showed that the man was not missing, but dead, and had been dead since 1958. This kicked the file to the TLAs (never mind which one) -

- Ok, the domestic equivalent of the **Peculiar Crimes Unit** (v. novels by Christopher Fowler).

• A suitable story was shared with the family concerning the man and body that appeared in Buffalonya. No facts were included in the story. The family, probably sensing the quicksand that their beloved Chuck Jim lived on, and not wanting to sink into the same hole that swallowed him up, thanked the contacting agents and declined to place any claim on the body. After a suitable length of time, the body on ice in the Eerie Coroner's Office will be interred in the public indigent section of a county cemetery to be chosen later. That release will be after the disposition of the entire **Mystery Man** matter. So far, nothing has been communicated to any local authorities, neither coroner nor cops.

• Chuck Jim, according to family (the only source we have, since whoever he was was using a dead man's name as cover), was an orphan of a shirt-tail relative and was taken in at an early age. He would come and go, and his children, now grown, would see him infrequently, and some never. His former wives have scattered like the Diaspora and are only a tad fewer than the Chosen People.

• The family gave the man a name, **Ben Willy Bridgis**, but nothing else. There is no known birth certificate or any other papers linked to the man whom they named and knew as Ben Willy Bridgis. Database searches yield no, repeat, no information on anyone named Ben Willy Bridgis. The implication is that this person lived his entire life off the grid. This man has been dropped down a deep hole at least once before.

• The Chuck Jim file is on hold and in a safe and very dark place that few know the location of. The inquiry is open but not likely to yield any more information that pertains to our matters, and the inquiring agency has been advised of our satisfaction of things as they stand. This is the preliminary step to dropping this guy into an even deeper and darker place no one will ever look into.

A final thought: A man who never was, who assumed another man's identity after that man died, will be very, very, very hard to trace in terms of who paid him to do a hit on whoever at the bookshop.

The lack of a DNA match, which is confirmed, slams shut one of the few doors that our inquiry into who is after the Tribe could have taken.

Tommy

Under the cloth in Buffalonya
|22December08|

Charles James "Chuck Jim" Reivers, despite the evil intent he bore the Tribe, in accepting money in exchange for murder, was still something of a brother. The elders of the Tribe could and did condemn his intentions toward us, but we were not surprised about the picture that had emerged in Tommy's profile.

Chuck Jim's darkest hour, the hour he first met Mr. Black, which was the hour that he went from **Quick** to **Dead**, reminds me -- don't ask me why -- of my own darkest hour. My darkest hour? That would be the time I spent as an apparent minister infiltrating small, liberal congregations in places including Buffalonya. The Rev. Mr. Black, and I, the Rev. Mr. White, worked as a team to collect names, addresses, and faces of members of activist churches, and we also in time became the ministers of such churches. That much you already know.

Domestic spying? Yeah. **Operation Beloved.**

Illegal? Sure, but a bit later ... and now, who knows, what with the Patriot Act and all.

Not illegal but repugnant and disgusting. In my view.

≈≈≈

You could say that Mr. Black and I were real patriots, and if you are using the word **patriot** pejoratively, go right ahead. At the time, I was under the sway of my handler, my father's legacy, someone else's rightist politics, and my own twisted conviction that I was helping make the world safe from leftists and other assorted crazies. Eve tells me that shrinks call it **reaction formation**. I was working covertly against my own shadow. Onion Man stuff.

Now I am free of all covert/political influences but my own, and those whom I trust to be not toxic but healing and positive for me, I have embraced my essential radical nature. But then, I was the enemy of those who were the enemy of what was going on in places such as Vietnam and in the Culture Wars that never were hotter than in the Nixon and Reagan years.

Operation Beloved was damaging to the soul of everyone whom we touched, and the institution of the Church as well. We deserve death for the damage that we did to good people who thought that they were exercising their right to free assembly and free speech, life and liberty, to name a few of those inalienable rights that leftists love so, according to rightists. And these same good people were welcoming us with a naive Christian love that we may never (should never?) see again in its pure form in our country. Cynics such as the Revs. Mr. Black and Mr. White forced gentle lambs to become as wise as serpents.

We, I say again, deserve to die for the work that we did, and the trust that we spit on and turned over to fledgling databases that have grown like cancer in the decades since.

One watchdog of the NSA, recently, said he is of the opinion that the State's ability to abridge liberty is now total.

Pop would be so proud. I would be so ashamed.

≈≈≈

We mocked God by pretending to be what we were not, and we laughed at the ease with which these good persons would open to us and give us access to their deepest secrets and all the rest, including church records. They welcomed us to their strategy sessions in church basements. We took notes and looked forward to debriefings. We deserved, and we still deserve, to die for this work alone amid all the ugly work over time that we did.

God should have sent lightning bolts to take us out, treating us like enemy combatants shorn of any protection from the State or its laws. We deserve to die like refugees caught on the road -- bloody and inert among blown-open suitcases and boxes tied with old belts. Face down in mud. Exposed.

We donned robes and put on stoles, and we crawled into the pulpit like snakes in the grass, and we led the people in prayers that we pushed with practiced ease past the barrier of our teeth.

We said, **This is the Word of the Lord**, and we survived.

And we laughed at the freedom with which we strode the halls of churches and received the exaggerated respect that real ministers earn and deserve. But God, in a serious bid to demonstrate a cosmic-grade sense of humor, led us to deeper and deeper encounter with God's people and with God's self.

God, who should have destroyed us, redeemed us and made us real, and called us to the work that we had pretended to be called to. First me, and in a photo-finish, Mr. Black.

Two minister-spooks made comfortless by our own machinations.

Deserving **death** but receiving **New Life**.

God called us in earnest intent to become what we had mocked and pretended to be for all those years of **Operation Beloved**.

O wretched men that we were, indeed, who would deliver us from that body of sin and death?

The only One who could.

And the shock, for me, and for Mr. Black, was so extreme that we were like a two-man **Burned-Over District**, smoking from holy fire, and useless, suddenly, to those who had called us to the shadows and sent us out to do harm to God's people. For when our handlers, in the dark, saw that we suddenly believed that we had been against all odds burned clean and burnished and made whole in God's light -- which they could not tolerate -- they turned on us like a bull turns on a bullfighter when the death-dealing sword hits bone, missing its mark.

It took about a New York minute to process our papers and punch our tickets for oblivion. **They** were vaguely amused, and **we** were dazed, like Paul on the road to Damascus. The church people whom we had served cynically were spared any further confusion or mistreatment, outside their awareness, when our handlers pulled the plug on our work under the cloth.

We had been blind, but effective, in ways that lead to death, and when the God whom we had worked against revealed to us who we had been messing with, and we knew that we were dead, and deserved death, and as quickly knew that we were loved, pardoned, and made clean, probably for the first time in our lives, we found ourselves alone, on an empty stage, and we knew in that instant that we had by our adroitness shorn ourselves of the only calling that we had ever known by the name of love and joy.

Blind like moles and naked, refined by fire, and exiled from all that we had ever understood, we made our way, separated one from the other now -- for the sight of one another was too, too painful -- into a light that we could not bear.

Shame at our new nakedness drove us even further from one another.

Eyes closed, we stumbled into the light, and slowly, each of us in his own way, worked out in fear and trembling what had happened and what we had left, and where we thought that we might go where someone would have to take us in. I took a room in a cheap and shabby apartment building, in the neighborhood of **Caspar's Books and That**.

I had heard of the place while still in the shadows.

Mr. Black, by his own roads, found the same sanctuary, as others had before us, such as our friends Mr. Red and Mister Ed, and the woman called Eve whom they worshiped and watched over like knights guarding their Lady.

≈ ≈ ≈

For a long time, Mr. Black could not and would not speak a kind or even neutral word to me, in a twisted way of dealing with the Love that had almost killed him, only to set him on a high place for a season in the wilderness, mirroring my own experience.

Perhaps my clinging to him drove him to this. I certainly bear half of the blame for our inability to share the love of God that had plucked us from the jaws of evil. Neither one of us could or would redeem the other with even a single, simple kind word.

Moles now, of the generic sort, we were blind to so many things.

In fact, the Mr. Black who disappeared and whom I mourned, for much of the last year, was still pushing me away every time we met and any time I sought to make a connection with him.

Not as violently, but still pushing.

At **Caspar's**, this was a daily ritual. The blind abusing the blind.

Mr. Black was one of two people in the universe who I felt might understand the blast-furnace **God of Burning Love** whom I had met and survived. The other person was Eve, and I look back and can see that Mr. Black, fighting the same fight that I was fighting, but without the love of a person like Eve, probably could not accept my vastly greater (but not earned) blessing. Mole no more.

We were not rivals for Eve's love, but I had found something that he needed as desperately as I did, and he hated me for that, for a long time, and when we were face to face after his dying to us and coming back, alive whom we had thought was dead, it was only then that he half-treated me like the brother that I am to him, and this has meant much to me, and far more than I could easily express, until now.

I doubt that he and I will speak of this soon, or at any length.

The mirror of God's love shows no image to the unloved, unloving.

We plan a decent burial or three
| 23December08 |

Eve and I talked at breakfast about the **Mystery Men Three**. One of us, and then the other, in what order I cannot recall, mentioned a need for proper burial -- or, more like, memorial services -- for the three victims.

"Closure would be good," Eve said, "for the quick and for the dead."

We drove down and walked into the **Roll In and Crawl Out**. Mr. Black was at his post at the bar, with David by his side. We led them to the backroom.

"I know you," David said, "and you, too," beerily smiling at Eve, who served up her best Buddha Girl smile.

"Heard any good ones lately?" I said.

"No," David said. "I've been floating on a sea of beer foam and trying to keep my throbbing head above the waves."

"The boy is a natural," Mr. Black said. "I've rarely seen a kid take to the suds the way that Davey Jones here does."

"Maybe it's time to pull the plug on the ocean of beer," I said. "What is the point, at this point?"

"You may have something there," Mr. Black said.

"Can we go home, **Daddy Bee**?" David said. "I miss my Jeanne. And the rest of the orphans."

I noticed that David was in possession of the only first name-equivalent Mr. Black had ever tolerated -- **Bee**. Not **King Bee**, either. Just **Bee**.

I wondered if David knew the honor that he had received.

"Tell you what, Dears," Eve said, "why not come up to **Caspar's** for a roundtable discussion AKA meeting of the F-Troop. We have a number of things to discuss, and your living situation can go on the agenda, Bee Dear."

"I can be as dear as you want," Mr. Black said, "but lose the old guy."

Eve smiled as any Buddha Girl would.

"Coming home will jack you into the network so you can catch up on the posts of late," I said. "We have new information you will find interesting."

"**Post toasties**," David said. "My favorite serial -- **Goose Grackles**."

Mr. Black nodded in a vague way.

"You refer to new information about **Chuck Jim**," Mr. Black said. "Tommy came by last night, and made like a jockey and gave us the crop."

"Tommy as jockey," I said. "Now that is an image."

"I'll put my little network on autopilot," Mr. Black said.

David smiled a crooked-mile smile that was a few rods short of a stile.

Long on style, though.

The boy does have style.

"I second that emotion," David said. "Undercover work has its moments, but they have not come to me yet. I can wait, though. Perhaps the moments came and went, and I was in the can."

F-Troop rides for the fallen
|24December08|

"This meeting of the F-Troop," I said, "will be in stitches."

"That's funny, Mr. Chair Sir," Jim said, "like a seersucker crutch."

"Yeah," OhJim, said, "I'm bobbin' and weavin'."

"Today's agenda," I said, "is turned over to the dead and departed -- the dear and not so dear."

"The gang is all here, Dear, except for the all-seeing and all-knowing Tommy," Eve said, "so you can tell them once and get it right."

"Yes, well," I said, "this is the deal. Eve and I have been talking about closure concerning the hapless dead guys that have gone by the name of the **Mystery Man Murder** victims. About closure."

"And so shall they be, forever," Jeanne said, "no matter what we find."

"Yeah," David said, from Jeanne's lap. "We call them the **Mystery Men**, but others will know them, Lord willing, as the **Mystery Man Murders**."

"Well," I said, "Eve's and my idea is that the three victims deserve a decent churchy service, and that we are the only ones who know their stories all the way to the end. And probably the only ones who ever will."

"And," Eve said, "Goose and I are of the opinion that the first victim, though he meant one or more of us ill, is also a brother. Something like Joseph's **coat-of-many-colors** brothers."

"After reading Tommy's profile of our not-so-dearly departed Chuck Jim, I can see what Goose Man means," Mr. Black said, "and though Chuck Jim meant it for evil, especially to me, God may well have meant it for good."

No one was surprised to see Mr. Black, the **Bee-Man**, and his sidekick David, the **Junior Bee-Man**, among us, since everyone reads my posts to the VPN blog.

"We certainly stand to gain in the **Karma Department**," Mister Ed said, "if we have a service for this Chuck Jim. I suppose that it is more about **deportment** than **department**, but let it pass, my friends. Just let it go."

No one had picked up on the distinction, I could see, so the letting it pass, passed without demur, to no one's demerit.

"I'm not used to this talk about closures," Jim said. "Reminds me of my days as a young man who was slow to learn the ways of lingerie and all those hooks and such."

"Yeah," OhJim said. "You still don't know **boulder** from **boulder-holder**."

"That might be a sweet confusion," Jeanne said. "The container and the thing contained. And it's an **over-the-shoulder boulder-holder**, I believe."

Jeanne gave my brothers her sideways smile.

They went all pink like fine lace at the bodice.

"Are you ready to vote?" I said. "Those in favor signify by the usual sign."

The vote was unanimous -- thumbs up and middle fingers in, the F-Troop salute. Mr. Black, the picture of dignity, nodded but kept his hands hidden.

"Next item of business, then," I said, "is to plan the memorial service -- who, what, where, when, why, and how."

"The **Five W's and the H**," Mister Ed said, "the journalist's six-fingered salute. I know them well. As well as I know **A E I O U and sometimes Y and W**. The two phrases, in a word, are consonant."

"I think that the first question," Eve said, "is who to invite and, then, where to have the gathering. The rest we can leave up to our two minister-equivalents, Lord willing, if they are willing."

"I am," I said, "and I see by his nod the Reverend Mr. Black is as well."

"And with one caveat, Mr. Foot-Stool Sir," Mr. Black said with his thin highway smile. "I think that we should speak directly to each victim's life and death."

I nodded with vigor.

"Who wants," I said, "to do Vic Number One -- Chuck Jim, hit man?"

"I will," Mr. Black said.

"Vic Number Two, Bill Zeohn, the hapless one?" I said.

"I will," Jeanne said.

"And Vic Number Three, the unknown homeless guy?" I said.

"I will," OhJim said.

"Really," I said.

"Yeah," OhJim said. "I mean no, not really, just in real time."

"As to Eve's questions," I said, "first -- who to invite?"

"Well," David said, "us, Tommy, and the four at the sub-tribe house."

"I can answer for my red-faced friend Mr. Red," Mister Ed said. "**Bleep youse every one, I'm of staying with Wild Billy to watch this shop.**"

"Ed channels Red, film at eleven," Jeanne said. "Nicely done, my elder friend and colleague."

Mister Ed, ever the sky-crane, bowed from the waist.

"And then the question of where," I said.

"Some fine and private place," Jim said.

"Yeah," OhJim said. "**Six Feet Under**, by Robert Graves. The grave's a fine and private place, certainly, but not nearly big enough."

"I know of a little church not too far from the Tribal House," I said, "and I'm sure that Baldi can secure its fine and private use on a week night."

"Sold," Eve said, "with the proviso that we make sure no one wanders in because they saw the lights and felt like getting down with the Christians."

"I think we can handle security," Jeanne said. "In fact, I know we can."

"Anyone want to invite Jane Carlotto?" I said. "On deepest background, only, of course."

"Ask Tommy for an opinion," Jeanne said. "It's ticklish. By coming, she would end up all tied up in the pretzel position."

"So am I," Jim said. "Ticklish. Especially in the pretzel position."

"Yeah," OhJim said, "me, too. I could draw you a stick-figure drawing with little Xs on the ticklish parts."

"Ask Tommy what?" Tommy said, walking in late, as usual.

"Ask Tommy if Jane Carlotto should be invited to a memorial service for the three murder victims of the **Mystery Man** series, on deep background," Jeanne said, shifting David on her lap so she could lick his ear lobe.

"I think that would be a good idea," Tommy said. "Jane is much, much more than a hack for the local rag. We go way back. I'll give her a call."

We gather in the name of ... what?
|25December08|

Baldi booked us for Xmas in the p.m.

The little church is made of a pinkish local quarried rock known as Medina sandstone. There is a stained glass window in the chancel that looks either like the Spirit descending as a dove or a wing-shot bird screaming to earth.

Mr. Black and I were the celebrants, in view of our covert experience

under the cloth, and we were nervous for several reasons --
- Our entry into the ranks of the God-convicted had brought to an end our covert activities in the church.
- Neither of us had led a church service of any sort since our sincere conversion and sudden departure from our flocks.
- We had not taken a poll, but we figured that the Tribe had a 50/50 split between orthodox and fairly unorthodox believers and those who were somewhere on a continuum that said **Indifferent to God** on the left pole and **Righteously Pissed at God** on the right pole.
- We wanted some music but didn't know if anyone played the piano, let alone the organ. It was not something we could call out for like pizza or maid service.

After we learned that Tommy was a piano player from way, way back, we got started. Tommy left Jane in a pew and sat down at the baby grand. I crawled into the pulpit, and invited the Tribe, sitting here and there in the first few pews, to find a hymnal and sing **Nearer My God to Thee**.

Tommy started in with an extended rolling introduction that had us smiling by the time he kicked in on the first verse, and we made a bit of noise, believers and others, together.

Now I know that half of you reading this will sit to the left, with the Christians, and half of you will tell the ushers that you want to sit on the right, with the Others, like people at a wedding. I hope you can bracket your feelings if they are negative for long enough to feel something of the moment that we were sharing.

It was hard enough to be there without you sneering at us, Friend.

It had been, in so many ways, a year from hell, and we were gathering in the one love that we had for each other, to touch something -- the face of God for some and the sensations of grief and awe, perhaps, for others.

And the rest, sitting with their anger.

Your anger?

Be there, now, with us, Onion Man. For once, feel while you cry.

What would you be feeling if you could ... be there?

Mr. Black stepped to the pulpit like a postman who knows your dog.

"Welcome, friends," Mr. Black said. "And now if Tommy can swing it, let's sing a few bars of **Drop-Kick Me, Jesus, Through the Goalposts of Life**."

Mr. Black meant it for humor, but Tommy meant it for real.

Who knew that he knew that song?

He played an intro and sang a few lines.

We were rolling on the floor laughing.

Not Holy Rollers, exactly, but having some fun. **ROFL.**

I waited until the Tribe was able to reach a more decorous place again, and said, "My brother and I invite you to join us in remembering the three **Mystery Man** brothers who died and were in their various ways mistreated in death. We come here not without stain ourselves but with hearts full for those who suffered and died. We will hear from three brothers and sisters who will remember each of the victims, and we will close with a prayer, each to God as we know him or her."

"Gotcha, Goose," Tommy said, with a flourish on the keys.

"First up," I said, "-- Mr. Black, who will talk about a friend and foe whom we now know as **Chuck Jim.**"

To bury Chuck Jim and to praise him
|26December08|

Mr. Black, from the pulpit, looked at us in glaring silence.

"I come," Mr. Black said, "to bury the man we know as **Chuck Jim**, not to praise him."

Mr. Black frowned. "That's not right."

He looked up for a while with that frozen highway smile of his.

"I come to both bury my foe and praise my brother," Mr. Black said.

"I first became aware of Charles James "Chuck Jim" Reivers AKA Ben Willy Bridgis AKA the **John Cash** AKA the first **Mystery Man Murder** victim when he stepped from his rented late-model Ford Crown Vic, back last spring.

"I was manning the bookshop, alone, at closing time. I had just killed the lights and was gathering my stuff by the lights from the street.

"A cold and hard rain had been falling all the day long, and the street was gleaming. The wind was stiff. There were patches of dirty snow.

"When I saw Chuck Jim open the trunk of his car and take out a sawed-off shotgun and hide it under his coat, I hit the back door at a run, and slipped around the side, behind him.

"Chuck Jim looked into the bookshop and rattled the locked front door. He banged on the plate glass and waited for a while. When he got back into his Crown Vic, I gave him a few seconds to pull away from the curb and ran to my truck and tailed him.

"Chuck Jim drove downtown, with me following. At President's Park, he parked. He got out of his car, quickly, and ran into the dark park, still in his leather coat. I parked, and pursued.

"I knew the park, and Chuck Jim didn't (I had noticed that his plates were from Pennsylvania), so I was able to come up behind him in the dark, where he had hoped to set a trap for his tail.

"The first thing that Chuck Jim knew was me slamming him in the chest. He went down hard, but he came up quick and was ready to rumble, but I had danced back into the shadows. When I slammed him in the chest again, he went down again, got up a bit slower, and began to stumble-run back toward his car.

"Chuck Jim could hear me, pounding hard behind him, and he looked back just as he broke into the street. That was his last act, in this life.

"That bus bore down on him, in the dark and rain, and he threw out his arms, as if to stop the bus or catch it.

"In a way, he was successful. He both caught the bus and stopped it, but the relative size difference of man and machine ensured one thing. Death.

"Knowing the park, I had pulled up in the shadows when Chuck Jim burst into the path of the bus.

"In the noise and confusion that followed, I slipped over to where I had parked my truck. I drove away, already knowing that I had to disappear for a time. The rest of that story is not part of Chuck Jim's story.

"That ends the story of my foe.

"But what of my brother?

"Chuck Jim, from what Tommy has been able to piece together, never quite made it onto the grid. Sound familiar? He was orphaned at a very early age and adopted, very informally, by shirt-tail kin, who gave him the name, never officially recorded, of **Ben Willy Bridgis**.

"In the fullness of time, Ben Willy visited a cemetery and found a marker with a name that he took for his own, **Charles James "Chuck Jim" Reivers**. That name, he got the documents for.

"We can only speculate about how he managed to lose his birth name and birth certificate. Perhaps he burned down the courthouse.

"He seems to have been that sort of guy, an outlaw for hire and a fairly shifty, resourceful character who knew how to stay in the game -- at least for the 50 years or so that he walked on this planet and -- we presume -- punched the ticket of many citizens who pissed off someone with enough money and coldness to pay for a contract killing. Our brother was not nice.

"Brother?

"I think so.

"No one in this room can cast the first stone, and no one of us is more clean or pure than this our ruthless brother who, like us, worked in the shadows for the bidding of others who compromised his soul, with his blessing and assistance.

"Child of God?

"Are you?

"I stand before you because I was quicker and because I was lucky.

"On his turf, I might have been dead. On my turf, you know the outcome.

"Tommy assures me that one cannot kill a dead man, and I say that the very real man I watched die, I killed in self-defense.

"God will judge, and until then may God watch between Chuck Jim and me while we are absent one from the other.

"Amen. And Merry Christmas."

Jeanne remembers a hapless man
| 27December08 |

Jeanne clicked to the pulpit.

She had worn her usual -- black, head to toe, from her hair to her old silk dress to her peep-toe pumps, with deep red accents at lips, toes, and fingertips.

Christmas colors, really.

Well, almost.

What, I wondered, would a refined Punk Princess with Goth leanings have to say about her subject, and who if anyone would she pray to.

"Billy Zeohn," Jeanne said, "was a cartoon version of a person. He was always in the way, and always taking pictures with his old print-film camera, and always with the flash attached and blazing. He was the sort of guy that you knew had probably been **Daddy's Little Fatty** as a child, unless, as was slightly more likely, Daddy was a drunk who had truly evil nicknames for a child he didn't care about, a wife he beat, and all the rest.

"Billy Zeohn, for all his many creepy edges, was a person.

"Billy Zeohn is dead, now, and if there ever had been an investigation into the circumstances of his death, which friend Tommy tells us was probably from natural causes, no one ever bothered to find out who Billy Zeohn was or what happened to him the night he died.

"We did find out that the camera was never loaded, that Billy used it as a way of getting close to the people that he was most interested in, and that that seemed to be women between the ages of 16 and death's door.

"When Tommy and David let themselves into Billy Zeohn's apartment, after Zeohn's death, they were assailed by paper, paper everywhere. They said that each room was covered in thicknesses of paper of any imaginable type, trodden into a carpet of pulp fibers in a rainbow of colors.

"They found ten-year-old library books that had strips of bacon inside, apparently used as bookmarks.

"They found no evidence that Billy had been a stalker, but many women downtown wondered at one time or another what they would do if this man turned his odd attention their way. His attention was always unwanted.

"It was easy to make fun of Billy, and most of us involved in the media in this city made fun of him at our whim.

"It was hard to interact with Billy, because his social skills were no better than his average daily living skills.

"Although Billy died young, he did die without any help, but after he died, someone hijacked his body and threw it into the street, in the middle of the night. Several cars and a bus ran over the body before anyone figured out what was going on, for it was a dark and stormy night.

"No one deserves this treatment, and no matter how ugly or odd or smelly, each one of us is a child of God.

"Was it God's joke on Billy to end his years in this repugnant way -- an ugly death for an ugly life?

"I would rather deny that God exists than to believe such things, but still the question remains -- who allows this sort of thing to happen?

"Billy Zeohn, as far as we know, will lay in a locker until the Coroner releases his body to a pauper's grave.

"The only picture that we have of him is a rough drawing that Tommy has made of an autopsy photo that shows him after the top of his head was cut off. Why? For practice, as far as we know.

"This brief and ambivalent remembrance will be as close as the memory of this man gets to any sort of permanence.

"Pray for his soul, pray for those who defiled his body, and pray for us all.

"And do not, ever, forget this man. Amen."

OhJim remembers two homeless guys
| 28December08 |

OhJim walked from the pews to the pulpit and turned back toward us.

At least I was not the most shabby dresser in the group.

OhJim had that honor. He won it by a cotton thread. Several threads, really, from tattered cuffs to raveled edges in general. His suit coat, though not of many colors, was of a certain age and condition. But OhJim carries his shabby self well, and I can think of no higher endorsements than those of Jeanne and Eve, who love my little brother for his wit and wisdom, and his true goodness.

OhJim took out a piece of paper and put it on the pulpit.

"I rise," OhJim said, "to remember a man whom I never knew. This man whom I volunteered to remember, on this **Night of All Nights**, to this date has no name, and if the past is the parent of the future, I am certain that no gestation period, of any length, will issue in a birth certificate for our fallen friend we do know as **Mystery Man Murder Victim Number Three**.

"We could call him the **John Cash Two -Too**, but maybe tomorrow.

"This ritual tonight is his last and possibly first shot at respect.

"Right now, he is front and center, on our minds and in our hearts, and if we ever forget him, he is more gone than just dead and gone.

"He becomes forgotten, as if he had never lived.

"If you will think back, this is what we know about him--

● "He seems to have been homeless, and was young and scruffy in a full beard.

● "After dying from natural causes, probably exposure, his body was dumped in a dumpster behind the bar that our own Mr. Black has virtually lived at for a number of months, and still does, while this Mystery Man Murder business sorts itself out endlessly, or so it might seem, some of the time.

● "Drawn on the outside of the dumpster that held his body was a symbol that we know as a secret society symbol known to countless persons in the covert ranks. The symbol depicts a coyote's face, in death. A shroud for an animal that doesn't look that lively even when he is alive.

● "After this third victim was found, and the coroner's workers and the detectives checked back in their evidence boxes, they found pieces of paper in the clothing of victims No. 1 and No. 2. Those pieces of paper bore the same symbol, that of the coyote in death.

"You may wonder why I asked to be the one to give this remembrance. After all, you know me as the **yeah** guy who chimes in with a second pun or one-liner when my brother Jim starts things off with a pun or a one-liner.

"If Jim is **wood-eye, wood-eye**, then I am **hare-lip, hare-lip**.

"You know me as an oft funny and almost always off-color straight man.

"I asked myself why I asked to give this eulogy, and this is what I decided.

"I too have been what others in their ignorance call **homeless** and I too have survived that life to no one's gladness but my own.

"I know the difference between **homeless** and **exile**, and I know that I was never in exile. That label sticks to hams that rise higher on the food chain than mine ever have or will.

"I know what it means to sleep under a bridge, to break into an abandoned warehouse to stay warm by making a fire that burns the place down while I stumble into the drunken night, looking for the next hole to sleep in.

"I know the numbness that leads to arson on a frigid night.

"I know what it is like to plan ahead -- but never past today, and not because it is a Zen thing but because without hope today is all there is.

"I knew that to dream was to wish for death and probably find it.

"I know what it is like to strike another hobo, to kick him in the head because he dropped the wine bottle and it broke with a swallow inside.

"Such treatment of **Tokay** was **not Ok.**

"I knew long before I reunited with my brothers it is best to mock and laugh at what terrifies you if you want to mock and laugh again tomorrow.

"And truth? Please.

"Truth is for those with the luxury of bed and board, and a warm place to -- well, you catch my drift, like those downwind from one breaking wind.

"I figure that our nameless brother in the dumpster knew more than just a few of these things that I know, and I am certain that it was not the first time that he slept in a dumpster.

"I realize that I have made this speech a lot about me, but in doing so I have somehow said some truth things about Vic Number Three, like one who flings mud and sees that some of it clings to the other.

"Amen."

Baldi adds a righteous richness
|29December08|

OhJim sat down.

We were stunned.

Who, including his brothers, knew?

OhJim, a homeless guy.

Pop would not have been proud, but we were grateful for our brother's candor and insights.

I nodded to Baldi Cleanue, whom I had asked to give a prayer at the end of the service. As Baldi walked to the pulpit, we sat with the stories that we had rededicated ourselves to and the three dead brothers whom we would always remember and never forget.

"I stand before you on this **Holy Night**," Baldi said, "as a self-retired but still committed minister of the Christian sort and a millionaire, many times over. What I am trying to say is that I don't need any of you. I don't need you to believe anything I believe or need you to say pious things to please me.

"The Lord, in the Lord's bounty, has freed me to free others from the need or desire to say the so-called right things to me, or in my presence. Thanks be to God for this gift of tolerance, borne of God's gifts of gold and silver, to me and to my wife, Luce.

"I don't usually talk about the wealth that Luce and I enjoy, but I don't usually find myself in a church with people like yourselves who will not try to part me from some of my gold. I'm loving this, because life is sweet when strange and wonderful things and people meet in God's House.

"I will offer a prayer that will bind no one's hands, heart, or mind.

"I will pray to the God whom we all know, or shun or deny.

"I will pray in the conviction that there is one God in diverse manifestations, and I will pray in a spirit that would get me kicked out of the **Minister-Boys Club**, may they rot in a hot place.

"Well, I could buy the club and give it back to them, several times over, and still have enough left over to do it again.

"I long since quit that club."

Baldi lifted both hands, palms up.

"Let us pray.

"Lord God, ruler of the universe, you set the stars in the sky and you set the planets in motion.

"You set our hearts on fire with the fire of your spirit, and you offer us truth if we would but ask and receive.

"We pray tonight for the insulted and injured. We pray for three brothers who were taken from the Quick and added to the Dead in bad time, and who in death were insulted and injured some more.

"We pray for the wisdom to remain apart from the ways of brothers and sisters who would condone such things, and for the wisdom to seek one another's counsel frequently lest we fall into grave error and become those things and persons whom we oppose and decry in our righteousness.

"Give us the courage to fight for what is right and proper and the discernment, together, to know when to keep our own counsel and avoid the snares of a system that rewards criminal minds and taxes with scorn and the boot those who would stand for a truly radical vision of justice and mercy.

"Help us, as our brother has said, to remember these our three brothers, because if we can forget them, others can forget us, and in the life to come, and before that **Great and Terrible Day** comes that will begin the end of what we now know, to be forgotten is worse than a death sentence.

"Be with us as we resume our lives of quiet advocacy, and help us to understand both the call and the sharp limits of our self-chosen roles as righteous Robin Hoods in a self-righteous world gone mad with self-interest.

"Deliver us from all High Sheriffs in the day of trouble.

"We pray all that we pray, in your **Holy Name**.

"Amen."

So said we all and were done.

I get a note from underground
| 30December08 |

On the Fifth Day of Christmas, I got a call from Luke Parmgartner. He wanted me to come and talk with him at his place of business.

Place of business?

His subterranean place of business. The **Tin-Hat Building**.

It was a bleak day of mid-winter, with snow like a blanket to hide under.

The wind was involved, with the snow, and they combined in an embrace that could kill you.

I drove over to the river and down to that ugly tin-clad building that shows no signs or indications of what is going on inside. I knew the drill, though, so I drove around to the back, and I buzzed at the back door.

May I help you, a Voice said. It was a pleasant female voice.

"Yes," I said. "I think I love you. Will you marry me?"

Bad input, the Voice said. **State your business.**

"Here to see Agent Luke," I said.

May I say who is at hand? the Voice said.

"Goose Grim," I said.

One moment, please, the Voice said.

I waited, and when I was done with that, I waited some more. Shivering. Finally, when I had re-upped for at least the third time, the door opened, and the Voice invited me to **step forward onto the black square and stand very still.**

The door clicked loudly shut behind me. Lights from an articulated harness that descended from the ceiling did a retina scan and took some pictures of me. The device beeped like a mouse trying to scat-sing. I expected it to invite me to stick out my tongue and say **ahhhhh**. With some final beeping and blinking, the harness retracted itself, and the Voice invited me to step forward.

Luke handed me a day pass and said, "You look like bleep. Follow me. I refuse your offer of marriage, by the way. Only because it would take me out of the running for Eve. That is my main consideration here."

"You look like bleep, too," I said. "Lead me on. Eve says hi back."

"We're going to my office," Luke said, "and I'll take you through the Ready Room, just so you can tell your grandkids -- if any -- that you saw it. I still can't see what she sees in a birdman like you."

Luke inclines to well-worn tweeds and chinos, with wing tips and hiking socks. He usually has a beat-up stingy-brim fedora on his huge head, brim up all around, and he inclines to stooping, because he is a lot taller than most of us. If he wears a tie, and he is supposed to, one can find it folded and tucked into his sport coat pocket up high by his chest. Luke always corresponds roughly and well with regulations.

Luke is probably within a few years of my age, a Baby Boomer but far, far from diapers -- or closer every day, I guess. Depends, actually, on the continent one inhabits. Or the incontinent, as it were.

Luke's bearlike friendliness hides an iron core that he uses to his advantage. Eve is somewhat susceptible to his well-aged charms, but I am not worried. I have a charm or two on my bracelet, too. Luke is hard to dislike.

The Ready Room, so named because it is ready for just about anything, is a regional center for border security. **Hum-int** ala **sig-int**. If it pulses, beeps, brays, or moves, along the border, the monitors in this pit of a building will register every nuance. And store it on tape.

We must keep a weather eye on those shifty Canadians, or, as Luke put it, on those shifty **foreigners**, on both sides, whom the Canadians welcomed with somewhat more zeal and sincerity than we do. We do not welcome those **mother-bleeping bastids** at all, thank you very much. Or so Luke says and so would those he works with at his particular TLA hidey-hole.

To Luke, **refugee**, **refuge**, and **refuse** are words of a common ancestry, and Luke's bedrock racism is not out of step with that of his cohort. Spooks in general distrust foreigners. Period. Spooks in general profile on outward appearance. Thus the preoccupation with audio and video. Video especially. If you look like a foreigner, Luke will always treat you like one and never stop that overdone agent's deference meant to say **Bleep**-you underneath.

Luke is an Ok guy. He just has not been redeemed, saved, or born again, like myself and the members of the Tribe. Luke holds to the old-tyme politics-as-religion, and it is good enough for him.

Like Tommy, Luke still lives in Spookistan.

Luke's lair was not a secret, exactly, but it was off limits to the general run of Americans, and as for others ... .

We took an elevator to get to the heart of the complex, down on the ground floor. The tin hat of the building was really only meant to cover the several-story, hardened silo of a hole in the ground that the government had dug for its spy equipment and operators.

The underground floors were secure, unlike the tin hat.

The Ready Room was the size of a small school gym.

Huge television screens ringed the room.

Someone smart had to tell you which screen showed what stretch of river or lake on our section of the border.

Techs at terminals, at the rate of one station per screen, tapped on keyboards and chased mice around on their little mouse pads. No one looked up, and there wasn't any chatter, just the hum that accompanies **Techistan** and the smell of refried air and stale corridors.

We walked through and out a door that led quickly to Luke's office. We squeezed inside, and Luke shut the door. He turned to me and grinned.

"You really know how to stir the chamber pot," Luke said. "I gotta hand it to you. Now we wait."

A mystery man appears
| 31December08 |

We sat for a long time, even longer than I had waited in the entry room. Luke's room is a typical spook's office, with huge metal lockers for file folders and a modular desk bolted to the wall, under a cabinet attached to the ceiling. The lights are the long tube kind, and the effect is bleak in a down-dragging sort of way. A season in this room would feel like a lifetime.

Luke seems oblivious.

Our chatter was so banal as to be not worth the repeating. We just went over the old social games -- why Eve had picked me over him and every other man, or woman, for that matter, Luke said, in the universe, and on and on, like that. Harmless patter, like a misting rain on a summer's day. Finally, there was a knock on the door, and Luke opened it.

In stepped a little man whom I had never seen before. He was young -- about 30, I would say -- and small -- petite, really, though such a word ill-fits the male frame -- though in his case it was apt. He had a small nose, small ears tight to his head, and slim fingers on raccoon-like hands.

His suit was expensive and hung from his spare frame like an expensive suit, actually.

"This," Luke said, "is a colleague, Mr. Trimlea. Mr. Trimlea, this is my old friend and enema Goose Grim."

We shook hands. I was mindful of his sharp fingernails.

"A pleasure," Mr. Trimlea said, in a voice that was far deeper than Mr. Trimlea appeared capable of producing. His smile, fleeting and understated, reminded me of a cat's tail twitch. Overall, Mr. Trimlea seemed like a sleek, dangerous little animal with very sharp teeth and claws.

"You may be wondering why I called this meeting," I said -- aiming for a chuckle or a grin.

"Not really," Mr. Trimlea said. "You are here, Mr. Grim, because I asked Luke to see that you would be. Simple as that."

"Mr. Trimlea," Luke said, "sits somewhere higher in the hierarchy than I do, and I sometimes carry his spear."

It was easy to see that the otherwise worldly and self-absorbed Luke, my friend, had more than met his match in this ferret-like superior being.

Mr. Trimlea was **not high, but mighty**, if you know what I mean, in short.

"Well," I said, "I'm here because I chose to be, and if you have something to say, I just might listen. And, just to be clear, here, you can stick your spear where the sun don't shine, for all I care."

Mr. Trimlea, though his face did not change, signaled something strangely positive with his eyes.

"Nicely put," Mr. Grim, he said. "Actually, Luke is the one who is hung up on strange metaphors, not me."

Bear-like Luke looked like a sick volcano that wanted to blow but had forgotten how to make magma.

"Metaphors aside," I said, "what's up? Give me the long and short of it."

Mr. Trimlea chose to ignore that barb, which raised my opinion of him.

Short men can be such a pain in the patoot.

"I represent certain interests," Mr. Trimlea said, "who wish to remain anonymous. They have authorized me to talk with you about matters that interest them, and if I do not miss my guess, you and your ... associates. I think you call yourselves the **Tribe** is it?"

The ferret man had my attention, and I chose to ignore the barb. I did file for later the question of who told him about the Tribe.

There was a knock. Luke, with a puzzled look, opened the door.

"Agent," Luke said.

"Agent," Tommy said.

Tommy poked Mr. Trimlea in the chest. Mr. Trimlea started to look uneasy, the way Tommy does when Jeanne looks at his ear lobe.

Tommy squared off, nose to nose with Luke. Neither was on tip-toes.

"And what is this weasel doing here?" Tommy said. "Any ideas?"

"Yeah," Luke said, "stop having dishes with garlic for lunch. We should go on down to the conference room, where we have a video to show."

Tommy, as he turned, winked at me.

"Where did you pick up these yardbirds, Goose Man?" Tommy said. "I knew I shouldn't have let you out to play by yourself. When will you learn that running solo is not wise when the other runners are upwardly nubile spooks such as our cute and harmless little friend here?"

"Well," I said, "do not harm the little guy. He looks like he might carry grudges and relish revenge. Still snowing and blowing outside?"

Tommy nodded.

"This little twerp? Revenge?" Tommy said, grabbing Mr. Trimlea by the head and knocking on his brow rapidly with his knuckles. "Rocky Raccoon, here, is actually an old friend."

Mr. Trimlea had gone limp while Tommy had him in the headlock, but as soon as Tommy let do, Mr. Trimlea stomped on Tommy's foot and hit him a smart blow to the zyphoid process. That had to hurt.

Mr. Trimlea actually broke into a smile, like a lab rat that knows, going in, that it is in the Control Group.

"Boy, boys," I said, "enough of this love fest. Luke and I are shocked."

"Wait until you see the video," Luke said. "It only gets worse."

Tommy threw his arm around Mr. Trimlea They led the way.

Home movies would be nice(r)
| 01January09 |

We filed into the conference room on the ground zero floor of the tin-hat building that houses the border security surveillance capabilities for our section of the ever-dangerous Canadian-U.S. border.

Tommy continued to set a tone of high jinks with his little buddy Mr. Trimlea. Luke and I were the sober ones, and not necessarily by choice. We spread out some, grateful for the additional space. Luke's office would give a sardine claustrophobia -- and that oily feeling like you get from breathing subway air.

"Sit, please, Mr. Grim," Mr. Trimlea said. "We have a video to show you that you will find of great interest, I believe. At least that is the opinion of Tommy and Luke, to name a few."

Mr. Trimlea picked up a remote, and video appeared on a screen at the end of the room. It looked like a CCTV feed or a surveillance tape. There was audio. At first, there was only a lot of noise, of this and that. The video was black and white, and reasonably sharp. I began to perk up when I picked out persons on the screen that I knew. Detectives Blucote and Schmidt were stars in the video, with another person, in a white lab coat.

"Mr. Grim," Mr. Trimlea said, freezing the image, "I will not tell you how we came into possession of this video, and I will not tell you why anyone thought it might be of benefit to set a covert watching/listening post in the Eerie County Coroner's Office or in the evidence locker at the downtown district police station. But as we continue, these are among the images that you will see."

"Noted," I said.

The detectives and the lab coat person were looking at a body on a slab.

"Where did you find this one?" Blucote said.

"In an alley downtown," the lab coat person said. "He just died, from what we can tell so far. We traced the fingerprints to a male subject, Billy Zeohn, with local address. Is this person known to you?"

"Oh, yes," Blucote said, "and we will take the body from here. You can adjust the paperwork."

"Gotcha," the lab coat person said. "I don't need or want to know where you are taking your new friend. Nor does Dr. Backstaff or your Chief."

"As you can see, Mr. Grim," Mr. Trimlea said, hitting the **pause**, "this is a provocative piece of video tape. We continue."

The tape resumed when Mr. Trimlea gestured with the remote. The date in the corner changed, though the same three persons -- Blucote, Schmidt, and the lab coat person -- were again the stars. They were looking at a body on the slab.

"Do you have any idea who this guy is?" Blucote said.

"No idea at all," the lab coat person said with a slight shrug of his head. "Some homeless guy by the looks of it. No hits on the prints. Obvious from his clothing and general lack of hygiene, **et cetera, et cetera** and so on."

"Well," Blucote said, "we will take him from here. The Lord hath need of this particular donkey's ass."

"Another provocative piece of video," Mr. Trimlea said.

"Noted, again," I said.

Mr. Trimlea lowered the remote after freezing the video on an image of the two detectives pushing the body on a gurney, out the door.

I already knew where the body was going.

"And now," Mr. Trimlea said, "we jump to the evidence locker, and some interesting footage."

The video showed the two detectives. It was the middle of the night, according to the time stamp. The two were working at a table with three evidence boxes in view.

"Take the paper and put it in a coat pocket or pants pocket. Make it look like we overlooked it the first time around. The coroner is supposed to announce tomorrow that his office has linked three bodies to the **Mystery Man** thing," Blucote said.

"Check," Schmidt said. "And I do mean check. I hope it is as big as the last one was."

"Yeah," Blucote said, "I've never been threatened, bribed, **and** coerced at the same time before."

"Any idea who **Mr. Big** is?" Schmidt said.

"Don't know bleep other than the fact that he has deep pockets and strange needs," Blucote said.

Mr. Trimlea froze the image.

"Mr. Grim," he said, "what we have here is a failure to communicate."

"And a whole lot of persistent moral failure," I said, "on the part of some startling persons charged with serving and defending. Someone has a problem, and it is a very big problem. Glad it's not my problem."

Getting down to the balance of power
|02January09|

"But I digress." I said. "Who has **a failure to communicate?**"

"It's an idiom from film," Mr. Trimlea said. "**Cool Hand Luke?**"

I looked at Luke with some degree of skepticism.

"And I'm an idiot," I said, "if I know what you are driving at."

"Let me try," Tommy said. "What we are saying, Goose Man, is that this is really your problem, as well as ours. It is your problem because someone is trying to cause trouble for you and your friends by diverting these bodies in hopes of embarrassing or exposing your quasi-criminal enterprise, and it is our problem because our superiors have assured us that this is our problem, lest someone decide it is their problem, too."

"Wake me up after the preliminaries are over," I said. "My attention is wandering. It seems like we need to be talking about a balance of power."

"Bingo," Tommy said. "What is it that anyone would gain by arranging three deaths to look like murders? And what is more, what would be gained if you and your friends were made to look like persons who were withholding information pertinent to a murder investigation? And finally, what would happen if one or more of you could be framed for one or more of these deaths that someone has tried to lay at your feet?"

"Ok," I said, "you have laid out our position, which from the beginning has been that someone is trying to make us uncomfortable at a minimum and dead at the extreme. Like I said. Power."

"Bingo," Tommy said. "So what would be some possible motives for seeking to put you-all in such powerless places?"

"Well," I said, "there is intimidation, there is embarrassment, there is exposure, there is jail time for withholding information, there is terroristic intent in sending a contract killer our way, and there is the risk that we will lose what we lightly refer to as **our exemption**. In a word, we would no longer be hidden in plain sight. We would be weak and nakedly exposed."

"In fact," Tommy said, "almost all of these things have happened as a result of the three deaths and how the investigation has gone. Your exemption seems to hang in the balance. How strong is the thread it hangs from?"

"Yes," I said, "and we are still pretty much the same quasi-criminal enterprise that we always were. There is one reason for that."

"Yes," Tommy said, "the Vault. Your power plant."

"Exactly," I said, "the Vault, and I can't believe you said that. So, let us simply stipulate that this mess has been a challenge of sorts to the Tribe. What then? The essence of who we are has not, and cannot, be touched. You know that, I know that, Luke knows that, and if **little mister pointy ears rooster** here does not know that, he has put himself in a lot more hot water than is good for him or his pretty feathers."

"Oh, please," Mr. Trimlea said, "I know as much, and possibly slight more, about you and your precious Tribe than you do."

"Oh, yeah," I said, "then tell me the name of my first pet."

"You didn't have one, Mr. Grim," Mr. Trimlea said, "because your Pop thought that the three of you -- that is, you, and your two brothers both named Jim -- were pets enough for anyone, yourselves included."

I was impressed.

"Tell me, then, where are we to go from here," I said. "I can see how it would be in my interest and in the interest of those whom I speak for, for all this crap to start rolling and tumbling downhill toward a sewer drain."

"That would be the general idea," Mr. Trimlea said, "but there is the small matter of who knows what and what those same persons have been doing to engineer evidence, alter evidence, plant evidence, and strew bribes around, paired with threats, like Johnny Appleseed channeling Attila the Hun."

"Don't quit your day job, Son, for any new job that includes similes or metaphors," I said. "But I am willing to let that pass. The main question, as you point out, has to do with the list of persons whose dirty tricks make the Tribe's withholding of evidence look like a juvenile coyness that is fetching and cute."

"Right," Luke said. "The list before winnowing includes the following, in descending order of ever-lessening importance and stature (sorry, **Mr. T**) --
- "The police commissioner,
- "The county coroner,
- "Someone high in the Coroner's Office,
- "Two city police force detectives,
- "And various unnamed helpers, either in spot situations or all along."

"Yes," I said, "and a separate but more than equal list has one name -- **Mr. Big** -- who at a minimum has coerced and/or suborned some or all of those on the other list to commit a list of illegal and unethical acts that would take an army of lawyers a month of Sundays to list, let alone look into. And don't forget that Mr. Big, who may be a person, or a constellation of persons, hired a contract killer and sent him against us."

"So far, so good," Tommy said, "but there is one question more."

"Yes," Mr. Trimlea said, "what do we do with this mess?"

"Well," I said, "the options are to go public and seek indictments, to do nothing and hope that the craziness will subside, or to confront the minions and make them stop doing the work of Mr. Big."

"Door No. One, Door No. Two, and Door No. Three," Tommy said.

"Our superiors," Mr. Trimlea said, "favor Door No. Three, and they want you and your associates, with the able assistance of these two agents here, to do the work of shutting down the rival web of criminal activity."

"Can I get back to you?" I said. "I will not make this decision on my own. I can see a high-stakes game developing, and I want my associates to have a full say in deciding whether to ante up or just fold 'em."

"You damn well better get back to us, and soon," Mr. Trimlea said. "Do not forget that we know where you live -- and a hell of a lot more."

"One thing only do you lack," I said, "that you cannot vault over, my **Little Friend**. Watch yourself, yourself."

We talk of minions and masters
| 03January09 |

"For a fairly young man, I'm an old fool," I said, "and I'm getting older by the nanosecond, the more I hang around your pals, especially that Trimlea."

"Don't let the bleepers get your down, Goose Guy," Tommy said. "You are in the catbird's seat on this one."

"Feels more like a bar stool up my patoot," I said.

Because it was.

Kinda.

We had stopped on the way back to the bookshop for a beer.

Not the **Roll In and Crawl Out**, mind you.

We had had enough of that dive for a season.

The snow still was falling.

It was a bad afternoon to be a stray dog, and the night was going to be worse, for all God's creatures.

"The question that I keep coming back to," I said, "is why did Mr. Big send the contract killer first and the local talent second."

"You mean," Tommy said, "that Mr. Big should have tried the least force necessary to begin with and should have bumped up the pressure as things went along, until the situation reached critical mass?"

"Well," I said, "that would make sense. Or if one hit man don't cut it, why not send two more as a team?"

"Maybe you are not as important as you think you are," Tommy said.

"That certainly could be," I said, "but I, and by that I mean **we** -- as in the Tribe -- are important enough to drive **Someone** to corrupt half of the local forces and a couple of high officials charged with serving and defending the people of the community."

"Well," Tommy said, "there is that. Maybe **They** are not done yet. Have you considered that option?"

"Am now," I said. "I think I see what you mean. Try this, try that, and try something else, while you make your millions and enjoy your spoils, and every once in a while you get a wild hair up your patoot about those over-the-hill bleepers who really could knock over the piss pot if they decided to. And you try something else, on the fly."

"Or," Tommy said, "this has been an interlude and a **Big Push** is coming. One that is planned and potent. Question is, what would that be, and where would it come from?"

"We're into the Zen thing," I said, "-- **ready and not ready, at the same time**. Bring it on. We will react. That means that we don't have to spend a lot of time and energy trying to anticipate moves that have not been made yet. We focus ourselves on the actual."

"And you stay ready and not ready, which sounds permanently uncomfortable," Tommy said.

"Not really," I said. "It feels like life as we know it and choose to live it. Look, if the Tribe had your resources, and sources, and the portfolio that you pack around, we would not need the Zen thing, but since we have nothing but our Vault and our quick reflexes, we stick with the Zen thing."

"Well, then, Grasshopper," Tommy said, "what is the next non-step?"

"We will run to meet what is already in motion, and already in front of us," I said. "I suspect that the others will agree that we gain a bunch by accepting the assignment to take you and Luke, and toss a spanner in the works. We need to stop the nonsense, in exchange for a **Get Out of Jail Free** card for all those who participated in the manufacturing of the **Mystery Man Murders**. It will be a nasty amnesty, but it will stop the madness, for a time."

"But what about **Mr. Big** AKA **Them** AKA **Someone**?" Tommy said. "You can cut off the snake heads but the Medusa will still be able to produce fresh ones."

"It's a two-part invention," I said. "The first part is stopping the minions. The second part is stopping the minions' masters. One can simply attack the minions when they become a bore or a bother, but if the minions' masters are relentless, and the minions are many, then at some point one must strike at the motherhouse of the masters of all those minions. We may be able to make a deal with the minions in exchange for information about their masters."

"I could get used," Tommy said, "to this pace of work."

F-Troop has a few reservations
|04January09|

"This meeting of the F-Troop will be in uproar," I said.

"Only if you wish it so, Mister Chair Sir," Jim said.

"Yeah," OhJim said, "and only if you click your heels and say, **There's no place like uproar**, over and over and over again."

"We have," I said, "corresponding members. Tommy you know. Luke you do not know. Give them seats. They are a bit behind."

"Oh, I don't know," Eve said. "Their seats have some size."

"That's what I said," I said. "Big lugs, big butts."

Luke smiled at Eve.

Eve gave Luke a very warm Buddha Girl smile.

"The Goosemeister does not want to admit that we know one another as well as we do, Eve," Luke said. "I think he has grown somewhat insecure."

"Mister Chair Sir," Jeanne said, "I for one, though I welcome Eve's evident friend Luke, would like to know something more substantial about him."

'You can call me **Agent**," Luke said. "Just like Tommy."

"I think that I will call you **ThreeBears**," Jeanne said. '"And for your own safety, I hope that you are not just like Tommy."

"Why **three**?" Luke said.

"Because,' Jeanne said, "you are a lot bigger than just one, and **TwoBears** sounds like something you cut up and add to a stew."

"**ThreeBears**, it is," Luke said. "And what shall I call you?"

"Jeanne," Jeanne said. "'And this youngster beside me, you will call David. Jim and OhJim, you know, at least by report, or echo, or by their puns that go before them like the little pissers they are. The other big-big substantial man in the room is Mister Ed, our resident retired journalist and current parliamentarian. Mr. Black, I assume you know by report or reputation, at the least."

"I wanted us all here at once," I said, "because I have had a trying time down by the river, at the **Tin-Hat Building**, the haunted one that spooky Luke works from. I met a strange and wonderful little spook called Mr. Trimlea, who seemed to be talking for persons even more strange and wonderful than he is."

"What the Goose Man is trying to say," Luke said, "is that we sandbagged him in the basement. No harm done, as you can see."

My briefing takes on a long-john feel
| 05January09 |

"What do you mean, Dear?" Eve said. "**Sandbagged** him how?"

"Well," Luke said, "I don't know what the others were intending, but my goal was to bring the Goose Guy to the decision point in one piece, with a generally positive outlook and a bare minimum of negativity, seasoned with a dash of good old high-quality B.S. -- and no visible bruises."

"Something like that," I said. "The sandbags were only half-full. What they did was to show me some surveillance tape footage of unknown provenance that shows a pattern of graft, corruption, and general misuse of moral obligation on the part of our police commissioner, coroner, two detectives whom we know well, and a host of local supporting characters."

"So good, so far," Tommy said. "Bingo."

"After showing me the tapes," I said, "which were of good quality, and complete with audio, I was asked to take back to you-all the desire on the part of Mr. Trimlea's superiors that we and Agents Tommy and Luke take on the task of dropping the **Mystery Man Murders** and all proofs of the various kinds of tampering with evidence and bodies down a dark and deep hole."

"I do not think that we should let you play outside by yourself any more," Jeanne said. "You seem to get into nothing but trouble."

"Yes," David said, "just play around with the pee pots like you used to."

"But," I said, "there is more. While in the basement with the spooks, I lined out for them three alternative approaches to the mess -- call in a special prosecutor, do nothing, or make the locals stop doing what they have been doing, by threatening them with exposure and rewarding them with silence if they make certain guarantees and demonstrate compliance."

"Well," Eve said, "for starters there is the moral question. You seem to be talking about the entire police and coroner offices, clear on up to elected and appointed leaders. I have no particular problem with making them stop their illegal acts, but how would we square that with any sense of moral responsibility such as our neighbors hold to, or aspire to, or acknowledge in the breech."

"And," Jeanne said, "there is the related question of how we would keep the lid on such a volatile story, if we found that we could square the moral questions with our Robin Hoodish ideals."

"Excellent questions," I said, "and ones that we will need to have good working answers for. I myself am concerned that the muzzling of the locals will do nothing about the shadowy characters who put them up to their dirty tricks aimed against us."

"And," David said, "we are drawing a blank so far on how to corner the **Big Fish** who make the minnows jump in our local waters."

"One thing that we have in our favor," I said, "is the access that Tommy and Luke bring to the table. Their being on loan for such a quasi-criminal enterprise as ours is proof that powerful persons in the TLA line favor an abatement of the craziness with scant attention to morality or legality."

"One more thing," Tommy said, "is this. I have Goose half-convinced that we have not seen the last of the craziness. If we do not act soon, and with enough juice to swing things our way, there may be an even more focused attempt on the Tribe and its fount of information."

"Down to the Vault, as usual," Mr. Black said. "I think I favor this action because we can gain a whole lot of new stuff to stuff into the Vault. If we broker deals that convince the locals to start acting like public servants again, we hold over them a huge club labeled **For the Public Good**. I like that. Plus, we get back our exemption, with interest."

"Well," I said, "don't stop now. What other questions do you have?"

"Well," David said, "there is the question of why the first attempt was to hire a hit man who ends up dead. Why then would you try to link two more bodies to that death and make it look like a serial killer is loose? Granted, it threw enough suspicion on Mr. Black to keep him, and us, at bay for a long time -- about six or eight months -- but why him and what was it that our enemies hoped to gain?"

"They certainly tied a bunch of tin cans to Mr. Black's patoot," Jeanne said, "and he had to lay low to keep from drawing any attention to himself. That had the effect of neutralizing our best operative (no offense to the rest of us)."

"Ok," Mr. Black said, "you are right, as far as you took it, but press the question. Why drive me into the shadows? It only made me more vigilant. I was a lot more effective in watching your backs, when you presumed that I was dead, than I would have been wandering around at **Caspar's**."

"If I may," Mister Ed said. "Either the point was to drive Mr. Black off, or the point was to pull off something that has not surfaced yet, or something not yet initiated, or something gained that we have not identified yet."

"All this speculation is good work, Dears," Eve said, "but the fact is, we can act to stop the immediate threat without knowing the answers to any of the questions that we have asked. I'm tempted to say that it isn't much to stop the locals only, but God Almighty, we're talking about a pattern of civic corruption that one does not encounter very often at the local community level. My gut says that we cannot go public on this."

"That was an indelicate noise," Jim said.

"Yeah," OhJim said, "and ambiguous until we got the pastiche."

"Yes," I said, ignoring the **Punnut Gallery**, "and we have to continue to embrace our essential nature -- we are a quasi-criminal enterprise -- for a number of reasons. First, we cannot **not** be covert, after all that we have done and not done, and not just concerning the **Mystery Man** stuff, but also the quasi-criminal and downright criminal enterprise that we were, are, and shall be. Second, the powers that animate the agents on loan want a covert resolution to this mess. We cannot win if we go against them. The victory would be ours, but the war to follow would light a mighty fire that would burn every one of us to a crisp."

"Ready to vote, Dear," Eve said.

There were nods all around.

"All those in favor," I said, "signify by the usual sign."

Everyone did.

"It's anonymous," Jim said.

"Yeah," OhJim said, "or unanimous."

"Next order of business," I said, "is how to begin, and all that."

"And I know just who to invite," Tommy said. "Let me make some calls."

The next question is *how*
|06January09|

"Now that we have put our necks in the noose," I said, "let us decide on the necessary arrangements."

"I have friends Jane Carlotto and Meme Shiva on the way," Tommy said. "Jane and Meme will provide a unique perspective, to say the least."

"A cop and a reporter," Jeanne said. "I guess that would be unique in the context of **keeping the bleeping lid on things**. At least this way, if the lid goes flying, we will have someone to chronicle the event and someone to read us our rights. Gee, Tommy! I should bite your ear more often."

"No need," Tommy said. "No need at all. I can understand why you would think that way. I'm thinking more in terms of who will be the next police commissioner and who can make that happen, with our assistance."

"Meme, I understand," Eve said. "She would make an excellent police commissioner, full of compassion and toughness, but what is Jane's role?"

"The power of the press," Tommy said. "The fuel that drives the engine of state ... local, national, and beyond."

"Just like old times, Goose Man, when a good reporter was an even better spook," Mr. Black said.

"Yeah," I said, "the more things change the more they stay the same."

Mr. Red stuck his head in the door, trying his best to parry Meme's nips and tucks and whispered comments.

"Two dames," he said. "Billy likes them. I have nothing to bleeping add."

Wild Billy, meowing, tail in the air, led Meme and Jane into the room.

"Welcome," I said, "and well-met."

Meme was dressed for work, which meant the blue uniform and leather jacket, with mounty cap, fur-lined, for her walking-the-beat job in the dead of winter. Jane's attire accented her thin but nasty frame. Jane could do nothing to hide her waif-like size or sluttish edges.

Meme smiled her sly smile of promise, and Jane did a thing with her mouth but not her eyes -- the next Zip Code over from a smile.

"I have briefed Meme and Jane," Tommy said. "They were outside waiting for my call. Ready to serve."

"Well," I said, "this is spooky. Police, press, TLAs, and Tribe -- a coalition of **disparate desperadoes** indeed."

"If you please," Tommy said, "Jane and Meme will liaise with me on their parts in our plan, for a speck of deniability for their more public roles, and to cover their ties with agencies that abhor any sort of trail or tie."

"Granted," I said. "Anyone opposed?"

"Only that Tommy gets to liaise with not only one beautiful woman but two," Jim said.

"Yeah," OhJim said, "talk about having your Kate and Edith, too."

Meme roared with laughter and made a feint in the direction of OhJim, who jumped behind his brother.

One had to make allowances for Meme's zeal. Red was our teacher here.

"You don't know your **liaising** from your **laying**, or is it **lying**," I said, "so zip it and don't fish it out again and play with it anymore."

"You can lie to whom you wish, and I will lie with whomever I choose," Tommy said. "It is as much a matter of style as of usage."

"Let it lay and lie, Father Goose," Jim said.

"Yeah," OhJim said. "Leave the laying to the Mothers."

"Two things," Jeanne said. "First, I am assuming that Tommy has vetted our friend Meme and is ready to affirm that she is right for the high-profile job that we are making available for her. Second, I am assuming that Jane, for whatever reasons she has, and she can keep them private, is not going to turn this caper into a bid for a Pulitzer while it is unfolding. Again, I look to Tommy for affirmation on this."

"Affirmed, and affirmed," Tommy said. "Meme checks out, and believe me, we used a big checklist, and Jane will not publish anything about this caper. Ever. Period."

"Jane and Meme are sisters," Luke said. "Nuff said, in my opinion."

Jane gave Jeanne her narrow, weak-ass smile.

"Some things are more important that Pulitzers," Jane said. "And some reporters are more than they seem."

"And that," Tommy said, "will have to be enough of that."

"I'm satisfied," Jeanne said.

My brothers just beamed.

They love it when ladies point out their runs and seams.

Next ... who, when, and where
|07January09|

The time was coming for pointed interpersonal action, but we had a few details to settle, such as who to lean on, who to do the leaning, and where this would go down. Some of us favored getting the suspects together at once and making things go our way in one push. Others thought that this would not fly.

Tommy, Luke, Mr. Black, and I were authorized to come back to the group with a plan. We shooed everyone away and went to work.

"This is the way I see it," I said. "We need to break the thing into two groups, and lean on the police commissioner and on the coroner, one after the other."

"Probably," Tommy said, "though we will have some leaks between the first and second efforts."

"An alternative," Luke said, "is to send a message to Mr. Big and let **him/her/they** sort out the details."

"I like that," I said. "It's like directing your prayers to the person at the top in the knowledge that those down the line will get their marching orders --or so one hopes, and prays."

"So," Mr. Black said, "what channel do we use? Or put another way, who is like God the Father in this scenario?"

"Get the Commissioner and the Coroner here together and make sure that they go on up the line," Tommy said.

"If we show them the tapes and tell them what we expect, they will take it from there," Luke said.

"Let's make it happen," I said.

Outside, the snow continued to come down and pile up.

We continued to dream of blue-sky warm days with no worries.

We win the war of words and images
|08January09|

The backroom was full to overflowing with the Good, Bad, and Ugly.

We were sitting in a circle.

That was the only way that we could fit in all we had either invited or coerced (Tommy's job, done well) into attending. In special seats -- special simply by virtue of who was sitting in them -- were Police Commissioner

Tom Tonolody and Dr. Bruce Backstaff, the county Coroner.

In cheap seats -- cheap because of who was sitting in them -- were Dets. Blucote and Schmidt.

Mr. Red and Wild Billy were at the front desk, with the door locked, the shades drawn, and the BACK IN 10 MINUTES sign in place.

"Lights," Tommy said.

"Gentlemen," Luke said, in the darkness, "we are your worst nightmare, so try to stay awake. Roll the video."

We watched the entire compilation of surveillance tapes that Tommy and Luke had put together from persons and places and clever listening appliances that no one wanted to know anything about. We watched the same tapes that I saw in the Tin-Hat Building with Mr. Trimlea and friends.

Remember the sequence?

First scene -- Dets. Blucote and Schmidt and the lab-coated man planting evidence while talking about diverting bodies and implicating the coroner and commissioner.

Second scene -- Blucote, Schmidt, and the lab coat person once more.

Third scene -- Blucote and Schmidt in the evidence locker at the police station downtown.

"Lights," Tommy said, when the tape stopped and the snow began to fall on the screen, just like outside. When the lights came up, no one was making eye contact. The chill inside was worse than outside.

"Gentlemen," I said, "we invited you here to give you two choices -- to ruin your lives and take away your careers as you know them or to retain your positions and learn how to actually serve and defend, with those in this room as your monitors and teachers."

Tonolody and Backstaff didn't say anything.

They tried to look tough but did not convince themselves or anyone else.

Blucote and Schmidt just looked sick.

The Tribe was seeing the tape for the first time, too, but they were empowered by what they saw.

"We want you, first, to take a message to the person or persons who have put you up to this," I said. "That message is this -- call off your minions and we stop looking for you. Continue, and we will ruin them, and find you. Stress that our resources are vast and effective. Tell them about the tape you saw and tell them that such thorough work points to a dangerous and numerous enemy."

"Second," Tommy said, "we are willing for the four of you to continue in your jobs, but with one difference."

"That difference," Luke said, "is this. You will find a way to defuse the **Mystery Man** investigation and tell some version of the truth about what happened. You will not continue to plant evidence, alter evidence, hijack bodies, or anything else outside the law."

"Furthermore," I said, "you will instruct the detectives and coroner's people on the case to work closely with me, the two agents before you, and our associates, those present in this room. We will clean up your mess and you will take the story that we craft for you to the media, specifically the **Daily Afterblatt, Lake Effect edition** and more specifically, their Senior Crime Reporter, Jane Carlotto."

"You really should be taking notes," Tommy said, "because there will be no transcript of this meeting but there will be problems for you if you forget any of what we tell you to do."

That was a white lie.

We were taping everything for the Vault and would do so every time we talked with these people.

We were not leaving any gold nuggets on the ground.

Needless to say, we had scanned our four visitors, without their knowing, for any evidence of wires.

"You, commissioner, will promote one Officer Meme Shiva to the new post of deputy commissioner, and you will sell the promotion to the mayor and the press and the public," Luke said. "And in private you will be subject to the Deputy Commissioner's wishes and commands. When you, or we, tire of your tenure in the top position, you will endorse your deputy as your replacement. You will announce the officer's promotion by close of business tomorrow."

"Any questions so far?" I said.

"Yeah," Commissioner Tonolody said. "What if I call my peeps and have this place leveled by a SWAT team?"

Tonolody got up, chest out, and ran his hands around inside the top of his slacks.

Tommy walked over to the commissioner and got right in his face.

For the commissioner's sake, even though I wished him under a bus, I did hope that Tommy hadn't had any garlic for lunch.

Fat chance, that.

"There is one answer to any smart-ass question any of you can ask. The tape that we showed you goes to all media with supporting documents and talking heads galore," Tommy said. "I can guarantee you significant jail time, loss of pension rights, and eternal damnation."

"You can choose to continue in your jobs, with certain corrections," I said, "or you can suffer a public lynching in the media. Your choice."

"Now," Tommy said, "the commissioner and coroner will go. We will be in touch. The detectives will stay."

The bigger fish swam out of the backroom and on out of the bookshop without saying anything further.

Nobody said good-bye.

A tinkle of the little bells on the front door, a meow or two from Wild Billy, and they were gone.

I knew we had them where we wanted them.

And I wondered if we would have to use any additional force to get them rolling in the right direction.

We probably have done worse

"Look," I said, "make yourselves comfortable. We have a lot to cover."

Blucote and Schmidt looked glum but not, for once, defiant.

"And stop moping, for crying out loud," Mr. Black said. "We probably have done worse. No doubt about it."

"Yeah," Blucote said, "we have, too."

"That's right," Schmidt said, "and probably worser."

"So," I said, "let us focus on cleaning up what cannot be taken back. Let's talk about what went down in the **Mystery Man** fiasco. Blucote?"

"We had no choice," Blucote said. "The commissioner called us in and told us what to do, day by day. He said it was his way or the highway, and no cop jobs or pensions if we walked. Plenty of cash if we did his bidding."

"That's right," Schmidt said. "No jobs, no pensions. Lots of cash."

"Did the commissioner ever tell you why he was lining things out the way he did?" Jeanne said.

"No, ma'am," Blucote said. "We asked, just once, and he said that we didn't want to know."

"That's right, ma'am," Schmidt said. "We didn't want to know."

"You can call me Jeanne," Jeanne said, "and her name is Eve."

Eve smiled a medium-strength Buddha Girl smile at the hapless pair.

"We will be working together from here on out, for as long as you stay on the force," Eve said. "We might as well resolve to respect one another. For us to be successful, you need to be successful, and the other way around."

"This will take some getting used to," Blucote said. "I thought that the stuff had hit the blades when you rolled that video tape. Like lights out."

"That's right," Schmidt said. "Hit the old fan. Lights out for us for sure."

"What," I said, "can you add to our general sense of what went down in the **Mystery Man** investigation? How soon after the bus vs. man accident outside President's Park did you start getting dirty orders from Tonolody?"

"Right away," Blucote said. "That visit we made here, early on? Tonolody told us to shake your tree, to see if anything fell down."

"That narrows things," Mr. Black said. "It infers that **Someone Big** got to Tonolody as soon as or even before their hit man turned up dead."

"Hit man?" Blucote said. "Why youse guys?"

"Yeah," Mr. Black said, "**us,** and we're going to give you some more, as a show of good faith. We are a target because of certain ugly information that we possess and that certain others know we possess. That's for one. Also, for seconds, I was the target of the hit man, and the hit man is the one that ended up plastered all over the front of the bus. I had a hand, and a foot, in his running into the street. He was trying to get away from me and back to his car. He tried to lead me into a trap in the dark, but I knew the park better than he did, and I drop-kicked him into a panic. He started running for his car. He turned to see where I was and couldn't stop in time when he looked back around. Self-defense. He intended to take me out."

"Mr. Black was alone and had just locked up the bookshop when he saw the guy pull up and get out of his car, and open the trunk, and hide a chopped shotgun under his coat," I said. "Mr. Black didn't look back, but ran out the back door and around the side, and then he tailed the vic down to the park."

"That explains some things," Blucote said.

"That's right," Schmidt said. "Sure does."

"Does what?" I said.

"Tonolody ordered us to make it look like we were actively investigating," Blucote said. "He ordered us to stay clear of any facts that we might find."

"That's right," Schmidt said. "We shunned facts. We did not touch them."

"That led to the coroner calling an inquest," I said.

"Yeah," Blucote said. "He wasn't dirty until later."

"When?" I said.

"When we had to doctor evidence," Blucote said. "Tonolody said he would have a chat with Backstaff and persuade him to play along. By then Tonolody had a wad of dirty bills in small and medium denominations, and he was pairing cash with threats to get his way. People started standing in line to get some of that wad and do his jobs. The coroner went to the head of the line."

"Maybe it's for nothing, but did you think of going public?" Jeanne said.

"Not really, Miss Jeanne," Blucote said. "Like we said, and you said, we have probably done worse. Where we drew the line in the past was not that far from bribes and tampering. We saw no upside to turning the bag upside down and shaking out all the sins of the past."

"Just curious," Jeanne said. "And **Miss Jeanne** has a nice ring. Miss Eve might like some of that, too."

"Like we all said," I said, "we work on different sides of the street, and we all are sworn to serve and defend, and we too have done ugly things to our own neighbors, let alone the community in general. Our goal, now, is to stop this particular madness and encourage everyone to do what they would want to do in their best selves."

"Tonolody, too?" Jeanne said.

"Yeah," I said, "but notice that he gets a shadow and Backstaff doesn't."

"Another thought," Mr. Black said. "I'm wondering if Tonolody will test our resolve, and if he does, how he will do it."

"I don't see him as a strong and brave guy," Blucote said. "He's malleable and prone to indecision. I don't know if he could come up with a plan."

"But what about the **Somebody Big** who is telling him what to do," Jeanne said. "What about him?"

"We can assume," I said, "that that is one mean bleeper."

"So," Jeanne said, "what is the plan, if **He/She/They** push back?"

Tommy seemed to come out of a reverie.

"I think," Tommy said, "that we won't have to deal with any new moves from the **Big Fish**. My sense of the data flowing in is that there has been no rise in **sig-int** in the quarters we are watching, and have been watching."

"Yeah," Luke said, "that's our sense, too. This chapter is just about over, except for the cover-up."

"And Tonolody may just be in more danger from the **Big Fish** than he is from us," Tommy said.

Luke just nodded.

Black/white and read all over
|10January09|

From a **Special Edition** of the **Daily Afterblatt, Lake Effect edition.**

Rapid turnover
Police commissioner names deputy commish, quits next day

By Jane Carlotto
Senior Crime Reporter

City Hall is abuzz today, after the erstwhile commissioner of Buffalonya police, Tom Tonolody, yesterday named a deputy commissioner from the patrol ranks -- foot patrol, no less --and followed this surprise with another.

This morning, bright and early, a clearly shaken Tonolody called a press conference and announced that he was resigning "for personal reasons."

The new deputy commissioner of police, Meme Shiva, was then named acting commissioner by action of Buffalonya Mayor Wing Dingus.

Meanwhile, the new chief was mum on reports that there had been a fracas on the top floor at the downtown district headquarters last evening.

Reports are conflicting, but a picture of chaos and drawn weapons is emerging, but slowly and only partially. No one in the know is talking.

What happened is not known just yet.

Dingus told this reporter today that "Office Shiva is an excellent choice for deputy and will, after the events of this morning, make an equally excellent commissioner. I have full confidence in her work and stand behind her all the way. I am particularly proud that Buffalonya becomes one of the few major cities in the country to have a woman as police commissioner."

There is some speculation as to whether Commissioner Shiva is the first woman in such a post, but she is at a minimum one of the first ethnic women in such a post, insiders are saying. Their tips are generally reliable.

Early reports from the Police Benevolent Association and the local police union are positive concerning the new chief.

One source who asked to be anonymous said that "a trained monkey would have given the previous chief a run for his money and would have won."

It is no secret, City Hall insiders say, that widespread low morale and rumblings about incompetence, paired with a de facto attitude that tied good cops' hands, has made the force an object of pity and scorn among peers across the country.

Sources inside the police department say that some sort of confrontation went down last night on the top floor of the police headquarters, site of the chief's office and the offices of other top cops.

"We had a situation here," one source said, "but that's just about all we will say at this point. Stay tuned."

At his press conference yesterday, Tonolody introduced Shiva, who has been the first walk-the-beat cop in a pilot program based on federal funding.

Shiva is well-known as a smart cop and as a favorite of the former chief.

"We are moving in the direction of strengthening the chain of command," Tonolody had said, "and I am both pleased and proud to announce the appointment of Officer Shiva as my deputy."

Tonolody had brushed aside questions about whether it would sit well with the old-boy network to see a female beat cop go to the head of the class from the last row of seats in the house.

At his follow-up press conference this morning, a clearly shaken Tonolody, with a calm and smiling Shiva at his side, said he had made his decision to resign overnight but he was certain it was the right decision.

""I'm out of here," Tonolody said, "and I leave the city in better hands."

Shiva praised her mentor and thanked him for his service to the city.

The mayor's office released a statement that said, "The mayor with regret, and with gladness for the term of meritorious service, sadly accepts the resignation of Chief Tonolody and concurs in his recommendation that Deputy Commissioner Shiva take over the chief's position, on a provisional basis."

When asked what that last bit meant, the mayor's spokesman, Greiner Greene, said that the mayor was making Shiva provisional chief and that if her performance in the coming weeks warranted, she would be made the permanent choice.

Chief Shiva inherits a force reeling from many months' worth of criticism over the so-called "Mystery Man Murders," three killings that have gone unsolved, with two of the three victims not even identified.

There is strife internally, and intra-department, with the coroner, Dr. Bruce Backstaff, a particularly vocal critic of the police department.

This is what really happened, sort of ...
| 11January09 |

Now that you have seen what Jane Carlotto wrote, with our coaching, here is my version of what happened, referencing the usual caveats about fact, truth, and the needs of the service. Trust me.

Tommy ended our initial debriefing of Dets. Blucote and Schmidt with the comment that Commissioner Tonolody was in more danger from the **Big Fish** who had forced him to force others to do dirty work in the **Mystery Man** matter than he was from us.

When Tommy said that, I look at Luke. And Luke looked at Tommy.

"Oh bleep!" Tommy said. "We better get over there, make sure he's Ok!"

The three of us went with the detectives in their ... **unmarked** ... Crown Vic, and the rest followed in Jeanne's Buick, the beater with many marks.

"Look, Blucote said, driving with his flashing blue beanie on the roof, swerving in and out of lanes of traffic, "we will get there about the time Tonolody has his press conference to promote the beat broad."

"That's right," Tommy said, "and that is a high-risk moment with everything after that an ever higher risk."

"Yeah," I said, "as soon as the **Bigs** hear about his naming a deputy, they will either want to talk with him or just tell someone to grease him."

"You think so?" Blucote said, narrowly missing a slowly moving old lady about the enter a crosswalk.

"Yeah," Luke said. "These guys don't mess. They just make them."

We pulled up at the downtown district building and walked in. Quickly.

"Turn right and right again," Blucote said. "We don't want to pile up at the security checkpoint. That's for losers and civilians."

"TLAs and two of your sweethearts," Blucote said to the duty officer at the door for cops.

We waltzed in.

Who knew what weapons we carried in?

I knew, but later on that.

"Any messages, Sarge?" Blucote said, moving us toward the elevator.

"The time when I have messages for you is the last time we talk," the desk sergeant said, "because I'll quit before I carry your lunch pail."

Waving a strategic finger in the air but not bothering to turn around, Blucote shooed us into the elevator and hit the button for the top floor.

"Let's check there first," Blucote said. "I don't think there has been an announcement yet. The desk sarge would have been all over that."

I called Eve on my cell and told her to get Jeanne to find out if a press conference had been called and for them to go there. We rode to the top floor, and the silence after the clanking and jerking was ominous. We sorted ourselves into pairs to cover the stairs and the elevator, with Tommy going to the commissioner's office solo.

I could see Tommy go in from my post with Luke at the elevator. The detectives were further off, flanking the door to the stairs. The bell on the elevator dinged and a pair of tough guys in suits got off and headed for the chief's office door, quickly, without giving us as much as a glance. Luke gave me a nod. We fell in behind the two and went halfway down the hallway.

When the two got to the office, there was a lot of noise and confusion.

We ran in, to find Tommy holding one glassy-eyed guy in a choke-hold.

The other guy was on the floor, silently screaming and holding his knee, which was sticking out at an alarming angle.

Luke, pocketing what looked like a techie plastic pistol, cuffed the guy Tommy had a hold on.

I told the secretary hiding under her desk to call for backup.

Tommy and Luke had put their TLA badges around their necks, so she was reasonably compliant. Trembling, too.

Luke tapped on the chief's door.

"What!" Tonolody said.

"Open up," Luke said. "You should see this."

Tonolody, followed by Deputy Commissioner Shiva, burst out of the door.

"What the --," Tonolody said.

"Yeah," I said. "We got to thinking about you and ran over, just in time."

"You didn't think at all," the heavy in cuffs said -- the one who could still talk. "There will be hell to pay for this. I can assure you of that."

Tommy finished frisking him and pocketed a knife and another plastic gun.

"I suppose that you're just here to check the fire extinguishers," Tommy said. "Dangerous work, I see."

That put a foot in the heavy's pie hole.

"These two are known to us," Tommy said. "We've been keeping an eye on them, at a distance, since they came into town yesterday along about sundown. They must have shaken their leash. **Evidentially**, it seems."

"I was about go down for the press conference," Tonolody said. "Do you think it's safe? It does not seem so."

"By all means go down," Tommy said. "We will hold these guys, and the others will have your back down there. There are no other bad guys about."

I called Eve on my cell and gave her an update.

Eve said our folk were inside and had seats around the room where the press conference was to be held in 15 minutes.

Tonolody looked like he had seen the inside of his casket.

No one likes the view from that height.

Shiva just grinned, like a tiger looking at her lunch.

I liked that about her.

"I'll go with youse," Luke said, "just so's you don't have to be alone."

Tommy and I remained in place.

"When the coppers come," Tommy said softly, "I'll do the talking."

What went down at the press confab
| 12January09 |

I was more than willing to let Tommy and his TLA badge, dangling from his neck like a **Hello! My name is Tommy** name tag at a dentist convention, do all the talking. Tommy has that toothy grin that inspires confidence.

Tommy told me in a low tone that he had made a quick pass to see if the two had wallets, but they had no identifying stuff along for the ride.

No surprise there.

Leaving the hobbled pair in good hands, we rushed downstairs. We wanted a covert show of force wherever the commissioner went, and we probably would have to discuss security for Deputy Commissioner Shiva, too. It was proving to be a silly sort of season, where the good guys, including Shiva, would need disinterested security as well as the usual internal controls.

One question banging on my awareness, like a drunken boyfriend who wants to come in, was this question of who and how to protect the two commissioners, chief and deputy. And at some level, I had a concern for the coroner, too. Whoever had put them up to all the dirty tricks and threats and bribes was not likely to go quietly away. I was, however, heartened that Tommy had recognized the two on the floor and that his associates had been watching them.

Could he be close to identifying the ones who sent them?

I hoped so.

The Tribe and friends would barely stretch to meet the security needs of three high-profile officials who could not trust anyone but who could trust us a bit more than the rest.

The two guys on the commissioner's floor had not talked much, and I was surprised that they were alive. This sort of heavy either delivered or took himself out. Tommy's recognizing them saved his life, the lives of the two behind the door, and the secretary, and the heavies themselves, though they had not yet thanked Tommy for his quick-witted response.

Tommy explained to me that their coming in without breaking stride spurred him to attack and that recognition followed closely on instinct. He took out the lead guy with a well-placed kick to the kneecap and slashed the other guy and grabbed him by the neck after he went down clutching his windpipe. It was a kung foo daily double.

We didn't expect to get anything from the two but it would not hurt for the cops to sweat them until someone put a hit on them in some cell. That was certain. The only question was the timing.

Their code said that they were already dead.

They might even do the work themselves. If they didn't, there was a shred of possibility that they would talk, at least a little, but no one of us needed to be holding out for that eventuality.

When an array of uniform and plain clothes cops flooded the office, Tommy's TLA badge was fifty times better than a **Get Out of Jail Free** card. With a minimum of fuss, we were on our way to the press conference.

In the elevator, Tommy did the talking, because Tommy was still dealing with a rush of hormones. When we walked into the big room that held the media and their cameras and microphones, we took positions at the corners in the back of the room -- cheap seats for media stars and wannabes but perfect for persons providing security.

Eve was center back, and Jeanne was mingling with her old friends right down front.

The detectives were flanking the central rows.

Jim and OhJim had elbowed their way to the center of the front row and stood like bald bookends, back to back, with a fine view of the stage and the crowd.

David was roaming.

Eve told us Jeanne understood that one of her tasks was to point out to Eve, via texting, anyone she did not recognize who was acting like media.

When Tonolody and Shiva walked in, to light applause from the few cops in attendance (and no one but Blucote and Schmidt providing security from what we could make out), the department flack introduced Tonolody.

We were as comfortable as one could be when the job was to thwart threats that had no preamble.

Despite the smackdown outside his office a few moments before, Tonolody looked reasonably calm in making the announcement concerning his new deputy.

It was only later in the evening, after a second huddle with us, that he formed his intention to resign the following morning.

Tonolody gets a deal he can't refuse
| 13January09 |

I had Jeanne slip Shiva a note that asked her to get the commissioner back to his office so that we could discuss his security.

We all assembled in his office, a few at a time.

The two detectives, the two agents, the three brothers, the two women of the Tribe, Deputy Commissioner Shiva, and David straggled in.

"Look," Tonolody said, "I don't enjoy these little talks at all."

"You're welcome," Tommy said, smiling like a shark in a floating meat market. "Those two were a heartbeat away from killing you and Shiva."

"What do you mean?" Tonolody said. "I thought that you knew them."

"Yes," Tommy said, "I knew them to be a free-lance hit team that we were keeping an eye on. We did not know their target or orders."

"Hit team?" Tonolody said. Suddenly he didn't look so good.

"The commissioner seems to be waking from a dream and diving into a nightmare," I said, "and that strikes me as a predictable response to the stimuli that have been present."

"Question is," Tommy said, "how many more teams will **They** send the commissioner's way, and what do we need to do to stop, interrupt, or redirect all that murderous energy?"

"If I step down," Tonolody said, "do you think that they will pursue me?"

"Chief," Shiva said, "they would have no reason to change their behavior. I think they are determined to kill you for stopping the games that they had you play on your new friends."

"My new friends?" Tonolody said.

"Chief," Shiva said, "these people here are the only ones in this building who, One, are aware of the threat you face and, Two, can keep you alive."

"Tell me what to do," Tonolody said. "I can't think straight anymore. I am suddenly just very tired."

"Well," Tommy said, "we can make you disappear and help you start a new life in another location, another country, even. We won't go through the courts, judges, and prosecutors, certainly, but my associates can make this happen through other channels."

"Does money and a house and car go with this?" Tonolody said.

"Let's go talk with some people I know," Tommy said, "who can answer all your questions big and small. Shall we?"

"Chief," Shiva said, "this is the only option, given what you have partici-pated in, and the power of the people that you have disappointed today. I say go with Agent Tommy and as soon as can be."

"Ok," Tonolody said. "I sure cannot go home or even stay here."

"Goose," Tommy said, "I want you and Luke to go with me, and I think the rest of you should go back to the bookshop. Goose will brief you later."

Tommy set himself on the point, walking ahead of Tonolody, whom Luke and I flanked -- he on the left and I on the right, and both of us a step behind the commissioner but almost touching him. We didn't care how odd it looked, though few persons saw us. We took the private exit and made our way quickly to a vehicle that Tommy had the keys to. Not one of your unmarked/marked Crown Vics with bad dark blue paint and those tiny hub caps and the discreet **Police Interceptor** nameplate on the trunk, in case you missed the other cues. Tommy led us to a mastodon of an SUV -- black on black, with tinted, bullet-proof windows, leather seats, and armor sheeting in the doors.

"Hang on, Gentlemen," Tommy said, and he shot into the traffic and headed for the Sky Bridge and points south along the lake. He spoke quietly into a Dick Tracy on his lapel, and five minutes later we pulled into a parking lot next to a new high-rise office complex.

"Come meet a friend of mine, Commissioner," Tommy said.

We walked into the foyer, and Tommy led us over to a door that he opened with his eyeballs -- retina scan -- and his splayed hands on a screen.

"One at a time, the Commissioner first," Tommy said, indicated the door that opened in response to his eyes and hands.

I went in last, and it was a lot like the Tin-Hat Building that Luke lurks in, with the articulated array that looked at my eyes and into my ears, for all I know, and finally decided that I was good to go into the inner sanctum.

Waiting for us was my old and dear friend Mr. T.

"This way, Commissioner, gentlemen," Trimlea said, and walked into a room with a conference table cut in a gigantic oval. The thing was way too small to play hockey on, but not by much.

"We have received Tommy's flash report on the events in your office," Trimlea said, "and the men in question are under heavy guard at the hospital. One we hope will talk, and the other will never talk again, but he may find it wise to write down his story. We shall see what happens there."

Tonolody just nodded.

He look bewildered and scared, like a freshly weaned kitten that discovers mama has claws.

"We are prepared," Trimlea said, "to help you relocate to a safe location, and we will help you in the transition -- and any family members that you wish to protect."

"There's no one else," Tonolody said, "except the dog. My ex-wife is remarried and the kids are grown and gone."

"So much the better," Trimlea said. "I'll take you on to my associates, and if you agree, we will send these three fine gentlemen back to the city to arrange the transfer of authority to your deputy. You will give a brief press conference first thing in the morning, to resign, then you will be on your way to a new life. From this point on, we guarantee your safety."

Tonolody nodded.

He would be in a better place, by morning, but the numb feeling of unreality would lift slowly, which would be a blessing for him and probably was more than he had earned or had coming.

One more press conference and he was free to enter his exile.

The second time around

I got back to the bookshop while everyone was still waiting to hear about the disappearance of our new friend -- Commissioner Tonolody as was.

"Did he bite?" Jeanne said.

"Yeah," Jim said, "but he had his shots."

"Yeah, yeah," OhJim said. "I bet he took shots at just about everyone."

"He took the relocation deal," I said. "By tomorrow night only God will know him as **Tom Tonolody**. Everyone else will forget his name and face."

"That's good," Eve said. "At least we don't have to watch him bleed out in public in a day or so, when **They** finally get a team in **that can hunt**."

"**Eve has said the magic word**," I said. "**-- watch,** which is what we will be joining Tommy and Luke at, in the morning. We have that one more watch, and let us make a plan so that he does not die on our watch. Now there just might be a bait-and-switch thing where a body identified as that of the ex-commissioner is burned in a fiery auto crash or the like, but that won't reflect on us, nor will it touch a hair on his head. It will incinerate his present identity, though."

"First things first, and the first thing," Jeanne said, "is to make sure that the police flak calls the press conference at the last minute, and only to those in the press room. He also can change the location at the last minute. We have surprise on our side. They don't know Tonolody is going to resign and they don't know they don't call the shots inside that building anymore."

"And we station ourselves as before, throughout the room, with Jeanne saying **one-two-three** on anyone she does not like the look of," I said. "I'll ask Tommy and Luke to get to the departmental press flak. We will be there as soon as the public door opens at 7 a.m."

"One other thing," Jeanne said, "and that is the safety of Shiva."

"Something tells me that we won't have to worry about Shiva the way we would about Tonolody. She isn't dirty. He was," David said.

"That begs the larger question," Eve said, "of when or if the forces of darkness will take a rest from their labors."

"Our vigilance, or level of watchfulness will not change," I said. "That is the price that we will be paying, as usual."

Ex-commissioner off, and away

Our digression to Jane's, and then my, view of recent events ends with the second press conference.

Jane gave the outline and left out the facts, as we desired.

We got to the downtown district building right after the public scanner door opened for business. When the dust finally settled, the room we chose was judged to be too small, so the department press flak switched back to the usual room. By that time, the camera people and talking heads from the television stations had caught up with the few print monkeys who had been dosing themselves with coffee and donuts in the press room.

Whatever.

The goal was to get the commissioner in front of the cameras long enough for the flak to introduce him with the warning that the Chief would have a short announcement and that he would not be answering questions.

That is how it happened.

Soon-to-be ex-Commissioner Tonolody, showing the strain of the events of the past 36 hours, read his statement -- resigning for personal reasons, etc., and making Shiva his replacement, subject to the mayor's concurrence -- and departed with Tommy and Luke. That left Shiva to bat away a few questions from the startled press corps. Shiva basically said that she was as surprised as anyone else, and that the press community could appreciate that she had a lot of work to do, as did they, if they wanted to get the news on the morning commute shows. All told, we were under the bright lights for about 10 minutes. We went back to the bookshop, looking forward to some serious **wordflay** and coffee drinking. Maybe we would make like cops, have some donuts.

As it turned out, that was exactly what we did.

Puns, pastries, and coffee
| 16January09 |

It seemed like a long time since I had been able to hang out and be fruit-ful with my buddies, in the backroom at the bookshop, with no other agenda than to laugh or to groan.

"Well," I said, "that was a flurry of activity, and no mistake."

"Yes, Dear," Eve said, "and we have been remiss in our laughing at adver-sity. We have simply put our heads down and worked. No chortling."

"Well," Jim said, "I've been laughing on the inside."

"Yeah," OhJim said. "I just had a chuckle as I was walking in."

"Why?" David said.

"**Why-questions**," OhJim said, "are generally unhelpful, young man."

"Who?" David said.

"Much better," OhJim said, "and I have no answer."

"And I," Jeanne said, "have no response."

"Fibber," Jim said.

"Yeah," OhJim said, "**Miss Mendacity**. You can't **not** respond to me."

"However," Jim said, "**mendacity** strikes me as gender-specific. What about the girls among us?"

"Ok," OhJim said, "how about **missdacity**?"

"So, it follows," Jim said, "that we would say **Missdacity**, as the noun of direct address for a fibbing Jeanne. Please sub for **Miss Mendacity**."

By this time, we all were smiling.

"Tomorrow," I said, "we will add some juicy stuff to the Vault."

"Sufficient unto the day, Dear," Eve said. "For now I'm ready for bed."

What is left / the plan what am
| 17January09 |

Email from Goose to Tommy --

Dear friend:

I find that the rising action seems to be finished, and the falling off has just begun. Barring any surprises, and who would be so silly as to bar surprises, we seem to be coming to the end of this story about my Tribe and the **Mystery Man Murders**. In the time between now and the next development -- which, as I say, is all but inevitable -- I plan to work on this narrative.

Yours in pleasant limbo
Goose

Email from Tommy to Brother Goose --

My elderly friend:

Just kidding. Your plan sounds fine, as far as it goes. Keep writing, and if anything emerges, blows up, or implodes, and you do not hear any reports, backfires, or small arms patter, I will let you know what is going on. Right now, all is quiet. I can say that the former commissioner is well on his way to a new life. And that is a bit more than I will ever be able to say about that. Shiva does well, and friends watch her back. Ditto Jane.

Yours at rest
Tommy

I have a talk with Mr. Black
| 18January09 |

"Thank you, my friend," I said, "for meeting on short notice."
We were sitting with beers at the **Roll in and Crawl Out**.
"No prob, Goose Man," Mr. Black said. "Anything for Eve's Goosy Guy."
"I hear you," I said, "and I know that you jest, but just a little bit, and the rest is all too true."
"You speak in riddles, Friend Fowl," Mr. Black said. "That is neither here nor there, but it will be getting dark sooner or later, and you won't be able to see the trail of breadcrumbs that you are sifting out as you go."
"Ok, Ok," I said. "Rather than force you to extend another flowery metaphor, I guess I'll just dust the flour off my hands and get to the point. Knead to know."
"Noted, with interest," Mr. Black said.
"Look," I said, "you and I go back a long way, and we share a powerful story that we have never much talked about. I want to talk about that story, and I am hoping for more of a reaction from you than **Bleep**-you, one word,

with the accent on the first syllable. I want you to get serious."

"I guess that I went through a phase of not wanting to deal with you or the past. Friends don't ask friends why or for apologies, right? But I'm new and improved now. So talk," Mr. Black said, "for your servant is listening."

We talk and listen
| 19January09 |

"I am willing to cast this as me talking and you listening," I said, "but I hope that you add your thoughts and feelings as we go along. Including **Bleep**-you, if it fits or feels right to you."

"Grab a root and dig," Mr. Black said. "I'm all ears."

"Ok," I said, "so I will start. There is more to Mr. White and Mr. Black than the colors needed to make a game board. We are also more than the absence of and the totality of color. And we are more than night and day, or spy vs. spy, or any other duality that black and white are heir to."

"Ok," Mr. Black said. "We are alike and not, at the same time."

"Right," I said, "and our handlers, back when we had them, valued them, hated them, and needed them, understood something about us that we did not understand about ourselves. It was, for me, only when I was cut loose and forced to come to grips with so many things, that I realized that in some way you and I are linked by what the metaphor of black and white can only suggest."

"Yeah," Mr. Black said. "I guess you are right, though it seems obscene somehow to talk about it."

"Maybe it is obscene," I said, "but I for one have a need to at least acknowledge that you are important to me and that you complete me in ways that I cannot do for myself with the elegance that you can. Losing you to death was a shattering experience for me."

"If this is leading up to a proposal of marriage," Mr. Black said, "I have to say out front that I'm just not the marrying kind, man or woman."

"Nor am I," I said, "but there is another thing that has gone by many names, and this other thing is that of which I refer to."

"And in a fairly oblique manner," Mr. Black said.

"Ok," I said, "let me be blunt. When I thought that you had been killed by that bus, I grieved in a way that I have never grieved before, even when I felt like I had lost everything about who I was. And when you marched into the bookshop, in your right mind, I went through the other side of that silence like a sling-shot rock. We have not talked of, or even alluded to, any of this experience."

"Noted, and alluded," Mr. Black said. "Nothing to add."

"I understand that this need of mine is my need," I said, "and I appreciate that you can sit and listen, with a minimum of discomfort."

"And I," Mr. Black said, "am a private man, slow to speech and wary of self-revelation. I am a man of few words, and even fewer emotions."

Spent, I simply nodded.
No change.
Still the **Onion Man**.
Both of us.

And then it was time to start on back
| 20January09 |

"There are things in this life that I will not talk about to any man, or any woman, for that matter," Mr. Black said, "and your topics touch upon those things of which I shall not speak, in this waking life. **Bleep**-you if you don't like it."

I nodded but held my tongue. Try it some time while looking into a mirror.

"Let us confine ourselves," Mr. Black said, "to what is by my definition, just given, secondary evidence. First, notice that I put my life on the line for the Tribe, even before that particular term became part of my lexicon. I was and am willing to die for those who find home at the bookshop."

I nodded.

"Second," Mr. Black said, "is this. I have not had the love of a good woman to help me heal from the wounds that I bore from our time in **Operation Beloved** and after. I have had, perhaps, a greater capacity for some things than you have, and at the same time I realize that my choices have made me distant and disconcerting, especially to my friends."

I nodded.

I held my tongue.

"Third," Mr. Black said, "I do acknowledge the power of friendship in my healing, and I ask my friends for understanding in the face of silence from me on what would help their understanding. I am not yet able to be any more plain or honest than that."

I nodded in awkward silence.

We shook hands -- firm, frowning, and solid -- in the way of old men.

No shoulder-touchy thing for us.

I do not expect to have another conversation like this one, with my old and dear friend Mr. Black, in this life.

What are the odds?

You can bet that we will find out.

So many questions remain.

≈ ≈ ≈

The **Grimoire's** end is its beginning -- like the self-swallowing snake of dreams, the **Uroborus**, eating itself from the tail forward in an ever-tightening circle like a noose.

Jon Rieley-Goddard works and lives in Buffalo, New York, with his wife, Cathy, and their three cats, Chica, Bella, and Slava. He is a writer, photographer, and minister. Before embracing the call of the Word, he was man of many words -- a copy editor on daily newspapers for 14 years.

The *Mystery Man Murders* is his first novel.

The Mystery Man Murders stands as the first novel in the series titled ***Grimoire - the Bros Grim Breakfast Serial - a story in pieces***.

Book Two (titled *The Double Daily Double Murders*) is in revision.

Book Three (titled *Operation Next of Kin*) is in process as we speak.

Visit http://thebrosgrim.com to read more about **Grimoire - the Bros Grim Breakfast Serial**.
Have some crime with your morning coffee ... .

Did you find a typo or other *oops*? The author appreciates help with these important matters and will be generous in return.
Email **boldface@baldybooks.com** with the details.

For the latest news from *BaldyBooks*, publisher of this series, visit http://baldybooks.com.

www.ingramcontent.com/pod-product-compliance
Lightning Source LLC
Chambersburg PA
CBHW030014180626
46810CB00001B/40